HEROES OF KARTH

HEROES OF KARTH

* * *

THE CURSE OF THE UNDEAD

Grant Hamilton
Edited by Ed Winters

Heroes of Karth Inc.
www.heroesofkarth.com
Facebook: heroesofkarth
Twitter: @heroesofkarth

Author: Grant Hamilton
Editor: Ed Winters
Designer: Toma Feizo Gas
Illustrator: Andrew Sonea
Maps: Toma Feizo Gas
ISBN: 0995295301
ISBN-13: 9780995295308

Acknowledgments

First and foremost this book is dedicated to my wife Carla who makes me who I am. I love you more than anything in this world. You take my fire and passion to amazing levels and you have been my strongest supporter and believer in the book, game and most importantly, in me.

This book is inspired by my children all of whom I love dearly. Matthew, Sarah, Britney and Gregory – I love you guys!! Matthew, grab life and run with your passions. Sarah, be true to yourself and remember you are never alone in this world. Britney, you are a wonderful person. You have been such a great sister to your brother and together the two of you have helped make each other unique and special individuals. I hope you keep that bond for the rest of your lives.

"Gregory, I am your father!" My son, my first book is dedicated to you.

Gregory, you make me so proud. The day in the car when you told me that even if they found a cure for autism you would not want it, really opened my eyes to the strength of your character. I agree with you son! You are a loving and amazing person. Don't ever change!!

To everyone else (there have been so many people) I thank you for your support and friendship.

Last but not least, this book would not be what it is today were it not for the contributions made by Ed Winters. The pages of the manuscript truly gained life as he massaged and molded my words and ideas while respecting my original intent. As a sounding board and friend he has helped me mature as a writer and has assisted in taking all my concepts to the next level.

To the Heroes of Karth!

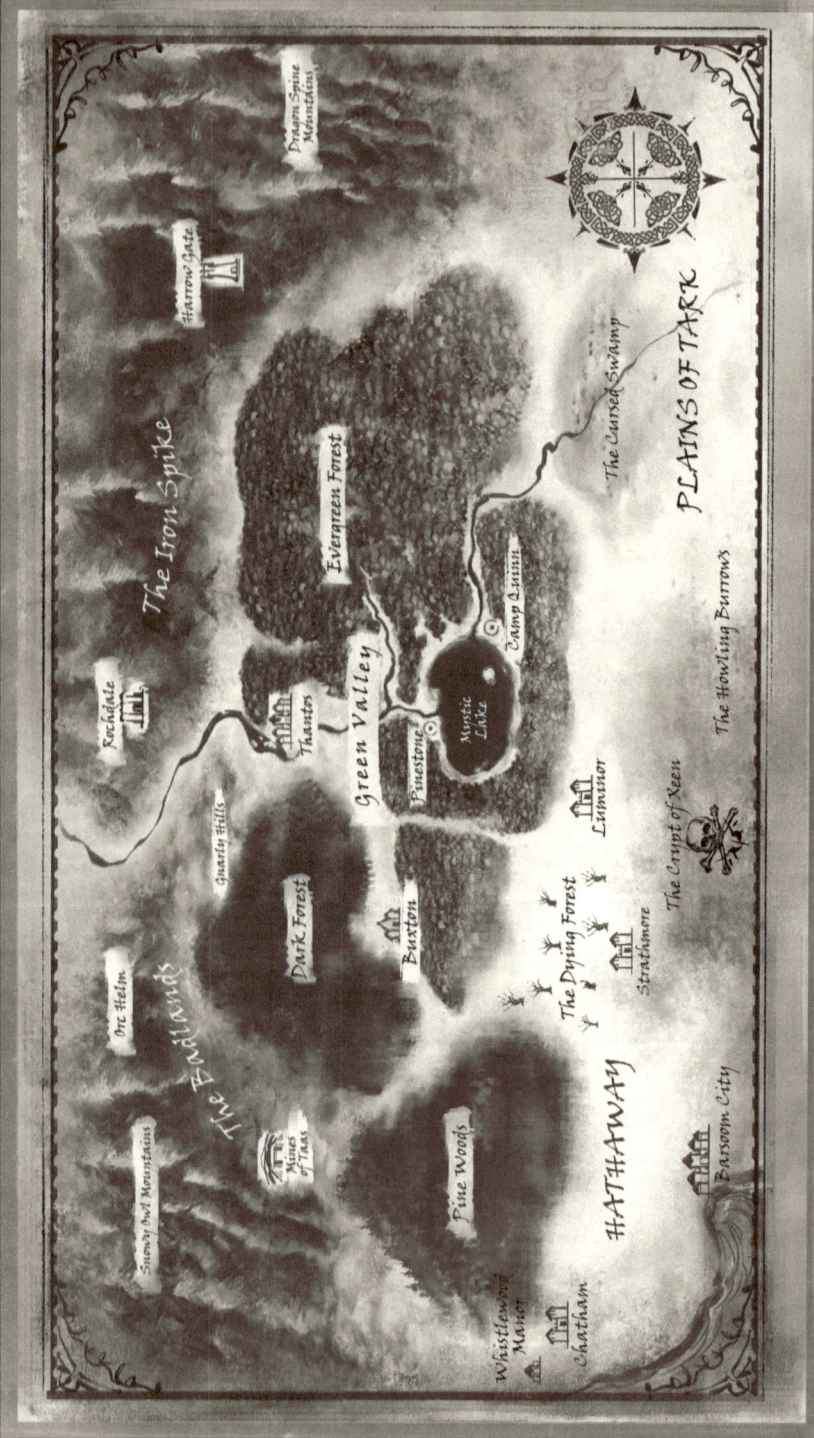

PROLOGUE

The agonizing twist of each surfacing memory pushes me further down redemption's path. I recall cherishing my life before it was ripped away to feed the beast. I see the scattered flashes of a family, of a wife and children no longer known and sense that they were an important part of my being. These memories have shown me that before being vanquished and reborn as an undead shade, I was a noble warrior. Images of past battles are crowding my thoughts, exposing the birth of my instinct to kill. Cutting through this enslaved and cloudy state of mind, I am connecting with my ancient past and finding endless facets to identify with besides my current monstrous form. I am the master of many lesser undead. I have killed countless living beings, darkening their essence and conscripting them to join the throng of undead as my new shade servants. If not for recent events, I am certain I would have continued doing the same thing I have done for what now seems an eternity – obeying my Master's commands.

I will never return to my previous physical form. My body rotted away long ago and all that remains is this shadowy creature without shape or weight. I cannot stand or touch the ground beneath me. Consisting of the darkness, I control and will it the same way a living being commands its hands to clench or its legs and feet to walk and run. Willing myself through the air as a shadow projects itself from a solid body, I flow across the ground. Wherever there is darkness I am able to melt and merge with it. My ethereal form may be the same as the rest of the dark creatures hovering together with no purpose, but I have become much more than a simple shade. Unlike the Dark Ones congregating around me, I am waiting, thinking, and biding my time. I am becoming my own master.

I can feel His continual gnawing, forcing me to obey. Like an addiction, when my Master beckons I must submit. He demands that I enable his plans, forcing the lesser undead to follow suit. My Master is the most powerful creature. In this existence, he controls us all. I have been His vassal for so long that it takes considerable effort to remember how to think for myself. This wellspring of memories has reacquainted me with fear. If my Master discovers that I am regaining free will, he will exert his power over me ten-fold, leaving no choice but to surrender to his domination. There is a part of me that would welcome that all-encompassing manipulation. But I will no longer be controlled.

The inability to remember my past torments my awakening mind. Memories of what has transpired during my time as a shade horrify me. As my psyche fills with the screams of the lives I have destroyed, I have been able to piece together many of the atrocities committed in His name, but so many more will remain lost in the flames of time. I accept responsibility for my actions, the guilt becoming bottomless. Swallowing these dark memories I demand they fade from my consciousness, but there is no reversing the unspeakable acts of genocide. When guilt overcomes me, I submerge into the depths of darkness, hiding the birth of my emotions from the other shades. Engulfed in this dark void, the emptiness washes away the evil memories, allowing me to focus on other things.

In those dark times I cling to sanity by the thinnest of threads, focusing on the one person I know who has proven true and selfless. A young elf boy named Llythwain has discovered a piece of my lost soul. Perhaps the memories of the innocent son I once held and guided were most eager to reach my consciousness. Combining the thoughts of Llythwain and the determination to right past wrongs, I am able to forgive myself enough to continue the quest for atonement. I will never forget my actions, nor forgive myself for the horrors I have inflicted. I will never stop searching for a way to make amends.

In this dangerous journey for reparation, I must succeed at finding the strength to resist the Master. In spite of my power as a shade, some things cannot be changed. The limits of my vision are simple tones of black and white and I am forever linked to blackness and death. My existence depends on draining other living creatures of their spiritual energy and choosing to ignore this thirst will be my doom. The lust will always exist within me and while I accept that I must kill and enslave others, the difference now is that I will attempt to choose my victims, killing only when necessary. This same lust for energy is what drives my Master forward. I will use everything I know about the undead against Him.

The One that commands us has many names, but his most infamous is Xeon, the Undead Shadow Dragon. To his shadowy servants he is simply known as Master. He still has control over me, but only when I allow it. I need to keep him from discovering the truth about this growing awareness. We have spent many lifetimes together traveling across the shadow-planes looking for suitable worlds to conquer. I am well known to him. Now the Dark Ones have been commanded to start the preparations for conquest of the world of Karth, and this is where I shall make my stand.

Congregating with the other shades while awaiting his next command, I am camouflaged by their darkness. Unlike them, I have a memory and conscience and am thinking for myself. I will never return to mindless anonymity, but for now it will protect me from his scrutiny. I cannot allow my Master to continue conquering and destroying worlds forever. I will try and save this world called Karth, but to succeed I must find individuals to help me. What happened to Llythwain has given me hope, shedding light on the beginnings of a plan that might just have a chance.

- Killian Acheron

ELF COUNCIL

Protected by the Snowy Owl Mountains in the west and the Dragon Spine Mountains to the east, Green Valley is home to elves, as well as eagles, wolves, raccoon, deer, and black bear. Radiating across the northwest corner of the valley is Evergreen Forest, a vibrant habitat lush with foliage and sacred to the elves. The fresh waters of the Skye River travel down from The Iron Spike through Green Valley, splitting Evergreen Forest and continuing southward into The Cursed Swamp. Spread along the river's rocky banks, moss covered redwoods and cool dark streams fill the forest and combine to create a thriving environment for all its inhabitants. Tucked within this ancient growth and hugging the riverbank is Thantos, the capital city of the elves. The fast flowing Skye departs Thantos over thunderous rapids located mere steps from the city gates, the river rushing to drain into Mystic Lake. The water's path along this route is deep and the many rapids run swift.

As the sun reaches the horizon beyond the Snowy Owl Mountains, the clouds begin disappearing into the darkening sky. The brilliant blue and gold of the setting sun is a rare and special spectacle, signaling to the elves that their goddesses Shifra and Silverymoon may be walking among the valley's residents this day. During these infrequent visits, the two celestial beings gain a better perspective on life below and are able to interact with the lands of their people.

"Silverleaf Forest is lost!" cried Shifra, Goddess of Light, stepping between the blackened trunks. The forest around her had become a rotting wasteland, the smell of decay thickening the air. Instructing her followers to monitor Silverleaf as its life drained away, they were now reporting that the destruction was almost complete. Although these lands are not of the elves alone, they often visit the forests that lie along their borders.

"Sister, the Curse of the Undead has turned Silverleaf into a place now known by the elves as Dying Forest," said Silverymoon, Goddess of Night.

"Do we not know who is responsible for this?"

"We know that the life crystals have blackened here," said Silverymoon. Moving away from her sister, she looked in the direction of Dark Forest. "And the goblins now have necromancers amongst them, just like the humans."

"Do you suspect it is necromancers at the heart of this destruction?"

"Their emergence just as the Curse comes upon us cannot be a coincidence," said Silverymoon. "Dark Forest is starting to show similar signs of decay."

"In addition to killing the forests, the Curse of the Undead appears to affect all living beings. They rise from death as undead creatures," said Shifra.

"I have seen that happening. The area affected by the curse is widening. Sister, what prevents the infection from spreading into Evergreen Forest?"

"The Moonguards are the protectors of the crystals and Evergreen Forest is their primary concern. They must be informed about the darkened crystals here!" said Shifra.

"Agreed. They might be able to discover a way to stop the curse from extending further."

"I have already alerted the priestesses, and the elves are addressing this at their council tomorrow," said Shifra, offering some small measure of comfort. "Come sister... the sun disappears and daylight fades. Let us return above before someone detects us..."

✳ ✳ ✳

"Council will reconvene in ten minutes!" Braigon Uanor heard the young town crier's voice booming across the courtyard. Not ready to return just yet, he found the sound irritating.

All morning he had presided over the council chamber, listening to various civil concerns. If it wasn't the gatherers recounting the amount of wood and plants they had harvested, it was the tradesmen reporting how much armor they had crafted or the tax collectors reporting that they were behind on their collections. He didn't care about any of those pedestrian concerns, yet as a lord he had an obligation to suffer through it all.

How do the kings of other realms do this? Strolling across the courtyard and walking beside the wooden palisades, he admired the tall guard towers built into the thick trunks of the redwoods and shook his head. When comparing to other nations Braigon always preferred the elven ways, where there were many lords to share the responsibilities involved in ruling the lands and people. However, it seemed that he was always the only lord left with duties at court. It was a rare occurrence when one of the other lords attended a council meeting.

I am sure it is because I was low-born into a worker family and did not inherit wealth. Flexing his muscles in irritation, Braigon ground his teeth. None of the other lords were half his size or strength and in his opinion, none were as handsome. Putting aside these petty annoyances, the rising irritation surprised him. He always preferred his lot in life to theirs, even if he was stuck chairing the council meetings.

Working his way through the courtyard, he passed through the crowd of elves buying goods at row upon row of stalls. It was time to get back to the council chambers before the afternoon session began. Scanning the scene one last time, his gaze fell upon a beast tamer selling her pets. Wrapped in a short skirt and laced hooded shirt, she wore snug knee-high boots that folded over at the top. Her attention to detail added some style to what would otherwise be considered common leather armor. Approaching her, Braigon's eyes captured every detail.

"My name is Braigon Uanor." Admiring her long dark brown hair and delicate hands, there was no doubt that he found her air of strength and confidence appealing. However, it was the warm smile greeting him when he first looked over that captured his soul. Her smile gave him a tingling sensation up and down his spine.

"Welcome Braigon Uanor. I am Cassandra Timber." Continuing to smile at him, she let her long hair fall forward so that he might notice it frame her features. Cassandra could not resist the opportunity to flirt with a lord and even if nothing came of it, this would be a great story to tell around the dinner table later that evening.

"It looks as though you are doing well Cassandra," said Braigon, examining the cages but unable to see any livestock.

As he looked away, she took the opportunity to continue flirting, moving a step closer. Braigon could feel the connection with her as she brushed against him.

"Thank you, yes. I have had a good day so far." She still had many of her larger cats left and wondered if he might be persuaded to buy a breeding pair. Noting the long sword at his side, her eyes rose to the white blonde hair that fell over his muscular shoulders, complementing the fine craftsmanship of his polished platemail and purple hooded cloak. *He must have money.*

"Do you have any stock left?" Braigon could not stop staring, drinking in her graceful movements. *Too obvious. Why is it so warm in here?* Her nearness was flustering him, and he struggled to recover.

"I have a few large cats left, did you want to inspect them?" It surprised her to see that the lord appeared nervous. His stare made it obvious that he found her more interesting than the pets.

"Council will reconvene in two minutes!" Calling out again, the town crier had circled back towards the beast tamer's stall. The voice reminded Braigon of his obligations.

"Forgive me, Cassandra. I must go back into Council." Braigon's face felt warm and it disappointed him to find this moment cut short when all he wanted to do was stay with her longer. "You may have guessed that I am a lord," he said, feeling awkward.

"I had a sneaking suspicion, Braigon." Cassandra raised an eyebrow as she noticed his arm muscles tightening. Pleased to see that he was confident and flirtatious as well, her heart began thumping in her chest. She did not know if she would ever have this chance again, and decided to make the most of it. Looking from his eyes to his mouth and back, she was hoping he might notice her attraction. Making sure that he felt like he was in control, she waited for him to speak.

"Please, wait for me in the courtyard. I would love to see your cats after the council session has ended." Gesturing towards the beasts curled beneath the wagon, Braigon did not have time to wait for her answer. Instead he hurried across the courtyard, exiting through a doorway into the council building. There were two guardsmen at the entrance waiting to escort him to his duties. Crossing the threshold behind the lord, they turned to Cassandra with impassive faces and closed the heavy door.

* * *

Rushing inside the stone council building to the main meeting area at the end of the hall, Braigon tried his best to shake the thoughts of Cassandra until later. It had only been a short time since the council session that morning, but walking down the hall he felt the power evoked by the council chamber. Leading up to the entrance was a hand knotted ochre-dyed runner, its golden tassels spreading in all directions like sprays of fine spider silk. Disappearing into the chamber, the runner stretched to the far side of the room. Framing either side of the doorway, green and brown banners hung from the ceiling, floating just above the floor. Embroidered in gold on each banner was an eagle, the sacred symbol of the elves.

Blue banners of The Allegiance hung next to the elf banners along each wall of the council chamber, together surrounding a platform that supported a massive oak table and thirteen ornate ladder-backed chairs. The front of the large table was open so that when a full council convened, the presiding lord and twelve representatives faced the gallery. On either side of the table were golden candelabras, each holding seven tallow candles. Large windows with opaque white stained glass illuminated the room. Filling the remaining space on either side of the chamber were rows of pine benches for spectators to observe the council proceedings.

Seating himself first at the center of the table, Braigon occupied the largest and most ornate chair. The other members of the council then sat in their customary spots to either side of him. Overhearing snippets of conversation as the room filled, he made a mental note of the attendees. As expected, there were many familiar faces.

Dressed in bright white hooded robes, both high priestesses of Thantos were the first to enter. It was interesting to see Inunis Brotah and Norin Tulaanos gossiping together while waiting for the proceedings to begin. The high priestesses were devout, their many holy skin markings demonstrating their high stature. The gods and goddesses only granted these symbols to those deemed worthy, and in the case of the high priestesses they covered most visible areas, including their faces. In spite of having known them for years, Braigon still found their exotic looks appealing. The lesser priestesses were also in full complement, with representatives arriving from the Townships of Buxton in the west and Luminor in the south.

Llaen Eilrah, Captain of the Rangers, was present along with a few of his Ranger scouts. Wearing green hooded cloaks with leather armor, they looked rugged and battle hardened. Accompanying Llaen was Razz Borrow, the elven Champion. Well respected as one of the best swordsmen in the land, Razz was slender but muscular, handsome, with a stern gaze and deliberate movements. His reputation and skill as champion had convinced many that not even the lords could match his dual weapon swordsmanship. The only one who might challenge him was Lenowyn Malaka, the assassin. On occasion the council employed her for special missions. The high priestesses had advised that she would attend the council meeting today, but Braigon had not seen her yet.

"What is the first order of business?" Braigon's voice was loud, cutting through the general babble in the chambers. Raising his hand, he signaled that council was starting. It was time to get things moving, as there was a lot to cover. As the gallery settled down, Norin began motioning for Llaen to approach.

"War is upon us," announced Llaen as he stood to address the council, becoming the center of attention. It had been a long time since he last attended a Council meeting and although scarred from years of battles and brawls, his face revealed his awkwardness in public speaking. The urgent tone of his bold statement caught all in attendance off-guard, and the room went silent. Looking around at those assembled, Llaen chose his words with care. Knowing that age and experience made everything he said more believable, he wanted to make sure that everyone understood.

"The Allegiance is at war with The Shard. Our allies, the dwarves and barbarians to the north are fighting against the orcs, hill giants and kobolds. We have detected goblins and spiders massing and they are roaming in Dark Forest." Motioning at his Rangers, Llaen continued after taking a deep breath. "The scouts have reported goblin patrols close to our borders. Each patrol appeared to have a necromancer with them. Rumors have it that they are the latest to join forces with The Shard."

"News of goblin activity is a concern for everyone, but worse still is that there are necromancers among them," said Braigon. Knowing that the priestesses saw necromancy as heresy, he made sure to state his position on the matter right away.

"By traveling with necromancers, Lord Uanor, the goblins have become much more formidable," said Llaen, pleased that Braigon appeared to be supporting him. Glancing at the high priestesses, he saw them nodding for him to continue. "The goblins are not an adversary to underestimate, especially if they have joined The Shard."

"The goblins warred with the elves a long time ago, and many of us died during that time," interrupted Braigon. "For decades now we have enjoyed peace. We do not want to face another war like that..."

"The Rangers are always bearers of ill tidings," whispered Norin, leaning over to Inunis. "But the Captain is loyal to me," she bragged. The priestesses were always scheming and playing at politics. Convincing Llaen to side with their interests was a valuable strategic addition to their machinations in council. Listening with one ear and nodding her head, Inunis was already in full agreement.

"Isn't your daughter married to a Ranger?" said Inunis out of the corner of her mouth, trying not to laugh. She knew full well that Norin's daughter Kalahni had married a Ranger. She also knew that Kalahni had even taken his last name, irking Norin even more. "What is his last name again?"

"The Rangers have worse news," said Llaen, speaking with force to silence the murmur in the chamber, only continuing when it was silent again.

The priestesses stopped their quiet bantering. Norin was not happy at having to hold her tongue. She had thought of a good retort and made a mental note of it so she could remember to use it the next time she had the opportunity to irritate Inunis.

"The Rangers encountered hunters in Dark Forest. They had just shot a deer and after confirming the kill, saw the animal return to life no longer looking or acting like a deer. It was covered in blood, with white eyes and a blank stare. The creature attacked with all its strength when the hunters approached. If not for the Rangers timely arrival, the hunters would have been in serious trouble. The deer appeared possessed and zombie-like, as if it had become evil; its sole purpose being to kill." Llaen looked around the room and could see that his words had caught everyone's attention. "The Rangers managed to kill the creature and it did not rise from the dead again. Upon seeing another deer, they killed it and the result was the same. It too rose from the dead."

Erupting in anxious conversation, the crowd quieted as Braigon signaled for silence. This occurrence was not news to the Council. There had been rumors of other similar happenings to the south. There were already unofficial reports that the Curse of the Undead was reaching into elven lands.

"What about to the east and south?" said Braigon. "Is there any more news of those areas since we last heard from the Rangers?"

"It appears that for now, those areas are quiet, Lord Uanor. The creatures in the swamps have not bothered anyone and the same holds true for the Howling Burrows," said Llaen. "We are fortunate to have peace with the swamp creatures and the jackals, as there is more than enough to deal with on the goblin and human borders. The report from Luminor is far worse."

"In the south the Curse has now spread into our lands. Inside Luminor an elder had passed on and within minutes he rose from the dead. In undead form he attacked and killed his own family. In turn, the family rose from the dead and those that had come to the defense of the family were also killed. In short order a large group of undead had risen. The Rangers managed to stop the spread of the creatures by killing them, but now Luminor is in a panic and the mistrust of neighbors and family is spreading. As an aside, the families of the undead are angry and feel the Rangers could have done more to save their kin." Llaen was from the township of Luminor, and it was clear that concern for his friends and family was weighing on him.

"It is the necromancers doing!" shouted Norin. "The goblin hunting parties have necromancers and are encroaching on our lands. Now inside our own borders the curse has begun spreading its infection. This cannot be considered a coincidence!"

"And the human lands have been overrun with this curse. Their forest is dying and they also have necros!" shouted Inunis. Good-natured ribbing aside, the priestesses were in complete agreement when it came to their disdain for necromancy. When she and Norin worked together, emphasizing each other's points, they were an effective combination of co-speakers. Jumping to her feet, Norin now assumed enough to start laying blame.

"The effect of the curse on human lands has been drastic and now it begins to defile our lands. The human necromancers must be in league with those of the goblins!"

The human Kingdom of Hathaway is the only safe coastal land and the humans have long been a part of The Allegiance. The elves depend on them for trade and the high priestesses know they need their ally, but this was still a good opportunity to raise more support against the necromancers.

"We must act now, before it is too late!" screeched Inunis, her eyes wild, arms flailing up and down.

"I say we must now strike against the goblin and human necromancers," said Norin, staring at Braigon and challenging him to act.

"This is grave news indeed," said Braigon, raising his hands again to silence the room. The level of emotion was rising beyond where he was comfortable and he could feel the tension in the air becoming thick with expectation.

"Is the mercenary leader present?" he asked, searching the faces looking back at him from the assembled gallery.

At Norin's signal, a gentleman wearing a top hat rose from the back of the crowd and made his way forward. Braigon and the elven leaders had known about the goblin movements for some time. They had made the decision to hire a mercenary company to venture on a secret mission into goblin lands and gather more information. In this way, the elves could avoid any blame for trespassing or spying. Even now, in light of everything revealed today, Braigon still felt that avoiding war was the preferred strategy.

"My name is Davissor Fergusson, Lord Uanor, and I am at your service!" Removing his hat and bowing before Braigon, the mercenary wore black silken outer garments with a white shirt, fancy red cloak and his signature black top hat. Davissor was a half-elf mage. He was also a businessman who sold the services of his adventurer-mercenaries to any who could afford his high prices. Calling the merry band of warriors 'The Heroes of Karth', they were most effective at their trade and had become famous throughout Allegiance lands. Given the seriousness of the current situation, the elf council had become less concerned about the cost.

"Mr. Ferguson, we have discussed this course of action amongst ourselves and have determined that your services are expensive," said Braigon, motioning to his assistant to lift two large bags of gems and gold onto the table. "We have also determined that we have no choice. As negotiated, you will receive the rest upon completion of your quest. You and your band of heroes will journey to The Badlands and work your way into the Mines of Taas to learn more about the goblin necromancers. You must find out if they are responsible for the Curse of the Undead!"

"Thank you, Lord Uanor. We shall not disappoint." Recognizing the elf lord's curt nod as his queue to leave, the mage turned on his heel and left the council chamber without another word.

"We need to take extra steps," announced Braigon, motioning for Llaen to step forward again. The elf lord was not about to take any chances, suspecting that war was unavoidable. "Captain, our borders with the goblins are too open. With today's news of this expanding curse, we must mobilize as if war is already upon us. Dispatch your Rangers without delay."

"Begin opening Camp Quinn as well. Any who wish can send their children to our hidden camp. They will be safer there. Those that stay must be ready to help with the preparations for war. We cannot risk being unprepared. We must act now!"

"Yes, Lord Uanor!" As the gallery gasped at the implication of their lord's words, Llaen glanced over at the high priestesses to gauge if they had already known how Braigon would react. Preparation for war was a drastic step for the peace-loving elves and a declaration such as this caught him by surprise.

Searching the assembled crowd, Braigon heard no argument from anyone. It was starting to sink in that the threat was real.

"Where is Lenowyn?" he said. Well-read and an assassin by trade, she was only used for missions of great importance. Her cunning and stealth were legendary among the elves. The crowd went silent as all heads turned to look around.

"I am here, Lord Uanor," a sultry voice replied from the shadows. Making the most of her entrance, Lenowyn took her time approaching the Council table.

It was obvious to any observer that she was an elf, but Lenowyn had an exotic mystique about her. She wore a black hooded cloak, hung low over her head. Her dress was skin tight, wrapping around her like a dark purple skin. Opening in the front, it revealed her smooth, pale complexion. An artisanal gold necklace and earrings complimented her sensual curving lips. The crowd remained silent as all eyes fixed on her shapely features.

Studying Lenowyn as she approached from across the room, Braigon could see her eyes gleaming from beneath the hood. They were deep green, and locked like steel claws on his face. *How could someone so beautiful be so dangerous?*

"Lenowyn, you shall journey south to Luminor and find out more about the Curse of the Undead."

"Lord Uanor, have the priestesses tried summoning their holy magic on the undead curse?" Shifting her cloak to reveal the hilts of the katana swords protruding over her shoulders, Lenowyn enjoyed reminding everyone that she was not just a pretty face. She had brought an arcane sword fighting style to the elves from far overseas years ago as part of her specialized assassin training. Those that wield the katana provoke fear in all who face them. *How easy it would be to kill him.*

"Yes, but their magic could not help them. Meet with the Rangers and priestesses and travel with them to Luminor to learn more. Continue with them and journey into the human lands. Gather more information about why their forest is dying and determine the level of human necromancer involvement."

"As you wish, Lord Uanor," whispered Lenowyn, making him strain to hear her. Flipping her hair as she turned on her heel, the assassin exited the main chamber. All eyes watched her leave.

"I would have a word before you go," said Norin as Lenowyn strolled past. The high priestess rose, hurrying out of the chamber after her charge. The priestess had been watching Lenowyn's interaction with Braigon and approved of her approach. The high priestess had often toyed with the idea of having her trained assassin become the wife of a lord.

"What is it?" asked Lenowyn, stopping in the foyer to wait for the older woman.

"When you get to the human lands and you find the necromancers, I think it best if you did not take any chances."

"No chances, Norin? I need more than word games to be successful."

"If you get the chance, I want all the necros killed! All of them! I do not care if they are not responsible for the curse!"

*　*　*

Carrying his advance payment, Davissor strode back into the courtyard. Reflecting on what had just transpired, he noticed a girl sitting next to some wagons, long after the other vendors had left for the day. Their eyes met as he approached.

"Are you coming from the council meeting?" she asked, her hopeful expression changing to disappointment as she saw the stranger's face.

"That is a distinct possibility, my dear. Who might you be and why are you sitting here alone?"

"My name is Cassandra. I am waiting for someone and was wondering how much longer the meeting would be."

"Not much longer I suppose. Good evening." Tipping his hat, Davissor hurried past her and out of the courtyard. There was no time for idle conversation tonight. When she was out of sight, the mage stopped and cast his Moongate spell.

"Par ipsu ori noom," chanted Davissor. A crackling hum, a flash of white light and the shimmering blue oval shaped portal appeared in front of him. Giving a final glance to make certain he was alone, Davissor entered the Moongate and in a heartbeat both he and the oval were gone.

*　*　*

"Well, well! He is finally back!" exclaimed Angus McVeigh with a wide grin. The gnome was the first to spot the Moongate shimmering in the corner. Jumping up and grabbing another tankard as Davissor stepped into the room, Angus was always happy to have another drinking partner.

"Aaargh! I will never get used to those blasted magic gateways," said Ragnar Thunderblade, wiping off the front of his copper light chainmail. Enjoying a mug of ale with Angus at the main table of their dining hall, the sudden crackling hum and flash of blue light had caused the dwarf to spill his beer.

A pair of charming rogues, Ragnar and Angus had been friends for quite some time before they agreed to join Davissor's mercenary company called the Heroes of Karth. Moving his red coat off the bench next to him, Angus motioned for Davissor to sit.

"Brothers!" exclaimed Davissor, grinning from ear to ear. Each hand held one of the large pouches that the elves had provided. "Guess what I have?" Throwing the pouches onto the large wooden table, Davissor slapped his friends on the shoulders as he squeezed into the seat between them.

"Ale money!" laughed Angus, jumping up on his chair. The mage had let the gold and gems spill out in a dazzling display. It was these moments that reminded the gnome why he had agreed to join this band of mercenaries. "Oh ho! Look at that, Ragnar!"

"Where are Ahira and Garrett?" asked Davissor, wanting everyone to see the commitment from the elves. There had been no opportunity to negotiate, as Braigon had agreed to the mage's starting amount, four times their normal rate. "This is an occasion worth toasting!"

"Oh, they are busy sparring at our training quarters," said Angus, taking another swig of his ale. "Let's fill them in on our good fortune later."

Davissor grinned, sloshing his tankard up in the air and they all raised their mugs in salute.

"To the Heroes of Karth!" they yelled in unison, taking a big gulp of ale to reaffirm their commitment to the team.

"I love you guys!" shouted Angus, ale dripping from his chin.

As the gnome danced a jig on his chair, Davissor and Ragnar clapped their hands to keep the beat, laughing as they drank the afternoon away.

II

ABDUCTION

On massive trunks stretching hundreds of feet towards the sky, the giant redwoods of Dark Forest creak and sway in the winds sweeping down from the Snowy Owl Mountains. Their dense canopy blocks out most of the sunlight, leaving the forest floor dark and moist. Cool dense air flowing around the base of the trees means that flying insects are unable to penetrate these woods and few birds or other animals exist within the forest range owing to the little food available. The lack of wildlife makes for quiet and peaceful surroundings. Elves enjoy visiting this forest and follow certain unwritten rules during visits, trying not to disturb their surroundings with unnecessary noise. They enjoy the tranquility that their world has created here and use it to find a more relaxed and spiritual existence. This day and this group of elves are different. These elves are trailing a goblin war party detected crossing into elven territory.

Spying on their movements for the last several days, the Rangers had been following the goblins from a respectful distance. Wanting to run this mission himself, Llaen had left Thantos as soon as the Council meeting had ended. Stiff from his long ride, he needed to act right away. This was not the time for resting. Laying out his plans with a stick on an open spot of loam, the captain had a simple strategy. "Llysander, take three Rangers with you to the left. Razz, take three scouts and flank right. Everyone remember that the Curse of the Undead has taken hold in Dark Forest. Try not to kill anything. We are seeking a single prisoner."

"You three follow me," whispered Llysander, signaling to the Rangers to make no sound. Dressed in identical green leather armor, hooded cloaks covered their heads. Peering down through the trees from their vantage point on higher ground, they could see several goblins resting in a narrow ravine. They were filling their skins from a small stream. One of the goblins had been riding a spider and had dismounted so the long-legged creature could also drink. Clothed in loose fitting tribal breeches and belted tunics with many shells and feathers sewn to the chest and arms, the green-skinned goblins, faces smeared with war paint, were similar in stature to elves. In general, their mouths were wider and their ears shorter. Watching them, Llysander recalled his experiences with goblins in the past. "The spider rider may be an archer."

"To me," hissed Razz at the scouts under his command. Glad to be back in the woods away from bustling city life, the anticipation of a possible fight was warming his blood and giving him a fresh high. In this era of peace, it had been years since he had tested his sword on flesh. Understanding the instruction not to kill, if it came down to a fight he was more than ready.

Razz wore a hooded green tunic with gold embroidering along its edges. His studded leather armor jutted out from underneath. When he unsheathed his two elf blades, there was no doubt in anyone's mind that they were thirsty.

"Archers, position to guard our rear." Glancing over his shoulder Llaen saw the bearded druid, Maedyn Taminah. Dressed in brown leather leggings and tunic and wearing a bear mask helm, this elf was taller than most and a few pounds overweight. To not shave was barbaric by elven standards and it was obvious that the druid had little concern for his attire, but he had been asked for the help of his spells. The Ranger Captain did not approve of the druid's independent attitude but restrained himself from saying anything inflammatory, as his preference was to avoid conflict within his team.

"I am ready," whispered Maedyn at the back of Llaen's head. Grinning at the Captain's obvious discomfort, he had seen the disapproving look before Llaen turned away. Watching Llysander's group of Rangers creep closer he could hear the three goblins talking amongst themselves in their native tongue.

"I am so hungry," complained the smallest goblin.

"When we can feast?" said the spider rider, echoing his companion.

"We are too close to the vile elf lands," snapped the largest of the three goblins. Holding a short bow, he was the leader of this small group. "We will feast when we get back to our main camp."

Signaling to the others, Llaen indicated that the big one would be their target.

"Se ebi fomi raws!" Unleashing his spell of summoning, Maedyn pointed in the direction of the two smaller goblins. A loud buzzing knifed down the ravine, gaining volume as the redwood forest erupted with a swarm of giant bees.

"Eeeeeeeeee!" squealed the smallest goblin.

"They are after me too!" yelled the spider rider. The swarm of bees split into two groups and bore down on the goblins.

"No running!" shouted the large goblin. "Stay and fight!" Nevertheless, with arms flailing the two others were already crashing full speed through the forest, the spider following right behind its rider.

"Now!" shouted Llaen. Jumping out on all sides with bows ready and trained on their target, the Rangers surrounded their quarry.

"Weaklings. Why not fight fair?" the goblin asked in broken Common tongue. Recognizing the futility of fighting this large group, the goblin didn't move. He stood eyeing his elven assailants with obvious hatred.

"Savage!" yelled Razz, sprinting up behind the goblin and swinging at his head. One hard blow from the hilt of his sword knocked their captive to the ground.

"Razz…" Llysander wanted to object to the hit from behind, but held his tongue.

"Bind the prisoner!" roared Razz, his eyes blazing with adrenaline as he stood over the prone captive. He was hoping the goblin would try to attack or escape. Ignoring Llysander even though he knew the Ranger disapproved of his action, Razz hated goblins as much as they hated him.

"Perfection!" said Llaen, pleased that there had been no bloodshed. Wanting a prisoner to interrogate, he had accomplished his mission in record time. "Let's move the prisoner back to Thantos for interrogation before any other goblins discover us. I would rather not have to fight a battle right now."

"Llaen before you leave, may I request a moment of your time?" Hating to ask for special treatment, Llysander spoke in low tones to his Captain as the rest of the Rangers prepared to head home. "I need to meet with my family to ensure their safety and prepare them, before war is upon us."

"I understand, my friend." Squeezing Llysander's shoulder, there was not a moment of hesitation in Llaen's voice. The Captain relied on him for support and had kept him away from home longer than usual. "Take the time you need, but try not to linger. Meet back at Clement's Peak where the other Rangers will regroup."

"Thank you, my Captain." Llysander's sense of duty to Llaen was strong and he was reluctant to leave his Ranger brothers, but his family needed him as well. In many ways it was a relief for him to return to Pinestone, the acreage he called home. Certain that war was coming, this might be his only chance to see his family for what could be a very long time.

"Let me travel with you, Llysander. I need to gather supplies and I believe Buxton is along the way to your home," said Maedyn, having overheard the Rangers' conversation. The druid was always happy to leave the social discomfort of the more regimented Rangers behind.

"Agreed, Maedyn." Looking to Llaen for help, Llysander saw only his knowing smile. "We will leave as soon as we are ready." The two Rangers felt the same way about Maedyn's appearance, but Llysander was happy having company on his journey, even if it was an unkempt druid.

✳ ✳ ✳

"Snow, come back here right NOW!" called Kalahni Lunas from just outside the doorway. Her magic bow and quiver of arrows hung close at hand inside the entrance. Even at home in Pinestone, she wore the blue leather skirt and matching darker blue hooded cloak of the Moonguard. Unlike the other Moonguards though, she kept a giant white cougar as a pet. This cat was a rarity even for the Rangers, who all seemed to enjoy keeping tamed beasts. Larger than most giant cougars, Snow weighed well over three hundred fifty pounds.

"I'll help you!" Playing alone in the garden, a young elf girl called out into the breeze. She inhaled the scent of the long-stemmed wild flowers that had seeded themselves that spring. A butterfly bounced and flittered about her head.

"Morrowyn, I swear your father knew exactly what he was doing when he picked her for me!" Kalahni smiled through her annoyance. Ranger beast training always starts by choosing two beasts for a trial period to guide compatibility. Following this procedure ensures that the bond between owner and chosen beast is strong. Llysander had recommended Snow over the other cat and as Kalahni was relying on his skill at training beasts, she had trusted her husband's choice. She was always able to find some humor in Snow's bad behavior because her preference had been the other cat. Kalahni liked reminding Llysander of this whenever he was home.

"He had to have known that this cat would be a handful." This was not the first time she had questioned his decision and was sure it would not be the last. Taking her time to walk back to the house, she laughed about some of her husband's past decisions and it reminded her of how much she missed him. Llysander had been away for a longer than normal length of time. *I will speak with Llaen about his time away, if I get the chance. Llysander needs to make his family a priority.*

"Come inside now please, Morrowyn," she said, knowing the cat would come back if they just left it alone.

"I've got her!" announced the girl in triumph, just as the butterfly was landing on her chest. Lifting it off her green hooded shirt with a gentle hand, she waved after it as it flew away. Approaching her as soon as Kalahni went inside, Snow had stared first at the tiny butterfly, and then back at the girl. Grabbing the cat by the collar, Morrowyn led her to the house.

"Oh thank you, Morrowyn!" said Kalahni. Brushing her daughter's golden hair to the side, she was glaring right at the cat. "Snow! Get inside!" This time Snow knew that playtime was over. Kalahni's tone told her that she had better start listening, and the cat scuttled through the doorway with her tail tucked down in case she received a sharp tap.

"Where is your brother, Morrowyn?"

"Not far, playing with the animals." Glancing in his direction, Morrowyn wished that she could join him on the edge of the forest right now. Llythwain needed extra care and her mother was always careful that someone had an eye on him at all times.

"Leave him be for now and come pray with me," said Kalahni, reading her daughter's mind. Having occurred to her that it had been a while since they last prayed, all this thinking about Llysander had made her heart ache.

What would my mother say if she knew about my lack of piety? I know she would not approve of how much I've changed. Her mother was a high priestess and would not provide much comfort to her daughter for missing prayer time. Following her own path, Kalahni had married a Ranger and become a Moonguard, moving away from Thantos to this idyllic acreage on the edge of Mystic Lake to raise a family.

"Are we saying the prayers that Nima taught us?" Morrowyn was hoping that wasn't the case. The prayer to the Goddess Shifra was a long ritual and she did not feel like doing it right now. Her thoughts jumped back to her brother, still playing outside. "Why doesn't Llythwain ever have to pray?"

Smiling at her without saying a word, Kalahni knew her daughter could answer that question for herself. It would be easy for the girl to be unhappy with her brother, but she understood that Llythwain was not the same as other children, even if she didn't always understand what that meant. Still though, at times it did not seem fair. Always happy to be with her mother, it didn't take Morrowyn long to relent and smile back.

"Today we will skip most of the Goddess Prayer and instead just recite the first part with the prayer for your father." Being wise enough not to force too much on her youngest child, Kalahni knew that would appease her daughter. As Morrowyn got older she would understand more, and the comparisons with her older brother would melt away.

"Make the sign of the four life crystals and let us say the Father's Prayer." Kneeling before their hearth and holding out her prayer beads, Kalahni made sure that Morrowyn was following suit with her own string of beads.

"O my Goddess, please watch over our fathers. Forgive us our sins and save us from the fires of below; Lead all souls above, especially those who have the most need of your mercy…" Closing their eyes, Kalahni and Morrowyn prayed with passion. They were both missing Llysander and gave extra emphasis and seriousness to the words so that Shifra might be more willing to hear them and grant their requests.

"Brpt!" Chirping in irritation, the young squirrel stopped to size up its pursuer. Scurrying along the dirt path that separated the grassy lawn from the garden, it had tired of playing and did not want any more food. The path led away from the house, disappearing into the woods that surrounded the clearing. The squirrel ran towards the forest and its own home.

"Come back here!" shouted Llythwain, flipping back the hood of his dark green cloak so that he could see which way the fleeing squirrel had gone. Chattering back at him, it was hurrying away down the pathway past the garden toward the trees. He was not done playing and ran towards where he last saw the creature moving. His quick eyes caught sight of it and he stood watching as it hopped and ran into the trees, its tail flipping around in the air. Feeling his heart thumping from the chase, he sensed that the squirrel had tired of this game, but he could not resist going after it and continued hunting his quarry.

Following the squirrel into the trees, Llythwain lost sight of his home as the forest closed in on all sides. There wasn't even a flash of color indicating that the clearing was just a few yards behind him. Single-minded in his pursuit, he found he had herded the squirrel into a ditch facing a wall of rocks, blocking it from any chance of escape.

"I have you cornered now!" Llythwain was proud of his tracking skills and he approached the creature to complete the chase. The squirrel sat motionless as he moved closer, staring at him with wide frozen eyes. The aspiring young Ranger's veins throbbed and he felt an unexpected burst of hot energy flow through him. The excitement of the chase and subsequent cornering of the tiny animal was elating, however his smile began fading when he realized the squirrel had stopped chirping and now sat frozen because it was lifeless.

How could this be? I did nothing! Horrified that he might have caused the death of a beautiful creature, Llythwain could hear his sister running through the clearing towards the trees. Embarrassed and shameful of what had just happened, he was pushing the squirrel out of sight behind the rocks as she came upon him.

"Llythwain! You leave that squirrel alone!" howled Morrowyn, stopping in her tracks at his sudden appearance in front of her. "I'll tell on you and then you'll be sorry you didn't listen." Having finished with her prayers, she rushed outside in time to see her brother sprinting into the woods after the little animal. Heading into the trees, he sometimes got annoyed when she followed him, but today she didn't care because she wanted his company. Morrowyn felt she knew Llythwain better than anyone and she was sure without a doubt that her brother loved her.

Dismissing what had happened to the squirrel, Llythwain smiled at his sister once he saw her insistence in chasing him. She often pulled him away from his dream world. The boy did not trust many people, but Morrowyn was someone with whom he could be himself without judgment. He sensed that it was her innocence that led him to trust her. She was kind and easy to understand, and he welcomed her friendship. When both of them were at Pinestone, they spent most of their time together. As is the case with many older brothers though, Llythwain also enjoyed taunting his younger sibling and was happy that she was now a part of this newest game.

"Release the Morrow!" yelled Llythwain, greeting his sister with the special nickname he had given her. "Try and find me!"

"Say hello to my big brother!" countered Morrowyn with her own catch phrase that she used whenever they were playing together. Capturing him before he vanished deeper into the woods was important because she knew that once he made it further into the undergrowth she would have a hard time finding him. She had spent many hours looking for her brother on more than one occasion this autumn. He was an excellent hider, especially in the forest. It was well known among the elves that Llythwain had a special skill at hiding. Hurrying after him as fast as she could, there was no way Morrowyn was letting him get away this time.

Upon reaching the edge of the mature pines he turned, pausing for a moment to make sure his sister could see where he was entering. Glancing up at the bright sun and wiping the sweat off his forehead, he was already thirsty and hungry and decided that he would keep it short so that they could be home in time for lunch. Teasing his sister as she ran after him, Llythwain entered the forest one slow step at a time, leading her in the direction of the beach.

"Llythwain! I won't look for you this time!" Morrowyn slowed to a walk as she neared the forest opening. Twisting a bunch of her hair together, she brushed back the long golden strands from her face while deciding which way she wanted to go.

"Llythwain, I can see you!" she continued to yell, even though she had no idea how far or which way he had gone. She decided to try walking in the direction of the water.

Llythwain lay still alongside the low ferny bushes that filled most of this part of the forest floor. Tiny black flies were everywhere around him and their constant buzzing in his ears and the repeated yelling of, "I can see you!" from his sister annoyed him in no time. Jumping up from his hiding spot, he was indignant. "You cannot see me!" he yelled, hurrying down a small, rocky path that took him closer to the beach.

"There you are!" yelled Morrowyn, grinning with satisfaction that the ploy to flush her brother out of his hiding spot had been successful. Appearing to have given up on the idea of running from her, she ran towards where he stood waiting. Getting closer though, she noticed that his long white blonde hair hung in front of his face as he stood frozen on the path. From beneath the hair Llythwain's wide eyes were staring at his sister in absolute horror.

"Do you have any more of these ropes, my friend?" The gnome was much shorter than everyone else, but had no shortage of personality. With a moustache and goatee framing his grinning mouth, it was obvious that Angus was happy to be back on the road and involved in another adventure. He was enjoying this shopping excursion in particular because they were billing the elves for everything. "What if we have to rappel down a mine shaft?"

"How about more of these tasty wafers?" interrupted Ahira Stonewell. Stomach rumbling in agreement, the burly dwarf had just finished breakfast, but already the thought of leaving on this journey was making him hungry. He loved eating fine food almost as much as he liked complaining. The dwarf was not looking forward to the small, uncooked meals that were commonplace on the road.

"Ran, please help the gnome and dwarf," said Ballan Thalian to his son. Ballan was the proprietor of the only general store in Buxton and he was always happy to see a busier day than normal. These new customers looked different than his regular ones but if he was being honest, he did not care. Their money looked the same.

"Strange boy! Doesn't look like an elf," blurted Ahira, not caring if he was rude. Putting back the wafers, he shot a disappointed glance at Angus. Watching as the boy scurried back and forth gathering the requested supplies, Ahira shook his head. "Don't drop anything!"

"My apologies, good sir. My wife is human." Never surprised at a dwarf's ability to be boorish, Ballan turned away from Ahira, addressing the mage again.

"Any other news from the Council session, Davissor?" The leader of the mercenary group had given him a requisition signed by Lord Uanor to supply the Heroes of Karth with anything they wanted. Ballan wanted to hear more about the mercenaries' mission, but Davissor was reluctant about revealing too much.

"Lord Uanor has declared a state of war and is recommending that parents send all children to Camp Quinn for their safety," said Davissor, sharing a snitch of gossip while he watched Ran rush back into the shop with more rope. "Will your son stay with you or will you be sending him away?"

"A good question. Most likely I will send him away with the others." Just yesterday the Rangers had stopped in Buxton, reading aloud the edict from Lord Uanor that everyone was to prepare for war. Ballan had spent the night pondering this very question and still did not know if he should keep his son with him or send him away with the other children. The boy was an able-bodied young teenager, but was also his only child.

"I see Llysander coming!" shouted Ran, running back outside. The boy had a teen crush on the Ranger's daughter, and he was hoping she was with him. It had been some time since he last saw her.

"Well boys, I think we have everything we need," said Davissor, straightening his jacket. "Let's move along. We've still got a lot of planning ahead of us." Seeing Ragnar and Garrett still poking through the weapons, the mage stopped and shook his head with a smirk. A stout bald dwarf with a thick brown beard and an eye patch, Ragnar was dressed in light bronze chain armor and a black silk tunic. Garrett was human and wore plate mail armor, a blue tunic and cloak. Lost in concentration as they picked up and continued testing various swords and bows, they were oblivious to the rest of the world. "Excuse me, gentlemen. Do you two wandering warriors need more time?"

"How about these daggers?" From across the room, Angus flipped three small knives through the air towards Davissor in quick succession. Thudding into the support beam behind him in a straight line, the wooden post was left vibrating from the impact. The gnome stood grinning as Ragnar, Garrett and Ahira all roared with laughter.

"Mr. McVeigh!" thundered Davissor, whirling on Angus in mock anger after straightening from the contortion of his avoidance. Seeing the gnome holding the knives and sensing his intent, the mage got ready to move ahead of time. However, he was unsure if the shopkeeper appreciated having daggers tossed around his store. "I shall turn you into a jackass and make you carry our supplies for the remainder of our journey!"

"Well boys! They don't call me "Dart" for nothing!" said Angus. Still grinning from ear to ear, he felt quite satisfied with his performance. "I must live up to my reputation, Davissor. You gave me the perfect opening."

"Please excuse my friend, Mr. Thalian. His nerves have been on edge since I told him about our mission to the Mines of Taas." Davissor shook his head, trying not to laugh. Hoping a quick reminder to the shopkeeper that they were on official elf business might help defuse the situation, he set about working the knives free from the wooden post.

"No worries, Davissor," said Ballan, smiling at the mercenaries laughing in his store. The shopkeeper held an appreciation for their camaraderie and if pressed for the truth he would have admitted wishing he could go with them on their mission. He was pretty sure it would be more fun than running a general store.

"I thought we called him Dart because he runs from every fight!" said Ahira. Garrett laughed again, even louder this time.

"Welcome back!" said Ran, excited as Llysander and Maedyn entered the shop. The Ranger and druid caught everyone's attention, quieting the conversation.

"Well hello and thank you, young Ran!" replied Llysander. "It is nice to be back in civilization." He looked Ballan's son up and down. "How are you doing? You look so much bigger than last I saw you."

"Is Morrowyn with you?" blurted Ran. Straightening his short brown hair, he pushed it back behind his ears as he was peering out the doorway.

"No, she isn't but don't worry, I'll tell her you said hello. And I'm sure you will have the chance to see her sooner than you might think." Llysander grinned at the memory of young crushes.

Noticing the strangers as soon as he stepped into the store, the Ranger guessed that they were adventurers of some description. A brown bearded dwarf with an eye patch and a human were looking at him with suspicion from across the shop. Another dwarf with red hair stood ten feet to his left. Bigger and stronger looking than Brownbeard, this one looked even taller standing next to a laughing gnome.

In front of Ballan was an elf fiddling with some daggers sticking out of a beam, in all probability the leader. Waving the shopkeeper away, Llysander let him know that there was no need to worry about serving he and Maedyn right away.

Walking around the shop with the druid, Llysander kept his eyes on the strangers and committed them to memory. Glancing over at the red haired dwarf, he recalled Llaen informing him before he left Dark Forest of the Council's plans to go to the Mines of Taas. *This must be that mercenary group. What a motley looking crew.*

"Well, I think we were able to fill everything on your requisition, Davissor. You should be all set to go on your Council mission now. I appreciate you coming to my store. Good luck to you, Sir!" Selling so much of his merchandise in one day made Ballan a happy elf.

"And a good day to you, sir!" replied Davissor. The mage lifted his top hat, performing a formal bow as was his custom. He quite enjoyed having a Ranger and druid as part of his audience.

"Come on, boys. Let's get out of here. I believe it may be time for a drink!" Angus was anxious to get started on their journey and was no longer in the mood for any more social graces.

"I'm with you, little brother," said Garrett. Trailing the rest of his group out of the store, he nodded at Ballan as he strode by.

"Well then, Llysander? How are you?" asked Ballan, turning his attention to the new customers.

"Hmm?" mumbled Llysander, only half acknowledging the shopkeeper as he watched the group leave. As Ballan spoke the Ranger was studying the human, the last of the strangers to leave the store. His blue cloak had the Hathaway emblem on it. *I bet he was a knight at some time in his past. I wonder what his story is.*

"Nice bunch of fellows, those mercenaries. They call themselves the Heroes of Karth."

"Have you heard Braigon's edict yet?" asked Llysander, returning his attention to Ballan. "We spotted signs of goblins not far from here. It's unfortunate but Buxton is likely the first place that they will attack."

"Yes I heard the troubling news. I think I will send Ran to Camp Quinn." Ballan hoped the Ranger would approve of that decision. "Will you be sending your children?"

"Camp Quinn!" Overhearing the name, Ran could not help repeating it aloud.

"I'm heading home now and plan to discuss it with Kalahni. There is a high probability that we will send our kids as well." Hearing the disappointment in Ran's voice, Llysander hoped he would feel better knowing that his friends would be at camp with him.

"Hurry Ran! Fetch Llysander's supplies!" called Ballan, snapping the boy out of his daydream. Finishing up with Maedyn's purchase, the shopkeeper walked outside with Llysander and the druid while waiting for his son to return.

Rushing towards the stairs, Ran went to get the bags of food that Llysander had ordered. Staring as he walked past and went down the stairs, the young man admired the Ranger's sheathed sword and long bow strapped across his back.

"It feels good to be back," repeated Llysander, looking around the town as they stood in front of the store.

"I know Kalahni will be happy to have you home. She talks about you every time she comes in for supplies."

"I only wish I could stay longer. With the threat of a war with the goblins, I will be even busier for the foreseeable future."

"I have the supplies," called Ran, hoping he wasn't too late to hear more news from the adults who were still talking outside.

"Ballan, how much do I owe you today?" Sifting through his pouch, Llysander withdrew a tied red handkerchief holding his coins.

"Whatever you think is a fair price, Llysander. There is no need to be generous today, as I made a great profit with the help of the mercenaries and am appreciative of your friendship."

"You are a true friend, Ballan. Thank you for helping Kalahni while I'm away." Counting out more than a fair price, Llysander squeezed the money into the shopkeeper's hand.

Gathering up their supplies, Llysander and Maedyn packed their horses and rode out of town towards Pinestone. Feeling his stomach tighten with every step, there was no doubt that Llysander missed his family and needed to see them again, but he wasn't looking forward to leaving them behind in the face of the coming storm.

* * *

"Llythwain, what's wrong!?" said Morrowyn, sensing his fear as she stood on the path close to her brother. Remaining cautious, she remembered that he had fooled her before. Stepping closer and half-expecting him to run away, she recognized that something was in fact wrong with him this time. He was blinking away tears, his face distorted with effort, and although his mouth was wide open he made no sound. The vague memory of an incident that happened a long time ago bubbled to the surface of her consciousness. Too young to understand or even care why her brother didn't speak about that time in their lives, she had almost forgotten that something terrible had happened to him. Watching him now, as a dark shadow was looming unseen behind her, she began to understand how he struggled all those years ago.

Dropping to his hands and knees, Llythwain froze in horror. The strain of holding back his tears took all his effort and he was unable to break the paralyzing fear that had overtaken him. Morrowyn did not understand that he was trying to warn her, and his emotions had stretched far beyond frustrated. He wanted to scream, to cry out to her, but between his shallow gasps for air the best he could muster was little more than a squeak. *RUN!*

"Stop it Llythwain! What is wrong? You are scaring me now!" Grabbing at her hair, Morrowyn twisted a handful in her nervous habit. Not knowing what to do to help her brother, she couldn't make out what he was trying to say and with all this excitement she was not thinking straight. Her heart was pumping in her ears like the drums at the solstice celebration, and running for help didn't occur to her. *Llythwain what is happening to you? I don't know what to do!*

Growing ever larger, the shadow readied its attack.

Slumping on the ground, Llythwain had stopped struggling and was silent. Only his eyes seemed alive and as they met hers, she started to realize that he was trying to warn her about something. *RUN!*

"If you are teasing me again Llythwain, it's not funny. Just stop now!" On the edge of tears, Morrowyn had no reason to know fear or suspect anything dangerous was happening. It was now too late for her to escape.

Oblivious to her surroundings and focused on Llythwain, Morrowyn saw his eyes close. As he disappeared from sight inside a rising shadow, the crunch of a snapping twig broke her concentration. Turning to see what made the noise, her expression changed from fear to horror.

"Llythwain!" she screamed, her nose filling with a fetid sweaty stench. She would have continued screaming but the shadow growled and Morrowyn felt a sharp thump against her head, sparks filling her eyes. As the pain from the impact intensified, darkness grew around her and she slipped down into unconsciousness.

The club's impact almost killed the girl, but a low groaning told the ogre she was still among the living. Shrugging his hairy shoulders, the ogre cared not whether she lived or died, although the thought of a live meal always held a certain appeal. Ever hungry, his stomach was already rumbling.

Crouching over his victim, the towering brute grabbed the elf girl by the feet and stuffed her into a large sack. Straightening his eight-foot tall frame, he twisted from side to side trying to locate the elf boy she had been talking to only a moment ago.

"Where is that boy?" he growled in his native tongue. Two more ogres thundered towards him. They also had sacks ready to fill with fresh meat. "Do you see him, Bigglum?"

Bigglum was the largest of the three ogres and had angry red pimples all over his face. The open sores bled as he scratched them in confusion. "Find him, Gurosh! He was just here!"

Standing upright, Bigglum was almost nine feet tall. As the chieftain of the ogres, he wore studded leather armor and had a chainmail shirt with shoulder pads made from skullcaps. His light-colored skin was pinker than that of his comrades and his belly was twice the size. "That small girl is not enough for all of us. Find that boy!"

Motioning at the third ogre in the group, Bigglum signaled for him to head around the trees towards the beach. "That boy must have run to the water, Zik. I bet he's a tasty boy who thinks he can escape us! Ha!" The chieftain rambled in excitement as both Gurosh and Zik circled step by step into the forest.

Zik was different than the other ogres. Dressing in light loose clothing and a woven poncho, he was wearing a boned necklace and in his right hand carried a large staff with three skulls nailed to the tip. He kept his grey hair shoulder length and wore a leather codpiece decorated with an elf bone shard. Zik was the ogre clan's magic wielding shaman.

Chanting as he stomped through the trees and ferns, Zik headed in the direction of the beach. Waving his staff over and back in half circular movements, the shaman's magic pulsed through his arm, white and yellow sparks flying in a spray from the largest skull on the staff.

Keeping his eyes closed, Llythwain lay in the exact spot that his sister had last seen him, in a slight depression beside the rocky path. He had no idea that the ogre chieftain was standing just a few feet away, but somehow he knew better than to move or make any sounds. Assuming that Morrowyn was already dead, he wanted nothing more than to cry out in anguish and run deep into the woods. It was only instinct, luck and the shadow cast from the ogre's large belly that had kept him alive to this point.

By now, Zik and Gurosh had finished their sweep of the immediate area. Lifting his left boot, Bigglum took another step forward, standing mere inches away from the boy's nose. The noise and vibration of the foot thumping so close to his body forced his eyes open. Seeing the ogre towering over him, Llythwain's muscles tensed as he held his breath and got ready to spring away. Not willing to trust that his luck at hiding would hold, he was certain that the ogre would soon step on him. This little game of hide and seek would then be over.

Riding the final miles to Pinestone, Llysander felt uneasy. Quickening their pace on the path along the edge of the forest that would take him home, he felt a squeezing tension crawling up the back of his neck and into his skull. Smelling the lake in the breeze that washed over them as they rode, he could hear it whispering their destination's nearness. The sky was clear, composed of blue darkening to purple at its greatest height, but he was paying little attention to the scenery today. Something wasn't right.

"What is going on with you, Llysander?" asked Maedyn, sensing his companion's unease and feeling the strangeness as well. The birds had gone silent and the travelers hadn't heard or seen a woodland creature for miles. "Why are we turning here?"

"I think it is clear that something is wrong, Maedyn. Let's investigate." It was necessary to follow the cleared path home from Buxton when on horseback, but Llysander found himself sliding off the main road, drawn toward the tree line by an inexplicable force.

"Llysander! Over here!" Maedyn had dismounted and was crouching with his eyes wide. Scanning the trees for movement, he was now not sure who might overhear him. Large footprints heading into the trees had caught his attention.

"They originated from over here, druid. It looks like there were three of them. What do you make of this? Who marked this location, and why?"

Painted on a large stone were rune markings, but the magic writing was not in the elf tongue. Llysander had seen elf rune markings many times before and understood that their use was to mark the location where a spellcaster could later gate.

"Those are ogre markings!" The crude marks were familiar to the druid, who had spent his life living close to the ogre realm. Kneeling in the tracks, the druid cast a quick enchantment, reversing the power of the rune stone. The markings disappeared, negating the magic held within. "I have removed the markings from the stone, but the real question is where are the ogres?"

"Kalahni!" Llysander realized how close ogres were to their home and a burst of adrenaline began coursing through his veins. The danger to his family was real. In one fluid movement the Ranger drew his bow and nocked an arrow.

"How could this be possible, Llysander? These ogres have traveled deep inside elf lands. Their boldness is shocking!"

"That does not matter right now. You must warn my wife! Transform and fly to my home while I track these ogres. They shall pay for this transgression with their lives!" Not waiting to hear Maedyn's response, Llysander darted into the trees. Following the ogre spoor, his heart raced and he became overwhelmed with dread. These tracks were leading him towards Pinestone.

"Trans Lup!" Maedyn appeared to jiggle in the sunlight, making a popping noise as he transformed into an eagle. Flapping with all his strength to rise above the trees, he headed straight in the direction of Llysander's home as fast as his wings would allow.

Tell me I am not too late. Stopping to study the trail, Llysander concentrated on the forest sounds around him. Using his Ranger training to compartmentalize each note, one by one he removed them from his consciousness as he worked to isolate any unusual noises. Inhaling the putrid and unnatural odor rising from the trail, his nose wrinkled in disgust.

"Llythwain!" Far off to his right, Llysander heard his daughter scream in horror. His heart jumped into his throat, leaving his chest empty and cold. He had never heard that visceral tone from her. Breaking into a sweat, he sprinted headlong towards her voice.

What is happening to our world? Speeding through the trees with his senses on high alert Llysander's mind wandered, trying to understand how ogres had managed to get past the Ranger patrols and mark a rune so deep in elven territory. Jerking his attention back to the possible upcoming scenarios with his children, he filed that thought away for a future discussion with Llaen.

Wanting nothing more than to call out and reassure them that he was there, Llysander stopped himself. He knew these woods well and was running to where he would best be able to do battle. Choking down his emotions to maintain the element of surprise, all the concerned father could do now was hope that his children would survive until he arrived to save them.

* * *

"How could the boy get away?" growled Gurosh. "Your magic should bring fear to even the greatest of warriors, Zik!" *How could this happen? Zik must be doing something wrong.*

Llythwain could not stay put any longer. The continued humming and rattling of the ogre were affecting his mind. The urge to run away had become too strong. Screaming as he jumped up, he bolted from underneath Bigglum's feet, darting into the forest he knew so well.

Shocked and surprised by the sudden noise and movement in the ferns right next to him, Bigglum stepped backwards off the path and lost his balance, landing on his back in the undergrowth.

"Get that boy!" Bigglum roared, his eyes widening with pain and shock as he sat upright.

"Yes chieftain!" yelled Gurosh, laughing out loud at the sight of Bigglum sitting on the ground with leaves in his armor, embarrassed to discover that the boy had been crouching beside him the entire time. Zik looked over at the warrior with a smug smile, knowing why the boy was running now. His magic had not betrayed him. The shaman knew that his spell would work.

"Leave the girl, Gurosh! Get that boy!"

"We'll get him!" said Gurosh, anger choking down his laughter. Furious at having to give up his catch, he could not ignore his chieftain's command without incurring his wrath. Hurrying over to where Bigglum was struggling to regain his feet, he dropped the bag carrying the elf girl. Spotting the boy running just beyond the trees to his left, the warrior loped after him at an ogre's fast pace.

"I will stop him, chieftain," said Zik, beginning his chant. "Ipsuli Kowli..."

Terrified beyond anything he had ever known, Llythwain turned and saw an ogre closing from behind. His head swiveling left and right, he was unable to process his surroundings as he raced through the forest. *What is that under those trees? Father?*

Twenty feet ahead of him and blending in with the undergrowth his widening eyes saw someone resembling his father crouched, an arrow nocked and ready to fire. Just as Llythwain opened his mouth to yell out, the spell cast by the shaman found its mark. Running full speed, his legs stopped working mid-stride and, now paralyzed, he dropped face first to the ground.

Llysander watched his son running right towards him, validating his choice of hiding spots. Making himself visible only to his son, it surprised him to see the boy drop like a stone without making a sound. Keeping his bow drawn, the Ranger could see an ogre waving his club and crashing through the trees not far behind. He wasn't sure what had just happened, but he could guarantee that the ogre would now pay a dizzying price for it. With Llythwain now lying on the ground, there was no chance that he would get in the way of the first shot.

"Die…" Llysander whispered under his breath. Letting the first arrow fly, he drew another in one fluid motion. This was the closest he had ever come to feeling pure hate, and he gritted his teeth while struggling to keep a steady hand.

Focused on chasing the elf boy, Gurosh saw him drop to the ground and readied to pounce. He failed to see either the elf in the trees or the arrow flying towards him. Arcing from the ground, the arrow plunged downward into the ogre's left eye socket, penetrating his brain and smashing into the back of his skull. The force of its impact knocked him flat on his back, emptying his lungs as his feet flew over his head. A second arrow found its mark in the back of the ogre's right leg as it flipped up in the air.

"Aaaaaagggg! Kill him! Kill him!" screamed Gurosh, wailing in pain and shock at the trees and sky. Rolling back and forth on the ground, the warrior was not sure where the arrow had come from, who had attacked him or even if there was more than one enemy.

I must get out of here now or I will die. Getting his feet back underneath his body, Gurosh heard another arrow whizz overhead, forcing him to hit the ground again. Shock and adrenaline were taking over now, the pain of the arrows protruding from his body disappearing into the mist of the instinct to survive.

"What just happened to Gurosh?" Seeing his warrior disappear and begin screaming, Bigglum heard a low hiss and with a thump an arrow penetrated his armor. The projectile did not pierce the ogre's chest cavity, but the deep laceration in the chieftain's breast and the continuing loud screams from his warrior were enough to convince him that it was time to make a hasty retreat.

"Never mind the boy! Zik! Get us out of here!" bellowed Bigglum, blood beginning to seep from under his armor. Looking back, he caught sight of Gurosh stumbling towards them, his face painted red with blood, an arrow protruding from his eye. Without knowing who or how many they faced, he wanted nothing more than to flee.

Despite his best efforts in the last minute, the shaman had failed to locate their attacker's hiding spot. He did not doubt for a moment that they were facing elves and he had no desire to retreat from them, but under these circumstances even if they only faced one elf they might as well just line themselves up for target practice. Ogres and elves despised each other as a matter of course, but Zik had a special kind of hate reserved for elves because they had natural resistances to his magic.

"Gurosh! Move faster or we will leave you here," growled Zik during a pause in the warrior's groaning. He had already cast the spell, creating a large oval gate. Dancing in front of them with its blue shimmering lights, the Moongate was humming and just about ready to transport. The shaman had marked the gate spell to take them back to his mountain stronghold, far away to the northwest.

"I go first!" yelled Bigglum, pushing his shaman out of the way. It was ogre protocol that the leader was the first to retreat from battle. Without a strong tribal chief, the ogres stood no chance against their enemies. Bigglum had proven his prowess in battle more than enough and all knew that to challenge him meant instant death. Zik jumped back as the ogre chieftain hurried into the portal.

The shaman looked back into the forest at the warrior stumbling towards him. Contemplating leaving and closing the gate before he reached it, Zik dismissed the thought. He did not like Gurosh, but would not dare be so brash with Bigglum waiting on the other side.

"Run faster Gurosh, or I will leave you to the elves!"

"Hold the light open, Zik!" pleaded Gurosh, not trusting that the shaman would wait for him. Screaming out again, he toppled to the ground as a third arrow slammed into his back. This arrow found a lung, blood soaking through the seams in his armor. Gasping for breath, the ogre found the strength to get up and move the last ten feet to reach the shaman and the Moongate.

Shuddering when he saw the gore covering his face and the arrow shaft still embedded in the warrior's head, Zik found it amazing that he was still alive.

"Hurry through the gate! I will use spells to heal you!" yelled Zik, hoping the warrior would not make it. "I can do nothing here!" Darting into the portal, there was a crackling noise for an instant and the shaman disappeared. With all his remaining strength Gurosh rushed towards the gate, but as another arrow struck him in the lower back he dropped to one knee and lost his footing.

With his first two arrows hitting their mark, Llysander knew that the ogre chasing Llythwain was on the ground and although still alive, was no longer a threat to his son. *A portal is opening! There is a shaman in this group.* To reveal his position would invite a battle where he would lose in an instant. One accurate fire spell would roast him alive. Relying on his Ranger training, the battle strategy with the highest degree of success was to remain hidden while raining death down upon the ogre heads.

Measuring the distance to the other two beasts, Llysander saw that the shaman was smart enough to stay where he thought he was out of range.

This big one must be their leader, but he's not as smart as the shaman. A hard accurate shot to the chest would puncture the leather armor and find his heart. Never missing at such short range, the Ranger let his arrow fly.

Bullseye! Llysander allowed himself a smile as he saw the arrow embed itself in the ogre's chest. It always elated him when his arrows found their mark. The beast's face registered the shock of the impact, but he recovered in no time and continued barking instructions at the shaman. *That should have had more of an effect. He must be protected by the shaman's magic.*

The blue Moongate manifested near the shaman. Carrying an odd-shaped cloth bag, the ogre leader was the first to escape. Llysander refocused on the closest ogre, who had risen from the ground and was now limping in the direction of the Moongate. An arrow to the left-center of the beast's back slammed him to the ground once more, but adrenaline gave him the strength to get back up and keep moving towards the portal. Loosing another arrow, he pierced the ogre's lower back but it was still not enough to put an end to its miserable life. The blood-covered beast fell headlong through the fading portal right after the shaman had disappeared.

"No!" shouted Llysander, jumping up as the Moongate disappeared and the forest went silent. Scanning the clearing around him, he realized that his daughter was gone.

Morrowyn must have been in the bag that the ogre was carrying! Llysander's blood ran cold as he looked for Llythwain. Attending to his son who was still lying prone on the ground, the Ranger realized that the best he could do was hope that his daughter managed to stay alive long enough for him to save her. *This fight is not over!*

III

SOUTHWARD BOUND

"Par ipsu ori noom," said Kethus Auberon, intoning the enchanted words. There was a humming noise, a flash of white light and the shimmering blue oval portal appeared in front of him. Standing to the side, he waited for the rest of the investigation team to pass through the Moongate.

The mage watched as Llaen, Razz and the six Rangers entered, followed by high priestess Brotah. When he had heard that a priestess was accompanying them, Kethus had hoped it might be his friend Ghilanna Ellifain. Noting the red hair cascading from inside the white robes though, the presence of the high priestess indicated the importance of this mission. Observing her from a distance and seeing her look with disdain upon the Rangers, he decided he did not like her much.

"That is everyone," said Lenowyn, trailing behind the high priestess.

"Excellent," said Kethus, choosing his words with care. The mage felt uneasy around this assassin and didn't want to say too much. Noting that she kept glancing in his direction, her natural edginess and piercing gaze made guilty thoughts rise to the surface of his mind. Having done nothing to upset her, he was starting to think she was planning an attack against him. *Perhaps it is all in my head. She knows nothing about me.* After watching Lenowyn enter the Moongate, the mage took a final look around and stepped through.

"Step no further! In the name of the High Council, identify yourselves!" commanded the startled guardsman, stepping in front of the arriving entourage with his sword drawn. Appearing on the platform near him, the guardsman observed a single armed figure exiting the Moongate's blue light. Seconds later several other armed shapes and a tall form in flowing white robes were stepping onto the platform. With the edict from Lord Uanor to prepare for war, the guards were nervous and edgy.

"It is Captain Eilrah and his team," countered Llaen, stepping forward into the light. He knew the guardsman well enough but appreciated the formalities on this surprise visit. The captain felt confident that no one here would become complacent in their duties at this platform.

Recognizing the Ranger uniforms standing in a group behind the Captain, the guardsman relaxed and waved the all clear signal to the guards in the watchtower above him. Llaen saw them lower their bows.

The platform in Luminor had shiny black stone steps leading to it on all sides, making arrivals and departures easier for the large groups that would sometimes use this Moongate. Most elven towns housed similar structures containing circular stones carved with magic runes. A Moongate was then conjured to that location by any magic user who bound their mark to the stone with their own set of magic runes.

"We have been sent here by Lord Uanor to investigate the Curse and were expecting that there would be another team meeting us here. Where are the others?"

Braigon had requested that Llaen lead this investigation as his personal representative. He had heard rumblings about the Curse for long enough and wanted his trusted captain to get a good look at things first hand. It was necessary to better understand what was happening and Braigon knew Llaen would provide him with an unbiased report.

"Tiliana and the Rangers are in the center of town, Captain," answered the guardsman in crisp tones. "There has been another death. This time we were able to trap the undead inside a house." Noting the high priestess in the group standing behind the captain, the guardsman felt relief. Tiliana was a young priestess and the guardsman had observed that her lack of experience did not allow her to help much.

"Guardsman, take us to this house of undead," ordered Llaen.

Leaving the platform, the team followed the guardsman down the cobblestone streets of Luminor. In spite of it being mid-morning, the streets were empty and it felt strange seeing the town so quiet. The few visible residents exchanged furtive whispers as they watched the team march past. Not knowing what was about to happen but fearing the worst, they shuttered their windows and disappeared behind locked doors.

Llaen had always liked visiting Luminor when he had time. Painted in dark colors with white trim, most of the two story houses had dark gray slate shingled roofs. The carved wooden lampposts lining the streets had floral ivy curling up from the ground. The architecture and cobblestone streets were magnificent, but these days neither visitors nor residents paid attention to any of it. An air of dread filled Luminor, unlike anything the townspeople had experienced before. Walking down the streets, Llaen could see the fear of the Curse in their faces. *I hope Inunis will be able to do something here*, the color of his thoughts matching the passing roofs.

"It is the third house on your left, Captain," the guardsman announced. The specific directions were unnecessary though, as a crowd of people were now surrounding the blighted home. Rangers stood guard on the perimeter, making sure the undead stayed inside the house and the onlookers stayed out. Dismissed by his captain, the guardsman turned away from the group, heading back towards his post at the Moongate without a backwards glance. The crowd began murmuring as soon as they saw the newcomers arrive.

"Llaen! Over here!" shouted Tiliana Oboron, only seeing the captain at first. The young priestess had been the first one sent to try and contain the undead. Pushing her way through the crowd, she walked towards Llaen and the group that she now saw was accompanying him.

"Tiliana! It is nice to see you…" Before Llaen could continue, Inunis stepped between them. She pulled her hood back with a flourish, revealing her identity to the young priestess and the rest of the assembled townspeople. The noisy crowd of onlookers erupted, as the high priestess had a fiery reputation. The townspeople were hopeful that perhaps now there might be a quick end to the Curse in Luminor. The chatter subsided as all eyes and ears focused on Inunis.

"High Priestess Brotah!" said Tiliana, casting her eyes down. Performing a deep bow to show her respect, she took a step back and waited for the expected reprimand. Standing behind Inunis now and offended by her rudeness, Llaen kept silent. His eyes met Tiliana's from behind the high priestess and he gave his friend a quick supportive smile. Dropping her eyes as she blushed at Llaen, Tiliana hoped Inunis hadn't noticed.

"Take me to them," the high priestess commanded, grasping her holy symbol with both hands and holding it up in front of her. Brandishing her religious symbol in front of her body, Inunis had more than enough power to keep the lesser undead from attacking. It was even possible for her to banish some of the less powerful forms. The creatures in Luminor were elves that had recently died, reanimating as undead. With flesh still clinging to their bones, they had become zombies. The high priestess had never experienced any problems controlling lesser undead, and zombies were one of the weakest forms.

"There are two of them," said Tiliana, knowing that Inunis was not listening to her warning. The priestess had tried banishing the undead, but her inexperience had left her unsuccessful. All she had been able to do was barricade them in their own house to keep them from attacking anyone else. She signaled to Llaen and the Rangers to remain close and observe.

"Let me through," ordered Lenowyn, glaring at the Rangers guarding the perimeter. The assassin's cold gaze convinced them to leave her alone. In addition to protecting the high priestess, Lenowyn wanted a front row seat to view the undead and their movements. Moving past the guards to stand with the two priestesses, she drew her katanas. *I'd better see how these things fight. I'm guessing they guard the necromancers.*

"I have unlocked the door," said Tiliana as she produced her own holy symbol, holding it at arm's length in front of her chest.

"I come to face you in the name of Goddess Shifra!" Drawing up to her full height, Inunis flung the door wide open and took a step inside the house. Gazing around the room, her intense gaze fixed on the zombies, grasping them with tendrils of her energy. She began gaining control of them within seconds.

"Mrrrroannn!" The zombie closest to Inunis made noise like a feral beast. It was mindless and unable to speak, but as soon as the high priestess entered the room the zombie could sense her spiritual energy. The creature thirsted for her life force, anxious to consume her energy to heal its own rotting flesh. Awkward on its feet, the zombie lunged towards Inunis, ready to attack.

"Back away. In the name of the Goddess Shifra obey me!" As the zombie slowed, Inunis was able to examine it. At first glance it looked like an elf woman, but its eyes were solid white. All color had drained from the body, its soul consumed by the Curse.

"This must be the daughter of the older looking zombie. It is likely that her father died of natural causes. When the Curse consumed him, he raised as a zombie, attacking and killing his own daughter. Now they are both undead," explained Inunis over the noise of the zombies. Gesturing with her holy symbol, both creatures staggered back unable to press forward. In spite of Inunis' superior spiritual strength, the zombies persisted with their attempt to attack her. *This curse is stronger than I had imagined.*

The moaning had increased tenfold. Working themselves into a deep frenzy with three living beings standing so close, the zombies' base instinct for survival kept pushing them to feed.

"Their lust for us is complete," noted Inunis, deciding not to waste any healing or bless spells trying to remove the curse. "The sight of the living is too much for them now. There is nothing we can do. Their souls now consumed, their spiritual energy is irretrievable." The zombies' frenzy was becoming more intense with the frustration of being unable to move forward. They were screaming with rage and bloodlust. The noise was deafening, sickening.

"Enough!" The high priestess's voice rose from deep inside her. Shocked that they could resist her power, Inunis could feel her control of these zombies loosening and it infuriated her. It was a personal affront to have a lesser undead dare to challenge her. "The Goddess Shifra banishes you!" Inunis focused her power as her face flushed with anger and effort.

Screaming louder in protest, without warning the zombies exploded with a loud popping sound.

"Damn!" said Lenowyn, surprised by the sudden zombie explosion. She wasn't sure what was going to happen here but was not expecting it to end like this. A spray of rotting flesh, blood and viscera enveloped the room. The assassin's reflexes were lightning quick and she tried dodging out of the blast's path, but was unable to escape the mist of gore painting the room red. Looking down at herself as she stood dripping on the floor, Lenowyn was furious. Her anger boiled over when she realized that both priestesses had been completely spared from wearing even a drop of the bloody mess. *What kind of pathetic magic is that?*

* * *

"How is it that an experienced mage does not have a rune marking to Strathmore?" Still irritated by the experience in Luminor, Lenowyn was shaking dried blood and entrails from her clothes and had been taking out her frustrations on Kethus as they traveled away from the town towards Dying Forest.

"Well, I have never been to Strathmore, so how could I have marked a rune to it?" said Kethus, having difficulty keeping a straight face at Lenowyn's obvious physical discomfort. He had almost laughed out loud when told about the events in the house in Luminor, but decided that keeping quiet and savoring the humor as they traveled on horseback through Dying Forest was preferable.

"Remember, Lord Uanor wants us to survey the lands and report everything we see. Traveling through Dying Forest is necessary to provide an accurate description," interrupted Llaen, examining the destruction surrounding them. The eerie silence filling the air was unsettling as he saw stumps and husks of what once was a vibrant living landscape. Trees had become dry and dark, as if a fire had burned through the forest. Even the earth was now pale and sandy like ash, yet no smoke or fire was ever reported. Over a period of only a few years, something had drained away the life force of almost every living organism here. Devoid of what the elves would consider normal wildlife, large vampire bats soared above them as the sun began disappearing. Llaen watched them circling overhead not far away, adding to the menacing feeling in the air as they appeared to move in unison with the team.

"Do not fire upon them," said Llaen, ordering his nervous Rangers to stand down. Stopping to draw his bow, Razz was taking aim at one of the larger creatures that had been swooping ever lower when Llaen spoke. "Under normal circumstances, vampire bats will not attack us during daylight unless provoked. If you were to shoot and kill one of them though, its death scream would bring many more. They hunger for our blood so we best not take too long getting to Strathmore. We do not want to travel out here after it gets dark."

"I sense many undead in this forest," said Inunis, shifting in her saddle, eyes closed in meditation. Braigon had requested she accompany the team to the human lands of Hathaway, feeling that her powers over the undead would be helpful. "Excited by our spiritual energy, they hunt us. We should maintain our pace and be vigilant."

Amazed at the state of the land around her, the speed with which the spiritual energy had drained from this forest came as a shock to Lenowyn. *Is this our fate now that the Curse has begun spreading to Green Valley?*

"Hold up!" shouted Razz, wrestling with his horse to stay on the path. Blocking their way was a large skeletal wolf, its yellow eyes glowing in the dusky light. An undead creature with a half-rotten carcass, the wolf-creature was more skeleton than zombie, a few strips of rotting flesh and matted fur still clinging to its dirty white bones.

"Watch out, Llaen!" Lenowyn reacted as the creature scuttled forward to attack now that the captain had trotted past Razz into the lead position. Drawing her katana and rushing to defend him, the wolf-creature was faster.

"What the...!" The creature sprang at Llaen so fast and from such distance that he had no time to draw his weapon. Its snapping jaws tore at the Ranger, biting deep into his right calf. His horse rearing as the creature's claws gouged it, the captain hung on with all his strength knowing that if he fell his life would be over. The undead wolf was far more powerful than any of them had expected and the burning in Llaen's leg from its bite was unbearable.

"Emu alif!" A burst of flame from Kethus's fingers struck the undead wolf broadside, shocking its body away from Llaen's horse. Landing on the ground with a thump, the creature began convulsing as small fingers of flame ate at its remaining flesh.

"Now you will die!" said Lenowyn, jumping off her horse to engage the creature before it could recover. With one precise stroke she severed its head from its body, the two parts continuing to spasm after they became separated.

"Thank you Lenowyn, Kethus." Righting himself on his horse, Llaen took deep breaths to help accept the pain as he examined his wound. Pulling a broken tooth from where he was bitten, he determined that the creature had pierced the flesh but did not cut any major veins. Of more concern were the edges of the wound that had already begun turning black. A simple bandage before they continued traveling would have to suffice.

"Don't worry about your wound, Llaen. I will heal you," said Inunis, her horse sidling up to the Captain's steed. Glancing at the team for effect, she closed her eyes while taking slow deep breaths. The high priestess placed her hands upon the Captain's leg and cast her magic. The wound filled with blue light and began to close. In moments the leg looked as though it had never seen injury. "We should not linger, there are many undead approaching us now."

"Thank you, Inunis. Your powers never cease to amaze me. Everyone, let's move now," said Llaen, noticing two rotting wolf-creatures skulking between the trees. The instinct to travel in packs appeared to hold true even in their undead state. The investigation team galloped away as fast as they could, seven howling wolf-creatures chasing close behind.

* * *

Riding hard for another hour, the team felt relieved to see Strathmore approaching. There had been dramatic changes to the landscape as they left the forest and its packs of undead wolves behind. The dark dead trees of the forest had given way to broad fields of knee high grasses. Along each side of the roadway wooden fences meant to keep livestock from straying were in varying stages of disrepair. The grasses inside the fences were high and unkempt; most of it was yellow and dead. There were no animals in sight and it was obvious that nothing had grazed most of these fields for some time. Scattered in the distance, a few farms dotted the countryside and further down the roadway they could see the twinkling lights of the village.

"We are almost there," said Llaen, allowing himself to relax at the end of the day's adventure. Years before this blight had begun creeping over the land, he recalled passing through this village on his way to the great port city of Barsoom. As a much younger elf, his excitement and eagerness for adventure could carry him for days at a time. Stiff from today's long ride, his muscles were aching and exhausted from keeping his senses on high alert. Nearing a farm, yelling and clanking of what sounded like an ongoing battle echoed through the air. Materializing out of dusk's early gloom, Llaen could make out a group of men with weapons drawn that appeared to be fighting something familiar. His tired brain refused to acknowledge the identity of their opponents.

"Come on, let's help them!" In the farmyard Lenowyn could see five swordsmen and a farmer struggling with what appeared to be a herd of cows. Drawing closer, the team saw that these animals had the same void look in their eyes as the forest wolf-creatures and the family in Luminor. This was an entire herd of undead zombie cows. The impact of the Curse appeared never-ending.

"I'll take the cows on the left," shouted Razz, racing after Lenowyn. Finding this situation amusing, the swordsman struggled to hide a smile. Honing his swordsmanship in practise every morning, play fighting was never a substitute for the real thing. He was glad to have the opportunity to swing his blades at live targets again. Real opponents always added an extra element of unpredictability, even if they were cows. With the fight now upon him, in an instant he switched from grinning at the absurdity of this situation to measuring his foes and planning their demise.

"The two by the farmer are mine!" shouted Lenowyn over the noise of the cow-creatures, running to assist the farmer. His only weapon was a pitchfork and it was obvious he was struggling to keep his opponents from gnawing on him.

"Mrrroooo!" Sensing Lenowyn's life energy, one of the zombie cows turned from the farmer to attack this new source of energy.

"Help... me!" Crying out with effort when he saw Lenowyn approaching out of the corner of his eye, even with only one cow facing him the farmer was losing the battle. The tines of his fork could not do much more than jab it full of holes as the heavy creature pushed him down. The cow was streaming blood as its head jerked up and down trying to bite him, its bell clanging over and over.

"Rangers, over here!" Looking for assistance, Lenowyn faced the cow and waited for an opening to strike. Swinging the katana with all her strength, she wanted to kill the undead cow-creature stamping its hooves in front of her as fast as she could to help the farmer dispatch his remaining bovine adversary before it killed him.

"I will heal the farmer!" Standing at the edge of the farmyard, Inunis cast her magic on the wounded farmer. His wounds began glowing as they healed and the man found strength trickling back into his muscles. But with its greater mass and undead lack of concern for its own well being, the cow-creature continued to prevail. It was still on top of him, thrashing and biting the farmer on his arms and legs. The zombie cow's flesh healed itself every time it bit him and stole a little bit more of his spiritual energy.

"Foul beast!" shouted Llaen, frustrated by the cow-creature's relentless style of attack. Charging into it at full speed, the Captain knocked the zombie cow away from the farmer, chopping at its neck with his long sword. The blow did not kill the creature but stunned it enough to allow the farmer to crawl out from beneath its weight.

"Can't you kill this thing?" Screaming as he regained his footing, the farmer was in complete shock. "What is happening to us?!"

"How are we even still alive?" a swordsman shouted out to no one in particular. Never having experienced the mindless fury of the undead, this swordsman was swinging his weapon for all he was worth, his arms growing numb from the effort.

"To battle!" Yelling in unison, the remaining Rangers raised their weapons as they joined the attack. Moving as a unit to help the swordsmen, they chopped at the cow-creatures over and over, sprays of blood and chunks of flesh flying into the air. Surprising them, the undead beasts did not slow under the assault. The proximity of the Rangers' life energy drove the cow zombies into an even deeper frenzy. Their relentless one-track minds continued pushing them to achieve their purpose. The creatures wanted to consume the living and feast on their spiritual energy.

"Kethus!" Inunis had finished evaluating the battle, creating a plan that she felt would turn the tides of this struggle. "I will gain the cows' focus. Create an explosion when they become distracted."

"You know my spells too well, Inunis." Reaching into his bag for the right spell components, the mage shouted a brief warning to the combatants. "Everyone get ready to retreat! On my signal!"

"Undead! Back away!" shouted Inunis, her voice rising from deep within her chest. Her steely eyes glaring at the undead creatures, she commanded the herd while holding up her holy symbol.

Ah ha! I'm not falling for this again! Having slaughtered the undead cow in front of her and sensing what the spellcasters were doing, Lenowyn went into an immediate full retreat. *It's nice to have a front row seat, but once was enough. I can let the rest of them have a turn.*

"Undead! Back away...! In the name of the Goddess Shifra, I compel you to obey me!" Stopping their attack at the sound of the words, every zombie cow head swiveled in unison to focus on the high priestess. Inunis took a step forward and like puppets, the entire herd took an awkward step backwards. The undead cows could feel their life energies throbbing as the priestess worked them. Unable to focus on more than one thing at a time, the herd stared at the holy symbol in Inunis' hands, retreating step by step as it moved towards them.

"No isi olpi xe!" chanted Kethus, beginning a whistle that seemed to grow from the ground all around the undead cows. Like the squealing of a thousand boiling campfire kettles, the noise intensified until it was deafening.

"Everyone move back now!" the mage shouted over the din, waving his arms as humans and elves scrambled out of the way. Seconds later the entire area erupted into flames. As the fireball rose into the night sky, the force of the blast was ripping the entire herd to shreds. A spray of blood mixed with large chunks of flesh and entrails flew in all directions. Unscathed by the gory debris, Inunis's white robes fluttered around her body. The pleasure she gained from witnessing the results of the mage's handiwork was obvious to anyone who happened to see her face in that moment.

"Not this time," said Lenowyn, stepping out from behind the mage. Stifling a chuckle at the sight of everyone's obvious disgust, her decision had been the correct one. Gazing at the carnage generated by Kethus' final act in the farmyard, it was a relief that the battle ended when it did. The undead cows were turning out to be much tougher fighters than she had imagined.

Inunis nodded her approval when she saw the assassin step out from behind the mage, having used him as protection from the flying gore of the explosion. Impressed by her quick thinking, it appeared to the priestess that Lenowyn was a quick study.

* * *

"Now you know why we do not trust any necromancers," said Inunis, loud enough that everyone in the room could hear her. Having already finished a few glasses of wine, the soothing liquid was loosening her tongue. "The undead are not something to invoke on a whim. Look at what they have done to your lands." Looking around the room with a cold glare, she took another sip from her glass.

After the battle with the herd of undead cows, the team of elves accompanied the swordsmen to Strathmore. Exhausted and tired, they went straight to the inn to bathe, have a few drinks and relax. The locals filling the adjacent tavern this evening found it quite surprising to see the newcomers sitting at their favorite tables. Extra chairs filled every available space, as everyone was eager to hear the tale of the farmer's battle with the zombies.

"Of course you are right, priestess." Speaking at the same volume as Inunis, Lenowyn made sure everyone in the room could hear her words. A few of the swordsmen from the battle were also here and she could tell they were recounting what had transpired at the farm. Lenowyn and Inunis hoped their loud conversation might present a clue that could lead the assassin to the necromancers.

"Does anyone think the necromancers have something to do with this undead nonsense?" In response to Lenowyn, a townsman yelled out to anyone who might answer.

"Who else could cause the undead to rise up as has been happening recently?" Wanting the conversation to continue with everyone overhearing, Lenowyn was watching to see if anyone would react. Skilled at reading body language, the assassin hoped to spot something suspicious.

"It's true, I cannot think of anyone other than a necromancer that could raise the dead," the townsman agreed. Nodding their heads, a few others followed suit in agreement. One group of patrons joined the townsman in a quiet conversation.

"The raising of the dead is unholy and has led to this curse. Humans have let necromancers practice this depraved act for too long and now it may be too late!" Full of vitriol and wine Inunis rose on unstable legs, glaring at the crowd of patrons who had by now stopped talking. The room stared back with wide eyes at this angry elven high priestess. The tension became palpable and in an instant the room felt more dangerous.

"More powerful undead can also raise the dead," a shabby older man at a corner table stated, oblivious to the sudden silence and discomfort of those around him. Squinting up at the high priestess, at once he seemed to realize that his mouth might have moved quicker than his brain was operating. Shifting in his chair, the man looked around for help as Inunis fixed her icy gaze on him.

"I did not realize we had someone here so knowledgeable on the topics of the undead and necromancy!" Her voice dripping with sarcasm, Inunis's eyes tore up and down the old man. He was older than she and it was clear he was past his prime. With only a thin fringe of brown hair circling his head, his large belly and round, nondescript features heightened the usual anonymity of his presence. Uncomfortable and squirming under the high priestess's scrutiny, he looked for any way out of this confrontation. Recognizing that he was harmless, Inunis did not care. The high priestess would not stand for any questioning and decided she was going to make an example of him.

"Priestess, I j-j-j-ust thought..." Wishing he could somehow undo his words, he knew it was now too late. Wilting into the corner chair, he could only pray the high priestess would be merciful.

"Oh, you just thought, did you? Perhaps your thoughts come from real knowledge. Maybe you are practicing necromancy in secret. Maybe it is you who is responsible for the Curse!" Waving her arms for emphasis, the priestess used her skills at working an audience to begin building consensus.

"N-n-n-no! I would never do such a thing..." Staring at the floor, sweat began darkening the man's armpits and he felt the contents of his stomach rising.

"So you do not deny being a necromancer then?"

"Not... a... necro... man... cer," the man wheezed, close to tears.

"Well... you claim you are not a necromancer, but I suspect you know of necromancy." Needing to raise suspicion, she used her words with precision. With many townspeople at the inn this night, gossip would soon spread and become distorted enough so that at least some might suspect him. Perhaps a real necromancer might come to his rescue.

"Not a necromancer, not a necromancer..." Staring at the floor, his reputation in ruins, he knew his wife would no longer approve of his visits to the inn.

"I think he protests too much. What do the rest of you think?" Dismissing him without another glance Inunis made a slow turn, looking at the crowd once again as she returned to her seat. Sitting down with a satisfied air and taking a sip of wine, the high priestess hoped that perhaps someone might make a mistake tonight. She just had to keep her eyes and ears open.

Watching the crowd as Inunis berated the old man, Lenowyn noticed a few of his friends clustered in quiet conversation. One of the men jumped up and slipped outside, looking over his shoulder at the group of elves as he left. Thinking it could be the breakthrough they were hoping for, she leaned over to Llaen. "I have to check on something."

Passing unseen through the crowd, Lenowyn exited through the same doorway as the man a moment earlier. The night was dark and the moon a yellow slit, working to the assassin's advantage. Keeping close to the edge of the street like a shadow on a black painted wall, her movements mirrored those of her quarry. Each time the man stopped to make sure he was alone Lenowyn read his intent and became motionless. Seeing no one, the man scurried deeper into the night.

Where are you off to in such a hurry, my little mouse? Lenowyn loved the warmth of the hunt. As silent as a breeze, moving from shadow to shadow, she pursued the man to what she hoped would be the location of her ultimate prize, a human necromancer.

✳ ✳ ✳

"Hello?" Thomas had left the inn in a hurry, heading straight to the graveyard. Looking for the caretaker, he was hoping to warn her about the elven strangers that had arrived in town. Her father had been the cemetery caretaker, and Thomas had been his friend for more than fifty years. He had died not too long ago, and with no other heirs the cemetery business had passed to his daughter.

"Is somebody there?" Unable to see far into the dark and foggy graveyard, Thomas walked down the stone pathway towards the caretaker's house. The gravestones on either side of the pathway never failed to unsettle him at night, even though he had been coming here for years. Thomas was sure he could hear moaning sounds and they seemed to be getting closer.

"Tabatha? Is that you?"

"Tabatha, are you ok? Please answer me!" The moaning was becoming louder and in an instant he felt quite vulnerable. The hair on his neck and arms was standing on end as he peered into the darkness.

"Watch out!" shouted a dark figure as it rushed past him. A blade hissed through the air, slicing into a creature that was staggering towards him out of the maze of gravestones. The blade found its mark, severing the creature's leg and dropping its body to the ground.

"Mrrrrroan!" Another zombie staggered into view from the other side of the pathway.

"Nooo! What is going on here?" His heart pounding like it was about to jump right out of his chest, Thomas wasn't sure who was with him in the graveyard or what was happening, all he could see was a dark shape darting around the gravestones like a dervish. Without warning the metal flashed like lightning, the steel blade cleaving its prey. "Tabatha?! Is that you?!"

"Mrrrrroan!" With its leg severed, the howling zombie continued towards Thomas as best it could. Crawling closer to the old man out of the dark, it clawed at his leg, trying to drag him down and consume his spiritual energy.

"Thomas! I'm here!" Woken by the noise in the quiet cemetery, Tabatha had sprinted to investigate the commotion. It was too dark to discern everything, but she recognized Thomas and knew from his tone that he was in trouble.

"Over here!" shouted Lenowyn. Three more zombies were approaching and she was already fighting two of them. *How many zombies are here?* Lenowyn kicked one creature backwards with a solid boot to its chest and as her leg dropped back to the ground she was already striking at another one.

"Mrrrrrroan!" The zombie howled as it pulled the much weaker old man to the ground. Sliding itself on top of him, it began ripping into his chest with its hands and mouth.

"Tabatha!" screamed Thomas, unable to hold the creature off. The burning pain was unlike anything he had ever experienced. Recognizing that he had already lost, Thomas was not offering much resistance to the eager zombie and was hoping for a quick death.

"Get off him!" shouted Tabatha, kicking the zombie hard across the head. The impact separating the head from the body, its skull rolled across the pathway onto the grass with its mouth still clacking open and closed. As the zombie's arms relaxed, Tabatha knelt down to help her friend. Pushing the now headless zombie corpse off him, she tried her best to comfort him in his final moments. "I'm here Thomas, be still now."

"Tabatha!" the old man whispered, his voice wet with blood. Life energy pouring out through his torn open chest, Thomas tried to pull Tabatha closer.

"You're a good friend, Thomas. Shhhhh… Be strong." Aware that her old family friend would soon be dead, the caretaker was dreading the inevitable effects that the Curse of the Undead would have upon his body. There was only one way to deal with a zombie, and that was an indignity she was unwilling to impart on someone as loyal as Thomas.

"Tabatha… there are elves at the inn…" Thomas could offer no further explanation. Tasting his own blood with every shallow breath, his world began turning black. Coughing as he tried to breathe, his eyes rolled back into his head.

"Raz par Del!" Upset and not thinking straight, the young necromancer cast a Raise Dead spell onto his now limp body instead of a Control Undead spell. So distracted by everything happening around her, she was not aware of what she had done.

"Mrrrrrroan!" Out of the mist, three zombies cornered Lenowyn, lusting after her spiritual energy. As a group they rushed at her, but were still unable to breach her defenses.

"Hey girl, I could use a little help over here," said Lenowyn, grunting with more than a little sarcasm. She knew someone named Tabatha had arrived and was helping the old man, but had lost sight of both of them in the dark as, twisting and turning she swung at the drooling undead. Bringing her sword down on the closest zombie she sliced off one of its arms, pushing past it through the armless opening. The zombies did not carry weapons, but with their larger numbers and surprising quick speed, Lenowyn did not want to be cornered again.

"I'm coming, stranger!" Taking a last look at Thomas lying on the ground in front of her, Tabatha could see that his eyes had already gone white, his skin becoming pale like parchment. The necromancer prepared herself and her short sword for a killing blow to the neck of what was once her old family friend.

"Tabatha?" Speaking though a froth of blood and confused by his surroundings, the old man had fresh memories of the black curtain of death but could once again hear the noises of the graveyard battle.

"What? Thomas!" Replaying what had just happened, Tabatha realized her mistake. Under normal circumstances, as soon as spiritual energy exited the physical form, a person was no longer alive. She had wanted to control the undead creature that Thomas was about to become, and she realized now that the wrong spell had been cast. Hearing the old man talking to her even though his eyes indicated he was a zombie raised a number of questions. The necromancer's mind whirled with the possibilities of this discovery. *The Raise Dead spell has somehow managed to keep the soul trapped in a zombie body! Could I use this to counteract the Curse?*

"Elves... blaming... necromancers... curse..." Choking out the words as a zombie, Thomas delivered the message to Tabatha that he had failed to say while still alive. His words gnawed at her heart. Tabatha hated hiding her true vocation and if the elves were hunting them, more than ever it seemed that her profession needed to remain a well-guarded secret.

"I have heard your warning, Thomas. Rest now, my friend." Her eyes filling with tears, she knew what she must do. Tabatha loved her old friend too much to keep his soul trapped in the zombie physical form. Taking full control of his undead body, she released her hold and the true zombie in the old man's body began stirring. Even before it could sense Tabatha's life energy she swung her sword hard across its throat, beheading the creature in a single merciful strike. The detached head rolled away from the body, more of Thomas' blood spilling onto the pathway.

"Watch out!" shouted Lenowyn after killing another of the zombies. Managing to get close to where the girl was crouching, she spun to face the remaining creatures and saw one of them lunging at the girl.

"Huh!" Turning her head at the sound of the stranger's voice, Tabatha saw the zombie rushing towards her. Bloody sword already in hand, her arm followed through with her swing as catlike, she jumped away from the old man's body. Her sword skewered the belly of the creature, knocking it off its already unstable feet.

"Die!" she screamed, channeling the raw emotions of having to behead her friend. Tabatha rushed the zombie before it could recover its balance, swinging her sword up and down, slicing it many times as tears ran down her face. Playing the drama of Thomas' last moments over in her mind, she continued hacking at the corpse in front of her. With each new strike her pain subsided a little more.

"Hey girl! I think it's dead already!" Killing the last zombie and hurrying towards the girl, Lenowyn now stepped forward into what little light was available. Watching her struggle to control the outburst of grief, the assassin's black hooded cloak hung low around her head, hiding most of her face from view.

Slowing her thrashing of the now long dead creature, Tabatha turned to face her unknown savior. Beneath the hood all she could see was a pair of deep green eyes staring back into her own. *This must be one of the elves that Thomas warned me about.*

"He was like family," said Tabatha, still in shock. Pulling off her glasses, she wiped at the tears that had mixed with the smears of blood on her face.

"I'm sorry for you and your friend." It was an awkward moment for Lenowyn and she struggled with her words. Grief counseling was not part of her usual duties. Turning away instead, the assassin let her years of training take over. "Be alert. There may be more zombies lurking behind these gravestones."

"You're right, of course. I'll try to keep my eyes open." Tabatha wasn't yet sure what this elf knew or what her purpose was for being here tonight. The last words from her old friend had warned her that elves were blaming necromancers for the Curse. She decided that not telling this one anything about her true profession was a wise idea.

"By the way, my name is Lenowyn," the elf said over her shoulder, walking along the path in front of the girl. On either side of the walkway tombstones stretched like rows of broken teeth disappearing into the mouth of darkness. Lenowyn scanned the area to determine if any more undead were moving. "I'm going to assume you have a name. Who are you?"

"Oh, I'm sorry! I'm Tabatha. Tabatha Shadowsong. I am the cemetery caretaker. I live not far from here and the noise of the fighting woke me."

"I was going for a walk to get some fresh air when I heard the same noises, so I came by to investigate," said Lenowyn. Based on what she glimpsed happen to the old man, she suspected that there might be more to Tabatha's story, but letting her suspicions go for the moment, Lenowyn focused on getting more answers. "Do you know where the zombies came from?"

"I have a pretty good idea!" Staring at the ruins of her cemetery and seeing the destroyed gravesites with dirt now piled high around them, Tabatha examined the empty wooden caskets that had been pulled out and torn open. The caretaker couldn't believe her eyes. "Someone has exhumed these corpses and raised them from the dead!"

"Wouldn't the Curse be causing them to rise from the dead?"

"These people were buried long before the Curse started affecting our town. Someone or something must have come and done this," said Tabatha. "We need to warn the guardsmen. Someone was robbing my graveyard of its bodies!"

"It looks like we interrupted them. Look! There are more graves dug up over there!" As Lenowyn's eyes adjusted to the gloom, she saw the extent of the destruction. "There are thirty or forty graves disturbed on that side of the cemetery and the footprints left by the zombies all head away from here. Based on the size of this place, there are enough bodies buried in this graveyard to form a small army of undead. It looks like we stumbled in here just in time to disturb the grave robbers before they could finish their work."

"We better warn the guardsmen right away," said Tabatha, worried that her graveyard might be further vandalised. Without waiting for Lenowyn, she turned and ran towards town.

* * *

"The tracks of the undead show them moving towards the southeast," said Llaen. Crouching between torn open graves, he saw nothing giving away the identity of the vandals. "Whatever caused these bodies to rise, it or they did not leave any tracks of their own."

"This is terrible! We need to figure out what caused this as soon as possible! If the Curse is the reason, then what will prevent all the other corpses in the cemetery from rising from their graves in due course?" said Mayor Downey, looking around as if expecting the rest of the dead to rise as they spoke. The mayor and a host of guardsmen had accompanied the team, Tabatha, and Lenowyn back to the graveyard to investigate the undead disturbance.

"I do not believe this is part of the Curse. I suspect there are necromancers behind it!" said Inunis, her voice rising above all others. Stumbling on the uneven ground, she was still feeling the effects of too much wine. Hoping nobody had noticed her drunken wobbling, the priestess tried finding a flat spot to stand.

"I respectfully disagree. Necromancers would have left some sign of their presence. We would see more than just the tracks of the undead walking away," said Llaen. "Another sure thing is that it would take a lot more than one person to raise this many dead bodies in so little time."

"I tend to agree with the Ranger," said the Mayor, choosing to ignore the high priestess's comments. "But if we find that this is in fact part of the Curse, we will have no choice but to dig up all the graves and burn the…"

"Marik! You can't dig up the graves. It isn't right!" interrupted Tabatha.

"The girl is right! Desecrating your cemetery is sacrilegious! If we follow the trail I am convinced it will lead us to the necromancers." Glaring at Llaen, his siding with a human against her appraisal of the situation was infuriating.

"Enough!" Asserting his authority, the mayor was not bending to anyone's will tonight. "I realize it is not the preferred option. Digging up and burning all the corpses is not what I want to do either. But if we have no other choice and the safety of the town is in jeopardy, I will order it regardless of it being right or sacrilegious."

"But Marik…" Starting to argue her point again, Tabatha fell silent when she saw the mayor's stern look and waving hand.

"Tabatha, please understand. This Curse is threatening our entire town. I realize that you are now the caretaker here, but your father was a good friend of mine for many years and I guarantee you that he would agree with me in this situation. Ranger, can you and your team help us track the undead creatures that got away?"

"Yes we can!" interrupted Inunis, answering before Llaen had a chance to open his mouth. "I am in charge of this team and we also need to understand the cause of what is going on with the undead!" Glaring at Llaen again, she dared him to try and take control.

"We will place the graveyard under armed guard, just in case. I will also send a dozen of my guards with you. But if I do not hear back from you soon, I will take the more drastic steps I have already outlined."

"You can't!" protested Tabatha. The caretaker looked at the mayor in disbelief, trying to convince him to rethink his plan through sheer force of emotion.

"I think it is best that Tabatha join your team as you search for more answers."

"What!" Tabatha could not believe what she was hearing. Feeling a gentle nudge on her shoulder, Tabatha saw Lenowyn hinting for her to stay quiet.

"She will be a welcome addition to our team," said Lenowyn, stepping in front of Tabatha. "I think it best if we leave right away while the trail is still warm."

"I completely agree!" Hoping to prove everyone wrong by discovering that the necromancers were in fact the perpetrators of the Curse, Inunis stepped beside Lenowyn looking ready to go. "Let's see what we can find, shall we?"

IV

THE SHAMAN'S LAIR

"A good morning it is," said Jujube, speaking to no one in particular. Yawning as he stretched the stiffness out of his body, the shaman's apprentice straightened his short brown robe and pulled the hood over his head to protect himself from the cool breeze now exploring his master's sanctuary. The mountain air was getting cooler every day now, hinting that winter was getting closer. Standing at the cave entrance, the goblin held onto the locked iron bars of the portcullis with both hands and watched the early morning fog burn away before his eyes as the sun warmed the stones around him. Looking out past the overhang of the cavern entrance, he could sense the mountain slopes extending further than his eyes could focus. Jujube had long lost count of the years he had spent in servitude to Zik, the ogre shaman.

"A good morning it is," he repeated. Jujube liked starting the day in a good mood and found the silence of the mountains relaxing. The shaman had been away for over a week and his apprentice was happiest alone, with the freedom to stroll as he pleased about his master's stronghold. The large cavern complex was huge in comparison to most of the other caves carved out of the side of the mountain. Turning away from the outside view, he paused for a moment to think about his upcoming day. "Master is coming home soon," he muttered, his expression dropping at the realization. His run of good days would soon be ending. Zik was never kind to his apprentice.

"Fssstz!" The spiritual energy-draining staff stuck in his belt made a buzzing crackle. Pretending that the noise was the magic staff responding to his words, the goblin smiled back at it. The master allowed him to talk to any of the prisoners as he pleased, but he preferred conversing with himself or the ogre's magic staff. That way he always got the answers he wanted without any argument. Years of solitary time had conditioned him to enjoy the sound of his own voice above all others.

"The goblin high shaman did not think Jujube good enough to ever be shaman," he said, bringing his mood down another notch. Each morning before Zik awoke, Jujube would sneak out of his bed to stand and gaze through the portcullis bars. Most of the time he thought about the life he once had before his tribe's high shaman had given him as a slave to the ogre. Today as he stood looking outside, he wondered if he would ever be on his own in the world again. Waving the staff about over his head, he imagined himself showing that high shaman his easy command of its power. Perhaps then, his life might be different. Finishing his morning ritual, he looked at the magic staff with affection, grasping it like a child holds a doll. "Come, you. We must get the chores done before Master comes back."

"First we get food from the pantry." With his feet slapping against the cold stone floor as he plodded into the kitchen, Jujube positioned the staff behind his back and looped it in his belt so he could grab the key ring. Flipping through the large cluster of keys, his impatient fiddling caused them to jingle as he searched for the pantry key. The master insisted that every door and cupboard were to remain locked at all times. That had been a painful lesson for the apprentice, but he was now careful to never forget the locking and unlocking as he completed his daily tasks, even when he was alone.

Being the keeper of the key to the kitchen larder gave the goblin access to plenty of food and he kept himself well fed. Jujube tossed a handful of dried berries into his mouth, smacking his lips while he prepared a simple breakfast for the prisoners. Loading a tray full of food, he locked the pantry behind him and sauntered down the hallway toward the jail cells. Whistling a tuneless air, his feet slapped out a rhythm on the floor.

"Stop that blasted whistling or I swear I will make you stop!" Threatening Jujube from inside the first cell, a voice yelled out in the common Shard tongue. A disheveled half-human, half-orc with brown curly hair plastered to his head was trying with little success to block out the noise of the goblin approaching his cell door. Exhausted and grumpy, Zik's potion-maker bounced up and down while shifting his position in bed. He had just finished working all night and was nowhere near ready to get up just yet.

"Mixer, you wake up right now! You better keep making those healing draughts for Master! He is coming back soon! Master will not be happy if they are not ready!" The goblin had never liked Mixer and it was obvious that the feeling was mutual. Before unlocking the thick wooden door to the cell, Jujube opened the sliding window panel and peeked inside. Not trusting the half-orc, the apprentice wanted to make sure that he was still shackled to the wall. Blinking his eyes wide as they got used to the smoky darkness, Jujube could see the potion maker's cauldron bubbling and stewing over the glowing red coals of the hearth.

Mixer must have worked all night. I hope he's tired. Jujube was a bit more cautious with the prisoners ever since an elf mage captive had tried to escape. He had blurry memories of the mage casting his sleep spell then rushing out of the cell. Before his face hit the floor while struggling against the spell's effects, Jujube remembered hearing the sound of running feet as the elf sped down the passageway to the front entrance. Shaking his head, he imagined how that elf must have felt when he realized there was no way of lifting the heavy portcullis. The master had feasted on elf mage that same night.

"Looks safe to me," said Jujube, reassuring himself while surveying things through the window opening. With the shackles visible on Mixer's leg and the potion-maker lying motionless on the bed, he felt comfortable enough to unlock and open the door. The key clicked in the lock and the door groaned as he pushed it open. Following the shaft of light from the passageway into the cell, he stepped through the doorway.

"I finished the potions!" Yelling as loud as he could, Mixer jumped up in bed as soon as the goblin took a second step into his cell, happy to have one over on the nasty little apprentice. His mouth cracked into a wide grin when he saw Jujube jump an honest foot off the ground at the sound of his voice. Pulling his blanket back over his head, Mixer tried covering his eyes and ears. "Now leave the food and go away!"

"You are not finished!" Jujube yelped, regaining his composure with great difficulty. "Your cauldron is still brewing. Potions need pouring. The ogres are on a raid. They will need many... more... POTIONS!" Tugging on the blanket as he yelled, the goblin tore it off and tossed it on the floor. Dressed in his leather patchwork clothing and apron the potion-maker's dirty, unkempt hair was long and bushy. Covered in potion ingredients, his light gray skin was filthy. Jujube could feel his nose wrinkling as the putrid smell of body odor rose like a cloud from the bed. There was nothing about Mixer that sat well with the goblin.

"I know what to do!" roared Mixer, still lying on his bed. Kicking his feet and swinging his arms in the air like a spoiled child, he did not want any reminding from his little green rival. Mixer hated following orders, and was forever hostile towards anyone who felt like competition.

Dropping the food on Mixer's table, Jujube pulled the energy-draining staff out from behind his back. "Jujube can't ♪ go ♪ just yet! It's time ♪ for Mixer's ♪ punish ♪ met," he sang, taunting the half-orc with abandon now. Sensing that the potion-maker's feathers were ruffling, he was enjoying the opportunity to harrass him.

To cast the magic spells necessary for making potions, a potion-maker needs lots of magic energy. Mixer's magic is powerful enough that he has the potential to wreak havoc if he were ever let loose within the master's stronghold. For this reason, the shaman keeps him locked up and makes sure that Jujube drains most of his magic energy every morning. This process ensures that Mixer cannot concoct anything unauthorized. He supplies the ogre tribe with healing draughts and fills the energy-draining staff with more than half of its magical energy on a daily basis.

"Ohhhhhhh, Mixer hates you, goblin! Hates youuuu!" Screeching in frustration, Mixer knew what was coming next. The ogres valued his potion-making abilities, and he had expected that his skills would guarantee him the freedom and power of the shaman's apprentice position. When the master had decided that Jujube would be the one wielding the energy-draining staff, the potion-maker had become incensed. He had never been able to hide his jealousy of the goblin since that day, and he made a point of spraying Jujube with hateful words at every opportunity. When he was alone and had calmed down, Mixer believed he understood why the master had made his choice. The goblin was completely inept, to the point of comedy. Poor simple Jujube posed no chance of a threat to the shaman.

"Hee hee hee! This doesn't hurt, does it?" Mocking his captive, Jujube pointed the staff at Mixer and willed it to drain him.

"Noooo!" Screeching again, Mixer had nowhere to hide. Enduring this punishment every day, he could never get used to the electrical shocks he received from the staff while it was draining him. Grimacing and squirming in agony, his magic power ebbed away.

"Ohhhh, poor Mixer!" Jujube kept laughing as the potion-maker writhed this way and that, trying in vain to protect his body from the paralyzing jolts. "You want me to stop?" He loved watching the potion-maker perform the involuntary dance while the staff drained him. Learning to control the rate by which the magical energy flowed into the staff, he made the process extra slow whenever it was Mixer's turn. Pulsing now, the staff seemed to move with a life of its own. It took a lot of strength to hold onto the staff when it was working, and his hand was trembling with effort. Only once the staff had drained all of its victim's magic would the process end. With the potion-maker now slumping on the ground next to his bed Jujube stepped closer, gloating over him with a wicked grin.

"One day friend... One day I promise I will kill you!" Threatening the goblin in a whisper as he glared up from the floor, it was all Mixer could do to find the strength to speak, but his eyes meant every word. The potion-maker would never forget the actions of his keeper.

"Master does not trust you with the staff. He doesn't. But he trusts me." Smug in his position, Jujube did not miss any chance to remind his adversary who was in control. *Mixer always looks disgusting and dirty. His cell looks the same. It is always littered with papers and potion bottles caked in dust and dirt.* Holding his breath as he looked with contempt around the cell, his eyes ended up back on Mixer. "Master would never pick you."

"I hate you, goblin. I make Master his potions! Why does he give you the staff to hold? It's not fair!" Croaking out his protest, the half-orc slid the rest of the way to the floor.

"All done, you!" Addressing the magic staff, Jujube watched it shimmer and pulse as the stolen energy swirled inside. With his morning visit to the potion-maker complete, the goblin exited the cell. Pulling as hard as he could on the heavy door, he closed it with a booming thud, locking it behind him.

"Master only trusts you with that staff because your magic is weak and you would not dare disobey him!" Still angry, Mixer continued his battle of words. "I will kill you one day and then the staff will be mine to hold." Struggling to stay awake, he pushed his back against the wall to try and sit up.

"Jujube is going now," the goblin sang from outside the door. Every time he was near Mixer, it seemed like it only took a moment for the potion-maker to threaten to kill him. It always reminded the goblin of just how evil he could be. Pausing in the passageway for a moment, Jujube could not remember hating anyone as much as he hated the hairy half-orc. The never-ending verbal battles were a constant reminder of that hatred, but maybe he knew something. Leaning against the wall, he wondered how much of Mixer's words about the master held truth. A moment later his eyes fell on the magic staff and he was smiling again. "Wiz is next!" he sang to no one in particular. Plodding down the corridor towards the next cell, he soon forgot all about his nemesis and the not so veiled threats.

Sliding the window panel open, Jujube peered inside the next cell to make sure the human wizard was on his blankets at the back of the room. Sitting cross-legged and content, eyes closed and facing the door, the wizard had long dirty gray and brown hair and beard. Wearing what was once a dark purple wizard's robe, it was now filthy and looked more brown than purple. Grinning at the cell door as his eyes popped open, it was the kind of grin one gets after finding a million gold pieces.

"Yoo hoo! Hello goblin! Are you peeking at me?" Jujube brought him food every day and the wizard was appreciative of his care. He might be crazy but he wasn't stupid.

"Goblin likes me, doesn't he?" The wizard was happier than usual because the shaman had been gone for over a week. The ogre was unpleasant when he visited and often pummeled him for no other reason than to be cruel.

"Wiz feeling good?" Whenever Wiz was happy, Jujube was able to get him to take over lots of his chores in exchange for the freedom of being outside his cell. Unlocking the door, he walked in and sat down next to Wiz on his bed of blankets.

"Wiz is good today, goblin!" he said as Jujube was unlocking his shackles. To demonstrate that everything was fine with his brain, Wiz began knocking on his head with a closed fist.

"Wiz's head looks good," said Jujube, acknowledging the head pounding and hoping it would stop before he hurt himself. Some days the wizard just sat on his bed, screaming from the pain inside his head. Jujube was much happier when the crazy human was feeling no pain.

The ogres had found the wizard wandering near the mountainside almost two years ago. When they first spotted him, they planned to make a game out of killing him. The shaman had been traveling with the group that day and after recognizing that the wizard's brain was not functioning as it should, guessed that he must have taken a powerful hit to the head. The shaman made the decision to keep the wizard as a prisoner in spite of what the others wanted to do with him.

During the two years that Wiz had been a prisoner, he had taught Jujube a little of the Allegiance common language and the apprentice had reciprocated, teaching him some of the Shard common tongue. The wizard and Mixer combined kept the magic staff full of energy. Those two prisoners alone provided enough energy that Jujube always had extra magic power available, which he enjoyed using in secret.

"You've come to take me away?" Jumping up and down with excitement, Wiz knew that the goblin was taking him out of his cell to do some chores. It was a chance for him to enjoy some limited freedom and spend time with his friend. Jujube had found that with help from the wizard he could finish his chores faster, giving himself free time to do whatever he wanted.

"Wiz, where is the staff I made you?" It had been necessary to empty the room of all furniture because if left alone for too long the wizard would destroy everything. With the room almost empty, there was a pile of blankets where he slept, a small bag to hold his few possessions and the long stick that Jujube had cut for him. He had become convinced that the wooden stick was his long lost staff of power. *Maybe he destroyed it and was hiding the broken pieces.* Jujube started pulling the blankets up to see if it was under them.

"I have it right here!" Giggling like a fool because Jujube had not picked up on his joke, Wiz had hidden the staff behind his back. Pulling out the wooden stick, he kissed it, lifting it over his head. "Oh, goblin! Today will be a good day!"

"Not funny, Wiz. You help me with chores. Come, you. Go to the broom closet. Sweep floors until I get back." Standing outside the wizard's cell, Jujube locked the door after the wizard came out and moved towards the other cellblock. Gripping his staff with both hands, Wiz now held it up in front of him and hurried in the opposite direction towards the kitchen broom closet.

"Wiz, you really are crazy!"

Walking down the darkened passageway into the second carved-out cavern, only one of the cells in this section had been in use since the elf mage had made his fatal mistake. Jujube was twirling his keys and fiddled with them as he approached the farthest door on his left. The noise of the keys turning in the lock of the cell door awoke the magic bones on the floor in the center of the cell. As he watched, the pale white bones animated and began assembling themselves into a skeleton. The completed rack of bones stood staring with blank holes for eyes, awaiting its next command. Jujube always wondered how his master had known that the staff could drain the skeleton of magical energies.

"Bones, go back to sleep!" said Jujube. Opening the cell door, he pointed the magic staff at the bones, activating its draining power. The bones immediately fell back to the ground in a heap. Feeling lazy at that moment, Jujube didn't drain it for more than a few seconds. Shrugging his shoulders with the decision, he decided that after he drained the wizard there would be more than enough power in the staff for his master. By leaving the majority of the energy in the magical skeleton, he knew that within a few short hours it would regain enough power to reassemble itself if anyone came within the proximity of the cell and tried opening the heavy door.

Being sure to lock the skeleton's door, Jujube left the cellblock and caught up with his crazy wizard sidekick. By the time he got back to the kitchen, Wiz already had the sweeping well underway. With the broom flying, he was humming a merry tune with no beginning or end. Watching the wizard work for a few seconds, the goblin tried making sense of the song with no success before preparing the master's meal in case he returned. Cinching the rope belt around his brown robe a little tighter, he grabbed a knife from the kitchen table and sliced the vegetables.

Dangling them over the fireplace, he then got skewers of meat ready for roasting, a quick chant lighting the logs ablaze. The meat began sizzling in an instant. Grabbing a keg of ale from the larder, Jujube lugged it over to the table.

"That food smells good," hinted the wizard, his stomach growling as he wandered back into the kitchen.

"Not ready!" said Jujube, pushing him away. The smell of the meat cooking had brought the human nosing around sooner than Jujube had expected.

"Take Mixer his food. Slide it under the door. Then we eat." Watching Wiz wander off with Mixer's dish, he wondered how much time remained before the master's return. Deciding to use power from the staff to finish some of the chores, he then had to replenish it in case the shaman appeared and needed it. Jujube left the kitchen unattended for a few minutes, hurrying to drain the skeleton of the rest of its magic energy.

"Wiz is hungry now!" Grinning when Jujube walked back into the kitchen, Wiz was already sitting at the table, waiting for his friend to dole out some food. He held a large kitchen knife and fork up by his ears.

"Ok, ok! Now we eat!" Using tongs to lift the meat skewers off the fire, he placed some on his plate. Carving off some scraps, he tossed them in Wiz's dish. The scraps were not a bad deal, considering that Mixer did not get half of what he just gave Wiz. Watching the wizard with amusement as he finished his meat and started licking the utensils, Jujube grabbed another portion for himself and stuffed the large morsels into his mouth. Tossing a few more small pieces to Wiz, he got up to clear their mess. The two of them then got back to cleaning, tackling the laboratory, storage rooms and the shaman's chamber.

* * *

"Whaaaak!" Jumping back out of the way, Jujube cracked his head against the edge of the bedframe. Walking into the shaman's chamber for a last cleaning check, he had heard a strange humming. As he bent to look under the bed for the source, a Moongate opened no more than a few feet from him. An angry ogre strode out of it, clutching an arrow protruding from his chest. The goblin's eyes widened as he stared up at the ogre towering over him, awestruck by the bloody violence of the scene. Frozen in place, Jujube did not move fast enough to get out of the way.

"Move! There are others coming through!" Not waiting for the goblin to react, the ogre slapped him out of the way with his free hand, sending the apprentice flying. In his haste to get away from the group of Rangers that they assumed were attacking them, the shaman had opened the gate into his private chambers instead of the main hall that the ogres used as a gathering place.

Slamming into the corner of the bed, Jujube slid down the wooden post in shock, landing on the floor with a thump. The force of his body hitting the bedpost had almost broken his back and he struggled to straighten himself out. Grimacing in pain, he gasped for breath as he was rolling as far away from the portal as he could. The ogre had stomped away from the Moongate to make room for his companions. It was obvious that he was anxious to start tending the arrow wound and tossed his bag on the ground next to where Jujube lay trying to stay out of sight.

Jarred awake as the bag hit the floor, Morrowyn started thrashing around in the clingy darkness. Her head and neck were throbbing, and the last thing she remembered was seeing a huge creature before feeling the thump of something pounding on her head. She fingered her scalp where it hurt the most. Her fingers felt wet and sticky when she pulled them away and she began to panic. Coming to her senses, she realized that she was inside some sort of cloth bag. *I'm trapped!*

"Let me out!" she cried, flailing her arms and legs up and down before losing all control of her emotions.

Who said that? Noticing the ogre's bag moving, Jujube cocked his head and listened, determining that the crying was coming from inside it. Looking around, he could see the shaman stepping through the portal. The buzzing and crackling from the Moongate was keeping the ogres from hearing the captive's wailing. All the noise and sudden action was making the goblin nervous. Jujube's quiet day had disappeared in a flash and he turned his head from side to side as he tried to decide what to do.

"Who are you?" whispered Jujube, not wanting to alert the ogres that he was speaking to their captive. In spite of the obvious tones of distress, he found the sound of this creature's voice fascinating. It sounded like how he had imagined a female might sound, speaking in the language of The Allegiance. Never having seen or heard an elf child before, he had no idea with who or what he was speaking.

"I am Morrowyn," the muffled voice replied. The struggling from inside the bag ceased at the sound of his voice, indicating to Jujube that the captive was coming to its senses. "Are you going to kill me?"

"Do not cry now, Mor-o-win!" Whispering was strange for him, but he felt a sudden sympathy for this creature. Jujube wished now that he had listened more when Wiz had been teaching him the common Allegiance language. Sneaking a glance over at the ogres, he saw a warrior fall through the portal. Blood covering his face and body, this ogre had many wounds. The others were still too distracted by whatever they had just escaped to notice Jujube speaking to the bag. "I won't eat you, but the ogres might."

"Nooooo, please don't let them eat me!" begged Morrowyn, sobbing in great loud breaths. Not knowing who or what she was talking to, the feeling of helplessness was overwhelming.

"No crying! No crying! They will hear you!" Speaking out of the side of his mouth, Jujube panicked but was trying hard not to look suspicious. He did not know that he was speaking with a child, but even if he did, he had no idea how to talk to one. So far his words seemed to only make things worse for this captive. The voice's reaction was far too uncontrollable for his liking. Fearing for the creature's life, the familiar fear for his own life began creeping back into his consciousness. The ogres would never approve of him talking to their captive. If they caught him, he would join the prisoner on the dinner table. In desperation, he formulated a plan that had little chance of success.

"Mor-o-win! They won't eat you if you show Master your magic!" Trying to talk without moving his mouth, Jujube turned his head to keep one eye on the ogres and saw the shaman cast a healing spell on Chest Wound. Arrow Eye still lay moaning and growling in a bloody mess on the floor, so Jujube needed to be quick with his scheme.

"What kind of magic do you know?"

"None!" gasped Morrowyn, fighting to hold back her sobbing. She was miles beyond afraid and as sure as the cold stones on which she lay, the elf girl knew she was as good as dead. Feeling like she was drowning, Morrowyn started grasping at her only chance for salvation, the mysterious voice outside of the bag. Her survival instinct took over and she began calming down, thinking of ways to help the voice in any way she could. In spite of her best efforts, Morrowyn's innocent honesty was not helping Jujube at all.

"No magic! Now what?" Talking to himself, Jujube hadn't meant to say those words aloud but now his idea well was running dry. Hearing the captive say she had no magic powers poked a huge hole in his master plan for survival. Not sure why he wanted to help this creature in the first place, he started second-guessing his actions again. It would be safer and easier to just back away from the bag right now and put as much distance as possible between him and the ogres' dinner.

"Please help me." Unsure how else to answer the voice, Morrowyn had to tell the truth about not having magic powers.

The intensity of her voice put Jujube in a panic. His eyes flashing around the room, he looked for a place to hide. Feeling the energy-draining staff pressing against his back, a reformulated plan solidified in his brain. So scared he could not think straight, he hoped she understood what he was about to say. "Do you want to live, Mor-o-win? You have magic, so use your magic. Start chanting like you are casting magic!" Figuring that he only had a few more moments before the ogres came looking for their prize, he didn't wait to hear her response. Pointing the magic staff at the bag, he released some of its energy. Watching the magic energy swirl in the air before disappearing into the bag, Jujube then cast his own magic, creating a glow around the bag before jumping into action.

"Master! The bag glows!"

The ogres were busy trying to remove the projectile from one of Arrow Eye's many wounds. Before the shaman could react, the injured ogre jumped up in a rage.

"Stinkin' elf!" he roared in pain. Peering around with his good eye, he grabbed his club as he rose. Raising it over his head, in four strides he reached the bag lying in a heap on the floor, aiming to smash the captive with all his might and anger.

It's an elf in the bag! Gasping out loud, his eyes now as wide as saucers and secure in the knowledge that despite his best efforts this elf was about to die, Jujube could hear the captive chanting nonsense words, unaware that her life was at its end.

"Gurosh! Stop now!" Seeing the glowing bag, the shaman knew right away that it was a minor light spell. All the same, he did not want Gurosh taking any unnecessary chances in his chambers. He wanted any power this girl had for his staff. "Do not touch her, Gurosh. Bigglum, I want her powers!"

"What Zik!?!" Roaring back at the shaman in frustration, Gurosh stopped just before he smashed the bag and captive flat. Instead he yelled incomprehensible gibberish, hammering his club onto a nearby bench as he glared with murder in his eyes at the goblin cowering on the floor.

"My staff, Jujube! Give it to me now!" Snapping the apprentice out of his daze of fear, Zik ignored Gurosh's tantrum. The one-eyed warrior was now looming over Jujube, and the goblin was more than happy moving as far away as possible.

Jujube's experience had taught him that angry ogres were unpredictable and would lash out at anything in their way. The warrior was now drooling and panting from the pain of his wounds and the rising force of his anger. It was an electric moment when anything could happen.

"Yes Master!" shouted Jujube, anticipating his master's request and hoping that Gurosh could see his importance to the shaman. Already holding the staff out for his master, he never took his wide eyes off Gurosh while delivering it. He had grown accustomed to Zik over the years, and the shaman's actions were very predictable. These other ogres were a complete mystery.

"Hurry up!" complained Zik, irritated that his apprentice was still paying attention to Gurosh.

"Your staff!" Groveling before his master, Jujube avoided direct eye contact as he held the staff up. It seemed that except for the close call with Gurosh, everything appeared to be unfolding just as the apprentice had imagined. The power lust in the shaman's eyes assured Jujube that his plan was working.

Snatching the staff and pointing it at the glowing bag, Zik had a look of sheer evil pleasure on his face. The magic staff began draining the elf of what little energy Jujube had just infused into her and Zik, not noticing how fast the staff completed its job, broke into a wicked smile when he heard her crying and begging him to stop.

"No one is to touch this elf, Gurosh. That includes you," ordered Bigglum, supporting his shaman. "She has magic and Zik wants it from her." Bigglum was now satisfied that the journey with his lieutenants into the elven lands was not a complete waste of time after all. This elf would make a nice addition to his prison.

"I caught her and I should be able to eat her!" growled Gurosh, facing Bigglum in protest. The pain from the arrow still protruding from his eye socket made him reckless and angry. Hungry and sore, he did not hesitate to speak his mind. Hearing the elf scream in pain when Zik was draining her magic had only served to make him hungrier for elf flesh. Grunting with effort, he had forced himself to stand back and watch as the glow from the bag dissipated and the kicking and struggling stopped.

"You would now challenge me, Gurosh?!" said Bigglum, displeased by the warrior's lack of respect. "Zik gets the elf. Do not make another mistake today." Glaring at the warrior, Bigglum waited until he dropped his eyes in defeat. Both of them knew that even when healthy, Gurosh was no match in a fair fight.

Under normal circumstances Bigglum would stay out of the day-to-day bickering between his lieutenants, but today Zik had shown his leadership under pressure. In truth, Bigglum was more supportive of him anyway, appreciating his council far more than that of Gurosh. With the shaman saving his life and the warrior failing to capture the elf boy, Bigglum's decision to reward Zik was easy.

"Take the bag to an empty cell!" Motioning for his apprentice to get busy, Zik looked over at Gurosh with a smug smile.

Forcing his bruised body to move again, Jujube grabbed the bag with both hands and scuttled off as fast as his legs would carry him. Allowing himself a weak smile as he left the chamber, he dragged the captive down the hall towards the cellblock. He had heard ogres arguing amongst themselves many times over the years, but had never had a personal stake in one of those fights. Playing the night's events over in his head, he was more than a little surprised to still be alive. Leaning against the wall Jujube closed his eyes, his legs feeling weak and rubbery. It was hard to comprehend how he had managed to make this all happen, and what the future held with another prisoner to watch over.

* * *

"Mommy?" Waking from a troubled sleep and feeling the cool wet cloth dabbing against her wounded scalp, for a moment Morrowyn thought she was at home in her bed. However, the roughness of the dabbing and the stinging from the cleaning of her wound made her realize that this was not her Mommy cradling her head. Her nightmare was ongoing.

"Who are you?" yelped Morrowyn, struggling to get away.

"Quiet! Master will come to check!" whispered Jujube, covering her mouth with his hand while listening for footsteps. Willing her to be quiet with his eyes, he released her only when he saw that she had relaxed and seemed to understand.

"I am Jujube. I am apprentice shaman!" He did his best to smile, not realizing how upset she was becoming. "You are... Mor-o-win?" The bag had muffled her voice and with all the excitement, he was unsure if that was exactly what she had said.

"I am... Mor..." Morrowyn stopped herself and took a deep breath. "Where am I?" The fear and confusion she had experienced in the bag were floating just below the surface of her consciousness. Feeling something heavy and cool on her leg she looked down and saw the shackle clamped around her ankle. Fear morphed into terror, and a flash of anger towards the goblin welled up inside of her like a hot tide.

"I am Morrowyn Lunas! My father is a powerful Ranger and he will come and rescue me!" Fast becoming furious, she wanted her goblin captor, this Jujube, to know that he was in trouble now. Glaring into his eyes, she looked at his stringy gray hair and green skin and almost laughed out loud. She would rather have the scrawny goblin as her captor rather than the angry, fat and smelly ogres, but the concept of captivity was going to take some getting used to.

"Your father never finds you! Now be quiet!" Jujube's words were hurtful, but that was the point. The elf's sudden burst of attitude was troubling and she needed to learn respect. The goblin knew from experience that the ogres would not stand for any brashness dribbling from her mouth. Considering all he had done for her this night, her words made him feel like the risks he took tonight with both their lives were not appreciated. He had saved her life and he still wasn't sure why.

"You're wrong! You're wrong!" Morrowyn's head dropping onto her arms, the loud sobbing started again and Jujube grimaced.

"You must not cry, Mor-o-win. The master does not like it!" Petting her head with an awkward hand, Jujube listened for any noise from the passageway.

When he finished dressing her wounds, the goblin rose and left the cell without saying another word, locking the door behind him. He could still hear her sobs echoing down the passageway long after he started plodding down the corridor to his own room. Thinking about the night's events, Jujube wondered if it was worth having another prisoner. Only time would tell.

V

MYSTIC LAKE

"Please try not to worry, my love. I promise that your father and I will find your sister." Hugging her son, Kalahni experienced a sickening feeling rising from her core. Traumatized by the ogres' recent capture of Morrowyn, Llythwain was struggling to control his emotions. Her affection for him went unnoticed and Kalahni could see the boy disappearing into his own world where she could never follow. She knew her son well enough not to become upset when he did not return her warmth or even acknowledge her words. She continued wearing a brave smile, curling her arm around his shoulders to calm the turmoil she knew was raging in his mind.

Following the ogres' hasty escape, his father had gathered him in his arms and carried him back to the house. As the shaman's spell wore off, Llythwain became agitated, pacing back and forth, trying to figure out how he could help Morrowyn. He considered his sister to be much more fragile than he ever was, and did not think she would last long under the cruel punishments meted out by the ogres, assuming she was even still alive. The deep scars on his arms were a constant reminder of the painful torture he had received from the goblins and ogres years ago when he had been the one kidnapped.

"But I can help with tracking!" Pulling back from his mother so that he could look at her face, Llythwain searched for acceptance. "Everyone says I am good at it!" Relentless in his self-torment and shouldering full responsibility for his sister's horrific capture, it was too much stimulation for his mind to process.

"You're right, my love. You are an excellent tracker!" Smiling but resolute, Kalahni was determined to not give in to his demands today. "But you are still too young to come with us. Llythwain remember that I have your father with me to do the tracking." Holding his eyes with hers to convince him that this discussion was now closed, Kalahni had already decided that she would give him no opportunity to negotiate. Recognizing that their chances of success in this rescue were slight, and if she and Llysander were not to return she did not want Llythwain losing his life as well.

"Have courage, my son! Put all your trust in your mother and I. We will find Morrowyn and return her to you!" Trying to reassure him and hoping that the words were not empty promises, Llysander paused to take a long look at his son as pangs of guilt and remorse filled his heart. There was no choice but to leave him with the other children bound for Camp Quinn, but both he and Kalahni were aware that their son needed them now more than ever. In spite of Llythwain's current emotional needs though, neither of them was willing to stay behind knowing that their daughter was in imminent and mortal danger. Morrowyn's safety would have to take precedence for now, and with luck they would return for their son and make everything right in his life again, as a family of four.

"Take your seat in the wagon, Llythwain. Be strong for us and take care of yourself." Llysander hugged his son goodbye. "I spoke with Ballan, and he assured me that Ran will also be at the camp. At least you will have a friend to keep you company."

"Please let me come with you," pleaded Llythwain, trying one last time, large tears rolling down his face. "I want to help find her."

"I'm sorry, Llythwain, but you are too young. We will hurry back as fast as we can," promised Kalahni, struggling with her own tears. Hugging him close again, she kissed his forehead and tried without success to dry his eyes. "Stay strong, my Llythwain," she whispered in his ear. Letting him go, she mounted her horse beside her husband. Llysander and Kalahni tried not to look at each other for fear they might give in to their son's desire to come with them.

"We will always love you, my son!" Llysander cried out as they trotted away from the wagon where the boy now sat, eyes glued to his parents. Waving to him, they hoped their hollow smiles looked reassuring. A group of seven Rangers and a druid were escorting the children evacuating from Green Valley to Camp Quinn. Located next to Mystic Lake, far south of Evergreen Forest, the camp was the elves' hidden sanctuary in times of trouble. Rumbling and bumping down the road the wagons started their journey with Rangers riding beside and behind them. Llysander looked back one more time and saw his son still waving. Facing forward again, he wondered if that was to be his final memory of him.

✳ ✳ ✳

Leaving the wagons and children behind, Llysander, Kalahni and Maedyn left Pinestone, following the same path through the forest that Llythwain and Morrowyn had taken the day before. This time though, Llysander was entering the forest dressed for war. Clad in the green battle armor of the Rangers, he had stuffed four score arrows into the two quivers strapped to his back. His helmet protruding from under the loose fitting hood, the breeze whipped his long white-blonde hair across his face. Other than the hot tears, he looked fierce and determined. Maedyn stayed back, adjusting his supplies and giving the distraught parents a moment to reflect on the coming challenges.

Reaching the exact spot where Morrowyn had been standing yesterday, Llysander inspected the droplets of blood that he knew without any doubt were hers. Standing amongst the tall trees he feared the worst, years of experience telling him that his daughter was already dead. Drawing his magic longsword from its scabbard, he focused his anger into a single diamond-hard point and thrust the blade into the air.

"Morrowyn! We love you! We will never give up! If you are still alive, be strong my daughter!" Shouting into the breeze bleeding around the trees, hoping that somehow it might carry his words to her ears, his mourning ran in rivulets now as pain overwhelmed him. Morrowyn had always joked that she never saw him cry, but now it took every effort to stop the flow of emotion in order to begin the search.

"Kneel with me and pray for our daughter!" said Kalahni, her voice hoarse. After a tense and emotional day yesterday and the difficulties she had just experienced saying goodbye to her son, Kalahni had sealed off her soul to everyone and everything. Llysander was never much of a believer, but in the face of this crisis she felt they both needed to pray that the goddesses would help look after Morrowyn. Not doing so would be leaving a potential support resource untapped.

Surprising her, Llysander fell to his knees without hesitation, holding the pommel of his sword and his wife's hand. Together they prayed with anguish to the elven goddesses that they might protect Morrowyn from the torture and indignities of the ogres. Llysander did not pray often, but today he prayed harder and louder than he ever had before.

"O my Goddess! Please watch over our daughter, Morrowyn. Forgive us our sins, save us from the fires of hell; and lead all souls to your kingdom of glory, especially those who have most need of your mercy…"

Taking his time opening his eyes, Llysander blinked in the flickering light and began wrapping his head around the journey that lay ahead of them. Gazing up at his wife, he saw her staring at him in shock.

"Llysander, the goddess has gifted your face with a sacred marking!" As they completed the prayer, Kalahni had opened her eyes to study her husband kneeling on the ground. Staring in disbelief she watched a small, crystal-shaped mark appear below his left eye. The moon goddess made it known that she had heard Llysander's prayers, acknowledging him with the crystal marking. As far as Kalahni had ever known, only a priestess or Moonguard received this recognition from Silverymoon. She could only take this as a good omen.

"How is this possible, Kalahni?" Feeling a slight tingling sensation on his face as he prayed, Llysander assumed it was an insect or leaf and ignored it. Touching his face with his fingertips, he then reached out to his wife. With newfound interest he studied her sacred markings. She had one on her forehead and another stretching along the side of her face, crystal and moon shapes held together by intertwining vines. Llysander had never considered it possible that one day a goddess would bless him. It left him feeling awestruck and overwhelmed.

"There can now be no doubt of Silverymoon's support of our mission," Kalahni reassured her husband. "Llysander, we must not lose any more daylight. Have you found the ogres' tracks from their sneaking about our forest?" Proud of her husband today and encouraged by the goddess's support, she felt a burst of confidence as her thoughts turned back to Morrowyn. Determined to find her daughter, the Moonguard's resolve was all she had left. Mounting her horse, Kalahni waited for her husband to join her.

Wrapped in dark blue plate armor molded to fit the curves of her body and a dark blue hooded cloak fastened at her throat with a moon-shaped brooch, she looked ready to fight an army of ogres. Sitting tall on her white warhorse, she held out the reins to her husband's mount. Her disbelief of the intruding ogres when Maedyn had first arrived and explained the runestone discovery flashed in her mind. The familiar feelings of panic and hopelessness had gripped her like a fist, refusing to let her go. Having lost Llythwain to the ogres a long time ago, only his safe return had restored a sense of normalcy to her life. Now it seemed that once again, something was forcing her to prove her strength. She was furious that this could happen twice to her family and her appreciation of the type of world in which they lived was deteriorating. Blinking back a sudden surge of emotion, she retreated to her fierce detached state. Until she saw with her own eyes that Morrowyn was no longer alive, Kalahni would continue looking for her even if it meant that she and every ogre in the land died in the process.

"As you guessed yesterday, the ogres did not gate into elven lands. There is a clear trail leading west out of the forest," said Llysander. Wiping away the rest of his tears, his hope had been that she would stay with Llythwain at Camp Quinn. It was easy for him to see past the emotional wall that she had built for herself. Their mutual bond was strong and each was aware the other was struggling with an enormous emotional burden. The Ranger knew she was as desperate as he to find Morrowyn, but traveling with his wife gave him another set of responsibilities. It was now necessary to split his focus between hunting for his daughter and concern for her safety and state of mind.

"It will be easy to follow the ogre spoor and discover the route they took to sneak here before we rendezvous with the Rangers at Clement's Peak. Assuming we still have a trail at that point, I will convince Llaen to provide a team to help us find Morrowyn." Llysander was still trying to work out the details of his plan, but he was convinced that getting help from the Rangers was their best chance.

"Llysander, my decision has not changed since yesterday. I will not be moving off the ogre trail to meet your Rangers at Clement's Peak. I plan to continue tracking the ogres that took Morrowyn while the trail stays warm."

"Kalahni, a rendezvous with the Rangers will only put us off course by a few days. In all honesty, the two of us stand little chance against these ogres, but by having the Rangers with us our chances increase tenfold. Why can't you see that?"

"I will mark a trail for you to follow as I track them, Llysander. Do not take too long with your Ranger friends. Your daughter's life may depend on it."

Over their years together, Llysander had taught Kalahni how to read and track a trail, and she had excelled as his student. He knew that tracking these ogres would not be a problem for her. Despite that knowledge, he was also aware that she did not want to be alone and needed his emotional and physical support. Kalahni was not willing to risk having the trail go cold under any circumstances, but now she needed her husband with her for more than his tracking abilities.

"Fine, Kalahni. We will do things as you wish." Sighing out his resignation, Llysander did not see any value in debating this further when he was not even sure there was a correct decision. Llaen had trusted him and knew he would return as soon as was possible, but he could not leave his wife alone on this journey. He was still convinced that he could convince his captain to let him have a small team of Rangers to assist with the rescue, but he said no more. Mounting his horse, Llysander rode out to Maedyn to inform him of their new course of action.

"We have a change in plans, Maedyn. Kalahni and I will not be traveling to Clement's Peak. Can you fly ahead and explain my position to Llaen?"

"Do not worry, Llysander. I believe you are making the right decision and I am sure they will understand." The druid had no idea how Llaen would react to Llysander disobeying his order to meet back with the other Rangers, but if there was ever a good excuse this had to be it. Maedyn squeezed the Ranger's shoulder in support, noticing the sacred mark on Llysander's face. Not wanting to pry further, with a few magic words he transformed into an eagle and flew away.

Kalahni heard her husband returning and was preparing for more discussion. Even though they had disagreed several times about how to approach rescuing Morrowyn, Llysander was not prepared to argue any more. When he indicated that they should start moving, she reached over to him, taking his hand into hers and squeezing it with all the warmth she could muster.

* * *

The air moving through Evergreen Forest was cool and when it hit the stored heat from the small lake it created a thick soup of vapor across the water's surface. The fog, lush green forest and high sword-like grasses made up most of the terrain across these otherwise untraveled lands. Much of the forest was impassable except for a few steep, narrow trails leading to ancient fishing spots along the water's edge. A stranger searching for Mystic Lake would be unhappy finding himself traveling through this rough and unforgiving terrain.

"Jaeyn, are you sure these boats will actually float?" asked Gaffer, looking at the canoe with a skeptical eye. A human forester from Hathaway, the older man had never seen a canoe before today. Gaffer had volunteered to go with Jaeyn to help prepare Camp Quinn for the children's arrival. Jaeyn was one of the Ranger Scouts assigned to watch over the camp.

"Elves have been using canoes to travel the rivers for a long time, Gaffer. It is surprising to see how fast they can go and how steady they are." Assigned the responsibility of watching over the children until word came that it was safe to return home, Jaeyn thought the children would appreciate having canoes available. The chances were good that they would be here for a while.

"I'll take your word for it, Jaeyn. We can keep all the paddles in the shed." Shaking his head and chuckling as he carried the paddles towards a small wooden shed built straddling the dock and the rocky shoreline, Gaffer was always amazed at the ingenuity of the elves.

"At least the children will be able to enjoy themselves. We'll also need something to keep ourselves occupied." Realizing that Gaffer was struggling to carry the paddles into the shed, Jaeyn ran to help the older man. They were too involved in the conversation to notice movement in the water.

"These rundown cabins sure don't help with the visual appeal of this place," noted Gaffer, enjoying his conversation with the Ranger. Loading the paddles into some empty barrels in the shed, he went back towards the edge of the dock to finish fastening the canoes to the pilings.

The thick fog on the lake made it hard to see beyond ten feet. It was early morning and all Gaffer could hear were the love songs of crickets and the buzzing of the odd fly. Small waves slopped against the sides of the dock, and the wooden platform banged out an uneven rhythm as it bumped up and down against its pilings. The old man didn't notice the bubbling splash in the water behind him.

"You don't suppose this camp is home to any ghosts, do you?" asked Gaffer, a chill running up his spine. Feeling uneasy at not being able to see much of the lake or the campground, he kept glancing over at the empty cabins dancing in and out of the mist. He had never considered himself a big believer in the supernatural, but something out here was unnerving him.

"The children's safety is our first consideration, my friend. Few know about Camp Quinn and even fewer are able to find their way through the forest to get here." Hurrying out of the shed and back to the dock, Jaeyn looked at what his new partner was doing. He was finding the old man a little tiresome but appreciated his help.

"Well, the whole place looks tired and run down, if I can be honest. I don't mind helping to fix it up." Straining to look out onto the lake, Gaffer went quiet when he thought he saw stirring in the water. Satisfied that there was nothing there, he continued. "I used to build houses when I was younger you know."

Idling in the water underneath the dock, a shadow was formulating a plan. Being careful not to make any sudden movements, it focused on the elf and human working above and waited.

"I didn't know that, Gaffer. Tomorrow I will bring in some tools then and we can get started," said Jaeyn, a little surprised that the old man would offer to help the way he did. "I think there may be some wood we can use stored in the supply hut. Let me go check while you finish tying up the canoes." Walking up the hill away from the docks towards the living quarters, the Ranger nodded his head. *I think I may have underestimated old Gaffer.*

"Can you also see if there are any measuring sticks?" Gaffer's mind was whirling as he thought about what they might need. The forester felt energized by getting the chance to build something again. "The shingles are also in need of repair, but we can't do much without accurate measurements."

"Okay, I won't be too long!"

As the Ranger disappeared around the corner of the main house, Gaffer was thinking he might enjoy volunteering at the camp after all. Bending back down to the canoes with renewed vigor, he fastened them to the pilings, concentrating on getting his knots tight enough so that the small crafts would not blow away if a storm showed up.

Watching the scene play out overhead, the dark shape tensed in anticipation. Sliding into position in the water on the opposite side of the dock from its target, the creature watched the elf walk away. Creeping up onto the dock, it was now crouched a few feet behind the old man. Kneeling and facing the canoes, its victim had no idea of the danger he was in.

Engrossed in his work, Gaffer was oblivious to his surroundings. *I am kind of interested in taking one of these canoes out to the island in the middle of the lake.*

Inching closer, the creature stalked its prey. It left a trail of wet tracks one at a time on the wooden slats of the dock as it crept into striking position. Tensed like a coiled spring, it was ready to attack at the perfect moment.

I'll fix this place up real nice if we have time. I might even repair the dock if there is enough wood. Whistling while he worked, Gaffer became aware that his legs were getting stiff from the time spent kneeling on the wooden dock. With an effort he stood, straightening his legs and repositioning himself to better reach the ropes dangling at the back of the canoe closest to him. Leaning out over the water, the old man was unaware of his vulnerability.

Reaching for the last rope, at last Gaffer sensed that something was wrong. At that moment the dark creature lunged forward, knocking the old man into the air above the lake with the momentum of its attack.

"Whuk!" Gaffer's lungs emptied as the impact of the dark shape shocked him before they plunged into the warm water. Feeling his attacker pushing him under the surface, the weight of the creature on his back gave him no chance to surface or call for help. A single splash disturbed the crickets, and in an instant the struggle was over. As the surface ripples spread out into the fog, the tracks on the dock had already dried and disappeared.

Seconds later the creature broke the surface tension once again to see if the returning elf had witnessed the attack. Seeing and hearing no one, it disappeared back into the depths of the lake with its now unmoving captive in tow.

* * *

Llysander and Kalahni had reached the edge of Dark Forest. Stopping only to rest the horses, they had followed the ogre trail for two solid days. Mirroring their mood, a heavy rain had started falling almost a day ago and continued with no signs of slowing down. Neither wanted to be the first to admit it, but both of them were getting quite tired and hungry.

"The tracks continue deep into Dark Forest, just as we suspected," said Kalahni, appreciating that her husband had instructed her in the finer points of tracking. Even with over a day of solid rain, she could still read the telltale signs of the ogres' passage. It was amazing what could be seen now that she knew where to look. In addition, just being alone with her husband seemed to make things more bearable. She would not allow herself to enjoy it for long however, as thoughts of Morrowyn in the ogre's grasp would stab her in the heart as soon as she turned her back to think about anything else. If it were not for their horses' need to rest and the coming stormy darkness, they would have continued chasing the ogres straight through another night.

"Being this close to the goblins, we should take turns resting and keeping watch," said Llysander from under his hood. "They are very active right now." Having had no serious rest since before the goblin hunt in Dark Forest, the rain was dampening what little positive spirit he carried with him. "You rest now. I will take first watch."

"Please Llysander, first forage around for something edible and I'll prepare us something to eat." It had been many hours since she had spoken any words that had nothing to do with their search, and it made her feel warmer knowing she could still care about something else. Noticing over the last few hours that her husband was not the same positive and optimistic individual she knew so well, Kalahni hoped that some food and rest would rejuvenate him. Encouraged by the change in her demeanor, Llysander took his wife in his arms.

"Kalahni, I can't stop thinking..." Quieting him with a hand on his mouth before he could say the awful words, she looked deep into his eyes.

"I know..." Grabbing his hands and pulling her husband close, Kalahni tried choking her emotions down but could no longer contain them. She was crying with no sound, large tears rolling with abandon down her face.

"Llysander, I feel the same way. We almost lost Llythwain to the ogres and now Morrowyn faces the same horrors or worse. I do not want to imagine what has happened to her, but how can I not think the worst?"

"We must believe she is alive and well, my love. She is stronger than most would give her credit. We must also believe that we will succeed at saving her."

"There you are. That's the Llysander I know and love." Kalahni saw a spark ignite in his eyes as they brightened at her words. All he needed was someone to look after, and someone looking after him. She brushed his cheek with the back of her hand, but as she looked at him with the warmth of her heart her expression changed to one of concern, shattering the moment. "Llysander! What's wrong?"

"Quiet!" Looking all around them, Llysander could hear unnatural rustling noises coming from the trees in a direct line behind his wife. Raising his longbow and nocking an arrow, he prepared to protect them from whatever was approaching. Following his lead Kalahni nocked her short bow, positioning herself behind and to the left of her husband.

"Prrrrrrrrrrrrrrrrrrreooow!" Purring with pride, Snow stepped out of the underbrush to greet her owners. It had taken several hours for her to break out of the cage. Following Llysander and Kalahni was easy for the big cat once she picked up their scent. It had taken her less than two days to catch up.

"Snow!" Although they had decided to leave her behind, seeing the giant white cougar standing in front of them right at this moment provided a welcome boost to their morale. The cat rushed to them, nuzzling and purring, her tail wagging back and forth with pleasure. For Kalahni it made everything seem more normal, as if they were back at Pinestone and the children were just outside playing together.

$$* \quad * \quad *$$

"How much longer until we get to the camp?" The wagons had been traveling for over a day and Llythwain was getting tired of bouncing around in his seat. He could still picture his mother riding away, dressed in her plate armor. It was the first time he had seen her dressed in battle gear, and he was still not sure how he felt about it.

To pass the time, he was experimenting with a makeshift sundial he had constructed before leaving home. It integrated a small compass his father had given him a year ago. Having seen maps of the land around Evergreen Forest, he knew that based on the noise from the river they were heading southeast. Using the compass to calibrate his sundial, he was able to determine their approximate direction and how long it was taking them. Calling on his memory of the map, Llythwain ended up with what he thought was a pretty good idea of where they were in the forest.

"A few more hours at least, Master Lunas," answered the Ranger closest to him. He had kept an eye on Llysander's son all day as they rolled along and the young elf had impressed him with his maturity and ingenuity.

"Based on our current direction and speed, the shadow from my sundial tells me a different story," said Llythwain, challenging the Ranger's comments. "Over the course of the day I have plotted this out, and I think we are almost there."

"Impressive! That is correct. It is not much further now!" Grinning as he brought the wagon carrying Llythwain and the other children around the next corner, the Ranger pulled the horses to a stop. "In fact, here we are!"

"I knew it!" Llythwain exclaimed in triumph while the rest of the children were yelling and screaming as they disembarked. However, before he could continue explaining how his tool worked, the entire group of Rangers fell back and left the wagon without another word.

"Llythwain!" shouted Ran as he raced outside, happy to see his friend. Standing outside the main lodge, he waited for Llythwain and Morrowyn to jump off the wagon carrying their kit. "Where is Morrowyn?" Ran didn't see her anywhere and knew by the expression on Llythwain's face that for some reason she was not with him.

"They took her!" The sight of his friend unleashed a torrent of emotions for Llythwain. Standing in front of the main lodge still holding his bags, tears flowed unchecked down his face.

"It's okay Llythwain. You don't have to say anything more. You can tell me later." Speaking just loud enough that only his friend could hear him, Ran noticed that the other children were staring at them and became embarrassed by Llythwain's sudden outburst of emotion.

"Okay Ran. I'm sorry." Gasping for breath, his whole body shaking with effort, Llythwain had trouble turning off his emotions once they started.

"Hey, I brought my ukulele!" Trying to distract Llythwain from his emotions, Ran held his instrument up with a goofy smile. A talented musician for his age, he had attached a leather cord on each end of the little guitar so that he could sling it over his back. Flipping it around by twirling the makeshift strap, in one quick motion it was in his arms, ready to play. Giving it a quick strum to make it sound happy and loud, the two friends strolled away from the main group with Llythwain's bags banging against his legs. Finding an unclaimed cabin made both of them a little happier, knowing that they could bunk together.

✳ ✳ ✳

The wind grew gusty and sharp as Llysander and Kalahni, accompanied now by Snow, traveled deeper into Dark Forest. It was as though the giant redwoods were grabbing the air from the sky and throwing fistfuls of it down at them as they passed by. Swirling all around from every direction, the wind whipped their hoods off and let the rain drench them. The limited visibility in goblin territory made the heavy rain even more uncomfortable. The horses had been spooking and were nervous at the level of noise around them, from the rain beating the ground to the howling of the wind in the canopy. Spider webs hung everywhere in the underbrush. Although the weather was nasty both Llysander and Kalahni knew that the rain was a blessing because it kept the giant spiders and goblins hunkering down.

Riding in silence, sometimes holding hands but more often alone with their thoughts, each of their minds alternated between brooding about what had happened and contemplating what the future held in store. A feeling of dread surrounded them, flavoring every waking minute.

As a seasoned Ranger, Llysander was finding this situation frustrating. Accustomed to providing all the answers for his wife, the reasons why this had happened to them again were eluding him. *We are good people. What did we do to deserve this fate?* Repeating that thought over and over, he rode through the rain and wind contemplating whether he was doing the right thing by acquiescing to his wife's demand to forgo assistance from the Rangers.

For Kalahni there was an impending sense of danger in this land of goblins, and it was becoming stronger as they traveled deeper into their territory. The unfamiliar surroundings, dark, wet and windy, were making her as nervous as the horses. She was an experienced Moonguard, trained by warriors and priestesses. More than a match against ogres and goblins, she was no stranger to battle. Many times in the past she had accompanied Llysander and the Rangers on small raids. Having Snow with them added to her sense of security, yet she knew the sheer number of goblins and ogres was the real concern. For the first time, she wondered if her husband's suggestion to get help from the Rangers might have been the correct decision. Making up her mind to not say anything more on the subject, Kalahni decided it was easier for her to cope this way.

Reaching down for the grip of her short bow, she squeezed the carved wood as tight as she could. The solid feel of the weapon helped renew her confidence in her abilities should they face an enemy. The bow contained magical crystals that increased her already formidable fighting skills. Her father had gifted it to her on the occasion of her becoming a Moonguard. Her mother had never approved of her choice of lifestyle, expecting her to take the vows of a priestess. An intelligent man, her father had sided with her mother, but in private was proud at how accomplished his daughter had become amongst her Moonguard peers. The gift of the magical bow was her father's only show of approval towards her choice of career and life.

"The horses are getting tired again!" Llysander had to shout with so much force that he hurt his throat. Even with that effort Kalahni had difficulty hearing him above the howling winds and drumming rain. Having reached the foothills some time ago, the continual up and down travel was wearing the animals out quicker than expected.

"Snow looks miserable!" shouted Kalahni, still surprised at how loyal and determined her pet was to have followed them into Dark Forest. Snow's tail and paws were muddy and she kept glancing over at her owners to see if they had any intention of hiding from this awful weather. Trying to avoid the largest puddles, it was becoming more difficult and pointless for her.

"Easy, Snow," said Llysander as they stood on the leeward side of a giant redwood. Looking down at the cat, Llysander knew now more than ever that choosing her had been the right decision. Standing under the dripping branches Snow looked back at him, waiting for something to happen.

"We should seek shelter. Do you agree?" Kalahni hoped he would concur. It was not only the horses that were getting tired. They had traveled for almost twelve hours straight, spotting the ogre trail with ease, even in the rain. Every so often, Llysander would request she hold her position so that he could search for signs that the creatures had passed.

Deciding to make for a known fork in the trail, Llysander guessed that the ogres would have done the same thing. Sometimes the best tracking came from knowing what was logical, and given that one of the forks led towards the mountains and the other took them deeper into Dark Forest, he came to the common sense conclusion that the beasts must have come from the mountains and mines that housed them.

"Follow me into the trees on our left, Kalahni. Maybe we can find a dry protected spot to rest until the rain dies down." Dismounting, they walked the horses and the big cat over the muddy ground through a clearing in the now hilly forest.

"Llysander! Look over there!" Pointing at a large opening in the hillside, Kalahni looked at its dark entrance in relief. The cave ahead of them looked large enough for the three of them with room to spare.

"There are many caves along these hills and I'm sure the Rangers have explored them all, yet I can recall no one reporting any of this size." Llysander was glad to find shelter from the rain but was suspicious of this cave's origins. Inspecting the entrance and cave floor as they drew closer revealed many large and recent tracks. The footprints disappeared deeper into the depths of the cavern. "It may have been natural processes that created this cave, but something or someone has enlarged it and dug a long deep passageway under the mountain ridge!"

"Do you think that this might be how the ogres got through to our lands undetected?" Straining to hear any unusual sounds as she scanned the darkness,

Kalahni wondered how she could ever fall asleep here, even with Llysander standing guard.

"It's a good question and appears to be the logical conclusion. Yet what kind of magic could create passageways so large and for such distances? This passageway looks like it could go on for miles!"

"Then we must travel through this tunnel to find Morrowyn!" In Kalahni's mind there was no question. Their decisions on this quest were either black or white. With this appearing to be a possible direct route to her captured daughter, she was finding it difficult to restrain herself from charging off right now. Discovering the tunnel had rejuvenated her, recharging her internal supply of energy.

"Kalahni wait! We cannot just run off into the darkness without letting someone know where we are!"

"Llysander! I must find Morrowyn! WE must find Morrowyn!"

"I know, Kalahni. Please trust me, I want to find her as much as you. But before we can go deep into the cave I must send word to the Rangers, advising them of our coordinates."

"What are you saying? How will you send word?" Llysander's grin told her that he had prepared something unexpected.

"I found some pixie dust!" Pulling out a tiny leather bag, few knew the ways of nature's creatures better than the druids and Rangers of Green Valley. For centuries, they had used pixie dust and a spell to facilitate long distance communication. By sprinkling the dust on a pool of water and invoking the magic, it created a direct link to the Land of Pixies. Any fairy creature could answer the call, and the pool would act as a viewing screen, similar to a crystal ball. Both the pixie and the spell caster could then see and hear each other.

"Be serious, Llysander! Where did you get that dust from?" Suspecting that he had stolen some from the Treasury, with a mother's patience she waited for her husband to come clean.

"Okay, okay. As I recall I may have borrowed some from Braigon. But there was a lot and I knew that it would come in handy!" Given their current discovery, he was glad to have scooped a little of the pixie dust as he walked through the Treasury when he was last there.

"Ei x'ip!" Speaking the magic words as the pixie dust fell, Llysander sprinkled it between his fingers into one of the pools of water created by the rain. The pool began swirling, rainbow colors snaking and twisting on the water's surface until a picture started forming in the puddle. Faint giggling noises were echoing within the cave, as if the pixies that answered the call were fluttering around them.

"Hello? Who is it?" Two winged pixies dressed in brown fabric were peering over what appeared to be a small stream. The sound of turbulent water was loud as one of the pixies stuck his head closer to get a better look at the elves on the other side of the pool. His bulging eyes and pointed ears filled the small pool in the cave.

Growling at the movement in the water, Snow's eyes were wide and her ears twitched at all the new sounds echoing off the cave walls. Raising her paw to poke at the puddle, Llysander knocked it away and motioned for her to be still.

"Move Blipp. I want to see too!" said the other pixie, pushing his face in front to get an eyeful of the callers.

"Hello! I am Llysander, a Ranger, and this is my wife Kalahni of the Moonguard." Waving to the pixies with one hand while her other arm rested on Llysander's shoulder, Kalahni smiled at the cute beings jostling above the pool while trying not to laugh.

"Hi Kalahni! Hi Llysander! My name is Blapp. You two sure are a cute couple!"

"Stop interrupting, Blapp! I answered the pool so I get to talk first!" Blipp bumped Blapp out of the way so that he could see the elves. "My apologies Llysander and Kalahni. It is a well-known rule amongst the pixies that whoever answers gets to do the talking. Please excuse my overzealous brother. Now, where were we? Oh yes. Hi there. My name is Blipp."

"He knows that already, Blipp!"

"Blapp! Why are you still talking?"

"Hello Blipp, Hello Blapp. I think I know your father! You look just like him. You two are not Blopp's sons are you?" Llysander went through a similar routine every time he contacted the pixies. They loved boasting about their family heritage.

Moving away to light a small fire so they could see better inside the dark cavern, Kalahni gave herself some time to get rid of the giggles in case the pixies thought her rude.

"Yes, Llysander! Our father is Blopp. He is a member of the Fairy Circle, you know."

"I know he is, Blipp. In fact I met him in person once, many years ago."

"Amazing!" Blipp and Blapp shouted in unison.

Kalahni shook her head at Llysander's ability to converse with these little beings. Over thirty years of marriage and Llysander was still able to surprise her with the things he had done.

It didn't take Blipp and Blapp too much longer to figure out how they could share the viewing area. Llysander gave them a brief recounting of their search for Morrowyn. Promising him that no matter who answered the pool, the next Ranger or druid that cast the spell would learn of Llysander and Kalahni's sad tale, including their whereabouts. Blipp and Blapp wished them both well and the images in the pool dissolved.

* * *

"Has there been any word from Llysander?" asked the Ranger Captain. Tullaos had arrived at Clement's Peak to take command while Llaen was on leave. Approaching Maedyn who was peering into a glowing puddle conversing with pixies, he was not impressed with his rumpled appearance. The captain had even noticed a foul odor emanating from where he was sitting, so he had kept his distance and left the druid to speak with the pixies on his own. Growing impatient, Tullaos stood closer to Maedyn to find out if the magic beings had any news.

"They found a cavern and passageway that they think might lead to the mines." The druid had known that Llysander had purloined some pixie dust, so Maedyn had wasted no time contacting the pixies once he had arrived at Clement's Peak. At first none of them had heard anything, but this last time he managed to find Blipp and Blapp, who told him everything he needed to know.

"The Shard have been busy." Hearing about Morrowyn's abduction by ogres right out of Evergreen Forest, Tullaos wanted nothing more than to act right away and help his fellow Ranger. Being only a captain though, he could not order the elves into goblin territory without first consulting the lords in Thantos. "Underground passageways would explain why we have not noticed the goblins and ogres moving about."

"Are you able to help Llysander and Kalahni, Captain?" Reading Tullaos's body language, Maedyn knew before he said anything that help would not be forthcoming.

"Druid, you know that one cannot just journey into goblin territory. If we do that we might as well declare war on The Shard right now, and that is above my level of authority."

"I understand that. Is there anything we can do for them?"

"I have heard and share your concerns, druid. Going against the standard protocol of peace between the elf and goblin nations, I will send a small team when it gets dark." Tullaos had never met Llysander, but he was not willing to sit back without offering some form of help to a fellow Ranger. It would take at least a few days before he could sort out what official direction the lords wished to take. Sending a small team of Rangers was the best he could do in the interim.

"Transform yourself. Fly off and watch over your friends." Catching another whiff of him, the captain decided that the best thing would be getting the druid out of his camp. He liked this part of his solution the best, protecting his sensitive nose by sending the druid to watch over the situation from above.

"Trans Lup!" Without hesitation Maedyn's physical form jiggled and with a loud pop transformed into an eagle. Flapping in the direction of the mines, he soared high into the clouds and soon lost sight of the Rangers far below. Alone at last, he always enjoyed soaring in and out of the low clouds. A small black bird swooped in close with a greeting and the druid acknowledged its greeting with a swoop of his own. Peering across the land, he was pleased to see that the rain that had been hanging over Dark Forest had stopped. Flying with speed towards where he understood the cavern was located, Maedyn started looking for his friends.

VI

THE HEROES OF KARTH

The deluge of rain that began earlier in the day was not showing any signs of letting up. If there had been any change at all it was to the wind, now whipping through the forest creating a howling orchestral movement that made communication near impossible at best. Leaning forward, the mercenaries kept slogging, one foot in front of the other.

"This rain and wind is unbelievable!" Like the rest of the group, the water had soaked right through Garrett's layers. He had grown tired of the continual trudging along the forest trail and was ready to stop for the night. It was lamentable then, that several hours ago the band of mercenaries had decided as a group not to stop and rest until they found a dry safe place to camp. Garrett no longer approved of this decision.

"I didn't think it was possible, but it might be raining even harder now," said Angus, echoing Garrett's grumbling. "And with night almost upon us, it is going to make further traveling difficult." The gnome was struggling to keep his lantern's flame from extinguishing with the wind blowing in gusts from every direction.

"An el luminous!" Without warning Davissor cast an illumination spell, lighting the blade of his katana. Blue-white light reflecting in all directions erupted from the full length of the sword, illuminating the smiling mage underneath the glowing weapon. Peering through the sheets of water, he could see spider webbing on most of the underbrush gaining life with the help of the wind. Rain droplets hanging on the fine threads acted as reflectors, making it appear as if the trees around them were full of tiny festive lights.

"Davissor! Warn me next time before you do that. You've blinded me!" growled Ahira. His heavy chain armor rattling in the rain, the warrior's plated shoulder pads rang out like muted cymbals as large drops falling from branches splattered them. The armor was not made for stomping around in this type of weather, and he was growing irritated at the thought of drying and oiling it before he slept. As his eyes adjusted to the light, mossy tree trunks and tall grasses became visible along either side of their path. Davissor's sword was brighter than any of their lanterns, but the dwarf was not in the mood for admiring the natural beauty of his surroundings at this moment.

"I agree! Can you dim that blasted firestick?" shouted Ragnar. The mage was already adjusting the light. The bandit pulled his dripping black hooded cape lower, covering his good eye. Shifting his eye patch, it was soaked from the rain and was irritating his skin. Chuckling to himself at the stereotypical gruffness of his fellow dwarf, being a thief by trade, Ragnar was much more reserved and quiet.

"Sincerest apologies, my merry band of complainers! It just takes a little fine tuning." As their leader and paymaster Davissor could and would taunt and tease at will, getting away with what some might consider offensive. The mage was the glue that held this motley group of miscreants together, and only he understood much about the arcane arts, surprising and bewildering his crew whenever he had the opportunity. "At least we don't have to worry about the lanterns blowing out for now. Perhaps with my good light we can find a spot to take cover from the storm."

On foot and in single file, Davissor led the way down the path, stepping with care over the slick patches of muddy ground. Due to the weather and tight quarters, they had decided against riding on horseback for this journey. Ragnar had drawn the short straw to manage their one packhorse, and he continued grumbling as he guided it along the narrow trail. On the one hand he did not like being the one saddled with packhorse duty, but on the other he didn't mind being the closest to the food. Bringing up the rear, he had used his specific skillset to pilfer a snack or three since leaving Buxton.

"I'm surprised we haven't seen much sign of goblins yet!" said Ahira, sounding more than a little disappointed. Carrying a great battle-axe over his shoulder, he fingered the haft as he marched. His technique was that of the berserker, running into battle with an uncontrollable bloodlust that ignited with little provocation. Refusing to carry a lantern, he explained that his eyes adjusted well to the darkness on their own. In truth he wanted nothing to do with anything that might slow him in a fight. "The rain is keeping the spiders away but I think we should have seen some goblins by now."

"Well, with the light from Davissor's firestick beaming our position to the entire forest, it's only a matter of time until someone comes to investigate," said Ragnar, smirking at his fellow dwarf.

Discussing possible routes to the mines before leaving Buxton, they all agreed that taking a direct path would guarantee them some fun with goblins. Now deep in goblin territory, the mercenaries found their unimpeded progress through this part of Dark Forest unsettling. They were itching for a confrontation, but it was difficult to remain on high alert for so many hours without any justification.

"It must be this blasted rain that is spoiling our fun!" Energized by the suggestion to look for shelter, Angus made an extra effort to penetrate the dripping gloom.

"Hey, let's look over there!" said Garrett, pointing off the path. The foothills were all around them now, with many rocky outcrops and boulders erupting from the trees. They headed towards the rocks to see if they could find a safe, dry spot. Walking around a cluster of large boulders that stuck out from the hills like broken bones, they came across a small cave opening tucked out of sight.

"Good eyes, Garrett! This weather has done wonders for your eyesight!" The mage stopped and signaled to the others to prepare an investigation. "Ahira, can you check if..."

"Already on it!" shouted Ahira, rushing past the others and charging into the cave.

"He's a little slow today. It must be the rain!" said Angus, rolling his eyes.

The mercenaries laughed as they waited for Ahira's report, quite accustomed to his undisciplined tactics. Skulking behind him into the cave, watching for the dwarf in the gloom, Angus liked taking advantage of Ahira's reckless charge into every battle. The warrior worked well as a distraction and improved Angus's chances for a covert opportunity to strike.

"No luck," a disappointed voice echoed out of the cave entrance. "There is nobody here!" None of them wanted a taste of combat more than Ahira, but they were all happy finding somewhere to escape from the wind and rain.

"Gah! I feel like a drowning rat!" Angus looked miserable as he stepped out from the cave opening, water pouring down his face and hair onto the red leather jacket he enjoyed wearing. Although having it made from the best leather meant that it kept him much drier than his companions, he thought it better to pretend to be in at least the same position as everyone else.

After finding a ledge that their packhorse could stand under for the night, the mercenaries hauled themselves and their gear into the cave. Davissor lit a fire near the entrance and as the air started warming up, the group commenced the long process of drying out.

"Oh yeah! Time for food and rest! And a puff or two from my pipe!" As Ragnar removed his black studded leather armor and propped it up to dry an apple fell from his breastplate, bouncing across the floor of the cave. Sneaking it from the saddlebags a few miles ago, he worried that the crunching sound might alert everyone that he was into the supplies and so put it away for later. The dwarf was starting to think he might never get the chance to eat it.

"I don't think any of us could ever have imagined this much rain," said Davissor, removing his black top hat and shaking off the water. "I will gate back to Buxton for some better protection against the weather while you boys rest here." Glancing back at the storm raging outside the cave entrance, he returned the hat to his head and began looking for a spot at the back of the cave on which to cast rune markings.

"Good thing you added those rune markings when we were in Buxton," said Garrett as he hung his clothes to dry by the fire.

"You really should take someone along for protection," said Angus, jumping to his feet. "I shall selflessly volunteer myself to accompany you." Knowing that Davissor would likely make an unscheduled visit to the tavern while in Buxton, he could still taste the ale they had sampled the last time they were there.

"Not this time, my well-pickled friend." They had left only three days ago and Davissor did not want anyone noticing that he was already back for more supplies. That kind of optics was bad for business. Some might look at their returning as unprofessional, like they didn't know what they were doing. Casting his gate spell without another word, he entered the Moongate before Angus or anyone else had the chance to argue further. There would be no entertaining frivolous suggestions tonight.

"I hate it when he goes by himself like that!" Angus frowned as the gate and Davissor disappeared with a crackling hum. In seconds the other mercenaries began laughing and whistling to get his attention. They knew what the gnome was after and surprised him by producing two kegs of the Buxton Tavern ale.

"My brothers!" His face beaming, Angus raised his arms in the air while performing a celebratory jig. "I love you guys!"

* * *

"Look there," whispered Toupa, the goblin champion and leader. "Follow that light." The goblin hunters were tracking a strange group traveling unbidden through their lands. Pulling his hood down closer to protect his face from the wind, with thirty hunters under his command and a shaman and necromancer at his disposal he was confident that this was more than enough strength to crush this small group of armed warriors. Grasping the hilt of his scimitar, he ran through the sword routine he would use to take down the elf leading the group. He found the thought of his sword slicing through the funny hat to split the elf's skull exciting until he remembered the necromancer's commands. With considerable reluctance he put his thoughts of a crushing victory aside.

"We attack!" Showing the impatience of a warrior, one of the hunters raised his spear, ready to engage the enemy alone if need be.

"Stop! The Dark One said no!" Pagga's voice froze the eager hunter in his tracks, reminding any others who might have forgotten about their orders. As the shaman, he worked with the champion to keep the scouts in check. Focusing his eyes on the light that Toupa had pointed out, he watched as the intruders moved around a large cluster of rocks. The war party had kept their distance, making sure that they did not lose sight of their quarry. "Look! They found the cave. They will rest now."

"Obey the Dark Ones," said Sooga, reminding the shaman and the others of their orders. "Obey the Dark Ones or die."

"I know the Dark Ones said no, but why not attack and wipe these intruders from our lands?" Looking over at the necromancer, Pagga studied Sooga's black robes, hoping for an answer. It was not always forthcoming, but he couldn't understand why they were letting these strangers come so close to the Mines tonight. Sooga was intimidating, his solid black eyes and unblinking gaze made him look as if he himself was an undead creature. Pagga shivered at the thought of what it must feel like to be a necromancer.

"No more questions!" Focusing on the shaman, Sooga started the life draining incantation. Spiritual energy started trickling from Pagga's body.

"Aaaaaaaag...! You're right! You're right! No questions! No questions!" As the agonizing pain of the spell began crushing him, Pagga was unable to speak a coherent sentence. It was all he could do to breathe and live.

It didn't take long for Sooga to sense Pagga's life force diminishing and growing dim. With the shaman's verbal show of obedience, he broke the spell by turning his deathly gaze towards the sky.

Gasping for air as he crouched on the ground trying not to black out, Pagga's strength began returning soon after the pain released him. Thinking about his position in the new goblin hierarchy, the shaman wondered about the future. The role of shaman used to be important. In the new order, necromancers ruled the goblin tribes and no one could contradict them, not shamans, hunter leaders or even the chieftain himself. The necromancers had become the voice of the Dark Ones. Twice they had demonstrated their power by destroying some of the strongest warriors without lifting a finger. Now no one dared challenge them.

"I will tell the Dark One where the intruders have stopped for the night," said Sooga in his deep monotone. Gifted the ability to silent talk by the Dark Ones, once he saw that the intruders had found a cave to rest in for the night he knew it was time to report back to his masters. *They have stopped in a cave. We are watching!*

Cloistered among the dark creatures, the powerful shade stirred from his meditative trance with the whisper from the necromancer. It was time to leave this place to get a closer look at those he followed. Killian Acheron let the goblin know that he had heard his call. *Do not engage them. I will be there soon.*

Remain here until I return! Commanding the dark creatures congregating about him, one command was all it took for Killian to enforce his will upon the dark legion. The shades obeyed without question, hovering together while waiting for his next directive.

Transporting himself to the shadow-plane, Killian strode along the onyx black road stretching without end before and behind him. Suspended in the never-ending darkness of the void, the road had only a faint glow distinguishing it from the black emptiness. The greater shades had the ability to travel immense distances by using the shadow-walking technique. It took all his concentration to will the road to take him where he wanted to go and he knew well not to hover close to the edges of the glowing road. One wrong step could set him adrift in the darkness. Nearing his destination, Killian could feel the presence of the goblin necromancer and hear the echoes of his voice.

"Where are the strangers?" Floating out from the shadows just behind Sooga, Killian startled the necromancer, causing him to lose his train of thought.

"In the cave below," said Sooga before reverting to silent talk. *"Follow the light."*

Pagga saw an unnatural shadow moving behind the necromancer. Sooga spoke aloud then went silent as he spoke to the Dark One using his mind. Watching them out of the corner of his eye and based on the way the necromancer was motioning towards the caves, he gathered that Sooga was filling the Dark One in on the status of the intruders.

"How many are there?" asked Killian. Moving past the necromancer to look at the location of the cave, the shade ignored the rest of the goblins now staring at him.

"Two dwarves, one human, one gnome, one elf. I think the elf is a mage. That means five."

Watching the necromancer use his fingers to help count something, Pagga wondered what they were discussing.

"A mage! Are they all in the cave?" He wanted to examine this group closer, but the mage could complicate things. Killian felt the slightest twinge of concern.

"*We sent a spiderling to look. The elf is gone,*" said Sooga, hoping the small spider was right. "*The elf is gone.*"

"*Stay here and keep the rest from attacking. Move only upon my signal.*" Speaking aloud in the goblin tongue so that all within earshot would understand exactly what he wanted, Killian was clear. "I will investigate this cave on my own. Do not interrupt me!"

"He will go on his own!" said Sooga, parroting the Dark One's words as the shade disappeared back into the shadows. "Everyone must watch the Dark One's power!" Waving his staff in the air, the necromancer motioned for the hunters to stay alert.

✴ ✴ ✴

"I musht shay, it wash nyshe of you to shurprishe me wit dat ale." Comfortable and drunk after consuming much more than his share, Angus passed a pipe back and forth with Ragnar as they kept watch while relaxing by the fire. The thunderous snoring of Ahira and Garrett echoing from the back of the cave provided them with a symphony of snorting and snuffling.

"It was my pleasure, brother." Ragnar rubbed his belly then belched, making the flames of the campfire flutter. He had a love of food, but enjoyed his ales and smoke even more.

"Do ya shink Davishor will bing more of dat ale?"

"Ohhhh, if I know Davissor..." said Ragnar, leaning back with a yawn. His eyes snapped wide as an icy breeze rushed past them, blowing out the campfire as it shot into the cave. Rolling to his feet, the dwarf fumbled for his short sword, gasping for breath. Leaning his back against the cool stone for support, he blinked into the darkness. *Blasted eye patch, I can't see a thing!*

"Hey! Who turned out da lightsh?" Stumbling to his feet, Angus felt a threatening presence all around him.

"Aaahaaa! What are you...?" Flinging his arms around as he awoke, Ahira growled into the chill dark. Hot needles of pain tore his face, his entire body falling numb. Struggling to sit up but disoriented in the blackness, the intense pain from the scratch across his face shocked him awake. Sucking in his breath, he tried to contain the burning sensation and get his wits about him. "Garrett! Are you still there?"

"Gaaaah! Something just bit me!" Feeling the sickening crunch as something dug into his neck, Garrett's body went cold and numb. Struggling to roll away in case whatever it was came back, he flopped about from side to side on the cave floor.

"Hey! You guys okay? What's going on in there?" Sobering up in no time in the cold cavern air, Angus used Ahira and Garrett's voices to orient himself. Creeping deeper into the cave with a dagger held in each hand, he slid along the cavern wall until he found a small recess in which to wait. The cave had gone cold and silent in the dark, the only noises he could hear being the labored breathing of his comrades.

"*You cannot hide from me, little one.*" The raspy whisper in his head tickled the backs of Angus's eyeballs. Feeling movement in the air, he threw the daggers in the direction where he sensed the presence of his assailant.

"I'm sure I hit it, fellas!" Angus heard sound of his daggers clattering on the cave floor instead of bouncing off the opposite wall, indicating that he had connected with something. His daggers though, did not seem to have had much effect.

"Woooooaaaaaahhhh!" Air began rushing past his ears and out of instinct the gnome put up his arms to defend himself. The counter attack from his assailant came on him like a twister and it was all Angus could do to remain on his feet. In seconds it was over. Surprised that the skirmish had been so brief, he took stock of his body. There was pain in his left wrist and it felt wet, but was not a critical wound.

Following Angus' voice, Ragnar snuck across the cave until he sensed that he was right behind the presence.

"Hey! Taste this!" Plunging his magic short sword into what he thought was the back of the dark creature, the dwarf knew without a doubt that he had connected.

Killian heard someone yell from behind him just before he felt a magic blade stabbing into his back. The burn of the sword lodged inside made him feel sick, and he knew right away that he was in trouble. Only magic could harm a shade, making this weapon a real threat to his continued existence. Warrior training taking over he dropped to the ground, rolling away to one side. As the weapon slipped out of his body, its blade left a gaping wound. With his life force evaporating into the night air, the shade would have to move fast.

"Over here! Over here!" shouted Ragnar, sensing the direction his opponent was taking.

"Watch out, brother! I have it here!" Ahira ran over near Ragnar's voice and swung his battle-axe in a wide arc, banging into the dark creature and pushing it backwards. His axe was not magical, but the force of his blow knocked the creature off balance. Dropping to the ground to avoid Ahira's swing, Ragnar listened for the results of the strike.

"Again!" Jumping up as he sensed the creature staggering backward, his sword flashed out, stabbing into it again. This time the creature screeched in pain. The sound of its scream echoed through the cave and out into the night.

"*Now feel my rage!*" screamed Killian into the magic sword wielding dwarf's head. Writhing in pain, the shade was furious. Underestimating the strength of the mercenaries had been a huge mistake, and now he had to get away as fast as possible. Charging at the dwarf, Killian thrashed at him with clawed fingers, his nails finding soft meat. Gripping the dwarf and pulling back, he felt the bloody heat of the mercenary's flesh ripping open.

"Feel this, you icy demon!" Ignoring the sting of the creature's attack, Ragnar thrust in front of him as he rushed forward, sinking his sword hilt-deep in the creature. The force of the attack sent them both tumbling to the floor of the cave. Pulling his blade backwards as they fell, the rogue freed it from the creature so that he could strike again.

"Screeeeeeeeeee!" The high-pitched scream cut through the air with such volume that everyone froze. Realizing that he had no choice but to signal the goblins, it was time for them to attack and cover his retreat. Staying to fight any longer would mean his destruction, and Killian took that moment of the mercenaries' aural shock to attempt a hasty withdrawal.

"Over here, boys!" Ragnar thrust his sword forward again but missed his target as the shade limped away from him. "I think it is trying to leave the cave!"

"It's mine! You're not going anywhere, beast!" Charging full tilt towards the cave entrance, Ahira rushed headlong right into the creature. Grabbing onto it, the dwarf wrestled with it as they stumbled to the ground just outside the cave entrance.

"It's mine too!" Charging forward, Angus surprised himself with his willingness to rush straight into the fight. The injury to his wrist had raised the gnome's hackles, and he wanted to inflict some damage on this creature as well.

Running to the cave opening, Ragnar could see Ahira wrestling on the ground with the dark creature and Angus stabbing at it as they rolled around. Hearing a cacophony of screaming and yelling, he looked up and saw a mass of goblins racing down the hills towards them. Dressed for battle, their faces and bodies painted in many colors, the hunters looked formidable and it was obvious they were thirsty for blood.

"Is Garrett still asleep or what?" Looking for a good opportunity to jump on top of the creature, Angus looked up and saw the advancing goblins. Changing his focus, he ran and stood shoulder to shoulder with Ragnar as they braced themselves for the upcoming assault.

"He must still be inside but it's too late to check on him!" The imminent attack of the goblins gave Ragnar no time for reflection. "I'll take the right flank."

"Ahira! Let him go! We are in urgent need of your special services!" Throwing his first dagger with deadly accuracy, Angus watched as his little knife sank to its hilt in the center of the nearest goblin's forehead. Tumbling to the ground the painted green hunter gurgled and was still. Spinning away, the gnome dodged a spear flying over his head.

Ahira had dropped his great axe during the flying tumble out of the cave. Not wanting to lose his advantage over the creature, he had let his axe go as he grabbed its neck, locking its arms down so that it was no longer ripping at him. Through a red mist, the berserker knew he was not strong enough to kill this screaming banshee, but felt he could hold it long enough for his friends to help him take it down and destroy it. Hearing Angus' sudden cry for help he pulled his attention from his enemy long enough to see the goblins bearing down on them. The dark creature was no longer fighting for anything but to flee, so Ahira's choice became obvious. Releasing his hold, he jumped backwards out of the creature's range and ran toward the location of his weapon.

"Screeeeeeeee!" another shrill pitch from the shade echoed across the dark hills as it limped away from the cave and the band of mercenaries. With several grievous wounds now bleeding out its life force, it was grateful to be free from the crazed dwarf's grasp. Retreating for the first time in his existence as a shade, Killian was having trouble moving as he disappeared into the night.

"Behind you!" Keeping an eye on Ragnar's back, Angus threw two more daggers at the crush of goblins now stabbing at the dwarf with their spears. Accurate again, one of the gnome's blades pierced a goblin throat, felling the attacker before it took another step.

"You got him, brother!" shouted Ragnar, thankful for the warning. Spinning his body ninety degrees, he had just enough room to swing his sword and decapitate the goblin behind him. Letting the momentum of the backhand swing carry his body around, he found himself facing another two attackers on his opposite side.

"We may be in trouble!" shouted Angus, as he felt a spear's point tickling his side. Instead of focusing on the pain, he countered with a dagger uppercut to the perpetrator. Stabbing the blade into the head of his attacker, the goblin was dead before it hit the ground.

"Don't worry, boys! I'm here now!" bellowed Ahira, swiping his now recovered axe downwards and chopping one of Angus' attackers almost in half.

"Nobody runs!" screamed Toupa, rallying his hunters. The goblins were looking for more direction after seeing the Dark One flee and their first wave of attack failing. Screaming out his war cry, the goblin champion charged at the crazy dwarf who had been wrestling with the Dark One. Striking him from the side with an overhand downwards slash, his scimitar cut deep into the dwarf's shoulder.

"Eeeeeyyaaaaaar!" Growling straight into the goblin's face as the blade slid out of his shoulder, the pain of that wound sent Ahira into an even greater frenzy. Spinning to face this new opponent, he slipped on the blood now soaking the ground, landing on his knees. The slip caught the goblin by surprise and his second mighty swing, a blow that would have connected with deadly force, ended up missing the dwarf altogether. From his knees, Ahira swung his axe upwards with all his might, sinking the blade all the way to its haft between the goblin's legs.

Toupa's eyes widened in pain and disbelief as, writhing on the gore-smeared blade of the dwarf's axe, he dropped to the ground. The goblin leader's ears could no longer hear the sounds of the battle, and the last thing he saw was the bloody feet of the dwarf stomping the ground in front of his face.

"Behind you, brother! What is this?" Two blood-covered zombies, goblins that Ahira had already killed, were now rushing the dwarf from behind. Angus had no time to watch how Ahira was doing because the goblins he had killed were also rising and charging at him. "What is going on here?"

"It must be the blasted Curse of the Undead!" Watching the goblins he had just killed rise from the ground to attack again as undead, they were blood-soaked horrific looking creatures and Ragnar's head was throbbing from the sound of their moaning.

"Right when I thought we were winning!" said Angus, ducking low to evade an attacking zombie. Turning to strike it hard in the gut, Angus found his short knives to be ineffective. "How am I going to kill these creatures?"

"I bet fire works wonders, boys! It looks like I got back just in time. Good thing I didn't stop at the tavern!" A two-foot tall flaming elemental darted past Angus, hugging the closest zombie for no more than a second before dropping its now smoldering carcass to the ground. Turning his head at the sound of Davissor's voice, Angus flashed him a grim smile, feeling like maybe the tables had just turned back in their favor.

"These creatures loved my sword so much, they wanted to feel it a second time!" Thrusting deep into one of the moaning zombies, Ragnar laughed as it performed a death dance on the end of his blade.

"Nice of you to join us, elf-mage!" bellowed Ahira as the blade of his axe arched over his head, slicing two undead goblins standing next to each other in half. Blood pulsing from his shoulder wound, the injury had little effect on his performance. He continued fighting as if he was in perfect physical condition.

Davissor's return bolstered everyone's morale. Rallying now that their leader was back, the mercenaries overcame the remaining goblins with ease. Seeing the fire elemental kill a second and third zombie with blasts of flame, the hunters scattered, fleeing back into the trees and hills.

"Well, we got our encounter, boys!" Exhausted to his core, Angus had no appetite for pursuing any goblins anywhere. Standing with his arms hanging at his sides he watched the goblins' scattered retreat. Even Ahira stood silent instead of charging after them, happy to see the goblins on the run.

"Where was Garrett this whole time?" asked Angus, examining the bodies of the zombies littering the ground.

"He is alive but not well," said Davissor. "I saw him lying unconscious when I returned and gave him a healing draught before coming to check on the rest of my heroes."

"We had better retreat back into the cave. I think we've had all the fun we can handle for one rainy evening." Even though he could not see them anymore, Ragnar's experience told him that the goblins were still lurking close by. Standing with his arms outstretched, he let the light rain wash away some of the goblin blood that covered him.

"Yes, let's retreat to the cave and regroup," agreed Davissor. "I will cast a wall of stone at the cave entrance to make sure that at least for the time being, no one will be able to attack us."

✳ ✳ ✳

"We lost the fight!" said Pagga, still in disbelief. More than half of the hunters were dead, including their leader.

"What are your orders, Dark One?" Having returned to the rendezvous point in defeat, the remaining hunters became nervous at Sooga's question, not wanting to hear an order to fight the strangers again.

"Retreat to the Mines of Taas and warn your kin. I will return to my kind and let them know of this turn of events."

"Mines!" ordered Sooga, not having to repeat himself. Vanishing in the dark, the goblins were more than happy getting away from both the strangers and the Dark One.

I have chosen my heroes well. Looking back towards the cave, Killian noted the wall of stone now blocking the cave's entrance. *The mage must have returned. Sleep well. You will all need your rest to prepare for the coming days.* The pain from his wounds was a throbbing reminder of just how much of a gamble he had taken tonight. Disappearing onto the shadow-plane, his first priority now was to heal. Beginning the task of hunting, he needed to drain some life force and rejuvenate himself before returning to the other shades. *No one must know I have been weakened.*

VII

THE CRYPT OF XEEN

"Master! The living discovered our presence in the graveyard, forcing our retreat," reported Gans Houlf. The greater shade had been unable to contact Killian, and it didn't take long for him to turn on his leader. Separating from the hive, he began exerting his strength as the new dominant shade. Gans felt emboldened, assuming the role as leader and controlling the swarm of shades now hovering in the upper chambers of the Crypt of Xeen waiting for their next orders. However, he had been unsuccessful at Xeon's first task. He had managed to gather a score of undead, but the dragon was expecting a much larger army and held him responsible for the poor result from the Strathmore excursion.

Furious with this worthless shade for failing at the graveyard, Xeon roared his displeasure. Finishing his feast of the crystals that he had ripped from his latest conquered world, the dragon stared into the blackness above, contacting the shade using his telepathic powers. Speaking with Gans instead of his chosen commander irritated him, but with no answer from Killian for a few days now, he had little choice. Stretching his massive boney wings and ascending out of his lair, Xeon's frustration was obvious. He needed to turn his attention to the assault on Karth. Soaring high above the ruins of this darkened world, soon his feasting here would be complete and he could apply his full focus to the next conquest. Casting his eyes across the deadened landscape, viewing the dark and lifeless trees and foliage, Xeon was pleased by the drastic effects the draining of crystals had on the landscape. *"Shade! Why do you exist? Where is Killian?!"*

"He was at the Mines of Taas investigating an intrusion and suffered grave injury, Master!" After not hearing from Killian for longer than expected, Gans had contacted the goblin necromancer, discovering that the shade leader may not have

survived. *"He disappeared after a battle with some mercenaries and the goblins have not heard from him since."*

"What mercenaries? Why is he fighting mercenaries on Karth?" Snarling at Gans' explanation, Xeon was unwilling to accept that his commander could have suffered a critical injury. Showing no remorse about the possible loss, he was only concerned about losing a strong general. Tendrils of power from his mind wrapped around the shade and began draining his life energy. *"Until we hear from him again you are in charge. Amass a larger army of undead. Return to the human town and kill everyone!"*

"Yes Master!!" Caught in the dragon's grip, Gans' energy was fading fast. Xeon's pull was relentless. Shrinking his mind into as small a form as possible to try and minimize the damage, the shade hung writhing from his master's onslaught. As his life force weakened, Gans began passing in and out of consciousness.

"Do not fail me, you worthless shade! Another performance matching this last one and I shall crush you like an insect, inflicting pain for eons to come!"

"Master, we will need help from King Ferrus and his minions!"

"Tell that mummy I will speak with him!" roared Xeon, stopping the assault on his new commander.

"Master, there is more..." Gans feared further punishment, but had no choice. *"There is a large group of humans and elves approaching the Crypt..."*

"Wretched shade! You caused this mess! I should destroy you now!" Erupting with a fresh burst of rage, Xeon restrained from attacking Gans with anything more than words this time. There needed to be someone left as his agent until he was able to give Karth his full attention. *"Advise the king of this threat right away. You must use his forces to destroy these humans and elves. I do not want the massed undead discovered yet!"*

* * *

"Killian! You exist? Where have you been?" Gans was both surprised and disappointed to hear from his leader. *"Our Master has ordered me to speak with King Ferrus."*

"Be patient, I am almost there."

Quickening his pace across the shadow bridge, Killian sped through the alternate plane of existence as he worked the bridge toward the crypt where the shades hovered together awaiting instructions. Knowing his prolonged absence would result in Gans taking command, Killian was ready to destroy him if he was not willing to relinquish his newfound power.

"I am on my way to see the mummy," said Gans, asserting his control. Confirmed as the new leader by Xeon he felt confident, tugging at Killian's mind and testing the strength of his former master instead of just relinquishing command. Stopping in the upper chambers of the crypt so as not to have this inevitable battle of wills in front of the king, Gans waited for Killian's reaction to the challenge.

"I am in command!" roared Killian with incredible ferocity. Challenging wills was normal practice among the undead, but insubordination of any kind infuriated him. Displeased with this affront to his authority, he would deal with Gans later when an opportunity presented itself. *"You will wait for me before seeing Ferrus!"*

"What?! Xeon has recognized me as leader now!" Surprised by the strength of the response from Killian, Gans had never felt as much power coming from his former master as he did right now. Not expecting such a show of strength when Killian was recovering from grievous wounds, Gans could feel the power of the shade leader's mind ripping his life energy away in chunks.

"You will obey me now! Our discussion is over!"

It had been necessary for Killian to take some recovery time after the encounter with the mercenaries in the cave. Refusing to kill innocent people for his own benefit, the hunt for prey became more selective. Due to the severity of his wounds, the recuperation had taken longer than expected. *"It is time for our meeting with King Ferrus! Shades! Meet us outside the king's chamber!"*

Killian did not waste any time reasserting himself and tore into Gans with a furious energy drain. Pausing at the crypt entrance to regain his composure, he blanked out any emotion and let his warrior instincts take over. *"Did you follow my orders to visit the Strathmore graveyard as I commanded before I left, Gans? Or should I just destroy you now?"*

"I followed your orders, master. We found ourselves forced into retreat." Wilting under Killian's onslaught, Gans relinquished any hope of authority. He could feel the strength of the attack still pulling his life energy away. *"We raised twenty skeletons and twelve zombies before leaving."*

"Pathetic cur. Did anyone see you or the other shades?"

"There were two humans and an elf. As you commanded, we did not engage them." Gans worried now that Killian might yet destroy him for his failure to get all the undead raised. *"We retreated with what undead we could before they came upon us."*

"We will need many more undead to satisfy Xeon," said Killian, squeezing Gans and the other shades now that they were all hovering together. *"Does King Ferrus know we are coming?"*

"He is in the burial chamber waiting for us." Feeling weak from Killian's constant drain on his energy, Gans was almost at the point of being useless. *"He already knows that Xeon wants his minions."*

"I will go first. Do not interrupt me. I will not hesitate to kill you." Dropping his hold on Gans's life force, Killian approached the crypt entrance before willing himself to merge with the darkness that covered the entryway. Two skeletal knights stood guard just inside, stirring to life the moment he entered. *"Shades! Be ready to act on my signal!"*

"Move aside." The skeletal knights were larger and stronger than most other undead, requiring a greater amount of strength to make them obey. Pushing past them and moving down the corridors, Killian passed many more skeletal warriors, undead ghosts, and ghouls. All were subservient to the greater shade's power and he took control of them with ease.

The darkening hallway and number of runes etched into the walls signaled he was almost at the inner chambers. Clearing his mind of any distractions, Killian prepared himself for this encounter with King Ferrus in his burial chamber. In previous dealings with the mummy it had taken all his strength to counter Ferrus's attempted domination. He braced for another battle of wills, but felt good about his chances for success.

"Come no closer!" Two skeletal knights guarding the door commanded the shade as he approached. Beyond the door was the burial chamber of their master. Killian had no influence over these undead with King Ferrus in such close proximity.

"Tell your king that Xeon demands an audience with him! I represent the shadow dragon on this world!" Unlike the two guards he had encountered at the crypt entrance, these undead creatures possessed magical weapons and armor. Providing Killian with a poignant reminder of having come so close to death not long ago, he grimaced at the memory.

"I will see you now," announced King Ferrus, willing the doors open as his knights stepped aside. Standing in the center of the chamber, the mummy had an entourage of skeletal knights on either side of him. Ferrus was a formidable creature to behold. Towering over eight feet tall, bandages were still wrapped around most of his body but his uncovered face revealed white eyes burning with demonic orange flames. One hand held a massive magic scimitar, its hilt studded with crystals. *"What word does the powerful Killian bring from the dragon Xeon, master of us all?"*

"Xeon has ordered that you provide me your undead to assist with the attack on the town of Strathmore. Shall I report your disobedience today?" Before he finished

speaking Killian could feel the mummy's mind engaging in the usual battle of wills. Unsure how Ferrus would react to Xeon's military demands, the dragon's unspoken expectation was that Killian would kill the mummy if he refused to cooperate.

"Prepare for battle!" The host of shades stepping out of the shadows and joining ranks behind him, Killian hoped that the strong show of numbers would avoid having to fulfill his master's command should Ferrus show an unwillingness to comply. Sensing the king's anger, the shade felt a sudden strong push for control. Countering the attack, he surprised the mummy with his level of ferocity and the battle for control began swaying back in his favor. Believing that he had Ferrus on the defensive, Killian further amped up his intensity.

"All right, we will help you, Killian. But what of the large group of elves and humans that nears my tomb?" Forced to relent, King Ferrus was not intimidated by the shades and felt confident that his undead forces would prevail against them in a fight, but having Killian overpower him with such ease was surprising and uncomfortable. *What has changed since our last meeting? The strength of this shade is overwhelming me. Perhaps Xeon has imbued him with some special power.*

"Will your shades help in the defence of my tomb, Killian?" Feeling his strength weakening, Ferrus became anxious to end the power struggle. Reaching the point of ordering his knights to attack, the shade's mental onslaught began subsiding with the mummy's tacit agreement to help Xeon attack Strathmore.

"We will kill the intruders and bolster our armies." Pulling back from crushing the mummy as soon as he got what he wanted, as much as Killian would have enjoyed squashing him, not facing the skeletal warriors with their magical blades so soon after his last fight came as a relief. *"Tell your forces to offer little resistance when the intruders enter the passageways. We will first close their escape routes then overwhelm them."*

* * *

"What is it?" asked Ted Heifer, Sheriff of Strathmore. He and some of his finest guards were accompanying the elves' investigation team as they followed the tracks of the undead for hours through the night. The human guardsmen were clad in chainmail armor and carried halberds, as this weapon was proving most effective against the zombies. As they wandered deeper into the sandy wasteland, vegetation became more and more sparse and the strong breeze worked its way around and through the team, filling every crack and orifice with dust from their footsteps.

"It is clear now that the tracks are leading us toward the Crypt of Xeen," said Llaen, covering his face to protect it from the sand and dust. "There is no longer any doubt in my mind. The undead are heading to the tomb of the old king!"

After losing the Holy Wars against Hathaway, King Ferrus had refused all efforts to eject him from this plane of existence. Entombed as a mummy in the Crypt of Xeen many years ago, the crypt had defied the desert's best attempts at covering his final resting place for all eternity. Built into the side of a large hill and covered by sedges and short grasses, a steep ramp pushed the tomb's entrance below ground, making it all but invisible from any distance to the passing traveler. As one drew closer though, the joints between the slave cut gray limestone blocks became obvious, having filled in with years of grime and dark moss. Scoured by wind and sand, the monument was an ancient and imposing structure.

"Are you sure the tracks head there?" asked Ted, fresh beads of sweat breaking out on his forehead. Shifting in his saddle the sheriff frowned, recalling the last time he had passed through this area. He and his friends had been scouting the area when they encountered hostile ghosts, and only Ted had escaped with his life. Rumors had swirled for years that many spectral creatures might exist within this crypt. His experience and the trail of the undead provided firm evidence that the rumors of something godless dwelling within the underground tomb were accurate.

"You may notice that there are no tracks heading away from it," said Llaen with a grim smile. "Perhaps the old king is going to try and retake his lands."

"Llaen, if that theory is even half correct, I should not just be warning the town. This is a serious matter that requires the attention of our king."

"I do not disagree, Ted. The source of the Curse of the Undead may not be so mysterious after all." Turning back towards the trail, Llaen was anxious to press onwards.

"Attention guards! It is my responsibility as sheriff to warn the town and kingdom. While I am gone you are to follow the Ranger Captain's orders as if they were my own. I will return as soon as possible. Do you understand?"

"Yes Sheriff!"

"Two of you stay here with the horses," ordered Llaen, not waiting for Ted's departure. "The rest of you follow me. Rangers split up on both my right and left flank."

"Good luck!" called Ted as an afterthought, turning in his saddle as he rode away. Unable to hear him in the whipping breeze, the team was already making a beeline towards the crypt entrance.

* * *

"Let's not be too eager to march right inside," said Kethus, examining the entrance to the crypt. "We can assume that there will be a welcoming committee. If I summon an elemental, it will help clear a path for us."

"There is no threat from the top," called a scout, signaling the all clear.

"I sense powerful undead at the entranceway!" Sweat beading on her forehead, Inunis knew they were in for a tough fight. Her holy symbol already in her hand, the priestess prayed in silence for her goddess's support.

"Lenowyn, let's move closer to the entrance," whispered Razz. A blade in each hand, he wanted to be in the first wave over the threshold.

"Good idea, Razz. I'll take the right side." Unsheathing her katanas, Lenowyn followed the champion's lead.

Staying back for now, Tabatha watched everyone move into position. She could hear the noises of the undead stirring. Her studies had shown that the undead could detect a living presence within a specific proximity. They did not need a direct line of sight to know that a potential meal was nearby.

"Stolanos flakos!" Waving his arms, Kethus then pointed at the ground. The sand began trembling, gravel and dust filling the air in front of him. As the sand elemental solidified, its humanoid shape developed from the swirling mass until it stood waiting for direction. A signal from the mage sent it erupting toward the entrance with thundering footsteps. As the summoner of the elemental, Kethus could see through the eyes of the creature as well as his own. When the elemental reached the top of the ramp, the mage could make out a wide stairwell below. Guarding the stairs were two large skeletal knights, alert and waiting for the living to come within range. These undead were not interested in the sand elemental moving towards them and would continue ignoring it unless it engaged them in battle. The skeletal knights' focus was on the living, giving the elemental the early advantage.

"Go!" yelled Lenowyn as the elemental crashed into the closest knight, knocking it backwards and slamming it into the wall. Darting in behind the dusty beast, Lenowyn and Razz were already slashing at the other undead knight as it stepped towards them. Led by Llaen, the Strathmore guardsmen charged in to support Razz and Lenowyn. The undead knights were relentless in their counter-attacks, bony arms swinging swords, bodies taking hit after hit. Pushing the knights backwards down the stairs, the team became buoyed by their initial successes. Reaching the bottom of the stairwell, the fight moved into a wide stone chamber, giving the guardsmen and Rangers more room to join. Each undead knight was now fighting several opponents at once.

"These undead are not affected by our attacks!" yelled Razz over the clanging of metal on metal. His eyes narrowing with concern, the elf watched the elemental drop to the ground as a pile of dust and sand, dispelled by several crushing blows from the undead knight it had faced.

"We will need magic to be effective against them!" Echoing his concerns, when Lenowyn glanced over her shoulder, she saw the silhouettes of Kethus and Inunis descending the stairs to the chamber. *It's about time!* In the spray of light from the entrance, she could see the other knight attempting to move closer to the stairs as it continued fighting the crowd of intruders.

"I come to face you in the name of the Goddess Shifra!" Facing the undead knight that had destroyed the elemental, Inunis held up her holy symbol. The skeleton stopped swinging at the Rangers and guardsmen, but instead of submitting to the priestess's control, it gathered its strong will and took slow menacing steps towards her.

"It is too difficult to control, Kethus! I would ask for your assistance!"

"Tis rubi em alif." Delivering a burst of flame from his fingers, Kethus knocked the undead knight backwards. "I've hurt it, Inunis! Try and turn it again!"

"Back away! In the name of the Goddess Shifra obey me!" Inunis could see that the skeleton's blackened eye sockets held an orange flicker, as if a fire burned inside its skull. Spawned from hell, this creature was not a typical undead. Weakening under her strong push for control, this time it staggered as it tried in vain to step forward. The creature paused, unaccustomed to being in a subservient position.

"I could use some help with this one too!" shouted Razz. Holding his own, he was now on the defensive against the continual hard blows from his undead adversary. Whenever he was able to land a strike against the skeletal knight, the impact didn't slow the creature at all.

"Our weapons are ineffective against these undead creatures!" shouted Llaen. Taking stock, he saw that Tabatha, the Strathmore guards and the Rangers had all joined the battle in the chamber. It was clear that the team was reaching the point of desperation. He began considering an exit strategy.

"This one is mine!" Sensing triumph, Inunis could feel her control over the skeleton growing. The knight had resisted her far longer than she would ever have imagined but as it became overwhelmed by so many concurrent attacks, she could feel its will succumbing. "The Goddess Shifra banishes you!"

Weapon and shield hanging useless while the orange glow in its eye sockets dimmed, the undead knight stood waiting for oblivion. With the sound of a popping campfire the bones disappeared in a cloud of dust, leaving only its dented armor behind to clatter on the floor.

"The other one is retreating," shouted Razz. The skeleton had begun attempting an escape as soon as its companion exploded.

"Eni otsi ifo law!" Casting a wall of stone to prevent the skeletal knight from escaping, Kethus gave the team the opportunity to finish it off. The combined weight of their attacks became more than the undead creature could defend against when the high priestess approached it with her holy symbol held out before her.

✳ ✳ ✳

"*They have killed both skeletal knights!*" In spite of Killian's order to lure the intruders towards the lower chambers, the skeletal knights had engaged the intruders and lost. Surprised by the knights' actions, Gans continued watching the intruders as they gathered themselves for a push deeper into the crypt.

"*My knights!*" The loss of two of the mummy's most powerful undead so soon came as a shock to him. Immune to normal weapons, these superior undead were not an easy acquisition.

"*All undead must follow my orders! The intruders are stronger than we expected!*" Enjoying that the mummy would be even unhappier with Xeon's orders now, Killian repeated his instructions. "*Comply with my commands now, Ferrus! Use the ghosts to lure them deeper or risk losing more of your precious army!*"

"*There is a high priestess with them, master!*" Horrified when he saw her destroy the knights with banishment, Gans retreated towards the undead horde waiting in the chambers below.

"*We will target her first, but not before we lure them completely into our trap.*" Positioning the rest of the shades on the darker side of the outer chamber, Killian waited for the battle to come to him. Lurking in the shadows close by was a host of ghouls. They were a large riotous pack of lesser undead, and it took great effort to keep them from wandering. Across the chamber he could see the mob of zombies and skeletons raised from the graveyard waiting for their next command. The other shades were controlling them. The undead trap appeared undefeatable.

"OoOoOoOoO!" The spectral wailing of the ghosts began percolating throughout the crypt. Commanded to call out into the darkness of the chambers, they invited the unwanted guests to come closer.

Peering out from the shadows, Gans saw the torches of the intruders approaching, and they appeared confident that their plan would be effective. This group may have taken down two powerful undead, but they did not seem experienced enough to appreciate the dangers they faced in the lower levels of an undead tomb. "*They are coming closer!*"

"*Lead them deeper! Let them come all the way down to the lower chambers before they realize the error of their arrogance. We will take their bodies and add them to our army!*" Falling back into his role as conqueror of worlds with ease, Killian reminded himself not to get too carried away. Hiding his true intentions would take a masterful performance, but he couldn't help feeling some small remorse.

There was next to no chance that this group would survive, but his actions were necessary to avoid suspicion and he would not compromise his true intentions.

"Once we add them to our armies, the Master told me to attack Strathmore. Has that plan changed since your return?"

"We will take command of King Ferrus' undead army first, Gans. Prepare to dispatch the mummy, on my signal. I do not trust his loyalty."

* * *

"I sense many undead in the chambers ahead of us!" hissed Inunis, but it was too late. The howling ghosts that had lured the team further into the deep chambers slid from the walls behind them, cutting off their only path of escape.

"OoEEoOEEOoEE!" Wailing louder, the ghosts charged the team, a writhing mass of spirits driving them further into the crypt. Many of the terrified guardsmen and Rangers dropped their weapons and ran, pressing their hands over their ears.

"Stop!! Stand your ground! This may be a trap!" Unable to command even his Rangers, Llaen could only watch as they ran towards their doom.

"Mrrrroannnn!" Zombies and skeletons rushed forward, attacking the fleeing guards and Rangers. Lust for spiritual energy driving them into a fury, the chamber became no more than a frenzied massacre.

"We must help them!" shouted Razz, charging forward to attack the horde of undead. Lenowyn was two steps behind him.

"At least we can kill these things with our blades!" Whirling back and forth, shiny blades singing through the stale air of the crypt, Lenowyn hacked at the undead in every direction. Llaen and the remaining Rangers joined her and Razz defending against the onslaught.

"Do not let the undead rush too far forward," commanded Killian, watching the bloodbath unfold. *"Let the whole group engage before I release the ghouls."*

"I will kill that priestess!" Rushing past the mage and attacking the priestess before she could join the fray, darkness filled the space around Gans. With his adversaries blinded by the suffocating blanket of blackness, the shade tore into her, his taloned hands and feet slashing at the priestess from every direction.

"Kethus! Help me!" Crying out as she felt the burn of the thrashing attacks tear into her body, the shade's talons dug deep into Inunis's side and exposed arm. Gasping in pain and desperation, she cast a magic shield to block the vicious attacks. It would not protect her for long. The priestess knew that her holy symbol would be of little help this time.

"Tis rubi em alif!" Kethus' burst of flame struck the shade from behind, knocking it off the priestess. "Can you turn it, Inunis?"

Watching the fighting swirl, Tabatha knew no one was paying any attention to her. Focusing on the two closest ghosts, she raised her hand and stepped forward, controlling them with ease. "Attack the undead. Leave the living alone!"

"OoOoOoOoo!" Confused for several moments, the mindless ghosts obeyed their new master. Spinning to face the undead mass around them, they began attacking the oncoming skeletons and zombies.

"We have to get out of here!" Swinging his weapons with a fury born of desperation, Razz looked over and saw ghouls joining the attack. "There are too many of them, Llaen! It's time to leave!" Most of the guards and Rangers had already fallen from the massive undead offensive and were rising as zombies.

"Retreat!" shouted Llaen, agreeing with Razz but knowing it was already a hopeless situation for his men. Slashing at another zombie, he let the fighting push him backwards towards Kethus.

"Look! The Curse of the Undead!" Gasping in horror, Lenowyn saw one of the fallen Rangers rising from the ground in front of her, his eyes now pale and lifeless. Backing up under the pressure of the onslaught, she now faced six undead pummeling her from all sides. There were too many blows for her to defend against and she began faltering.

"Lenowyn! Fight! I cannot assist!" Watching her take hit after hit, Razz was battling four undead and struggling to defend against their furious assault.

"Back away! In the name of the Goddess Shifra, obey me!" Using all her strength, Inunis had little control over the shade but had for the moment managed to slow it and the other undead, preventing them from overwhelming her. "Kethus! We need a Moongate now!"

"Par ipsu ori noom." Without hesitation Kethus conjured a shimmering blue portal. "Everyone! Jump through the gate as fast as possible! It won't last long!" The mage rushed into the portal of light, not waiting to see who would join him.

"Everyone who can must leave now! We cannot wait for you!" Rushing past three ghouls grabbing at him with their clawed and bony hands, Llaen dove into the portal headfirst, hoping the others would follow his lead.

Hearing the crackling buzz of the Moongate, Razz turned from his attackers and bolted. Looking around as he ran, he saw at least a dozen undead rushing towards Tabatha. There was little he could do for either her or Lenowyn, who was not going down without a fight. Stopping to beat back the zombies following him, Razz turned again and leapt at full speed through the portal.

Sprinting right behind him, Inunis observed the horde of undead surrounding Lenowyn and knew there was no longer any hope for her assassin. Retreating through the Moongate just before it closed, the last thing Inunis saw was Lenowyn's sword swinging above the mass of undead bodies piling on top of her.

* * *

"*Leave these two for Ferrus!*" commanded Killian, calling off the shades that were closing on the human female necromancer.

"*I can kill her if you let me, master!*" Thirsting for more energy and another kill, Gans would not dare disobey Killian. The shade retreated with the rest of his kind into the shadows to join their master watching the conclusion of the battle.

"What just happened?" Regaining her feet, Lenowyn saw the zombies that had been tearing at her just moments ago now appeared to be attacking other zombies.

The crackling sound of the Moongate gave her hope. Turning away from the fight, she ran towards the noise. Inunis' robes were fading in the shimmering blue light, but before Lenowyn could get to it the gate disappeared. The sound of footsteps behind her brought reality crashing back down on her head as she stared at the missed opportunity for salvation. Spinning around and swinging her katana hard against a charging ghoul, she dropped the creature in its tracks. Looking around for an escape route, it was confusing to see the undead fighting each other. Hearing a female voice giving the creatures orders, she began to understand.

"Who dares disturb the sanctity of my tomb?!" Storming out of his burial chamber, King Ferrus roared into the depths of the crypt. Killing the few remaining guards and Rangers himself, it pleased the undead king to see them rise into new zombie recruits.

"*I will take care of these two stragglers myself!*" Glaring at the human necromancer with pure hatred for her power over his army, the mummy took stock of his remaining troops and concluded that his undead army had made too many sacrifices in this battle. "*No one will engage these two but me!*"

"Lenowyn! Over here! Hurry!" Tabatha had a dozen undead under her control and they rushed to the assassin's defence.

"You don't have to ask me twice!" Surrounded by her new undead escort, Lenowyn pushed her way beside Tabatha.

"Stop your attack!" Tabatha was unable to achieve complete control of all the lesser undead in the chamber. But turning away those not already under her control, only Ferrus and his two bodyguards continued advancing.

"I cannot believe you are a necromancer!" Incredulous with the simplicity with which the human had fooled her, Lenowyn stared at Tabatha shaking her head. "You are the cause of the undead curse!"

"I can stop controlling them if you want. Get ready to run or fight."

"Hang on, that's ok. We need their help." Darting forward and striking the closest skeletal knight hard across the chest, Lenowyn remembered that the greater undead were immune to her weapons. Jumping back into position, she understood in that instant that it no longer mattered whether Tabatha was a necromancer or not. The advancing skeletal knights and the mummy were too strong to defend against.

"There is no way I can control the more powerful undead! Defend against the mummy, Lenowyn. I'll have my zombies attack the skeletal knights."

"Whatever you're going to do, Tabatha, you need to do it fast. My swords are ineffective here!"

"Undead! Destroy the knights!" If the undead could keep the knights busy and Lenowyn could slow the mummy, Tabatha thought that maybe they could escape with their lives.

Swinging with all her remaining strength, Lenowyn slashed at the mummy twice. Her attack had no effect on the brute. Switching tactics out of necessity, she took a defensive stance as the mummy approached her, hoping it might slow him down.

"The zombies are no match for the skeletal knights, Lenowyn!" There were only a few zombies left remaining under Tabatha's control. "I will send the ghouls. Maybe they will be more effective."

Furious with the skeletal knights for killing the last of the zombies, King Ferrus couldn't believe that the ghouls were now taking the zombies' place and attacking the knights. This battle was becoming far too expensive. "*Stop! Do not kill my ghouls!*"

"I am in trouble! Tabatha!" Lenowyn had lost her footing on the blood slick floor and dropped to the ground. Keeping her blade up in defence against the onslaught of blows from the mummy, her strength was almost gone.

Seeing the elf's weakness exposed, the mummy wrenched the katana from her tired hands. Turning it around, he drove it into her stomach and out her back, twisting it up towards her chest.

"Tabatha! Help… uhhhh…" Blood pouring from the gaping wounds, Lenowyn felt cold as her life energy gushed away.

Running to Lenowyn's side when she saw her go down, Tabatha ignored the mummy standing victorious over the elf. Cradling her head, the necromancer held her breath as death began crawling up and over her fallen comrade.

"No! No! Noo!" Casting her Raise Dead spell mere moments before Lenowyn's final breath, Tabatha closed her eyes and squeezed Lenowyn's hand. Within seconds after dying, the Curse began the elf's undead conversion. The skeletal knights stomped closer to Tabatha, preparing to finish her for their master.

When she felt Lenowyn stirring, Tabatha rose and danced away from the approaching knights before they could strike. Surrounding herself with the ghouls under her control, she waited to see the results of her spell.

As her eyes snapped open, Lenowyn groaned and rose, standing between Tabatha and the undead attackers. Covered in blood and confused by her return from the dead, she snatched her katana out of the stunned mummy's hands, her undead eyes glaring at him as she stepped in front of Tabatha to protect her.

How is this possible? Astonished by what he had just witnessed, King Ferrus tried putting it into perspective. All deaths brought new undead, but the elf had kept her soul. That meant that there was a loophole in the Curse. They needed to inform Xeon as soon as possible. This was a big threat to their plan and if all the necromancers learned of it, they could ruin the entirety of the Master's careful maneuvering.

"Lenowyn! Let's get out of here!" Not waiting for the mummy's reaction, both Tabatha and the undead elf assassin backed away, retreating down the empty passageway faster than the knights or mummy could follow.

"*Stay here!*" Ordering the shades to leave the fugitives alone, Killian was just as amazed as King Ferrus. "*She can control the undead. I don't want to take the chance of putting any stronger undead under her control.*"

"*For once I agree with Killian. Never mind them for now!*" The skeletal knights had started after the fugitives but the ghouls still under Tabatha's control had positioned themselves to block the chase. Ferrus was unhappy letting the necromancer escape but he was not prepared to risk losing more of his undead army. Instead, he focused on getting all the ghouls back under his control. The necromancer would pay with her life at a later date.

The mummy and the rest of the undead faded out of sight as Lenowyn and Tabatha stumbled to the stairwell and climbed back to the crypt's main level. Not thinking straight and weakened from her conversion, Lenowyn was struggling with the pace. Letting basic survival instincts take over, she willed her legs to move as if they had a mind of their own.

"*You have done well tonight, necromancer. Your discovery may be the answer we seek to the Curse of the Undead!*"

Unsure who was speaking, Tabatha did not even care to try and return the communication. Her mind was in shock at the day's events and only the will to survive kept her running now. Turning to see if anyone was following them, she continued leading Lenowyn away from what she knew was their certain doom.

VIII

NO ESCAPE

"Worthless elf beads." Rifling through the elf girl's possessions and finding only a string of simple prayer beads, Zik stuffed the find into his pouch and turned his attention back to the study of new spells.

The shaman had spent two days recovering from the close call in the forest, but today the cold mountain air had woken him early. Instead of going back to sleep he chose to continue practicing spells stolen in another raid not long ago. Standing at the large table in his bedchamber, he hadn't had to move far as this was also his laboratory. The room contained a large desk with many shelves holding his spell books and devices used for inscribing his scrolls.

Swirling his arms above his head, Zik practiced a transformation spell turning him into a bearlike figure while maintaining his ability to talk and cast further magic. Jujube waited and watched without making a sound, staying out of the way but ready to help the shaman in any way possible.

"Trans bur ap!" Watching his arms as the transfiguration started, his skin began pulsing and bubbling. Without warning a persistent background noise wormed its way into his subconscious, forcing him to stop the spell before it had completed.

"What is that noise?" Pounding on the table as his short temper boiled over and now stuck in partial bear form, the shaman glowered at his apprentice. Jujube's eyes widened with the unwanted attention, having felt firsthand the results when anything interrupted his master's magic studies. The mewling coming from down the hallway appeared to be invading every corner of the chamber.

"Master... it is the elf girl! I will silence her!" Hoping that the ogre wouldn't notice, Jujube had made sure he slipped out of the shaman's range when the sound first tickled his ears. For the last two days Morrowyn had been silent, eating only crumbs. For some unknown reason today she resumed crying, and Jujube knew it would result in trouble for her. The shaman would not tolerate any noise or interruption.

"There will be no crying in my prison, goblin!" Looking to punish his apprentice for the interruption and seeing Jujube cringing on the other side of the room, Zik knocked the spell book and other components away and charged out of his chamber. The cave had gone silent at the sound of his angry roaring, and his feet thundering against the cold stone floor added emphasis to his anger.

Exhausted as usual, the potion-maker had startled awake at the sound of Zik's loud bellowing. Still groggy with sleep, he had no idea what was happening but felt relief when the uproar passed right by his cell. Mixer had been here long enough to know the results of angering the ogre.

Morrowyn stood frozen in her cell, hearing the angry snarls getting louder as Zik approached her cell. She thought about hiding but couldn't move. Jujube had warned her about crying around the ogre, and she was now wishing with all her heart that she had listened. Holding back any more tears, she fought the fear freezing the blood in her veins.

"Open the gate, NOW!" Stopping Zik in his tracks just outside Morrowyn's cell, a loud voice yelled out from down the hall.

"What do you want?" roared Zik, not happy hearing Gurosh yelling orders at his guards. The warrior's appearance added fuel to the already raging fire inside him and the shaman made note that the extra adrenaline from the bear form pumping through him made flexing his muscles a pleasurable experience. Hammering a half-transformed paw hard against Morrowyn's cell door, his claws dug deep into the wood. Not sure what was happening, he turned to hear what Gurosh's interruption was about.

Without making so much as a squeak, Morrowyn fell backwards onto her bed, afraid that the ogre would smash right through the door. Closing her eyes, she had never felt so vulnerable. *Please let him go away and I will never make another sound!*

"The chieftain wants to see you, Zik!" Striding into the shaman's lair as soon as the gate had risen, Gurosh had seen the shaman storm by on his way to the prisoner's area and was curious about the commotion.

"What are you doing here? I did not ask for you!" Not caring what Gurosh wanted and never appreciating uninvited visits, the bear-shaman approached the warrior and stood in front of him clenching and unclenching his fists.

"Our Chieftain summons us!" Glaring with his one good eye, Gurosh grinned into the face of his adversary. Catching the shaman in bear form surprised him, the addition of fur and claws making Zik appear more formidable, but he still felt he was the stronger of the two. *One day I will test my strength against Zik and prove to Bigglum who is stronger.*

The damage from the arrow that pierced his eye was permanent and Gurosh had accused the shaman of not using all his powers to heal him. There was no love lost between the two ogres before he lost his eye, but now the warrior had a personal vendetta against him. Planning to wait until the most opportune moment to exact his revenge, he would enjoy his retribution.

"What are you up to Gurosh?" Annoyed at the interruption, Zik hated leaving halfway through learning a new spell, but if the chieftain was calling he had little choice. Studying the sneering warrior, the shaman was not surprised when he ignored the question.

"Jujube! Clean up my mess!" The goblin scurried out from the kitchen and back into the shaman's quarters. "Make sure my chamber is clean before I return!"

"I clean it now, Master!"

"When I see you again I want my supper ready, goblin. It better be good or I'll have you for the second course!" Bumping past Gurosh as he left, the two ogres stomped out of the cavern, the portcullis slamming down behind them.

Clinging to the mountainside, various huts of all sizes sat helter-skelter in the ogre village. At the center of the settlement and constructed against the tall granite wall of the mountain's side was a stone tower, spreading outwards one hundred feet in a half circle and over two hundred feet tall. Resembling an open-mouthed skull, the carved entranceway to the great hall was unlike anything else in the land, its doorway resting inside the gaping maw. On top of the tower sat a massive nest of sticks and mud where hippogriffs watched over the mountainside, reporting any activity to the chieftain.

The warrior and shaman did not speak as they marched to the chieftain's tower. Guarding the entrance, two dark knights dressed in black plate armor stood watching the shaman and warrior arrive. Matching their impassive stares with his disfigured glare, Gurosh's intolerance for protocol was evident. He hated waiting while the guards announced his arrival before allowing him entry.

"The chieftain grows impatient, Gurosh. You know better than to keep our leader waiting." Unwilling to relinquish the battle of wills to the one-eyed warrior, the dark knight did not waver as he stood blocking the entrance.

"Hurry! Run and tell him that Gurosh and Zik are here!" Making no effort to swallow his irritation, even though Bigglum demanded full respect from everyone who entered his main hall the warrior refused to follow all of the protocol.

Why has Bigglum summoned us? Zik replayed the events of the past week trying to gather some clues for their meeting today, but was unable to come up with anything specific. *What has Gurosh done?*

As the heavy door swung open they could see inside the Great Hall. On the walls, orange war banners stretching over twenty feet in length greeted them. The clenched fist emblem of the ogres, embroidered in thick cream-colored wool, filled their centers. Gurosh noticed the recent addition of a smaller red banner with the Shard emblem in black stitching. At the back of the hall a colossal carved granite throne flanked by piles of the chewed and whitened skulls from all races sat on a raised platform. Things had changed since his last time in the Great Hall.

The main chamber was full of onlookers today, including an orc and a hill giant. All present turned to look at Zik and Gurosh as they entered and stood waiting for the official invitation from the chieftain. Sitting on his throne, Bigglum beckoned them forward. Dark knights standing at intervals smashed padded clubs onto metal shields as the newcomers approached the throne, the noise reverberating throughout the tower. Another dark knight motioned for them to stand a respectful distance from the chieftain and wait for his summons. Standing on either side of his throne, Bigglum's aides eyed Zik and Gurosh as the chieftain continued listening to the latest updates from one of his scouts. Bigglum let the scout continue, not caring that his lieutenants were waiting for his signal.

"Step forward!" Bigglum dismissed the scout with a wave as he faced the room.

"Greetings mighty chieftain, slayer of elven champions and eater of human princesses!" proclaimed Gurosh, listing some of Bigglum's more infamous deeds. Pleased with the results of his earlier private meeting with the chieftain, the warrior was looking forward to Zik's reaction.

"Hail! Oh mighty chieftain, ruler of the Snowy Owl Mountains and destroyer of all who oppose you. Your shaman answers the call and welcomes your orders!" Zik liked letting Gurosh go first, as it was easier to one up him. The look on Bigglum's face today confirmed that theory once again. Flattery was helpful when it came to their chieftain and he had a greater flair for speaking than Gurosh, who never seemed able to win their word battles.

"I will get right to the point, Zik. There have been reports that there is a band of adventurers in our realm, and it appears they are heading for the Mines of Taas."

"How many are there? Is it the elves?" The shaman's eyes narrowed. Perhaps their kidnapping of the elf girl had elicited this, but he had not thought anyone would ever bè so bold. The elves seemed adverse to war and it would be surprising indeed if these trespassers were following elven orders.

"Our scouts report five or six warriors with one elf among them, but these adventurers fly no banner. It does not appear that the elves of Green Valley are behind this and it is possible that they are working on their own."

"Bah! Cowards!" A true warrior from head to heart, hearing this about elves did not surprise Gurosh. He had always considered that race to be cowards and fools. "They have sent others to do their dirty work for them!"

"Cowards!" murmured the crowd, agreeing with Gurosh. Feeling encouraged by their support, the warrior was about to continue speaking but Bigglum silenced him with a disapproving glare. Choking down his remaining words, he reminded himself that interrupting the chieftain was never recommended.

"You are correct, Gurosh. The elves have proven themselves weak and foolish." Bigglum courted the crowd by creating consensus and exerting his leadership. Glaring around the room as he spoke, the chieftain waited for silence, ensuring all present heard his wisdom. "But they are smart enough to send others in their place, as it helps avoid an open declaration of war."

"What would you request we do about this band of intruders approaching us?" Frowning at Gurosh, Zik was unsure where this conversation was heading. "Our front lines are goblins and while they will take a heavy blow if these are strong warriors, superior numbers should prove enough to overwhelm a small group."

"In an unfortunate turn, the goblins have already had one confrontation, losing more than half of their war party! It appears that a mage accompanies these warriors. It will take more than simple goblins to dispose of them."

"A mage! That complicates our defense." Considering what he had just been told and having battled mages before, Zik appreciated the real threat even one seasoned mage could bring to a fight. Becoming uncomfortable with the conclusions he was drawing, the shaman could see where this was leading. He waited for his chieftain to make the announcement, already planning his strategy.

"Gurosh has volunteered to seek out the band of adventurers and dispose of them. He has asked that you help him on this hunt and I have agreed that you should go. He will need your Moongates to reach the mines and then your main task will be the destruction of this mage."

"Yes, mighty chieftain! As you wish!" Knowing that Bigglum had already made up his mind, the shaman would not fight his decision.

Grinning at Zik's uncomfortable expression and waiting for further instructions, Gurosh faced Bigglum, his demeanor betraying his obvious enjoyment.

"Take a group of ogre warriors and scouts with you and bring me that mage's head, Gurosh! Do not fail me! The cost of failure is high! You leave for the mines now."

∗   ∗   ∗

When Zik returned from his meeting, there had been no interest in eating what Jujube had prepared for him. Growling with anger, the shaman had packed various items in a sack and left without another word. Jujube was unsure if the ogre was returning, but waited until the shadows had grown longer and darkness covered the mountains before putting away the meal that he had prepared. It was not the first time this had happened. Elated with his master leaving on another mission so soon after returning from the last one, the goblin had a bounce in his step as he completed his nightly routine. He enjoyed every bit of freedom he could get these days.

"Ok you, come with me." Grabbing the magic staff from the ogre's table, Jujube strolled down the corridor with the staff crackling and shimmering in his hands.

Having already drained Mixer of his magic for the day, he snuck up on the front gate and peered around looking for any sign of the ogre. Satisfied that his master wasn't in sight, he headed for the cellblock to complete his rounds.

"She is an elf isn't she?" Interrupting Jujube's quiet conversation with the staff, the potion-maker was having a hard time controlling his excitement. There was no answer from the goblin, and Mixer grabbed his hair in frustration as the apprentice ignored him. "Let me out right now so I can see her!"

After the ogre's angry roars had awakened him earlier in the day and the crying had stopped, Mixer assumed that whoever was disrupting the shaman had become dinner. That was just the way things worked in the ogre's prison, and the faster new prisoners learned where they fit into the pecking order, the longer they lived. Of course, Mixer was aware that there were always exceptions.

"I don't trust you, Mixer. You'll kill her! I decide when you stay in and when you come out. Which is never." The noise of the girl's continued blubbering was making Jujube irritable. Looking back down the hallway at Mixer's cell, the goblin could just see the tip of the half-orc's nose as he tried peering through the little window to catch a glimpse of the new prisoner.

How can I make her understand? No more crying! This is your life now so you must accept it and learn how to live! Waving the staff around in front of him, Jujube tried figuring out a way to help the girl survive without jeopardizing his own life. It would not be easy.

"No! Jujube please! Mixer likes elves. Just let me out so I can see her! What color is her hair? Can you tell me that much?" Pacing back and forth in his room, he grabbed his mixing spoon and bent it out of frustration. Hating the power Jujube held over him, for the last two days the goblin had been tending to the new prisoner, ignoring everything else except the daily energy draining sessions. He figured the girl had become sick and was always sleeping, but he could not get any information to satisfy his craving. Already jealous that Jujube had the wizard for company, now the little goblin had this new girl as well.

"Listen Mixer. You better get making the master his potions and forget about the elf girl!" Wondering how he could teach her magic, Jujube fiddled through his pouch looking for ingredients that might help inspire an idea for what he could teach her first. Not knowing much real magic, all the apprentice had mastered were a few simple parlor tricks. *If this elf does not learn magic, it might be safer for me if I let Mixer kill her!* Worrying about what the ogre might do if he found out his apprentice had lied about her having magic, he reasoned that for now it would just be better not letting Morrowyn and Mixer out of their cells at the same time. Maybe if she learned some magic and could demonstrate her potential, Zik would not be so upset.

"How is Wiz today?" Glad to be away from Mixer, when Jujube peered into Wiz's cell, the human was jumping to his feet. For the last few days he had not spent much time with anyone but the girl and the wizard was showing signs of loneliness. There had been no choice, as Morrowyn had a bad fever and was near death.

"Jujube let me out today please?" The wizard was not used to the lack of attention, but he knew better than to make an issue out of it. Pressing his face against the bars in his small window, he watched the goblin fiddling with his keys. The human ached from being without proper exercise and conversation.

"Not today Wiz. Must help the girl get better. You must be patient!" Feeling bad for the wizard, he pulled out the magic staff and started filling it with the human's power.

"Wiz should sleep now. It will be better tomorrow!" Pulling the staff down now that his chore was complete, Jujube hoped that the wizard would understand.

"Oh, I'll be patient!" Slapping his pillow, it was uncharacteristic for Wiz to speak in a sarcastic tone, but he was unable to help himself. Even with the knowledge that if the ogre ever saw him out of his cell he could expect a beating, he was not happy having Jujube continue to ignore him.

"You shush now, Wiz!" The crying from the girl's cell had stopped and Jujube thought maybe she was asleep. "If she sleeps, you might wake her."

For the past two days the girl had been close to death. Looking in through the cell window, he could see the bed along the far side of the cell, but could not see her lying in it. Pushing back some of the rancid gray hair hanging over his eyes, he took another look. Quiet now and crouching at the foot of the bed, the girl glared back at him.

"Oh! It is you!" Recognizing her captor with a start as the door swung open, Morrowyn tried not to look too relieved. "I thought you were the ogre bear!" Trying hard not to laugh at how she could mistake a short goblin for a huge ogre, after the shaman's outburst earlier she now feared him more than anything she had ever known.

"You thought I was an ogre?" Understanding how she could make that kind of error was beyond Jujube's comprehension.

"No I meant... never mind." Leaning back on her dirty pillow and feeling better since the middle of the day when her fever broke, she was even able to get out of bed and stand for a while. Memories of the goblin caring for her kept crossing her mind and she knew that he had in all likelihood saved her life, but she couldn't forgive him for putting her in shackles. This goblin was one of the creatures that held her captive, and in her mind he was just as evil as the ogre. The goblin's power over her was frightening. The shackles jingling when she moved was a continual reminder that she was his prisoner. Every time she heard them the feelings of anxiety began escalating and she would start crying.

"Why are you keeping me here? I have nothing for you."

"Jujube is happy to see you feeling better, Mor-o-win! You are the ogre's slave now. I am his apprentice."

"I am not a slave!" Trying to ignore the shackles on her leg as tears welled in her eyes, Morrowyn found herself backed into a corner. "I will escape this filthy cell and my father will make you all pay for this!"

"I told you there is no escape! You must stop thinking like that! If the ogre finds you out of your cell he will eat you on the spot." The reality was harsh but Jujube hoped the harshness would help her understand. "We are far up in the mountains. You could never find your way back home and your father will never find you here."

"I don't believe you!" In spite of this verbal sparring with the goblin, Morrowyn was starting to believe that his words were in fact the truth.

"The master will want to see you soon. We must teach you some magic so you don't get eaten." Patting her head like she was his pet, Jujube hoped his words were getting through.

"No, no, no! I don't want to get eaten!" Gasping between sobs, the memory of the ogre smashing on her door earlier flashed through her mind.

"An el luminous!" Turning his finger in a circular motion the goblin watched as a crepuscular glow from the leg of her bed began illuminating the cell. "Watch me now and listen to what I say," he said, repeating the incantation and movement of the simple spell at a slow speed for Morrowyn to follow. Holding out the energy draining staff, he imbued her with some of its magical spiritual energy. "Now you have power flowing through you. Feel its energy and learn how to use it to create magic. If you make the light grow stronger, you will live a long time and won't get eaten."

The constant crying and hostility towards him left Jujube exhausted. Hoping that she had paid attention, he turned and left her to practice on her own.

∗ ∗ ∗

This sunrise would mark the fifth day since Kalahni and Llysander had set out on their quest. Traveling inside the ogre tunnel for almost two full days, they felt a huge relief when they saw light streaming in from the opening on the other side and walked out into the fresh air without problems. Resting in the tunnel had not been possible for either of them. If the ogres had appeared, they had nowhere to run, but Kalahni's intuition told her that things would get harder still. Working their way up the rocky hills before they rested in the growing dusk, the pair ate a light meal and took turns sleeping.

Kalahni and Snow sat on a large flat-topped boulder, keeping each other company while Llysander slept. It was a good vantage point from where they could spot anyone approaching. The darkness was shifting before their eyes, the sky filling with purple and blue shades. As the moon faded from view, she watched the sun begin its slow dance on the horizon.

Sleeping was not an option for Kalahni these days, with her mind consumed not only by thoughts of Morrowyn's capture but also remembering Llythwain's face when he realized that she was leaving him behind. Wanting to comfort him and make promises that everything would be okay, she knew that her son's thought processes worked in a different way than those of other children and he understood things in a much more literal fashion. There was no way she would ever lie to him or sweeten her words. Over the last few years he had regained trust in his mother again, and she refused to jeopardize the work it had taken bringing him back just for the sake of a few false hopes. She had told him the truth and reassured him that Morrowyn's capture was not his fault, but what she feared most was that he would blame himself while she wasn't there helping him deal with it.

Watching the gradual sunrise gave her a lot of thinking time. It was difficult to imagine that her entire family was shouldering the blame for something that was not any of their faults. Accepting that particular truth had made her feel a little better inside, and blame was no longer foremost on her mind. Time spent trying to assign attribution was only dividing her family. Clear and decisive action was all that mattered now. The instincts and wisdom of a mother were helping ground her in reality.

The pine trees gave off the sharp pleasant aroma of the outdoors. Cool mountain winds reminded her that the mines were getting closer. It was time to move on.

"Llysander, wake up." Her lips brushing his ear, Kalahni rubbed his shoulders and felt the large muscles underneath his shirt. This physique is not common amongst the elves, but she found it attractive on him. Her husband stretched himself awake while she was massaging his head.

"Kalahni? You didn't wake me for my turn? Was everything okay on your watch?" Shaking off the tatters of his night's sleep, Llysander was more than a little concerned by her exhausted appearance.

"Everything was quiet. I made us breakfast. Let's eat so we can continue following the ogre trail. The rain you spoke of last night hangs in the sky, but it was peaceful earlier. I wish we could have seen the sunrise together, but I decided it was more important for you to sleep."

"Look out past the trees." Taking the food she offered, Llysander pointed in the direction they had to travel. "Just where the next set of hills lies are the Mines of Taas. The ogres must have come through there!"

"Do we go into the mines or around them?" Fixing her eyes on the direction he was pointing, Kalahni was eager for action.

"To be honest, I am not sure. I have never been this far into goblin territory. They may live beyond the mines. Or they might live underground."

"Then we must go into the mines."

"Let's find the entrance and decide from there." Dreading either option, Llysander knew their chances of success were slim no matter which way they went. If entering the mines was the next step of their foolhardy plan, it was becoming more evident to him that they didn't have a plan at all. Clinging to his hope that the Rangers would have already mobilized and somehow arrive to save the day, at this point his hope was fading fast.

* * *

Refusing to try the simple spell while Jujube was in her cell, Morrowyn hated her captor. Rejecting to his face whatever help he offered, she still could not help watching every detail of his magic lesson out of the corner of her eye. Alone in her tiny cell, she could do little else besides sleep, cry and think about home. The memory of Jujube telling her that the ogre would eat her would then replay itself and that kept her thinking about the spell. Practicing the chanting and movements over and over in her head, the spell was becoming imprinted in her mind. *I will practice when that goblin is not around in case the ogre comes back.*

"Why?!" Shouting at the walls, she couldn't believe the state of her accommodations. Her cell was damp and smelled of mold. The slimy walls were strewn with cobwebs and dust, and the only furniture consisted of her small bed, a desk and a chair. The dried and over-spiced food that she refused to eat was piling up on the desk. Accustomed to eating meals cooked with love by her mother, Morrowyn's brain wasn't yet hungry enough to choke down the soft vegetables, flat bread and spicy meat. Her stomach had a different opinion, but so far her head continued to overrule it. Grabbing her blanket, she pulled it over her head and her nose wrinkled. The blanket was dry, but came complete with many stains and funny odors. Missing her mother and family, images of home began crowding her mind's eye.

"Where are my beads?" Thinking that praying might bring her mother closer, she had managed a few short verses but struggled without her beads to help her focus. Every passing moment in this dungeon brought the futility of her situation closer to home.

Studying her cell in detail, she noticed some old bones slumped behind the cell door. Images of the hungry ogre began dancing behind her eyes, and she shook her head to try and dispel them. The reality of her captivity did not sit well with her and she lost herself again in tears of disbelief.

"Hey little girl! What are you crying about? Is that nasty goblin hurting you?" Accustomed to the relative silence of the ogre's prison, the constant crying from the girl was getting on Mixer's nerves. For days he had not been out of his cell and he knew why. Mixer had always hated elves and this was just another reason. *That whiny little brat will no longer cry if I get my way.*

"Who are you?" Hearing the new voice seep in from the hallway, Morrowyn's sobbing choked to a halt. The voice was strange, with a thick accent and raspy tone. Welcoming the concern from a stranger outside her cell, she got up out of bed and stood on her toes at the door trying to see out the small window. "Are you a prisoner here too?"

Surprised at having elicited a response, Mixer allowed himself a smile. Wondering what advantage he could gain from talking with the girl, his brain was working hard to decide his next move. *At the least I can gain her trust and kill her if she doesn't stop crying!* Chuckling at the thought, this change in circumstance would help spice up his normal boring routine.

"My name is Mixer and I am a prisoner too, just like you!" he replied in as sweet a tone as he could muster. "How could that nasty goblin and evil ogre lock up a girl like you? How awful! I feel horrible for you. Please tell me your name." Holding his breath, he was proud of his acting routine and snickered into his hand. This was so much more fun than making the same healing potions over and over again each day.

"Silence! No speaking with the girl!" Yelling down the hallway, Jujube's feet echoed louder as he hurried towards Mixer's cell. Throwing open the cell door, he pointed the magic staff at the potion-maker and started draining him at full power. *At least I got here before Mixer had a chance to learn anything he shouldn't from the elf girl.*

"Your name? What is your name girl?" Groaning in pain from the draining shocks, Mixer played this to maximum effect.

"Stop it Jujube! You are hurting him!" Still standing at the doorway, she could just see Jujube standing with the staff in his hand. "My name is Morrowyn!" Guessing that the draining would not kill Mixer, she still feared for her new friend's health. *How could anyone be so mean? That goblin is so nasty!*

"Don't worry, Mixer. He won't kill you." Uncertain about Jujube's real intentions with the staff, she didn't think he was the type to murder anyone.

"Do not speak with that one, Mor-o-win. He is dangerous!" Getting angry with her now, the girl was being disobedient and for that she needed punishment. Noticing her hands gripping the bars of the cell window, the goblin took three quick steps towards her and gave her fingers a hard rap with the staff. Not for the first time, Jujube was questioning the wisdom of having the girl added as a new prisoner in his cellblock.

"Aaaiii! You are mean!" wailed Morrowyn as she jumped back onto her bed. Her fingers were now throbbing, and bruises were already forming. Pictures of home came flooding back into her mind as she closed her eyes and wished this all away. Gasping for air as she sobbed, she hid herself back under her dirty blanket.

"Practice making the light stronger with your magic!" said Jujube, being quiet so Mixer would not hear and stir up more trouble. "And remember to tell no one of our secret or the ogre will eat you for sure!"

IX

NIGHTMARES REVISITED

"Draeg! Bring me another slave!" Standing in a small cavern branching off the larger passageway, Sooga had brought a dozen slaves with him on this excursion deep into the Dragon Spine Mountains. The Dark Ones had ordered the goblins to finish these tunnels by summer's end so they could start digging the tunnels under the Snowy Owl Mountains before winter arrived. Children being more obedient, less of a threat and short enough to walk through small tunnels without difficulty, were the most common slaves used for the tunneling.

Draeg was busy beating one of the prisoners with his club. Hearing a voice but unsure of the instruction, he smiled when he saw the necromancer motioning for another slave. The goblins forced the young captives to handle the unstable explosives, taking all the risks while setting the charges. The explosives used for cutting through the walls of rock were unreliable and many children lost their lives in the process. The goblin foreman was determined to finish his tunnel no matter what the cost.

"You! Come!" Motioning at the shackled human child standing beside Llythwain, the goblin knew enough of the common Allegiance language to make himself understood. This boy had seen other slaves perform the task and did not need any further instructing. Picking up a small keg of explosive powder, he carried it into the small side passage without hesitation, disappearing from view.

"Aaahhm…" Mumbling and shifting, Llythwain paced left and right on the spot in the line-up. Fidgeting and waving his arms, his distress had become unmanageable. He hadn't even gotten to know the human boy's name.

"Quiet elf!" Sneering at this strange elf boy, Draeg approached with his club raised. Moving within range, he swung hard and struck him on his right side.

"Noooo!" screamed Llythwain, crying out in pain. Unable to understand why the goblin was being so cruel, he covered his face as the blows continued raining down. Pain was a powerful reminder that the goblins were in charge. Choking back any more screaming, he hoped the beating would end soon, but the silence only further enraged his captor. This cruel goblin wanted nothing more than to hear the elf scream.

"Beg for life!" roared Draeg, a spray of white foam flying from his mouth. Waving his club, he looked around to see if any of the other goblins were watching his display of ferocity. Slumping to the ground, the elf boy was bloody and bruised. Draeg continued flailing him until a loud explosion grabbed everyone's attention. Dust and rock flew out of the small passageway that the human had entered a few moments ago. The boy had not returned prior to the blast.

"Draeg! Bring me another slave!"

Not wanting his fun to end just yet, Draeg pointed at the human slave that had been standing on the elf child's other side. Deciding that they were losing too many prisoners, the necromancer dismissed that child with a wave, pointing at the elf that the goblin had been abusing. He was half-dead anyway.

"As you wish, Sooga."

Panting from the excruciating pain, Llythwain looked up when the guard stopped the beating and saw the goblin leader pointing right at him. Struggling to his feet when the goblin tugged his arm then pushed him forward, he limped over and selected the explosives. He was glad to be the one carrying the keg into the passageway now. Blood soaked his clothes and he could see it dripping down his arms as he bent down to pick up the small wooden barrel. Lubricating his hands, it made gripping the keg difficult. Arching backwards to get leverage and maintain his balance, Llythwain began limping into the passageway.

"I wait for you, elf!" Swinging his club and smashing it into the ground, Draeg made sure the elf knew what was waiting for him if he came back.

Grimacing at the sight and sound of the guard's threats, Llythwain hurried down the passageway as fast as he could to avoid any extra trouble from the goblin leader. Through the dust still hanging in the air he saw the rubble and the human corpse lying mangled on the ground. Visual confirmation of the boy's death made him sad.

* * *

"Llythwain, wake up. You'll miss breakfast." Tugging on his friend's shirt, Ran knew that he was struggling with nightmares by the way he was tossing and turning in his sleep. Leaving his friend alone to sleep awhile longer, he wandered outside to watch the sun rise over the lake. After another hour or so, he came back and shook Llythwain awake before breakfast hour was over.

"I was having a bad dream." Looking around their room, Llythwain tried orienting himself but still felt groggy. The nightmares had started after the ogres took Morrowyn. The experience of that day awakened memories that were better left asleep.

"Guess what, Llythwain? I was down by the lake earlier. They have the canoes out now!" Being an only child, Ran liked having his freedom. Frustrated by his new role with Llythwain, he didn't like looking after someone else. Watching him drifting away again, it reminded him that his friend was different and needed more attention than others. "Hurry up, Llythwain. Breakfast will be over soon."

Hopping out of bed and splashing some cold water on his face from the bowl left on the dresser, Llythwain followed Ran outside. The two friends hurried along the path to the largest log cabin. Two stories tall, the cabin stood on solid wooden stilts as thick as an elf was tall. Climbing up the center stairs, the boys ran across the walkway, trailing their hands along the log railings. The double doors of the main entrance hung open, inviting everyone to enter. Inside there were long tables with split tree trunk benches providing enough seating for over a hundred. Hungry children bustled past them into the almost full seats. The fresh aroma of smoked meat, baked beans and scrambled eggs filled the air. Adjusting to life at camp, Llythwain and Ran remembered enough from yesterday's orientation to hurry into the lines ahead of any children lagging behind.

"Come on Llythwain!" said Ran, shouting encouragement. He could hardly wait to eat.

"This food smells quite good!" agreed Llythwain, delighted that his first night and morning at the camp had not been such a bad experience, not counting the nightmares. Hurrying to catch up with Ran, the boys got their food and found seats together without delay. The cabins reminded Llythwain of trips he had taken with his father whenever he was on leave from his Ranger duties. "Did you say you saw canoes down by the lake, Ran?"

"Yup! I saw Jaeyn taking them out before breakfast!" Sitting close to the exit, Ran motioned for Llythwain and pointed at the canoes beside the dock. Beyond the shore they could also see Mystic Lake waking. The night's mist covering the lake was beginning to dissipate in places and the boys could see the vastness of the water stretching away towards destinations unknown. Gobbling down their food and laughing at each other, they were anxious to explore their new environment.

Hurrying out of the main cabin, they headed straight towards the shore. Fingers of fog from the lake still permeated the forest, but navigating the trail was easy for these two forest-dwellers. They could hear the voices of a few children ahead of them talking with Jaeyn, the young Ranger Scout who was in charge of activities at the camp. His head shaved on either side, he wore his hair in a spiked strip down the center of his scalp. Jaeyn was not like any of the Rangers Llythwain had seen before. Younger than most, it was obvious he enjoyed talking and laughing with everyone. Noticing Llythwain staring at him, he winked with a smile. Waving the fishing rods in his hand, he motioned for everyone to gather around. Llythwain and Ran soon found themselves jostling with the others as they selected fishing equipment.

"This lake is a great place for fishing. Be careful and have fun today. Let's see who can catch the first fish and then who can catch the biggest!" Encouraging the children to take part in activities was a large part of his role at camp and today the children were in a good mood, making his job easier. The sudden disappearance of Gaffer was troubling, but he preoccupied himself with helping the children adjust. The Ranger's gut feeling was that something must have scared him off, and he could not accept the other Rangers' explanation that the old guy just gave up and returned to town. Smiling at the children spreading out and looking for the best spot, he walked by Llythwain and Ran and handed the boys some bait.

"Thank you, Jaeyn!" they replied in unison. The dock stretched over forty feet, providing plenty of room for many young fishers at the same time. Grabbing their fishing rods and bait, the boys moved to the farthest end of the dock away from the other children.

"Aren't you throwing in your line, Llythwain?"

Llythwain stood staring into the water, mesmerized by the many small tadpoles swimming back and forth. Marveling at the way the waves brushed hard against the dock and pushed the canoes back and forth, the lake was peaceful and helped make being away from his family somewhat bearable. Snapping out of his trance at the sound of Ran's voice, he baited his hook, dropping his line into the water on the opposite side of the dock from his friend.

"Sorry Ran," said Llythwain, smiling and happy just to have a friend. Now that the fog was lifting, he could see farther out onto the lake. Near the center, the rocky cliffs of a small island towered above the water. The two boys cast their lines out and began fishing in comfortable silence.

"Have you ever ridden in a canoe before?" asked Llythwain, breaking the silence after a few short minutes. Already restless and kind of bored he reached down, wiggling his fingers in the warm water. Pondering the heat rising from the lake, he wondered what could cause it to be so warm.

"You mean those funny looking boats?" Replying with a note of sarcasm, Ran was pointing at the canoes near the docks. "Of course! My father took me canoeing lots of times. You don't have to be a Ranger's son to learn how a canoe works, you know!"

"Did you want to take a canoe ride today?" Not noticing Ran's tone and excited by his idea, Llythwain wanted to go canoeing right away but wasn't comfortable going alone. It felt like they had been fishing for some time now and his active mind needed more stimulation. "We can bring the fishing stuff with us!"

Lifting his line out of the water, it didn't take Ran long to grow annoyed with the disruptions.

"I think it is going to rain soon. We better wait until tomorrow." Flipping his line back into the water, Ran turned away from Llythwain to let him know the discussion was over. Noticing how quiet his friend got when he said he didn't want to go, he nonetheless felt that waiting was the right decision. It was a nice day so far but the clouds were building and it looked like a storm might form overhead. The other part of the story was that Jaeyn had told Ran they could not use the canoes yet, but Llythwain didn't know anything about that conversation.

"Ohhh, okay. Tomorrow then." Looking at the sky, he had also noted the rolling clouds. It was disappointing, but he reasoned that tomorrow would come soon enough. Brightening after thinking things through, he stretched out his arm looking for a promise from his friend. Ran shook on it and they both went back to fishing.

The morning sped by as the creature worked hard at its morning foraging. Keeping the prisoner alive in the cave on the island made finding sufficient food more stressful and the doppelganger would be happy when it could finally dispose of the captive. *Only for a little longer.*

Moving along the southern shore of the island, it looked for crabs, clams or grubs. Fishing was always an option, but it had a preference for juicy grubs and there seemed to be an abundance of them on this island.

"My name is Gaffer." Mind-melding with the old man for the first time last night, the creature was already beginning to imitate his vocal inflections. Its skin was also changing as the doppelganger began the process of morphing its body to mirror the captive's shape.

"These changes need to happen faster," the creature hissed. Lifting its head to look out across the lake, it could make out a large number of people standing on the dock at the camp. Crouching down onto its belly, it crawled back along the shore without risking discovery.

What is going on over there? Peering back at the campground from the southern tip of the island, the creature was amazed by all the activity. The temptation to take a closer look was strong. Disappearing behind the rock face, it retreated to its cave and fed the prisoner some grubs. *I must wait for the foggy morning or the dark night before risking a closer look.*

∗ ∗ ∗

Grimacing with back spasms, his arms shaking from fatigue, the continual trips into the tunnels carrying heavy kegs of explosives had taken a toll on Llythwain's body. Riding an unprecedented string of luck, none of the small barrels had exploded before he returned from placing them in the tunnel. The group of slaves with whom he had been standing shackled were cheering him on every time he walked out of the tunnel alive, but the lack of food and loss of blood had prevented him from lifting any more. Rather than let the guard beat the life out of this one, the leader sent him away to recuperate from his wounds and now, instead of toiling in the tunnels, he was cooking for the ogres. There was less chance of dying but the continual work was not helping his recovery much.

Heffer's servants worked all morning preparing meals for their journey to Harrow Gate, as food had always helped calm the ogre's nerves. A snack before their departure was unavoidable.

"Elf! More food!" Smacking his new slave with a large stick while motioning at the cauldron swinging above the fire, the slave lord had woken to Xeon's summoning and it made him nervous. Nothing good ever came from the undead dragon's call.

Jumping into action, Llythwain's eyes widened when he heard the nine foot tall ogre roaring at him again, but since he couldn't understand what was being said he had to guess what the angry beast wanted done. Walking by a window and looking out into the dark sky, he scooped a huge bowl of steaming chunky broth. The smell was revolting and he struggled with its weight, but somehow got the bowl onto the ogre's table. Stepping back into his appointed spot as one of several servants, he became lost in thought while blocking out the sound and sight of the ogre stuffing his mouth. Staring up at the dark cavern's ceiling, images of happy days at Pinestone began cycling through his mind once again. *How could this have happened to me?*

"Elf! More!" His mouth still full and dripping with grease, Heffer could not get enough of this soup. Scooping the last chunks out of the bowl, the ogre shoved the greasy container across the table and pointed at the fire again. "I like you, slave! You may be a dumb elf but you know what I want!"

The ogre's voice broke Llythwain from his thoughts. Frowning at the thought of smelling another puddle of this vile slop, he picked up the empty bowl and walked back to the fire. Looking at the ogre out of the corner of his eye, he decided that his disagreeable personality fit his look. Hearing footsteps entering the room, Llythwain froze when he recognized the voices that accompanied them. The goblins from the tunnel stood in the doorway and while he couldn't understand what they were saying, he could see them begin motioning in his direction. He had no desire to resume explosive duty. Serving the ogre, no matter how disgusting the food looked and smelled, was a far better job and his heart sank at the possibility of returning to the tunnels.

"We need our slaves back, Heffer!" Sooga strode into the room past the elf at the fire and stood over the table. The necromancer was running out of slaves and demanded a return of at least some that the slave lord had taken as servants. This was not the first time the necromancer had asked Heffer to return the slaves and he tried reasoning with the ogre again. "The dragon wants the tunnels finished and we are running out of time. We need more help getting this work done!" Noticing the elf boy holding the bowl, Draeg took up a position closer to the fire.

"You shouldn't have been so cruel, Sooga." Seeing the bruising and blood on the slaves when they arrived, it was obvious that the goblins were abusing them. Heffer was not willing to lose out on new servants, knowing that these incompetent goblins were killing them without a second thought.

Looking over at the elf boy, Draeg began growling and bared his teeth with evil intent. Assuming this was the one who had cried to the ogre, he couldn't wait to get him alone again.

"Guards!" Rushing into the chamber, Heffer's guards menaced the goblins that were threatening their leader and his slaves, ready to act with violence if that was his next instruction. Deciding that he didn't like the goblin's attitude, the ogre was not waiting for this meeting to get out of hand.

Intimidated by the huge ogre standing over him, Draeg took a step away from the elf boy and looked for the best escape route if the ogres became aggressive.

"Heffer, I am forced to use the kobolds!" The necromancer was not intimidated by the guards standing within a hand's breadth behind him. "They demand payment and refuse my instructions!"

"Then pay them and stop crying to me with your problems! I am leaving to see the dragon and will be taking the servants with me! All of them!" Thinking that the necromancer might still try taking his servants away, Heffer decided that leaving now was a good idea. Springing up from his chair, the ogre stood with his guards and motioned for them to take the servants away. "We are leaving now. That is all!"

"The Dark Ones will hear about this, Heffer! Are you sure you want that?"

"Hahaha! You are funny, goblin. I am sure they will love hearing how you have been killing the slaves without reason!" Hoping that Sooga wasn't stupid enough to push things further, an argument as petty as this would not result in anything positive for either of them. Ushering all the servants outside to the main passageway, the ogre and his entourage marched towards the outer cavern complex where his wagons were already packed and ready.

Heaving himself into the back of the lead wagon, Heffer signaled for the rider to start moving. Looking back at the necromancer, the slave broker was smiling with his mouth but had pure hate in his eyes. The guards loaded the servants onto the other wagons and secured them in iron cages for the long ride. Llythwain and the other slaves sat like animals, surrounded by tied bundles of food. As the wagon train rolled out of the cavern, Sooga and Draeg fast became a distant memory.

* * *

"Where are they taking us, Marko?" Whispering once they were far enough from the tunnels, the boys in Llythwain's wagon felt comfortable that no one was watching. Listening to the two human boys in front of him, Llythwain chose to rest and said nothing. Confined in separate cages, the children kept an eye on the ogres and watched the scenery sliding by outside their bars.

"We are going to Harrow Gate. That is where the Dark Ones have a gateway to their own world. Terrance, you don't need to be afraid."

"Tell me more about what the dragon looks like!" Hearing rumors from some of the older slaves about the dark master that commanded everyone, Terrance was very afraid.

"Have you ever seen a Dark One? The dragon is not like the rest of them. His powers are so great he can change his shape whenever he wants." Marko had been a servant of Heffer's for some time and had seen many unbelievable things. "The last time I went on a trip like this, we traveled to a gigantic wooden ship that floated in the night air. I saw him on there in the form of a shadow dragon."

"How do you know he can change his shape, Marko?"

"I met him when he was in human form and he changed his shape right in front of me."

"Are we going on that ship?" Listening to Marko explain things, Llythwain found this boy's level of knowledge intriguing.

"The portal at Harrow Gate takes you to the shadow world. This alternate plane of existence is a dark void and they travel through the air in floating ships. We might have to go on the ship again. But they don't tell me their plans!" Shrugging off the elf's question, Marko had about reached the limits of his knowledge.

"What's your name?"

"I'm Llythwain," the elf replied with a shy smile, making extra sure none of the ogres could hear him. He liked Marko right away and wanted his friendship.

"Don't worry. Talking is okay as long as we are quiet," whispered Terrance, noticing the worried look on Llythwain's face.

"We are high up in the mountains right now." Looking through the bars of his cage Llythwain could see the wheels of their wagon knocking loose rocks from the road, sending them plummeting down the side of the mountain.

"Harrow Gate is on the highest peak," said Marko, looking at the star-filled sky. "You can already feel the air getting colder. We still have a long way to go."

"The air feels refreshing," said Llythwain, filling his lungs with the night's crispness. It felt like a long time since he had been above ground.

As the wagons rolled and creaked their way through the peaks of the Dragon Spine Mountains, Marko explained that they were traveling along a roadway that goblins had built many years ago. It extended for at least a hundred miles along the top of the mountains and at times consisted only of wooden bridges stretching from one mountain peak to the next.

"That's the third lamppost," he said. The wooden bridge they had just crossed was still rocking back and forth in the stiff breeze. The children had all been holding their breath as the wood beams and ropes flexed and groaned under the weight of the wagons and supplies.

"Do they ever burn out?" asked Terrance, his voice cracking from the stress of the crossing.

"Those lamps were the creation of ogre mages many years ago. They are magical and are always lit." Stone pillars two feet in diameter rose ten feet to a copper bowl covered in a glass casing that contained the perpetual fire lighting the road. Enjoying his role as tour guide, Marko continued pointing out landmarks and highlights as they rolled along.

"No! No! No!" Screaming as he sat up in bed, a lightning storm had arrived at Camp Quinn and the loud claps of thunder were intruding on Llythwain's dreams. Blinking his bleary eyes, it took him several minutes to realize that he had been having a nightmare.

"Don't worry, Llythwain. It's just a thunderstorm!" Smiling up at his friend from the table, Ran was glad the storm had woken him up. Being alone with the lightning was making him uneasy.

"This storm will not be letting up any time soon," said Llythwain, yawning as he tried to push the tattered memories of his nightmare away. Looking out the window from the upper bunk, he watched the rain pouring down the glass. For some reason it made him think about his parents, wondering if they were getting wet from this same storm and if they would ever find Morrowyn.

"If the rain doesn't stop, we won't be anywhere near a canoe." Interrupting Llythwain's thoughts Ran fiddled with his ukulele, strumming a few random chords as he watched his friend stare out the window. It was obvious that he was getting agitated and fidgety at the thought of being stuck inside.

"If we don't go tomorrow we can always go the next day." Fond memories of outings with his father surfaced every time Llythwain thought about the canoes. The escape would help bury the constant worry about his sister and parents. Hoping that the storm would let up soon, he decided they would be canoeing sooner versus later.

"Hey! Sit back and listen to my new song!" Strumming his little guitar, Ran concentrated on remembering this new combination of chords.

Leaning back on his pillow, Llythwain listened to Ran strum his instrument. His friend was a gifted musician and he found that the cascading notes had a calming effect. Waking up in turmoil almost every day was taking its toll and he was glad to have found something that would quiet his mind. The nightmares were coming more often than they ever had before, forcing him to remember more of his past.

His brain had buried the awful memories of the ogre and goblin enslavement deep in his subconscious mind. Morrowyn's capture was dragging them kicking and screaming back to the surface and they were sticking with him long after he woke up, amplifying his already nervous habits. Sensing that further horrific scenes were still hidden, he wasn't sure how much more he could handle.

"Why do you scream when you sleep, Llythwain? Are you worrying about Morrowyn?" Muting his instrument for a moment, this question had been burning in the back of Ran's mind ever since that first night.

"Yes… No… I don't know…" Worrying about his sister and parents had become a preoccupation, but Ran reminded him of the boys in his dream. Terrance and Marko had become his friends and he wondered if they were still alive. Somehow Llythwain doubted it.

"It's okay, take your time. We have all day," teased Ran, snapping him out of his persistent daydream.

"I was eleven when they took me." Not noticing Ran's teasing, Llythwain felt his heart pounding in his ears. Remembering the worried look on his mother's face when she talked about leaving him behind to search for Morrowyn, he wished now that there was some way of letting her know that he was all right. He had never told her what had happened to him during his captivity, and he hoped she wouldn't mind him sharing it with his friend first. Wiping away the beginnings of tears before Ran noticed, his thoughts raced back in time. Taking a deep breath, he dove into his memories headfirst.

"Who took you where, Llythwain?"

"I was playing outside when they attacked me." Memories began rushing to the surface of his consciousness and he tried controlling their release with little success.

"Who attacked you?" Becoming impatient, Ran could see Llythwain's hands flopping back and forth, and he could tell that his friend was struggling with something big.

"Ran, the stories of ogres abducting children are true!"

"What? How do you know that?" Putting the pieces together, with Morrowyn gone and the children now living at Camp Quinn, the story was becoming more obvious by the minute but Ran's youthful brain refused to accept it.

"They were so cruel. You would not believe the things I have seen and felt." Releasing these memories felt good even though it meant reliving them. His hands were trembling and sweaty, but Llythwain forced himself to continue. "They shackled us together with chains. The goblins made us slaves in the tunnels."

"Goblins! Llythwain, are you serious?" Grasping the word as it reached his ears, Ran was more familiar with the stories of goblins than ogres. His father had taken him on a trip with some Rangers a few years ago on what should have been a fun outing when they ran into a goblin war party and had killed one that was threatening them. Its corpse had become a source of morbid fascination for Ran in the weeks following the encounter. It was the current threat of goblins that was taking them away from their normal life. "What did the goblins do to you?"

"The goblins were way worse than the ogres. We never did anything to them, but they hated all of us." Remembering the boy getting killed by explosives and the constant beatings he received, Llythwain was staring right through Ran. His whole body shaking now, it seemed as though the memories had held their freshness well all these years.

"Hey Llythwain, go easy. We can talk more about it tomorrow." Seeing his friend shaking on the bed, Ran realized it was time to talk about something else. Tapping him on his back, he brought his friend back into the present.

"Thanks for listening Ran!" Turning back to the window, Llythwain stared outside watching the rain pour down the glass. Not talking about this anymore was a relief, and his mind jumped back to the friends that he had met when he was a slave. Hypnotized by the rain pounding on the roof of their cabin, his eyes became heavy and he dozed off again.

* * *

"That is the biggest castle I have ever seen!" Looking out at the structure in awe, Llythwain was having a hard time containing his emotions. The other boys remained silent thinking about what might happen to them next.

"They kept us in the barracks near the big tower the last time I was here," said Marko, pointing at a squat building off to the left. Bumping up and down over the threshold as they entered the inner courtyard of Harrow Gate, the wagons jerked to an abrupt stop.

"Is this where Xeon lives?" Becoming more scared by the second, Terrence could see ogres everywhere. The sound of the gates slamming closed startled all of them back into silence.

"I don't know for sure, but I don't think so. You will see many shadow creatures here. They are cruel beasts." Watching an ogre tie up the wagons, Marko's tone became dead serious. "Just keep your eyes down, your ears open, and hope they don't notice you."

"They can't be any more cruel than the goblins," said Llythwain. All three boys nodded in agreement. Escaping goblin torments at least for a little while was a welcome relief.

Holding up his hand to warn the others to stay quiet, Marko had noticed that while they were talking a shade had approached Heffer.

"Xeon has sent me to retrieve your medallion so he can recharge it." Surprised by the unexpected request, Heffer's eyes grew wide when he realized that he had forgotten it in his chamber. The fuss with Sooga had occupied his mind just as he was leaving and caused him to rush away.

"Which one of you slaves packed my medallion?" Heffer had seen many ogres killed for similar absent-mindedness when they wasted the shadow creature's time. Trying to hide his nervousness around the shade, Heffer heaved himself out of the wagon and approached the caged boys.

"What should we do?" Terrance had gone white as he stared at the angry ogre glaring down at them. None of them being fluent in the Shard tongue, they had no idea what the beast was saying.

"Servants! Where is my medallion!?" Approaching the elf's cage, he flung open the door and pulled him out by the hair.

Llythwain did not know what the ogre was angry about. The beast was growling at him, but he was now petrified with fear. Unable to move, his mind was a complete blank and he stared back at the ogre without making a sound.

"Useless elf! You left it with the goblins!" Swinging his arm back, Heffer smacked Llythwain across the head with a powerful swipe of his hand. Expecting the hit, it was natural to roll with the blow almost at the same time as the ogre's hand struck him. There was no avoiding it however, and Llythwain bounced across the ground in pain, blood bubbling from his mouth.

"Uuuuhhh! Marko, what can I do?" Hoping his new friend might have a way to stop the ogre from killing him, Llythwain's ears were ringing from the impact and if Marko said anything he couldn't hear it. Lying on the ground covering his head and pulling his legs up, the act of submission only enraged the ogre further.

"Insolence!" the ogre roared, pretending he understood what the elf had said. Knowing that the shadow creatures could read thoughts, Heffer wanted to kill the elf in an attempt to distract the shade from the truth. Channeling his fury, he focused all his energy on anger, blocking all other thoughts out of his head. Striking the elf child harder and harder, the slaver beat the boy into the ground as he put on a show for the shade.

"Ogre! Enough!"

Heffer did not dare disobey the shade's command, watching him stride around the wagon. Panting now, dripping with spit and sweat, he backed away from his crumpled victim.

"I do not have time for your delays, ogre. Give me the boy and I will take him to fetch your medallion."

Confused by the shade's request, Heffer felt that perhaps his actions had created a favorable outcome. The shadow creature did not seem angry with him at all. Maybe he was in Xeon's favor and that was why the dragon had summoned him here today. Maybe this would be a good day after all.

"Get up elf. You will go with him," said Heffer, picking Llythwain up and pushing him forward. "Get the medallion that you forgot, and do not make another mistake!"

Not knowing what the ogre wanted him to do, Llythwain had to make a move but his mind froze his body. *What should I do?*

"*Come to me if you want to live today.*" Hearing a strange whisper inside his head, Llythwain knew right away it was the shade. Understanding what it was saying, he turned without fear and walked on stiffening legs to the dark creature's side.

Heffer and the slaves watched stunned as the elf boy became engulfed by waves of darkness. Before anyone could move, he and the shadow creature were gone.

X

THE MINES OF TAAS

Looking left and right, not sure if he had gone blind or died, Garrett remembered resting in the cave after drinking a little too much. There was a biting crunch and the next thing he recalled was everything going dark. Fingering his neck, he could feel the wetness of a wound. That didn't feel like a dream.

Am I still inside the cave or is this the afterlife? Looking down at his feet, he was standing on a smooth and shiny black road suspended in the deeper blackness, radiating a faint glow. As his eyes adjusted he observed the road stretching as far as he could see and it seemed to twist and turn in response to his thoughts. *What is this place?*

"*Warrior! Hear me now!*" Echoing inside the mercenary's head, Killian began taking control. During the confusion of the battle in the cave, he had infused much more of the shade venom into the human than he had intended. There was a point where he thought this man would not survive, but it seemed as though the mercenary was regaining consciousness.

"*Who or what are you? Show yourself!*" Taking a step to challenge the speaker, Garrett stumbled forward.

"*I am your master. You will know who I am when I am ready to reveal that information.*" Exerting his will and boring deep into the knight's subconscious just as he would with any other undead, Killian sensed that he was strong but the shade's power was persistent.

"You are mistaken. I have no master!" said Garrett, fighting hard against whatever was gnawing at his mind. Resisting the power of the strange voice, before long he found himself growing tired from this constant battle of wills. *"What is it you wish of me?"*

"I will break you and your friends. Soon you will all feel the venom burn. Then you will obey me without question."

"What are you talking about?" Unable to tell if he was dreaming, Garrett bristled, unwilling to accept some voice pushing him around. *"You picked the wrong crew to mess with if that is your plan."*

"Human, you are still not ready," said Killian, the pull against the knight taking longer than he expected. It was time to end this communication. *"Rest now. You will remember nothing when you awaken."*

"I will remember nothing…"

"You won't break the Heroes of Karth. Don't waste your time."

"I want you all to reinforce my words when Ahira returns. This is not the place for rash decisions. Please exercise patience and watch for my Moongate. Eli bisi vini in rut." Looking at each of his mercenaries in the eye and making sure they understood, Davissor cast his spell of invisibility and headed towards the mine. No one was to make any moves until he summoned them.

Leaving the campsite on a trail towards the mine entrance, there were no goblins to be seen but Davissor was certain there would be many in the tunnels. *The goblins that attacked us may have fled, but it's guaranteed that they would have sent word to others by now. Reinforcements could be waiting anywhere.*

"Blast! Where did Davissor get to now?" Striding into the campsite, Ahira didn't see the mage but already knew the answer to his question.

"We finished working out the plan," said Angus, fast becoming exasperated with the short-tempered dwarf. "Davissor used invisibility and went alone. Where were you?"

"What! The mage said we would all sneak into the mines. I don't recall anything about it being just him or invisible spells!"

"Calm down, Ahira! It's not your time!" said Ragnar, trying to head off the inevitable explosion. Working himself into a rage, Ahira already held his battle-axe ready.

"There will be too many goblins for a frontal attack this time, brother," said Angus. "Let's just wait for Davissor's Moongate, as he asked us."

"Ahira, listen for a change." Patting him on the back, Garrett smiled and hoped it wasn't too late to calm him down. Standing here with his friends, he was just starting to enjoy the feeling of health again. Rubbing his neck where the laceration once oozed, he found it amazing how Davissor's potion healed his skin without even so much as a scar.

* * *

Gaping like an open wound, Davissor saw that the goblins had scraped the entrance to the mines into the bottom of a large hill close to the mountainside. Hidden from view by trees and hills on either side, well-worn pathways threaded away between the hills in all directions and as he worked his way along the side of the trail, the mage came across a large group of goblins consisting of both peons carrying pick axes and armed warriors. *Good thing we decided against rushing in the front door!*

"Stay alert! They are close!" Retreating to the mines after battling the mercenaries in the cave, Sooga had received word on their enemy's location from hunters positioned higher in the hills. Assuming that a frontal attack was imminent, the necromancer gathered all available peons and warriors to defend the mines from these formidable intruders.

Jumping into the bushes to let the goblins march past, Davissor strolled up to the mine entrance undetected. Hearing voices and the clanking of metal implements echoing from deep inside the cavern, he stopped inside the ragged entrance as his eyes adjusted to the gloom. Crude rails snaked away into the darkness and a mine cart lay overturned on piles of rubble not far inside.

Well, it's quite obvious that many goblins have been through here. The amount of garbage they leave behind is unbelievable!

Picking his way down the tunnel with care, thirty steps in and he found it widening into some kind of processing area with many goblin peons breaking up the larger chunks of rock that others were dumping beside the cart rails. *That looks like a lovely job. I wonder where I sign up!* Following the rails until he was alone, he lit the tip of his katana with a dim glow before continuing his exploration. Looking like a firefly bouncing through the air, the tip of his sword cast just enough light to keep the mage from stumbling on the uneven floor.

"Mmmroan!" A zombie stirred at Davissor's approach. It could not see the mage but sensed the life energy of a living creature nearby.

"Quiet!" Irritated that Sooga had assigned him this menial task, Halob hated watching over the mindless zombies brought back from the last battle. The young necromancer didn't raise his head or look at the three zombie servants as they began stirring, failing to notice the firefly's glow extinguish.

"Mmmroan!" Another of the zombies growled as it shuffled about at random. The three undead couldn't pinpoint the location of the living energy but were staggering around the cavern searching for the source.

"Follow me now!" Unaware that the zombies had just cornered the energy source, the necromancer rose to leave. Ceasing their hunt at his command, the undead turned away.

Raising his blade, Davissor was ready to repel the zombie attack. Breathing a sigh of relief that the zombies were now shuffling to keep up with the necromancer, he decided that following this group as they stumbled through the tunnel was as good a plan as any. Descending deeper into a large gallery, Davissor stayed close and was inspecting the goblin handiwork when he bumped into the rearmost zombie. The mage froze as the zombies restarted their baleful moaning, but Davissor soon realized that he was not the target this time.

"Get back!" In a fit of rage Halob beat the zombies away with his fists. Pushing past the cowering creatures he knocked away a large piece of rock, revealing the glow of blue crystals.

Energy crystals! Surprised and concerned that the goblin mines contained the coveted translucent stones, these were powerful sources of spiritual energy and kept all creatures rejuvenated. Davissor had even seen them used to restore magical powers.

"Aaaaahhhh! The power!" Gripping the crystals with both hands, Halob writhed in ecstasy as his body flushed with blue energy. "This will please the master!" The moaning zombies feasted on stray crystal energy escaping as the goblin raped it from its glassy enclosure.

"Mrrroan!" Gobbling up any energy they could capture before it dissipated, in no time their rotted corpses had almost healed, returning their physical form to near pre-death state except for the blankness in their eyes.

What kind of parasitic creature does that? Watching the necromancer draining the crystals of their energy offended Davissor to his very core. Never having seen crystals drained like this and unaware that such an act was possible, he wondered how it was that the goblin could contain so much energy at once.

Throwing his hands in the air, Halob released the crystals and stepped back from the stone outcrop, his wild eyes glowing blue with excitement and stolen energy. Without another sound he rushed away, the zombies in hot pursuit.

"These crystals are empty and black!" Speaking aloud, Davissor forgot himself when he stepped up to take a closer look at the desecration. Replaying the sight of the zombies' physical forms rejuvenating as they absorbed stray spiritual energy, he filed that information away for future use. *If this is what the goblins are doing down here, the future of our very existence is being put at risk!* Taking a quick look back down the tunnel, he watched the necromancer and his undead disappearing into the darkness. *I think it's time to gate everyone in so they can take a look and try to understand what we are up against.*

Ranging out in front of Snow and Kalahni to get a better look at the entrance to the mines, Llysander had noticed goblins scouting from the hilltops not far from their position. Expecting there to be guards at the mines, what surprised him were two dwarves and a human lurking on the side of the trail ahead.

Freezing when she saw his quick hand signal, Kalahni crouched and tried to figure out what her husband had spotted. Following his finger, she saw him pointing at several goblin positions higher in the hills, but that didn't seem to be where he was focusing. A low growl escaped Snow as she sensed the danger, but a stern look from Kalahni ended any more noise from the big cat.

"What do you see?" she whispered, crawling up to Llysander's position and nocking an arrow in her short bow.

"Luck is with us, Kalahni! There is an adventuring party with dwarves and a human ahead of us."

"That is not luck, husband. Shifra is helping us!"

"And what might be a Shifra?" asked a voice from the bushes behind them.

The sound startled them and as Kalahni turned, in one fluid movement she let her arrow fly. Seeing the source of the voice, at the last moment she pulled up just enough, grabbing Snow before the cat pounced. Her arrow shot by the voice's head, thudding deep into a tree branch narrowly missing her target.

"Whoa!" shouted a gnome, jumping to the side and exaggerating his near death experience. "Is that the new elven greeting to Allegiance friends these days?" Grinning from ear to ear as he stepped out from his hiding spot, the gnome was scouting the immediate area expecting to find trouble. Discovering two elves instead was a pleasant surprise.

"My apologies, good gnome! I thought you were a goblin sneaking up on us."

"That's a funny one, my dear. Do I look green to you?" Raising an eyebrow, the gnome stood with his hands on his hips. "So what brings two elves and their pet cat to the Mines of Taas? I'm guessing you're not out for a relaxing stroll to reconnect with your beautiful natural surroundings."

"Gnome, we did not mean to offend you. Please forgive us." Hoping to run into the band of heroes hired by the council, Llysander recognized one of the mercenaries from the store in Buxton.

"Wait a minute. I know who you are! You are the Ranger I saw at the outfitters! I hope you're not following us, because we don't know where we're going."

"That is correct. I am Llysander of the Rangers. This is my wife Kalahni of the Moonguard. And this is Snow. I remember you from the store as well." Extending his hand in friendship, he laughed as the gnome shook it with vigor.

"I am Angus McVeigh, lately of the Heroes of Karth! Come meet the rest of my crew." Keeping his head down, he disappeared into the underbrush.

"Are you going into the mines, Angus?" Anxious to keep looking for Morrowyn, Kalahni needed immediate confirmation. The gnome kept going, not answering or waiting to see if they followed.

* * *

"Hey! Look what Angus found!" exclaimed Garrett, surprised when he saw two elves and a large cat sneaking back to their camp with his friend.

"What the hell are they doing here?" said Ahira, frowning at this added complication. "I don't like cats." Looking right at Snow, he made sure she saw his axe. Growling at the obvious threat Snow froze, waiting for Llysander or Kalahni to provide some guidance.

Resting his hand on her head, Llysander gave her subtle reassurance that she was safe.

"I found them approaching us from the rear. I think they were planning on going into the mines on their own!"

"Hi there!" said Ragnar, flashing a quick smile at Kalahni. "Angus, you are amazing! We can always count on you to find a party, even way out here in the middle of nowhere!" Looking over at Ahira, he could see by his frown that the burly dwarf had not finished speaking his mind. "Please go easy on them, Ahira!"

"The mine on your own? That is the craziest thing I have ever heard!" snorted the dwarf. "Two elves against an entire army of goblins? Have you two taken leave of your senses? Even I wouldn't risk that!"

"Why do you have to be like that, brother?" Waiting for the elves' response, Angus could tell that Ahira's words had upset Kalahni.

"He makes a good point though," said Garrett with an apologetic smile. "Is it true? Was that your plan?"

"Of course it's true!" Exasperated by the group disbelief, Kalahni was ready to go on her own. "Ogres took our daughter and we think they came from these mines. What would you brave and mighty warriors expect us to do?"

"I was... We were hoping we might run into you and join your team," said Llysander. "We have also sent word to the Rangers. We were just scouting the entrance when..."

"Guys! Davissor's Moongate!" They all heard the humming crackle before the Moongate shimmered into existence, but Angus's words galvanized them into action. "Let's go! Grab the stuff and let the pack horse go free."

"Enjoy the rest of your day, folks!" Picking up a bunch of their supplies, Ahira was unapologetic. "We'd love to hang around and chat but it's not the best time for a tea party."

"These elves are your responsibility, Angus!" said Garrett, watching Ahira disappear into the Moongate. Looking back a last time, Garrett shrugged and followed the dwarf.

"Wait for us! We are coming with you!" Grabbing what they could carry, the elves set their horses free to wander the area and ran back to the Moongate.

"Davissor is not going to approve of this, Angus!" Furrowing his eyebrows as he jumped into the Moongate, Ragnar knew that the gnome had already made up his mind to invite the elves to join them.

"Coming?" said Angus, waving them to move quicker before the gate disappeared. Davissor might close it once the others had enough time to explain that he was bringing guests. Wasting no time, Kalahni rushed in first, followed by Llysander and Snow. Taking a last look around, Angus jumped in with a smile. He loved a little controversy.

"We have been sitting here doing nothing for too long!" complained Wagger. Waiting on the hilltop with the other nervous goblins, the hunter had held his bow ready for almost the entire day.

"I thought you said you saw them?" said Booma. "Why are they not here yet?"

"I am not sure. Maybe we should go see what is keeping them."

"No! That's what they want us to do!" said Terpa. Part of the group that had worn defeat the first time they faced these warriors, he had no appetite left to go out looking for them.

"Didn't Sooga's spell detect them?" asked Booma.

"Maybe they are hiding in the bushes. Booma, why don't you and Wagger go have a look."

"Bogg says we must wait until Sooga says go," said Booma, sounding disappointed. Looking down the hill, he watched their Champion and leader striding with purpose towards the necromancer. More muscular than most goblin warriors, Bogg's horned helmet had one tusk broken, showing his great experience in combat. The war paint and tattoos adorning his large chest told the story of his mighty prowess. Seeing him stop beside Sooga to discuss their plan, it was obvious to Booma that his leader had no fear of the necromancer. "It's better to stay and wait."

"How much longer must we wait here, Sooga?" As the new leader, Bogg was still not comfortable handling the mass of hunters and warriors growing impatient while they waited for an attack. Noticing that they were all watching his every move, he looked right at them and snarled until they looked away.

"We will wait here until we hear from the ogres!" Irritated by the questioning of his subordinate, something seemed wrong to Sooga as well. "I will reach the ogre shaman and find out what he wants from us."

Relieved that the necromancer was going to do something, Bogg was glad he might soon have some answers. These goblins didn't yet know him as a leader and were watching his interaction with the necromancer. So far he had pushed the boundaries enough to appear strong to them while not upsetting Sooga, which was never a good thing.

"There is no sign of the adventurers, Zik. What do you want the goblins to do?"

"Let them get inside the mines. Mass your hunters along the main corridor, Sooga. We will come at them from the other side. Make sure your warriors know who they are aiming at."

Sooga did not like the tone from the shaman but decided against making an issue of it. Under normal circumstances that kind of insolence would call for a harsher rebuttal but the necromancer did not have time to address this minor affront to his authority. Controlling his emotions, he relayed Zik's message. "It is time to move out, Bogg! We will wait for the intruders in the main hall!"

"You two! Come here!" Spinning to catch Wagger and Booma eavesdropping on his conversation with the necromancer, Bogg decided they needed some extra duties.

"I am ready!" Wagger shot down the hill first, eager for anything to stave off the boredom.

"You and Booma will gather the others. We wait for the intruders inside."

"Yes master!" answered Wagger, his eyes widening when Bogg awarded them the extra responsibility. Eager to engage the mysterious warriors that Terpa had told them about, the hunters did not waste another moment. Screaming and waving, they rallied the rest of the goblins to follow, moving as a group down the hill into the mines.

* * *

"Hummida, hummidaaa…" Ignoring Sooga's voice as he continued meditating, Zik needed this spell to show him what the adventurers were doing.

"Gurosh! This fire doesn't burn bright enough. Bring more wood!" The images Zik was conjuring from the flames were already disappearing. The ogres rummaged through their packs for more wood. Waving at the warriors to hurry, the shaman only had so much time before he had to start his incantation over again.

"More wood for the fire, master shaman!" Placing a few logs in the pit, a warrior stoked the flames.

"Come on, Zik! Where are they now?" Becoming impatient, Gurosh knew the mines were vast and wandering without direction through the twists and turns of its many tunnels would be slow going. The labyrinth of pathways meant that even with his knowledge of the area, one wrong turn could cause them to miss the intruders altogether. The shaman's magic would be the key to their success. The flames could reveal much about their adversaries' location. As he watched, the images were getting clearer.

"Hummidaaa…" Voices began swirling out of the heat. *Now we will see who dares come into the mines uninvited.* Fanning the flames with a piece of cloth, Zik could see humanoid shapes dancing along the blackening logs. In a flash the flames erupted, roaring toward the cavern ceiling. The warriors took a step back as tongues of flame appeared to obey the shaman's commands. Following the chanting rhythm, a bird's eye view of the intruders came into focus. Summoning his courage and stepping closer, Gurosh recognised the combination of mine carts and landmarks in the fiery images. He began formulating a plan.

"It is nice to meet you," said the elf warrior as he shook the mage's hand. "I am Llysander of the Rangers and this is my wife Kalahni. She is a Moonguard."

"Hello to you both. I am Davissor, leader of the Heroes of Karth mercenary band." Surprised by the elves and their large cat preceding Angus through the Moongate, the mage recognized that their skills added strength to his group. "Ragnar tells me that the two of you have demonstrated an interest in joining our adventuring party."

"My wife and I have been tracking the ogres that kidnapped our daughter. We were hoping to join you because together we stand a better chance of rescuing her."

"Since you are already standing here it appears the choice was not mine to make." Davissor maintained his natural politeness, even tipping his hat and bowing at the two newcomers, but hiding his real concern was difficult.

"There is no doubt that your skills as Ranger and Moonguard could be of great help in our endeavor. However, if we agree that helping you find your daughter is a worthwhile task, you need to understand that your inclusion on our team does not provide an equal share of any treasure, although there is an expectation of your assistance in any battle-related scenarios."

"Fear not, Davissor. We will accept whatever treasures you and your team see fit to share with us," interjected Kalahni. "We only care about the safe return of our daughter."

Nodding his understanding, Davissor shook hands with the elves to seal the deal now that they all understood each other.

"I have seen enough," said Zik as he stepped back from the fire. "So our enemy has two more in their group and they seek the elven girl I hold captive. Ho ho! That girl may prove even more useful than I anticipated."

"I knew that elf was trouble, Zik! I should have eaten her when I had the chance."

"Let's move to the lower area of the mines so we can crush them from both sides." Smirking at Gurosh as he reached into his pouch, Zik fingered the necklace of beads that he had taken from the elf girl's pouch. "Maybe when we get back you can have her as part of your victory celebration."

* * *

"Look at what is happening to these crystals!" Taking the group over to the darkened stones, in actual fact Davissor was quite happy having a Moonguard present. Connected as she was with nature and spiritual energy, he hoped she could shed some light on the necromancer's actions. "I am certain that in the time since the goblin touched them, the darkened crystals have blackened those adjacent."

"Oh Shifra! The crystals are blackening!" Horrified at the sight of what was once a beautiful container of spiritual energy, Kalahni couldn't believe what she was seeing. "The darkened one is draining the life from the others. Why would anyone do this to our sacred crystals?"

"Sorry, what is so shocking here?" Being taller, Garrett looked over the top of the assembled team, but something in his chest kept pulling him closer. "You are saying that darkened crystals are a bad thing?"

"These energy crystals have a spiritual connection with all living things in the world." Touching the dark crystals, Kalahni shivered as they sucked at her fingertips. She could feel them draining her life force. "These crystals contain a different kind of energy now. It feels toxic."

"Hey Garrett? You okay brother?" As Garrett got closer to the crystals, Angus noticed him swaying from side to side.

"Huh? I'm... fine." Feeling weak as he neared the darkened crystals, Garrett reached out to touch them and could feel energy flowing into his body. He felt stronger, although his head was now throbbing and dizzy. The crystals grew darker, as if he was draining its remaining energy. With no in depth knowledge of crystal properties and not wanting to alarm the others, he shrugged it off. *I'll be okay. I'm still tired from the attack in the caves.*

"What the...?! Hey! Check this out!" Not far from where the group was standing, Angus discovered some empty mining carts sitting on the rails in the next tunnel. *Boo hoo! All this crystals dying stuff is too serious for me.* Looking for a way to lighten the mood, the reckless gnome jumped into one of the carts. "I bet these carts are magical!"

"Angus wait!" yelled Davissor, but it was too late. As the gnome jumped inside the cart, it began rolling down the rails.

"What are you doing!" said Ahira, stumbling out of the way as the cart picked up speed. "We don't have time for this!"

"You fool! I'm coming with you!" Jumping headfirst into the cart as it thundered past, Ragnar waved and shrugged as he and Angus sped away.

"Angus! Use the levers to control the speed!" shouted Davissor, hoping his voice made it over the noise of the cart's wheels on the metal rails.

Having a natural knack for gadgets, as soon as he saw them Angus had figured that the mine carts would move on their own. What impressed him right now was the speed that they were reaching. In no time he and Ragnar were out of sight.

Looking back at Llysander, Snow saw him wave and she took off after them. The cat was fast, but there was no way she was catching that cart.

"Let her go," said Llysander, stopping Kalahni as she started to call the cat back. "Perhaps she can lead us to them. That Angus sure is an interesting fellow." The Ranger shook his head at the sheer irresponsibility of playing around in the enemy mines.

"What the hell?" Whipping around with his battle-axe ready, Ahira searched for an enemy. "Did you hear that, Davissor?!"

"I'm afraid not, Ahira. What is it?"

"They will ambush you."

"There it is again!" Realizing the voice was inside his head, this time he was angry because someone had decided his mind would be the easiest to attack. "Someone is talking to me in my head!"

"What is it saying, Ahira?" Thinking he had been hallucinating all this time, Garrett hadn't told the others he had been hearing voices as well. "I think something was talking in my head as well!"

"That they are going to ambush us!"

"You must prepare yourselves!"

"Vax Flam!" Lighting the tip of his katana, Davissor illuminated enough of the cavern to allow him to search without causing a spectacle in case a goblin was walking by. Sticking his sword into every nook and corner, the mage made sure that this wasn't some sort of parlor trick by someone hidden deep in the recesses of the cavern.

"Is the voice still there, Ahira?"

"No, it's gone now. It better not try that again if it wants to live! I would just as soon chop my own head off as hear that nasty noise again!" Lifting his axe, Ahira swung it through the air around him in case the invisible creature was standing close by.

"Hey boys! There might be ghosts down there! Be careful!" Bellowing after Angus and Ragnar even though he could no longer see them or even hear the cart, Ahira stopped yelling when Snow ran back into the cavern. The cat was staring at everyone in disbelief, wondering why they were not following her.

"Snow has a point. I guess we should start moving." Walking over to another of the carts, Davissor climbed in and braced himself. "Getting separated was not part of my plan. I will be drinking all of Angus's ale ration tonight!"

"I say we avoid those tunnels altogether!" voted Garrett, knowing already that no one would agree with him. His skin had become pale and his hair was standing on end. The knight had no longstanding fear of the otherworld, but his experiences with the crystals and the voice in his head were giving him second thoughts.

"Garrett! We cannot disregard that warning!" said Davissor, knowing that there was something going on with the knight as well. "There is a good chance you will feel better once we are on our way!"

"Maybe that voice is trying to trick us, to keep us away," said Ahira, shrugging his shoulders.

"Hurry everyone! Get in the cart and let's roll down that tunnel. Our brothers cannot take on the entirety of the goblin and ogre nations alone! My friend, let's prepare our surprise entrance, just in case."

"Grand idea, Davissor. I've got it covered." Pilfering through his pack Ahira produced several sticks of dynamite, their fuses twisted together. "Hello old friends. I've missed you."

"Are these guys for real?" Whispering as she leaned over to Llysander, Kalahni whistled for Snow. The cat's ears perked up and she trotted over, purring like thunder.

"We need their help, Kalahni. Let's give this a chance, because our other options don't look good."

"Point taken. But if we don't find anything soon I think we must take our leave of them."

"Are you two coming, or will you wait here and continue whispering?" Looking right at Kalahni, Davissor had overheard part of the conversation and it irritated him. *If these two don't want to be traveling with us they can just head off right now.*

Dropping her head to hide her reddening face, Kalahni wasted no more time and climbed into the cart.

Llysander jumped in the back, motioning for Snow to lead the way. Picking up speed, soon they were rushing headlong down the passageway, following Snow into the dark and hostile tunnel.

XI

NEWS OF THE UNDEAD

"Council will reconvene in ten minutes!" Hearing the young town crier, Braigon smiled at the memory of when he met Cassandra for the first time. "I better get to the council chambers."

"Poor Braigon," said Cassandra with genuine sympathy. "All the worries on one elf's shoulders."

"In fact, most of the lords will be attending this time."

"Impressive! I bet that won't be awkward." Strolling with Braigon through the courtyard, Cassandra admired the stone palisades and tall guard towers.

"It seems that preparations for war have changed everyone's priorities." Turning to watch his girlfriend's movements, he recalled that it was not that long ago that he had met her in this exact spot in the courtyard. Reaching out to stroke her long dark brown hair, he gazed into her eyes. She was smiling back at him and Braigon wondered if she was thinking the same thing.

"I'm glad I waited for you," said Cassandra, reading his thoughts. Letting her hair fall forward, she toyed with his mind. "I almost left you know."

"But you chose to wait!"

"I chose right... I think." Grabbing his arm, she gave him a quick kiss. "You better hurry. Your escort is waiting for you."

"Forgive me. I have to go back into council," clowned Braigon, recalling the last time he had hurried away. "Did you know that I am a lord?" Braigon flexed his muscles, the corners of his eyes wrinkling with delight.

"Nice. And a funny one at that!" Laughing out loud, she watched him head away with the guards.

"I'll see you back at the palace. Don't forget to wait for me!" Hurrying away, Braigon exited the courtyard through the same doorway as that day, two guardsmen in tow.

Hurrying through the stretch of hallways to the main meeting chamber, Braigon reflected on recent events. This was already the second council session since his decision and subsequent proclamation that the elves were to prepare for war. The other lords had voiced their displeasure at his lack of consultation, but after hearing the ongoing reports of destruction across the land, there was no longer a dissenting voice among them. Striding into the main chamber he made a quick mental note of the attendance. In addition to the usual banners and symbols, the personal banners of the other lords in attendance now hung on each wall.

"Good day gentlemen." Greeting his peers with a shallow bow as he approached the council table, Braigon stood near his regular seat at the center of the table. The other lords were already seated and looked a little uncomfortable with the upcoming proceedings.

"Lord Uanor," the lords replied in unison. Lord Duaner Parthos, Lord Alanor Ramos and Lord Lavanor Ferri rose from their chairs and returned Braigon's courtesy.

"Lord Uanor, please run the Council session," suggested Duaner. "You have the most experience at court."

"Of course, Lord Parthos." Seeing agreement on each of their faces, Braigon seated himself in the center chair as usual. *Some things will never change.*

As was his habit, he watched with interest as the room filled. The priestesses were in full complement as usual with representatives from the Townships of Buxton from the west and Luminor from the south. Inunis Brotah and Norin Tulaanos were in deep discussions. Braigon recalled how shaken Inunis had been when she gated back to Thantos with the report of what had transpired on their mission. Llaen and Razz sat farther towards the back of the room, looking tired and worried. This time Kethus was with them instead of their usual accompaniment of Rangers. Braigon already knew the nature of their business and was hoping for more answers today.

"What is the first order of business?" Raising his hand to signal that council was starting, he brought the chamber to order. Signaling at Llaen, Norin gave him permission to approach. Llaen stood with effort as all eyes turned to watch him come forward.

"Lenowyn is dead," said Llaen, holding his eyes on Braigon. The Council Chamber was silent. "The Crypt of Xeen has become a nest of undead and evil. Zombies, ghosts, skeletons, ghouls, their numbers are incredible. We killed more than I could count, but still they overpowered our team."

"We will need a new assassin to replace her," whispered Norin.

"The next one better be more reliable. This one was good, but not good enough," agreed Inunis. "The Rangers were not much better either."

"Lenowyn and the Rangers gave their lives trying to get you answers about the Undead Curse!" roared Llaen after overhearing part of the high priestesses's comments. "How dare you tarnish their memory with your catty commentary?"

"And what was it you found out in the Crypts, my good Captain?" said Norin, unperturbed by the Captain of the Guard's anger and putting the room's attention back on him.

"The human lands are deteriorating, as the Undead Curse is infecting their towns." The weight of losing the Rangers, the human guards and especially Lenowyn sat like a sack of lead on his shoulders. "Something was raising the dead from Strathmore's cemetery and the trail led us to the Crypt. We think someone or something is creating an army of undead. We believe King Ferrus is somehow linked."

"I believe the necromancers are responsible!" interrupted Inunis. "The humans are in danger of losing their towns to the undead and this crypt is the obvious source! Allied with The Shard, they are now infecting our lands with their necromancers!"

"Llaen, do you agree with Inunis? Do you think the Crypt is the home base for the necromancers?" Having more faith in his captain than any priestess, Braigon's full attention was on Llaen's words.

"It seems plausible, Lord Uanor. I am not sure if human necromancers have any involvement, but the source may be this Crypt."

"Is there any news from the Heroes of Karth?" asked Lord Ramos. Turning to face Braigon for the answer, it hadn't taken long for his peers to feel comfortable at the council table.

"We have not heard from the Heroes yet. We should not make an official declaration of war against The Shard without some proof of aggression. Many questions about The Shard and their now having necromancers remain unanswered. So far they have not attacked us."

"What about the ogres who took my granddaughter from Pinestone? Does that not count as aggression?" Having already spoken with the other lords in private to help influence the proceedings, Norin felt that now was the time to convince everyone to help save her granddaughter and daughter. Walking with purpose towards the council table and looking towards the other lords for support, she made her case. "How many more of us do they have to attack before we act? My daughter faces them alone with her husband, and there has been no help from his vaunted Rangers. It is obvious to all that the necromancers are behind the Curse! What special sign are we waiting for?"

"Norin, I promise we will help your daughter find her child," said Lord Parthos in a calm voice.

"Lord Parthos, we are not even sure where they are," said Braigon.

"Actually Lord Uanor, we know exactly where they are!" Pulling a bag of pixie dust from his belt, Lord Parthos tossed it on the table for emphasis.

"Llysander has some pixie dust and managed to send us a message. It appears that the ogres have a secret tunnel that leads towards the Mines of Taas. Llysander and Kalahni have tracked them through the tunnels and intend on entering the mines."

"We can't just leave them to deal with the goblins and ogres on their own!" shouted Maedyn. Still upset by the Rangers treatment when he asked them to send help, he was hoping that there might now be a chance.

"We need to help them now!" Trying not to catch his eye, Norin could not believe she was agreeing with a druid, but this was her family and she was willing to accept his support for now. *These are strange times indeed.*

"I am confident that this will bring war upon us!" warned Braigon, as he saw agreement on the faces in the room. "Be certain of the path upon which you are about to tread."

"By abducting Norin's granddaughter, The Shard has already started this war," stated Lord Parthos. "Inaction now will make us appear weak and indecisive. We must act to end this threat before they become further emboldened."

"Lord Uanor, we have no choice," agreed Lord Ferri. Raising their right hands over their heads to indicate their acceptance of this plan, the three lords waited for Braigon's decision.

"Then war it is!" concurred Braigon, raising his right hand in unison with the other lords at the table. "Llaen, send two patrols towards the Mines. One is to investigate Shard activity and one is to help Llysander and Kalahni. We will begin mustering our defenses, as our borders must not remain undefended. We will wait for reports from the patrols and the Heroes of Karth before we plan our attack."

"And what of the crypt, Lord Uanor?" asked Llaen. "Do we help the humans?"

"We will have enough to deal with in a war against The Shard," said Braigon, looking at the other lords to make sure they were in agreement. "For now the humans are on their own. But send an emissary to request they do something about the crypt."

"At once, Lord Uanor!"

∗ ∗ ∗

"Still no one follows us!" Twisting to look in the direction they had just come, Lenowyn was having a difficult time focusing. Feeling disoriented and unsure of each step, soaked in her own blood, she struggled with their fast pace. Staying close to Tabatha, she stumbled through the dark tunnels of the crypt, surprised by the lack of pursuit.

"Lenowyn, you need to focus on nothing but me. Please try and stay with me."

"I am trying, Tabatha." Looking down at herself, Lenowyn was only just beginning to grasp that the ability to run with a large hole in her midsection meant that only magic was keeping her alive. In spite of the obvious, the elf was unable to comprehend that she was dead and existing as a zombie.

"When we are safe I will try and heal your wounds. Don't focus on anything but following me right now."

"Mrroan..." Out of the darkness the echo of a nearby zombie sensing Tabatha's approach startled them.

"Careful! More zombies!" hissed Lenowyn. Reaching for her katana, she gathered the strength to protect them.

"Don't worry, Lenowyn. I can control them."

"It is so obvious now. A necromancer working as a graveyard caretaker." Shaking her head at how simple it had been for the girl to fool her, Lenowyn was gaining a better understanding of their situation and Tabatha's role in what had happened today.

"Undead! Follow me." Taking control of the three zombies as they stumbled towards her, Tabatha had never controlled so many undead as she had today. Marveling at how easy it had become and ignoring Lenowyn's snide remarks, Tabatha climbed the stairs into the upper chamber where they had first entered the crypt. They had almost made it. Pushing past Lenowyn, the zombies stayed close to their new master.

"I should have seen it sooner. I'm not as skilled as I thought I was." Dragging her body up the last stairs into the cool night air, the moonlight highlighted the grievous wounds on her body. Lenowyn still wasn't quite grasping how it was possible for her to continue walking, but certain things were on the verge of clicking together.

"Guard us!" commanded Tabatha. The zombies turned and faced away from her, their white soulless eyes peering into the night. If she and Lenowyn were to have any chance of seeing Strathmore again, Tabatha knew she would need to address her companion's wounds. "I will heal you now, Lenowyn. Come over here."

Without a word, she found herself obeying Tabatha. Lenowyn felt the slight tug in her mind at Tabatha's command, but the act of mindless obedience was so foreign that her natural indignance threatened to overwhelm her. "Wait! Stop! Are you controlling me?"

"I'm trying not to, Lenowyn, but you are undead and that's just the way it works. Give in for now and I can explain it all later."

"What do you mean I'm undead?" Looking down at the gaping hole in her stomach, the events of the night rushed back into Lenowyn's mind. The realization that she had died in the crypt became as plain to see as the flaps of skin hanging from her wounds.

"This will make things better," said Tabatha, reassuring her friend. She applied some magical healing salves to the most hideous of Lenowyn's wounds and within a minute or two the hole in the elf's stomach had disappeared. "That should help you keep up, but we must travel faster."

"What have you done to me?" Backing away from the necromancer, Lenowyn realized that she still held her katana and started preparing for battle. Studying the zombies' position, she wasn't sure if she would be able to strike them down before the necromancer could counter, but she would give her best accounting.

"Hey, Lenowyn! I saved you! This may not be a perfect solution but if you'd rather, I can release your soul right now." Releasing the slight hold she had on Lenowyn's mind, Tabatha waited for the obvious reaction.

"Wait! I'm not ready to go," pleaded Lenowyn, feeling her soul struggling to free itself from her body. Understanding her predicament even more now, she tried reconciling her emotions with her warrior's mindset. The assassin had never been under anyone's control before.

"Lenowyn, the rules are simple. If you raise your katana against me again, I will release your soul." Re-establishing her hold on the elf, Tabatha turned away in the direction of

Strathmore. "Follow me," she commanded her zombies. Six steps later, she realized her companion was not following. "Lenowyn! What now?"

"Necromancers are evil." Putting her katana away in case Tabatha followed through on her threat to release her soul, Lenowyn stood rooted in place. "I do not want to go with you."

"Lenowyn, please come with me to Strathmore. I must return to the graveyard. Once I know everything is okay in town, we will find the other necromancers and maybe they can figure out a way of reversing the undead curse."

"What will happen if I don't follow you?"

"I'm not sure. I've never tried any of this before. I didn't even know this was possible until the night I met you. Can we go now?"

"I can't stay with a necromancer, Tabatha. I must approach my own kind for help."

"Well, I'm sorry to hear that, but I can no longer wait for you. Mark my words, I think that is a terrible idea, but you are free to do as you wish." Turning away from the crypt and Lenowyn, Tabatha jogged towards the trees. Looking back to see if the elf was following the zombies, there was no sign of her. Lenowyn had vanished in the darkness.

✳ ✳ ✳

"Move, boys! I have important information for the mayor," said Strathmore's sheriff, waving the guards in front of the mayor's large mansion out of the way. Striding right past them through the gates, he made his way down the garden path straight to the main entrance with one of the guards running behind him.

"Wait here," puffed the guard, disappearing through the front door as he called for the Mayor.

"Ted! What brings you back so soon? Why are you not with the rest of the team? Don't tell me...!"

"Mayor, we found proof that it was creatures from the crypt that made the dead walk in the graveyard! We're pretty sure that there is no chance that the corpses could raise from the dead on their own. The elf captain took the team and went into the crypt to investigate further. I came back to let you know what we had discovered."

"That is good news indeed, Ted. Excellent work!" The sheriff's chest puffed up with pride. "But it still means our graveyard is a target. What if they return for more bodies?"

"I guess I didn't think of that," the sheriff mumbled as his chest was deflating, upset that he hadn't thought things all the way through again. Motioning for him to follow, Mayor Downey led Ted away from the mansion and began walking towards the center of town. The two men walked in silence, the mayor mulling over his options and Ted thinking about answers to the mayor's questions. Stopping in the middle of the street, the mayor turned to his sheriff and took a deep breath.

"Ted, I think that in order to ensure the safety of the town we have no choice but to destroy all the dead bodies in the graveyard." Turning on his heel, Mayor Downey resumed walking towards City Hall with Ted four steps behind him.

"But Mayor, that is sacrilegious!"

"Now Ted, I already have the priest's agreement. They will perform a special cremation ceremony that should satisfy any accusations of impiousness."

"Well I suppose..." Knowing that Tabatha was going to be unhappy, Ted was sure the task of telling her would be his alone. Envisioning the scene when she heard what had happened, as they rounded the next corner he stopped dead in his tracks.

A mob of townspeople was gathering at City Hall, some carrying long torches and the rest with shovels and pitchforks. They were loading a wagon with timber while two priests visited with each of them.

"Just so you know, Ted, we are loading the wagons tonight and will be digging up the bodies tomorrow." Revealing the breadth of his plans, Mayor Downey kept walking without looking back at his sheriff. "It looks like you got back just in time."

* * *

"We spotted Tabatha at the graveyard!" said the guardsman, puffing out his report to the sheriff and mayor. Standing at the front of the column and about to lead the townspeople through the streets of Strathmore, the two men knew they had waited too long.

"Blast," said the sheriff. "I was hoping we wouldn't have to deal with this. Were the guardsmen and elves with her?"

"We didn't see them. But I can verify that Tabatha is not alone."

"What do you mean? Speak up man!" Irritated by any possible wrinkle in his plan, the mayor was not in the mood for any guessing games this early in the morning.

"Tabatha has three zombies with her, sir! They appear to be under her control. She threatened us and demanded we leave her graveyard!"

"What's that you say!? Her graveyard! The nerve of this girl!" Shaking his head, the mayor could not believe the start of his day. "Ted, get your men together. It appears we have a little issue to clear up before we can have our cremation ceremony."

"Guardsmen!" Raising his voice above the murmuring of the crowd and pointing at some of his men, Ted saw that the mayor was already marching down the street towards the graveyard alone. "You three stay with the wagons and townspeople until we deal with this. The rest of you come with me!"

"Zombies under her control! Did you know she was practicing the necromancy stuff, Ted?"

"Of course not!" Having known and respected Tabatha's father for many years, at no time did Ted suspect anything like necromancy in their family.

"Are twenty guardsmen enough?" said the mayor under his breath, looking back at the troops as they marched through the streets of town. Weapons glinting in the early morning light, the guardsmen looked formidable but they all found the news that Tabatha was a necromancer shocking. None of them were looking forward to fighting zombies, even if there were only three.

Arriving at the graveyard, their eyes widened as they saw a large mob of zombies waiting at the gates with Tabatha standing in front of them. The guardsmen were not ready for this kind of resistance and Ted began hearing the voices of dissent rising in the air behind him.

"Where did all these zombies come from?!" Counting at least a dozen zombies standing with Tabatha, Ted frowned at the guard that had reported the incident. "I thought you said there were three zombies. It looks like you need some help with your counting, young man!"

"Everyone be careful," shouted the mayor, holding up his hand to get the guardsmen's attention. "Remember that the Curse of the Undead is in effect. Any of you who dies will rise against us."

"That is far enough!" Holding up her sword in defiance, Tabatha stepped forward to challenge the mayor and sheriff.

"Tabatha! What are you doing?" shouted Ted. "Are you prepared to kill the living townspeople to protect the dead ones?"

"I won't... we won't, let you destroy the graveyard!" Motioning at her zombie mob, the necromancer knew that the guards would not be excited about facing the zombies in battle.

"We will do what must be done for the safety of this town!" raged the mayor, his emotions getting the better of him. "Necromancy is not now, nor was it ever, permitted in my town!"

"Disrupting the graves is wrong and I will not let it happen, mayor!" Feeling goosebumps rising on her arms, Tabatha sensed the situation beginning to spiral out of control.

"What you are doing here is wrong, girl! I will not have you tell me what to do in my town!" Signaling Ted to prepare his attack, the mayor was not going to give up his authority without a fight.

Hesitating before he sent anyone ahead, Ted wasn't yet sure of the best way of fighting the zombies that stood with Tabatha. Seeing that the guardsmen looked distressed by the sight of all the undead under her control, he didn't think an all out frontal assault was the best maneuver but it didn't look like there were many alternatives.

"Tabatha please! This is your last chance!" Motioning his guards to be ready, the sheriff knew this day was not going to end well.

"Wait! Stop!" From the shadows just behind the zombies a slight figure emerged, its small voice splitting the tension. "You are all in trouble! An army of undead is on the way to attack your town!"

"Hold your ground!" ordered the sheriff, holding up his hand. Looking over at the mayor, he waited for instructions.

"Who are you, where did you come from, and how do you know what you know?" Staring at this ragged elf, Mayor Downey thought she looked familiar.

"I am Lenowyn Malaka. I was with the team tasked with investigating the crypt."

"I remember you, Lenowyn. What happened to you? Where is the rest of your team?"

"Dead for the most part." Closing her eyes to try and chase the vivid memories away, Lenowyn was still in a state of shock from the events at the crypt. "Some managed to gate away, but I do not know of their whereabouts."

"What of this army of undead approaching Strathmore? How can we prepare ourselves?" said Ted, impatient to find out more details.

"There is a large massed group of undead from the crypt moving in this direction only a few hours behind me. If I had to guess I'd say they are coming to finish what they started in the graveyard. And more."

"I believe what you are saying, Lenowyn. It appears that our efforts today have come too late." Stepping forward, the mayor turned to address the guardsmen waiting for his signal. "Gentlemen, it is quite possible that our town is already doomed! In a few hours we will be set upon by an army of undead. If any of you wish to walk away, I understand. Collect your families and leave at once! No one will stand in your way."

"Not yet! Not if we stand together!" shouted Tabatha, waving her sword. "It's true I'm a necromancer, but you all know me. I am not evil! I can command the undead to help us defend the town!"

"Ted, as mayor I need your council now. How do you feel we should proceed?"

"Marik, the way I see it, we have two options. We either turn and run or we stand and fight." Addressing his guardsmen, Ted looked each of his men in the eye. "I agree with our mayor. If any of you would like to leave, now is the time. I can't say how successful our fight against an army of undead will be, so if you choose to protect your family by leaving, no one will think any less of you. My choice is to stay and fight. Strathmore is where I was born and Strathmore is where I will die!"

One by one the guardsmen held up their weapons. "We choose to defend Strathmore, Sheriff!"

"Very well then. I commend you all for putting your personal safety on the line to defend our town." Feeling proud of the sheriff and his men, the mayor wasted no time. "Sheriff, get your men organized! The time for hugs and tears is over! What are you waiting for?"

"Thanks for coming back, Lenowyn. I thought that I might have lost you forever."

"Don't thank me, Tabatha. I didn't come back to save you. I came back to save myself." Lifting her skirt, Lenowyn displayed the rotting black flesh around her wounds. "It seems my body can't stray too far from you without falling apart. We are in this together whether I want to be or not."

"I will heal you again once we are alone, Lenowyn. In spite of your thoughts, I'm still happy you are here."

"Can you tell me something first? Why did you save me?"

"Oh, I don't know." Putting her arm around Lenowyn's undead shoulders, Tabatha pulled her close. "Thank you for coming back Lenowyn, whatever your reasons. Let's go back to my house where I can heal your body beyond the reach of any prying eyes."

XII

DARK FRIENDSHIPS

"Wolf th'gil!" Repeating the invocation and concentrating as hard as she could while moving her hands just like Jujube had shown her, for hours on end Morrowyn had practised the light spell. Following the goblin's instructions was irritating and exhausting, but she recognized the simple truth that her life was in danger if she had no useful purpose other than being the ogre's next meal. After all this time and effort, it still surprised her when without warning she found some small level of success. The light persisted and even grew a little brighter, its glow revealing a smile on her face for the first time since becoming a captive. Magic was fast becoming a passion for the young elf girl.

"Mixer, are you awake?" Sharing this success with her new friend was tempting, in spite of the goblin's explicit instructions to keep her magic knowledge a secret from everyone. Whispering so she didn't wake her captor, Jujube was asleep in a room at the end of the corridor.

"Morrowyn? Oh Morrowyn. What a pretty name!" Cackling under his breath, the potion-maker grinned as he wiped the sleep out of his eyes. *It is still dark! Who does this girl think she is, waking me up in the middle of the night?*

"Mixer! I knew you'd still be awake!" Jumping up from her bed and standing at the cell door, without thinking Morrowyn motioned with her fingers towards the bedpost, dimming the light emanating from it. Grabbing the rusty bars in the small window on the door, she pulled herself up to try and catch a glimpse of Mixer in the darkness.

"What do you look like?"

"Well Morrowyn, I am a half-orc, half-human with dark brown hair, light gray skin and beautiful bright blue eyes. My clothes are so old and tattered from being in this lockup that they no longer resemble the magnificent front buttoned white shirt and hide stitched brown pants that they once were." *I hate the small talk already. This girl's voice is quite annoying!*

"Mixer, that outfit sounds grand. I am wearing a green skirt with hooded shirt, my hair is gold colored and my eyes are silvery green!"

"You sound so beautiful, Morrowyn!" Biting his finger to keep the disingenuous tone out of his voice, he shook his head. *Who cares what you look like! You are as good as dead in this prison. The ogre only cares what you taste like!*

"Is your mother the human side?" Assuming that he was more human than orc, Morrowyn wanted to be sure. She had never met an orc before but remembered many awful stories describing them as cruel slavers.

"Oh yes Morrowyn. Of course my mother is human. You might even say that I am human too.

"How did your mother and father meet?"

"Well, my mother was attacked and raped by orcs, then left for dead. That was so long ago. I miss my mother." *Oh my, what did I just say? There is no way this girl will fall for that line.*

"I miss my mother too!" Stifling an empathetic sob, Morrowyn struggled to remain composed as images of her family began flashing through her mind. It occurred to her that other creatures might also have families and feel alone and sad being away from them.

"Little girl? Little girl! No more crying! We cannot cry!" *All right, go easy on her. A little bit of sugar will go a long way tonight.*

"I'm sorry, Mixer," said Morrowyn, worrying now that she might have offended him. "Are you mad at me?" To a seasoned dissembler it was more than evident that his words and tone were full of pretense, but she was so desperate for a friend that she heard none of that.

"Of course not, Morrowyn. How could I be mad at my new friend? I just think it is better for you not to cry as the ogre will get mad at you again!" *This girl will believe anything! Ok, now settle down and try being her friend.*

"Ok Mixer. Yes, that makes sense." Gulping back more tears past the lump in her throat, she made an effort to settle down. "I will try harder not to cry."

"There you go now, my new friend. See? It is that easy!"

"Thank you, Mixer." Feeling a little better now, the dim glow from the bedpost was a reminder of her most recent success. Remembering why she called out to him, Morrowyn illuminated her room a bit more with a wave of her hand.

"Morrowyn? Where is that light coming from?"

"I was just practising magic!" she said, trying not to sound too proud of her accomplishment.

"Elf magic! So you are a caster?" *I need to have that magic! What else can this girl do? She sounds so young though. How much could she really know?*

"Yes I am. I can cast elf magic!!" Hoping he didn't ask too many more questions, it wasn't in her nature to lie, but Jujube's warning had made her cautious. *I don't think Mixer would hurt me. He seems pretty nice. Anyway, I think it's the goblin that is the problem.*

"Well, I know lots of magic too!" said Mixer, not wanting to be outdone at any time by anyone. The possibility of Morrowyn's magic-casting abilities made her an instant threat to his position within the ogre's prisoner hierarchy. *If this girl took my position as potion-maker, I could become dinner for the ogre or worse, a useless lump like that wizard.* Feeling an instant flush of hatred, before it could exit his mouth he covered his feelings with another fabrication. "You and I share lots in common, Morrowyn. I make lots and lots of potions, but I like to practice casting magic."

"Maybe we can practice magic together someday, Mixer!" As the words left her mouth she became unsure if what she had just suggested was the wisest thing, but her desire for a friend was so strong and he seemed like her only choice.

"I would love practicing magic with you, my new best friend! I wish I could convince the mean goblin to let me see you, but I'm sure he will never trust me..." Sifting through his things for his old recipe book, Mixer's mind was whirling with possibilities as he started formulating a plan.

"He is so mean!" said Morrowyn. "But I might be able to convince him."

"You think so? I wonder if you can." Finding the recipe book, he flung it open to what appeared as blank pages. A wave from his hands revealed their hidden words. *What else can I talk about with her? I want this to keep going.*

"Oh yes! I have a way with him!"

"Where are you from, dear?" Reading through the recipe from his book as he talked and listened, Mixer smiled when he saw that everything he needed was right there in his cell.

"I am from Evergreen Forest! We have a ranch near Mystic Lake called Pinestone. It is my favorite place in the world."

"Go on..." said Mixer, rattling around as he setup his workbench and beakers to prepare the ingredients for the spell. *There is enough for just one spell. I must get this right the first time! Keep talking, elf. I don't care what you say, just keep talking.*

"My father is a Ranger and my mother is a Moonguard!" Excited to have a willing and interested listener, there was no longer any doubt in her mind that he was a good friend. "My father is not home often but my brother and I enjoy helping our mother as much as we can."

"They sound like a real nice family!" All this babbling was making it hard for him to concentrate but the potion was almost ready, its ingredients simmering and bubbling in the cauldron. *I need silence now! Easy! Easy. Just keep being nice. Don't be mad. Be nice.*

"My brother and I are best friends," said Morrowyn, smiling at the thought of Llythwain. "He acts different than the other elves but is still pretty normal."

"How nice for you! Or for him! Or both of you!" Becoming bored with all the chatter, he was now wishing she would just fall asleep. Tapping at the smaller beaker, the potion-maker tried hurrying the liquid's conversion into a gas, then back into a liquid. The compound slid its way through the tubes and distilled the finished product into his empty beaker on the other side of the coiled tubes. The wait was frustrating but he knew the result would be worth it.

"What? What is nice, Mixer?" Questioning if he was even listening, she heard the tone in his voice rising and sensed he was becoming agitated. *If he is going to get mad at me all the time, maybe I don't need him as my friend after all.*

"Ummmmm, you and your brother getting along so well?" Hearing her annoyance, he smoothed out his voice and hoped it would be enough to placate her. *Don't ruin it now. Stay calm, be friendly. She is yours if you just stay calm. What can I talk about now? Think!*

"Do you have any pets, Morrowyn?"

"Snow!" Blurting out the name without thinking, she missed her cat so much.

"Snow? What are you babbling about now?" *This girl may not have recovered from hitting her head. She may not be that useful after all.*

"That is my cat's name," said Morrowyn, looking for a way to end the conversation. She had a strange feeling that Mixer was acting different than normal with her.

"There it is!" Ignoring Morrowyn and the growing awkwardness between them, Mixer saw that the ingredients had transformed and enough liquid had accumulated in the beaker for him to call this charm potion a success. Lifting the beaker to his mouth he swallowed the entire contents in one gulp, burping as it bubbled going down.

"What are you working on in there, Mixer?"

"You will know soon enough, Morrowyn!" The effects of the potion made him feel euphoric. *It's working! Oh this will be so much fun!*

"What are you doing? What is happening?" Grabbing the edge of her bed, Morrowyn's room began spinning, even the smallest ray of light becoming as bright as the mid-day sun.

"You sound tired dear. I think a rest will do you good. Stop talking with me now and go to sleep."

"What? No! I'm not tired!" Without warning she yawned and felt her energy levels dropping fast. The voice coming from Mixer's cell had changed, its sweetness compelling her to listen. *I'm so happy to have a friend here. I never imagined that happening.*

"It is getting late, Morrowyn. You should go to bed now don't you think? Why don't you sleep for awhile and we can talk more tomorrow." *I can't believe that this potion was useful! The goblin will be so surprised!* Mixer's potion imbued a loyal and friendly disposition on the first person hearing his voice. Wanting to use it against the goblin lackey one day, this would be a much more effective plan.

"Well, I am feeling tired now. You must be right. You are so nice, Mixer! I can't wait to talk with you again."

"I am your best friend, Morrowyn." Droning on in hypnotic tones that made the elf think of the sweetest birdsong she had ever heard, Mixer kept repeating the words that his recipe said would guarantee success. "Trust. Comfort. Friendship… Trust. Comfort. Friendship."

"Thank you for being my friend, Mixer." Putting her head on the pillow, she couldn't stop yawning.

"Go to sleep like a good little girl. Mixer will talk with you more tomorrow." *Hurry up! Hurry up! I don't think I can take much more of this nice talk. Tomorrow I'll be able to just be myself and she will think I am the nicest friend she has ever had, no matter what I say or how I say it!*

"So tired…" Fading away, Morrowyn's eyes closed as her breathing deepened.

"Morrowyn? Morrowyn! Are you there?" Cackling out loud Mixer began planning how he would use the charmed elf girl to his advantage. This friendship would help him exact his revenge on Jujube while also gaining control of the master shaman's staff. This was turning into a good day indeed.

What is wrong with that girl? Why does she like Mixer so much? She should like me! I'm the one who takes care of her. I'm the one who brings her food. I'm the one who teaches her magic. He has done nothing to help. He will kill her if he gets the chance, I know it! Pacing back and forth across the main hall, Jujube couldn't believe what he was hearing this morning. When he let Wiz out to help with the chores, the wizard found the goblin's distracted pacing amusing.

Elated when the goblin opened the door to let him walk about and have some company, the endless days spent alone were far too long for Wiz and the hours of boredom preyed on his fragile mind. Walking alongside the apprentice, he mimicked his every move and facial expression. Despite the wizard's occasional snicker or snort, Jujube was oblivious to his unwanted shadow.

"Mor-o-win has been laughing and talking with Mixer all morning!" said Jujube, banging his hand on the table.

"Hehe!" Playing the fool and enjoying the imitation game, Wiz continued his clowning around.

"She is acting like he is her best friend and treating me like her worst enemy! I have been so nice to her! Why is she not nice back?"

"Sweeping time!" said Wiz, hopping to the closet for the broom.

"Wiz, I don't trust him! If Mixer finds out that Mor-o-win doesn't know any magic, he might tell the shaman. If the ogre finds out, the elf might not be the only one who becomes dinner!"

"Wiz doesn't trust Mixer either. That one has a mean soul."

"I have to make sure that Mixer does not find out that Mor-o-win knows no magic!"

"Wiz saw the light fade and then grow brighter last night. She knows some magic now."

"What? Wiz, was the light coming from Mor-o-win's room?"

"Yes, yes. Wiz saw it shining! Very pretty indeed!"

"This is such good news my friend." Placing a hand on the wizard's shoulder, Jujube's mind raced. "We must show her another spell today, Wiz. Mor-o-win is making a good apprentice!" The goblin ran off looking for his spell book.

"If the master finds out that Mor-o-win doesn't know magic, I will be his next dinner," he shouted, racing away. Laughing at the goblin's panic, Wiz shook his head before resuming his frenzied sweeping.

Pausing at the cellblock entrance, Jujube could not hear any talking going on between Morrowyn and Mixer. It was time for draining the captives of their spiritual energy and as he reached Mixer's cell door, he saw the potion-maker's face pressed against the bars of the window watching him. The half-orc's features twisted into a contemptuous sneer when he saw the goblin take notice.

"Morrowyn hates you, goblin."

"Time for the staff!" said Jujube, staring hard at Mixer. "Don't worry, I'll make it hurt as much as I can!"

"Drain me of my energy while you can goblin. Soon I will hold the staff and I will make sure the ogre eats you alive, one bite at a time."

Ignoring the half-orc's empty threat, Jujube took particular pleasure in draining the potion-maker of every drop of his energy. Halting once Mixer was within an inch of dying, the goblin watched him lose his grip on the bars and slump to the ground unconscious.

With you asleep I can talk to Mor-o-win without your help. The sound of shuffling from her cell broke his train of thought.

"Hey! Why were you hurting him? He didn't do anything to you!" No longer hearing the noise of the staff draining her friend, Morrowyn worried that Jujube would use the staff on her next.

"Hello Mor-o-win!" Putting the staff away, he waved with a smile and approached her cell. *Why can't she see that Mixer is a liar and will only hurt her?*

"Go away. You are mean." Her voice trembling at the thought of what she was about to do, she put her thoughts together and waited.

"He will be ok. Do not worry about him. I have drained him many times before. I think he is starting to like it!"

"Why are you so mean to him?"

"Because I do not trust him! And neither should you!"

"Well, I do trust him! You would find that he is very nice if you just gave him a chance."

"What! No Mor-o-win!" Changing the subject, Jujube wasn't about to give up on her yet. "Wiz tells me you have been practicing the spell I showed you."

"Yes I have! It was easy for me."

"I am so happy, Mor-o-win. You are doing good! Now Jujube needs to teach you more." Unlocking the door the goblin walked in and sat down beside her on the bed.

"I want to make a deal."

"You want to what? What kind of deal?" *Mixer must have had something to do with this!*

"I will work hard to learn more of your spells if you let me spend time with Mixer!" Holding her breath as soon as she said the words, she could see a storm rolling across the goblin's face.

"Mor-o-win, you do not know him like I do. If you do not learn any more of my spells, the ogre will eat you and Mixer will not care! I am the one who cares!"

"Please!! He is my friend. I am so lonely and he is nice to me and we can talk about our families and he likes pets and he misses his mother and…"

"Fine, fine, fine! That's just fine! But remember, spells must remain our secret. There is no telling Mixer or anyone else! If the master finds out you have no magic, he will eat you, one bite at a time!"

"Okay, I promise not to tell anyone, even Mixer," she said, exhilarated by her successful negotiation. *Mixer will be so proud of me. I can't wait to tell him!*

"I will teach you two more spells today. Watch me." Sifting through his component bag for some small bone shards and pieces of sparkstone, Jujube was happy that at least now she seemed eager to learn.

"Show me!" Clapping her hands and holding back the excitement of gaining this knowledge, the feeling of power Morrowyn received as the magic energy coursed through her body was intoxicating. Studying how Jujube rattled the bone shards, it occurred to her that this was the first time she wasn't worrying about being a captive and away from home.

"You must make the darkness your friend and control the fire as if they were both a part of your being. Just like the light spell, once you have mastered them you will never forget."

"Darkness and fire! Thank you, Jujube!" Her eyes as big as dinner plates, it was hard to contain herself as she watched him demonstrate the lesson.

"ss' en krad!" With a slight shift of his hands, the room became darker. "Did you see?"

"Oh my... Let me try..." Reaching for the bone shards, she ran through the motions in her mind.

"Wait!" Rubbing two stone pieces together, Jujube snapped them with his fingers.

"But I want..."

"Erif!" Interrupting her, the magic word ignited a flame on the tip of Jujube's thumb, illuminating his hand and face.

Drinking in every detail, Morrowyn captured even the slightest movement and the timing of the pauses. These motions controlled the release of spiritual energy from the body necessary for casting all spells. Understanding this point deep in her heart, she watched him repeat the spells over and over again.

Leaving Morrowyn to practice on her own, Jujube had tired himself out and went to bed early. He had spent almost half a day showing her the two new spells while worrying the whole time about what this deal he struck would bring for he and the girl. His intuition was screaming that it would not be good.

* * *

"What's this thing for? Standing in Mixer's cell, Morrowyn was rooting through the beakers and flasks with a child-like wonder for even the most mundane objects. Amongst the bottles she had found a small bowl and stubby stirring stick carved out of bone.

"That is none of your concern!" said Mixer, not accustomed to anyone touching his things or being in his space. *If this girl breaks anything I might just kill her right now. If the goblin says anything about it maybe I'll take my chances and kill him too!*

"Fzzzt!" Reminding him that Jujube had refused to leave the girl unattended, Mixer heard the magic staff crackle and saw the goblin's shadow on the floor outside his cell.

"Please be careful, my dear! I wouldn't want you getting hurt."

"Can you show me how to make potions, Mixer?" Desiring to learn as much about magic as possible, she kept poking into dark corners of the potion-maker's cell that were best left unexplored. Never in her life had Morrowyn imagined that someone could live in a room this cluttered and dirty, but it was all so interesting and new that she paid no attention to his moodiness.

"In reality, what kind of potion do you think someone with your limited skills can make?" Knowing that the charm potion would let him speak any way he wanted, Mixer chuckled at his not so subtle rudeness.

"Well, what kinds of potions are there?" Hoping that he would know about different types of healing draughts, the only potions she had any knowledge of were the healing draughts and cure poison salves the elves used.

"My recipe book has all kinds of potions. All of which are too difficult for a silly elf girl." Picking up his big black potion recipe book, he patted the dust from its hard leather cover. There was at least one hundred recipes hidden in this tome, and the potion-maker was proud to say that he had made them all at one time or another.

Pleased with the way the charm potion worked its magic on the girl, the glossy look in her eyes was all the proof Mixer needed to see that Morrowyn was under its spell. Keeping up the acting charade was too much for a half-orc used to being rude and abusive. Anything he said would seem much sweeter now that she was under the charm's influence.

"My father can make healing potions and poison remedies!" She felt proud of that fact and hoped this might give Mixer the confidence he needed to show her how to make some.

"His pitiful elf magic could not compare to anything in my recipes!" Laughing at this innocent trying to one-up him, all the same Mixer felt threatened that she may have magical knowledge he did not. It wasn't taking long for his irritation to bubble up. The potion's effects were helping him to see this situation from a different perspective though, and he began to recognize the depth of the opportunity at hand. His mood began sweetening as he relished the thought of learning some elf magic.

"Oh please Mixer! Please show me how to make some potions. I need to know about making healing draughts!"

"Will you trade me elf magic, Morrowyn? I can give you what you desire, but I want to know what I get in return."

The potion had put her under a light trance and Morrowyn had allowed it to affect her even though elves had a natural resistance to charms. There was also a truth element in this potion and while the magic was driving her to be honest with him, the threat of losing her secret was stronger. Swooning and light-headed, she began pushing back against the charm's power.

"Elf girl! I asked if you have magic to trade with me. I need an answer now!"

Morrowyn froze, nodding without saying a word. She wanted to learn more magic and the potion pushed her forward. Resistance caused her head to spin and sharp pain crackled across her temples.

"That's better! If you want to learn anything from me you best answer my questions faster in the future. Do you understand?"

She nodded without argument.

"Show me how you make heals first, Mixer. Then I'll show you how my elf magic works!" It had taken a minute for the rough effects of the potion to work their way out of Morrowyn's head, but now she was feeling fine again. Still uncomfortable with lying to her friend, she felt ok with a small fib. After all, she did know the little bit of magic that Jujube had shown her. She was just hoping it was the elf magic that Mixer kept talking about.

"You better stick to our bargain! I will not tolerate any cheating!"

"Erif!" Rubbing the two stone shards that Jujube had given her and snapping the pieces together with her fingers, a tiny flame ignited on her hand. She willed the flame to grow larger until it illuminated the space around her. There was a candle on the table, so she used her hand to light it before extinguishing the flame on her fingers.

"Elf magic! I want it!" Imagining how easy stealing all her knowledge would be, Mixer couldn't wait for the girl to enrich him with her secrets.

Sweat beading on Morrowyn's brow, her amazement at the fire spell mirrored Mixer's level of excitement. That was only the second time she had managed to get it working.

"Ok Morrowyn, I will show you how we make a heal potion. Then you must show me your magic! That is fair!"

"Oh thank you, Mixer!" Grabbing and hugging the potion-maker, Morrowyn felt relief that her little ruse had worked so far. "We will be friends for a long, long time!"

XIII

A FISHING TRIP

Looking outside as he sat up in bed, the sun was already up and there was not a cloud in the sky. Jaeyn wanted to prepare the canoes before any of the children arrived and hurried through breakfast before heading down to the lake. Expecting a torrent of rain, he had spent a long time getting the canoes stored in case any of the children wanted to use them this morning. Pulling all the canoes further up the shore last night had prevented them from floating away during the storm. On his way to the waterfront he ran right into Llythwain and Ran, who had skipped breakfast to get an early start on the day.

"Hi Jaeyn!" called Llythwain with a wave as soon as he spotted the Ranger.

"Are we okay to go out on the lake today?" asked Ran, following two steps behind. As eager as Llythwain to get in a canoe, he wanted to go fishing this morning. After the previous day spent cooped up in the cabin, he needed to expend some energy.

"Yes lads, you will be fine. It is still foggy but you should have no problems if you don't take any unnecessary chances. I will hang a red lantern on the dock so you can orient yourselves."

Reaching the shore first, Llythwain had already started poking around, running from canoe to canoe. Turning away and following Jaeyn onto the dock, Ran chose their fishing gear.

"I picked out a good sturdy canoe for us, Ran!" Jumping up and down with pleasure, Llythwain paid no attention that his enthusiasm was making his friend a little uncomfortable.

"After a rainfall it is normal for the fish to be hungry, so you boys should do well." Recognizing that Llythwain was different than the other children, Jaeyn decided that he was just happy seeing the boy enjoy himself.

"Let's get going, Llythwain! Calm down!" Carrying all the gear was awkward and Ran would have appreciated some help. With the canoe loaded and ready, he hopped in and waited for his friend to join him.

"Okay, Ran! I am ready!" The canoe Llythwain had picked out was along the shallow beach away from the deeper waters of the dock. Taking a couple of deep breaths to calm down, he wasted no time climbing into the canoe. The boys began paddling perpendicular to the shore, keeping it in sight.

"You are too close to shore! The bigger fish live in the deeper water!"

"I know!" shouted Llythwain, mirroring Ran's snarkiness. Jaeyn meant well, but Llythwain wasn't interested in any advice just yet. He wanted to do this on his own.

"Good luck! Be safe!" Watching the boys disappear into the foggy blanket, Jaeyn turned back towards the camp and readied himself for the coming rush of young fishers.

Squinting into the blanket of fog, Ran was already nervous. The water was as smooth as glass, but he could only see a few feet into its dark depths, and not being able to see anything around them beyond the wall of white was making him uncomfortable. Trying to sound normal, he didn't want Llythwain sensing he was a little scared already.

"Llythwain, do you think it's safe to be out here this early?"

"Jaeyn said he would hang a red lantern on the dock to help us get back, so don't worry." Pointing in the direction they just came, he motioned for Ran to follow his finger. The faint red light shining in the mist was the Ranger's beacon marking their starting point. Keeping the light behind them, the boys paddled towards where they thought the island sat.

"What was that?" Thumping on the canoe with his foot, Ran tried fooling his friend. Llythwain saw him do it, and both boys laughed at their mutual uneasiness. Enjoying the feeling of their muscles working, they grew more confident as they warmed up. *Splash, stroke, thump, splash, stroke, bump, splash, stroke, thump.* Concentrating on the task at hand, the rhythm of their paddling began calming their minds.

"Let's fish over there!" said Llythwain, tired of paddling all of a sudden and excited to have located what he felt would be a good fishing spot.

"Looks good to me. I'll paddle us over while you get ready." Motioning for him to prepare his line, this area of the water looked the same as all the rest to Ran, but if Llythwain thought this was the best spot there was no reason not to try it. Turning his paddle sideways, he stopped the canoe right where his friend thought they should try their luck.

"I bet I get a fish first!" said Llythwain, laughing as he plopped his baited line into the water before Ran could put his paddle down.

"Llythwain, don't you ever get tired of being wrong?" Taunting his friend right back, Ran loaded his hook with bait and dropped it in the water on the opposite side of the canoe. Settling down to wait for the big one, they started jigging their lines up and down while keeping an eye on each other's techniques. Concentrating on what they were doing and not wanting to scare the fish, the conversation and giggles tailed away.

The slight bobbing of the canoe and the quiet calm of the lake were hypnotic, and Llythwain's thoughts began drifting. Against his will, more memories of his troubled past started bubbling to the surface and overwhelming his already raw subconscious.

* * *

Compelled to approach and enter the shadowy creature, his mind had fallen under the shade's influence. Enveloped by clinging darkness, Llythwain appeared to be floating in a tenebrous sphere while living strands of the shade curled about him, supporting his weight. He felt motion as they traveled, but his disembodied mind was now numb to the real possibility of imminent death.

Traveling inside the creature's shadow essence was the strangest sensation that Llythwain had ever experienced. Its energy was cold and the crackling jolts made his body jump and twist, yet somehow he found the sensations comforting. His natural curiosity taking over, he was in awe of the creature's brute strength.

Snatching glimpses of the outside through the wisps of shadow, a black ribbon appeared to be moving as they did. *Where are we? Is this a nightmare?*

"We are on the shadow bridge heading back to the mine to get the ogre's medallion." Hearing the boy's thoughts as he was probing his mind, Killian continued pressing him. *"What is your name?"*

"My name is Llythwain." Having someone looking through all his innermost thoughts was uncomfortable and he tried stopping all activity in his head.

"I am Killian. You cannot hide your thoughts from me. What do you think I am looking for, Llythwain?" Surprised at how easy it was for the boy to communicate with him, he felt at ease with this elf child as unfamiliar emotions began crowding his mind. Trying to ascertain the source of his feelings, he was unsuccessful. The concepts were still too foreign.

"I think you want to know if the ogre was the one that forgot the medallion. Why does that matter?"

"Very perceptive." Not accustomed to anyone questioning him, instead of being angry he felt a strange inner calm. There was something different about this elf and somehow his feelings towards him had become almost nurturing.

"Why do you care about this ogre, Llythwain?" Probing the boy's thoughts, Killian could see that he was in fact concerned about creating trouble for the ogre. The compassion of the child for his captor surprised the shade.

"I'm not sure. He was my master I guess. He was better to me than the goblins in the mines. Are you going to kill him just for forgetting the medallion?"

"If I feel like killing him I will do so." It was a casual answer, but Killian was unhappy with the direction the conversation was taking. Reflecting on all the possibilities open in regards to the ogre, he felt like this boy was the one reading minds. Upset with himself for allowing this manipulation to happen, he stopped communicating and switched his thoughts back to shadow-walking. Concentrating on the onyx road, he twisted its direction towards the mine and enjoyed the awkward silence.

"We are almost at our destination." Unable to remain silent, Killian found it odd that he wanted to hear more of what this boy had to say.

"Wouldn't you feel bad if you killed him for a medallion?" Not realizing that this line of questioning was making the shade uncomfortable, the overwhelming sense of fear paralyzing Llythwain had long since faded and his natural empathy and curiosity were taking over.

"I do not care about the medallion, Llythwain. The ogre's usefulness is almost at its end. My Master will decide his fate." Divulging his plans to anyone was not habitual, but doing so this time made him consider them further. The shade had the sudden realization that some might consider his actions cruel and unfeeling, and for some strange reason that seemed bothersome today. There was no possible way for the leader of an undead horde to reconcile these opposing viewpoints.

Releasing the elf from his shadowy bindings and examining him closer, another strange thought percolated to the surface of Killian's now troubled mind. *"You remind me of someone."*

"Who?"

"Why do you not fear me?" Ignoring Llythwain's question as he continued picking through the boy's mind, with his entire mindscape spread out for the shade to study, Killian was still unable to pinpoint the source of his own rising emotions.

"Well, you seem nice enough to me!" Enjoying his conversation with the shade, it felt like a lifetime since one creature or another hadn't been screaming or barking at him. Waiting for the shade's approval to retrieve the medallion from the ogre's quarters, Llythwain sensed the shade's preoccupation and waited for his attention.

Overwhelmed by the sudden freedom to think for himself, Killian wanted nothing more than to withdraw into the mindless hive to consider his next move. He decided that he had better not let any of the other shades discover his new skills or this new phenomenon would find its way back to his master in no time. Realizing that the elf was waiting for his command, he snapped out his orders without thinking. *"Hurry boy! Fetch your master's medallion! Do not take long!"*

"Yes master shadow!" Running to the ogre's chamber, Llythwain couldn't believe that he had become friends with a shade. Unlocking the chest that held the medallion, he tried forgetting about his feelings towards Killian in case that angered him. The creature was proving to be nothing like how his friends had described shades.

"I have the medallion, Killian!"

Wrapping the elf back up in his shadowy embrace, the shade prepared to leave.

"Why did you save me from the ogre, Killian?"

"My master has told me to find a servant."

"You want to make me your servant?" Worrying about what he had heard about the shades and their venomous bite, Llythwain felt an instant pang of fear.

"An astute assumption, Llythwain." With his mind already made up about the elf boy and certain that his decision was a good one, the shadow venom would need administering soon. He had to be careful about injecting too much poison into him though. It would be a delicate operation and one misstep would kill the child on the spot, but Killian was unfamiliar with failure.

✳ ✳ ✳

"We have visitors!" said the scaly creature, practicing the old man's voice to perfection. Glancing up into the morning mist, it saw the two boys encroaching on its space and with narrowing eyes it contemplated how to proceed. These boys were fishing and might never come any closer, but it was busy with the prisoner and did not have time for distractions. Wanting to swim out and kill both of them, it knew that others at the camp would sound the alarm about their disappearance and start searching the area. The creature wanted to remain undiscovered for now.

I'll kill one of you and make it look like an accident. Moving off the rock it perched on, the creature slipped away from the small island in the middle of the lake, submerging without a sound. The thrill of the hunt was beginning again.

Bloodlust made the creature reckless. Able to hold its breath for long periods when necessary, it swam under the canoe without filling its lungs. Knowing what it wanted to do, the creature wasn't concerned about any physical limitations.

"This is a great spot, Llythwain! Every time I put my line in I get another bite!"

"Something told me it would be good here! We've already caught seven fish. We'll be feeding the whole camp tonight!" crowed Llythwain. "I love fishing. It's so relaxing out here on the water."

"I have another bite! I think it's a real big one!" Scrambling to get turned around again, the strength of the pull on his line required all Ran's attention.

Feeling the line in its hand tighten, the creature tugged one more time then swam to the other line. Making sure not to pull too hard, it tied the two lines together and let them go under the canoe.

"Ran! I have a big bite too!" Leaning back to keep the line taut, Llythwain's heart was beating faster and faster.

"Keep it tight, Llythwain! Don't lose that fish! I'm doing the same thing!"

"This fish is pulling so hard!" shouted Llythwain, struggling with the control of his fishing line.

"I want to catch this fish right now!!" Leaning forward to gain some leverage, Ran tugged back with all his might, hoping he could show this fish who was the boss of the lake.

"Whoa! Ran!!" Not being ready for the sudden strong pull on his line, Llythwain lost his balance, tipping headfirst into the water.

"Llythwain!" Forgetting all about the fish as he heard the splash of his friend falling overboard, Ran dropped his line. Peering under the canoe he saw nothing but darkness and dove into the water. Splashing about and swimming around the area, he found no sign of his friend.

As soon as he realized he was going overboard, Llythwain took a deep breath and let go of his line. The water was warm and not unpleasant, but he had the sudden sensation that he wasn't floating back to the surface. Opening his eyes, his blood turned cold as he saw a bulgy-eyed green creature floating overtop of him and holding him down. Grappling with the creature's long arms as they tried wrapping around him, Llythwain sank deeper.

Pleased that the plan had worked, the creature just wanted to stay above the boy and weigh him down until he drowned. It wouldn't take long until the struggles subsided and it could resume the task of learning the old man's ways.

Unable to get past the creature and back to the surface, Llythwain refused to give up. The struggle was taxing his supply of air though, and he was feeling lightheaded. When the creature turned its head to look back at the surface, he saw his chance. With a mighty kick against the creature's chest, he shot towards the bottom of the lake. Swimming with all his strength, he put some distance between himself and his mysterious assailant.

The creature growled as the elf kicked away and disappeared into the deeper gloom. Recovering from the kick, it chased after its victim. It didn't matter how far down the elf swam, the creature just wanted to watch him die.

Panicking as he searched for a quick way back to the surface, Llythwain's lungs were screaming for oxygen. As he thrashed about in the darkness, his brain began the short process of preparing itself to die.

"Llythwain! Keep swimming downwards. Find the cavern opening and you'll find air."

"Killian?" Almost unconscious and with nothing left to lose, he swam towards what he could now see was a small opening on the lake bottom.

✳ ✳ ✳

Entering the dragon's courtyard, Heffer got the distinct feeling this meeting would not go well. After the elf had left with the shade, another shadow servant had arrived informing him that Xeon was demanding an immediate audience. The door to the courtyard swung open and two guards beckoned the slave lord follow them without delay. Spread across the throne room, the master of all was waiting. In dragon form the beast was massive, stretching over one hundred feet in length. Formidable scales the size of shields rattled as he swivelled his head to view the ogre now cowering before him. Heffer's only defense was making himself seem small and pathetic.

"Greetings ambassador!" roared Xeon, the volume of the dragon's thoughts filling every crevice of the ogre's mind. *"Where is my medallion?"*

Dropping to his knees, Heffer pressed his face to the floor and closed his eyes. His worst fears were coming true and he knew what was going to happen next. The ogre began trembling when he realized that this would be his last living day.

"Killian took my servant to fet... yeeeeeahhhh!" Beginning his explanation, Heffer felt the paralysis of the dragon's assault overtake him. As his life began rushing away, the ogre felt himself weakening, his blood draining from every orifice.

"You should have kept it with you, worthless insect! This is not the first time you have made this mistake. You are wasting my time!"

"Master...Please!" Heffer was desperate to find any reason to live. Death hovered over his shoulder and as his internal organs began exploding, the ogre lost consciousness.

"Useless ogre!" roared Xeon, disgusted by the grovelling display. *"You do not deserve to live!!"* Baring its teeth as the last bit of life hemorrhaged from the ogre, the dragon continued draining him until the body lay heaped like bloody meat.

"I am here, Master!" Stepping out of the shadows, Killian and Llythwain had watched the drama of the ogre's last moments play out before them. Heffer's body first twitched and jerked, then became still and cold under the strain of Xeon's terrorizing assault.

"*Master!*" Kneeling before Xeon as if nothing had happened, the shade could sense his fury. The dragon vibrated with intense energy after having made a fresh kill.

"*The medallion, Killian! Give it to me!*"

Motioning Llythwain forward, the shade stood back and watched the exchange. The dragon was already agitated and one wrong word by the elf would seal his doom.

"*Yes master shade.*" Gripping the medallion with two hands, Llythwain stepped towards the dragon. Afraid that he might scream, he sensed that if he were to flinch the dragon would tear him apart.

"Who are you, worm?" said Xeon, the chambers trembling with the deep growling voice. Grabbing Llythwain before he could run away, the dragon held him up for examination. Killian and the guards stared in awe as the sound of Xeon's voice was not often heard.

"*I am Llythwain!*" The sight of Heffer's dead body was shocking and he couldn't stop glancing between it and the dragon. The ogre had been large and powerful, and seeing him lying dead was more than his fear would let him comprehend. As he and Killian had traveled, he had pictured seeing the dragon, but nothing could have prepared him for the reality of staring at it from this close. Twisting in the dragon's grip, he tried lessening the pressure that was squeezing the air out of his lungs.

"He speaks in silence!?" Grabbing the medallion out of the elf's outstretched hands, Xeon tossed him aside. Sliding to a stop in front of Killian, he sat on the floor to catch his breath.

"I intend on taking him as one of my shades, Master!"

"He is young and is not likely to survive your venom."

"Your assessment is accurate, Master. But he will make a powerful shade if he survives!"

"As you wish, Killian!" Dismissing them, the dragon turned his attention back to the ogre, who had by now risen from death as an undead zombie. He still had a use, even in death.

Bowing as he left, Killian knew better than to waste Xeon's time. Engulfing himself and Llythwain in darkness again, he transported back onto the shadow bridge.

Still gasping and overwhelmed, Llythwain assumed he would be rejoining the slaves again and was looking forward to relating his terrifying story to his new friends.

"My master approves of you."

"He is massive."

"Be silent now, Llythwain." Focusing on the long journey ahead of them, Killian had much to consider.

∗ ∗ ∗

Rising to the surface, the creature hissed with elation now that the elf was dead. Chasing the boy close to the bottom of the lake, it had run out of air and had no choice but to leave the hunt behind. Satisfied that there was nowhere for the elf to go, it was time for the creature to turn its attention to more pressing matters.

They will look for his body. I must prepare for that. Bobbing in the swells, the creature saw no sign of the canoe or the other boy. Sliding through the water back to the island, it rushed to check on its captive.

"Mmmmmmrp!" Struggling when he heard the creature approaching, Gaffer's heart started pounding at the sight of it. Gagged and bound, the old man had reached the point where he would rather be dead than alive.

Deciding that the captive was at the end of his useful life, the creature thought that now would be the best time to take his place. There was no more information that the old man could provide and the creature had come close to perfecting his mannerisms. Stripping the human of his clothes, the doppelganger began the process of assuming the victim's physical form.

"Mmmmmmrp!" Standing naked and cold, Gaffer watched the creature's skin and shape bubble and mutate. The passing minutes seemed like an eternity as he came to recognize the creature's new shape as his own. Old and new Gaffer stood staring at one another, and as the old man cowered, miserable and confused, he watched as his own hands reached out to wrap around his throat. He didn't have the strength left to scream as blackness overcame him and he began the long fall down death's empty well.

Dragging the old man's body behind some rocks deep in the cave, the doppelganger stretched and flexed, taking a few minutes to get comfortable in its new form. Pleased with the transfigurement, the plan for the old man's body was simple. Rejoin and mingle with the elves at the camp until he found a suitable candidate, perhaps someone with considerable power and influence, then take their place. Running over the story it had prepared to tell the elves about the reason for the old man's disappearance and miraculous return, doppelganger/Gaffer climbed into a canoe it had stolen from the camp days before and began paddling towards the dock. Drawing closer it could hear the commotion of the search parties mustering on the bank. Some were already getting into canoes to search for the missing elf boy.

"What's happening?" said the doppelganger/Gaffer to the first elves it approached. "Are we under attack?" Looking confused and offering its help to search for the boy, it first wanted to check in with Jaeyn, who was standing on the docks by the boathouse waving him over.

* * *

"Uh… uh… no…!" Moaning and coughing as he began to gain consciousness, Llythwain's head was pounding and he was grateful that wherever he lay was dark. The space was warm though and he found it difficult to breathe the stuffy humid air.

"*Killian?*" Memories of his past that he had suppressed were bubbling closer to the surface more often now and here in the dark it was hard to differentiate memories from reality. Not ready to move just yet, he could hear nothing but the pounding of his heart.

"*Who is Killian? And who are you?*" Surprised to receive a reply from the young elf, the creature had been alone for a long time and wanted to learn much from this visitor. Anxious to pepper the stranger with questions, the thought occurred to it that this visit could be a short one if the boy discovered what he was speaking with. Staying hidden behind rocks deep in the cavern, the creature cast a blanket of darkness in the cave complex as a further precaution.

"*I am Llythwain. Killian used to speak to me like this.*" Answering the question both for himself and whomever he was speaking with, he had been hoping it was Killian waiting for him beneath the lake and wondered if this creature would help or try to keep him stuck here forever. His heart sank a little at the thought.

"*So Llythwain? Will you tell me about Killian?*" Spending years alone had dulled its once charismatic conversational skills, but they were getting sharper by the minute as its mind warmed up. Riddles had always been its specialty, and this boy seemed to be full of them. Sensing the elf's panic as he fled the doppelganger, the creature had hoped to inject a little excitement into this otherwise boring existence by guiding him towards the crack in the lakebed. Even if the boy died or escaped, it would provide food for thought for many years to come.

Noticing that his eyes had adapted somewhat to the darkness, Llythwain stood to stretch his legs and explore his surroundings. It was obvious that he was standing in a large cave, but he was unable to discover anything in the thick blackness. Stepping with care, Llythwain guessed that the deeper darkness was unnatural and was created by the creature he was conversing with for concealment purposes.

"Do not come any closer, Llythwain."

"Killian is my... friend." Trying to answer the initial question, he struggled with his words. *Don't worry I won't come any closer."*

"If he is your friend, why do you hesitate?"

"I think we were friends... I have trouble remembering my past." Becoming quiet as soon as he heard the creature's words, its reaction puzzled him and made his head throb as he tried to come up with an answer.

"Interesting, Llythwain!! What happened to you that you cannot remember?"

"I have been through a lot," replied Llythwain, using his parents' words. *"First I was kidnapped by ogres and now my sister has been taken by them."* As images of Morrowyn began flooding his mind, large tears rolled down his cheeks.

"There is no need to get upset. You will find it easier to talk if you keep your emotions in check." Using a light hypnosis to calm the boy, the creature had no interest in tears and drama. Shifting from one foot to the other, the ground trembled under its weight.

"Who are you?" said Llythwain, speaking out loud when he felt the cave floor move under his feet. "Why won't you let me see you?"

"Forgive my rudeness. My name is Xamiss. I am so very grateful to have a visitor after being alone for so many years. Do not fear me, Llythwain. I will not hurt you." Remaining hidden behind the darkness that blocked him from view, the creature gazed down at the young elf.

"Do you know Killian? How can I find him again?"

"I am sorry Llythwain, I do not know him. I have been trapped down here for many years and haven't had the opportunity to meet with many people at all."

"I'm sorry, Xamiss. I had no idea you couldn't leave this place."

"Don't worry, Llythwain. There was no way for you to know." Surprised by the young elf's advanced sense of empathy, Xamiss became motivated to help Llythwain through the emotional struggles with his past.

"Xamiss, my father is a Ranger. I can let him know your situation. I am sure he can get someone to come and help you get out!"

"No! Llythwain, you must promise not to tell anyone I am here!" Speaking a little louder than he had intended, Xamiss' booming voice echoed into the depths of the cave and Llythwain stepped back covering his ears. "The world is not ready to have me in it yet. You are young and wouldn't understand. Others would see things in a different light and treat me as a threat."

"Don't worry, Xamiss. Your secret will always be safe with me."

XIV

UNEXPECTED HELP

"Start the waters!" commanded Thraka, signaling his servants to rotate the windlass raising the enormous steel stoppers. Steaming water began filling the oracular pool in the main hall near the shining copper throne, spilling into the channel below the lock. Finding the technology of the kobolds fascinating, part of the agreement made when they became allies was employing their engineers to design and construct this massive metallic city complex for all the goblin gods.

"Open all the valves!" shouted Eremix, the yellow eyes of the Spirit Walker glowing from deep within his wrinkled visage. Looking down the long complex to the machinery controlling the valves, he could see more Spirit Walkers performing assigned tasks. Each was identifiable by their dark gray and purple hooded robes and large crystal necklaces. Thraka deployed the Spirit Walkers to act as ambassadors between gods and mortals. These special servants were the ruler's way of sidestepping the Pact of the Gods, which prevented any direct intervention with those below.

"The pool is ready, Master!" called Oramix when it had filled with the scalding liquid. Glistening with beads of sweat and water from the heat and clouds of steam, the Spirit Walkers were willing to endure any discomfort while the gods in attendance were above such mortal travails.

"What is he doing now?" whispered the God of the Hunt to those standing near him. Like many of the other gods, Goran did not support the changes Thraka had put in place. It hadn't taken long, but it seemed that their age-old traditions began disappearing once their ruler took Zanna as his wife.

"This fool is using his magic puddle to look into the future again," said Sannog, shaking his head. The God of Darkness bore an intense dislike for Thraka's leadership and was working hard behind the scenes to gain support from the other gods in the event of a power struggle.

"What if he discovers your alliance with the shadow dragon?" Worrying more about himself than anyone else, Goran peered into the pool and tried to learn something. Glancing up he could see Thraka's enthrallment with whatever he was seeing.

"Quiet! Do not speak of this here! That knowledge is even kept from our necromancers!" Angry now that Goran spoke of his plans so close to Thraka's ears, Sannog regretted letting him know. "He will not discover anything from them nor from the Spirit Walker's visions, as long as no one else informs him!"

"Why can't I see anything in this pool?" said Goran, annoyed at having to wait for the ceremony to finish until he could hear what Thraka had learned.

"You already know it is only the ruler commanding the Spirit Walkers that can benefit from their visions!" Finding Goran tiresome and boorish, the God of Darkness was jealous of Thraka's position and felt he would be better suited to rule the gods. In fact, the dragon had promised Sannog that soon he would indeed reach his goal, he would just need to be patient. Once anointed as ruler, the Spirit Walkers would have an obligation to bow to his will and give him the power of future sight. *If they refuse to honor me as ruler, I will replace them with my necromancers!* Thraka's voice jarred him back into the present.

"The visions have finished. I have seen the future! There will be a long war with the elves."

"War!" Cheering for the opportunities of battle, the crowd of gods became silent under the weight of Thraka's dark stare. Their ruler did not have the same appetite for conflict as he once did.

"What else did you see?" said Kor. The God of Thievery knew that the rogues would want inclusion as soon as possible.

"There will be a new shaman hero emerging with powerful allies," revealed Thraka, hiding a grin as he saw the looks of amazement on their faces. Unsure of how much he wanted to unveil today, the ruler had seen that this new hero would be in grave danger and need the protection of those in attendance. "The rogues must keep this shaman protected. There will be some who will see this hero as a threat!"

"I will send word through the rogue networks." Understanding Thraka's body language, Kor knew to discuss more with his ruler in private.

"These proceedings are complete!" Dismissing the crowd of gods, Thraka stepped away from the water's edge.

"Drain the water!" shouted Zira, one of the few female Spirit Walkers. Accorded high levels of respect for her skills as an ambassador, she was a leader within the Spirit Walker fraternity.

"Oramix and Zira! Gate now to the Mines of Taas!" commanded Thraka. "Pooga and Zik the ogre shaman will both need rescuing. They have important roles to play before the goblins can rise in stature on Karth!"

"We will ensure their destined paths will come to fruition," said Oramix. Sharing Thraka's vision from the pool, the Spirit Walkers already knew where they would be most effective.

Chanting under her breath, Zira cast a Moongate and without another word the two purple-robed servants disappeared into the bluish portal.

"Goran! Follow them!" hissed Sannog. "Do not let anyone know you are there. If my necromancers are in trouble you must help them as best you can, but do not risk Thraka learning about our interference."

*   *   *

Lurching to the left and right as they sped along the tracks, the team followed Angus and Ragnar on their wild ride deeper into the mine. Using caution as his guide, Davissor controlled their descent as they chased after their compatriots. Rumbling past smaller side caverns they could hear the moaning and screaming of ghosts, but saw no sign that Angus or Ragnar had disembarked from their cart.

"Can't you see anything yet?" asked Ahira, annoyed that he got stuck in the middle of the cart and trying to push his way to the outside. Realizing that no one else was able to see a thing in the inky blackness either, he was pretty sure he had heard the voice in his head again, but there was too much noise and he was unable to make out what it was saying.

"No Ahira, I still do not see them," shouted Davissor, raising his voice over the sound of the rushing air and rumbling wheels. "I'll speed up and maybe we can catch them. Hang on!"

"These carts are incredible!" Grinning at Kalahni like an excited child, Llysander found the magical ride thrilling, providing him some temporary relief from the seriousness of their mission. Davissor's added boost of enchantment lit the tracks as they sped along after Snow and the two rogues, although the wheels sent echoes flying in all directions and gave them no chance to surprise anyone.

"I have to admit Lysander, this is a fun ride." Holding her bow in case there was trouble, Kalahni held onto the cart with one hand as they twisted left and right through the darkness.

"Look! Over there!" shouted Llysander, catching a glimpse of Snow on a ledge up above them as they passed close to her. "Why is she up there?"

"I see their cart ahead!" said Garrett, oblivious to the confused looks in the cart. Not even the elves could see farther than a few feet into the blackness. Roaring through the tunnel, the knight had felt an eerie sensation come over him and he was pretty sure they were not alone.

"Whose crazy idea was it to make this cart go faster?" barked Ahira. Trying to stay focused in spite of his rattling teeth, he missed out on the glimpse of Snow moving along the small ledge above them.

"An el luminous!" Illuminating a wide area around them, Davissor's lit sword cast crazy shadows across the walls as they charged past.

"Davissor slow down!" Sticking his head over the side of the cart, Ahira saw the cart barrelling towards the end of the line. "LOOK OUT!!!"

"What? Hello!" With little time to react, Davissor noticed the overturned cart lying across the tracks ahead.

"Piotis iwoni!" Releasing his spell, the mage brought the cart to a smooth, quick stop inches before impact. Turning back to look at the rest of the passengers, he grinned at their terrified looks and white knuckled grips.

"Everybody out! The good times are over!" Waiting for the inevitable reaction, Davissor stifled a belly laugh. "Is something wrong, brother?"

"Blasted mage!" roared Ahira, relieved to have avoided what he thought was going to be a disastrous ending to their fun ride but not appreciating Davissor's sense of humor one bit.

"Prrrroew!" Stepping out of her hiding place, Snow stood alongside the now abandoned cart, her tail wagging back and forth as the team disembarked.

"Snow found them!" said Kalahni, interrupting the dwarf before he could continue his barking. The cat led them away from the rails and up towards a small pathway branching off from the main tunnel.

Snickering at the chaos surrounding this team of mercenaries, Llysander knew operating like this was fun but he made sure not to forget the seriousness of the situation. "We better be ready for anything. The goblins love an ambush."

"They could still be right here," said Garrett, staring at the overturned cart. Not hearing any sounds coming from underneath it, his emotions flew up and down like they were still on the cart ride. Drawing his sword, the tall knight flung back his cape as he strode to Angus and Ragnar's overturned ride and used his free arm to lift it enough to inspect the tub. There was no one beneath it.

"Garrett! Stay quiet!" cautioned Davissor when the knight dropped the cart with a bang and stood up. "Up above us..." Pointing to a small opening in the wall, Davissor started climbing towards it.

"I'll check ahead!" Pushing past the mage and racing after Snow, Ahira swung his battle-axe over his head as he bolted up the rocky passageway towards the opening.

"Ahira! Wait for me!" shouted Garrett. Hurrying to the top behind the burly dwarf, the mercenaries found that the opening led into a massive cave complex extending far beyond the light from any magical sword.

"Snow senses something," whispered Llysander, following right behind them with his longbow ready.

Not far ahead Snow stood growling, the hair on her neck and back standing straight up. Creeping forward on her own, every muscle in her body was taut and ready to defend this group from the hidden enemy.

"Snow stay with us," whispered Kalahni, feeling more comfortable with the cat by her side. Motioning at her husband, they crept forward together just to the right of Ahira and Garrett. Looking back, she saw the mage hurrying up the path after them.

*   *   *

"Ragnar don't go too far," cautioned Angus. "The others won't know where we are. I'm pretty sure I heard them back there."

"Come on, Angus! The voice said to come through here! I bet Garrett and Ahira heard it as well." Neither of them could resist the pull in their heads as the voice guided them out of the main tunnel. The cavern labyrinth they were in now was massive, stalactites and stalagmites growing from the ceiling and floor.

Peering around the chamber where he saw a shadowy figure, Angus could not see any signs of recent passage. Energy crystals cast a faint glow from within some of the rocks along the cavern walls, providing a minimal amount of light.

"Now where did that ghosty get to?" Moving deeper between the stony formations with his sword ready, Ragnar was eager for a scrap.

"I don't like it, brother. It is too quiet in here." Readying his daggers, Angus' senses were on high alert. He and Ragnar had trained together as rogues to move from shadow to shadow in an effort to remain hidden. Noticing how well they seemed to meld with the darkness now, he was finding their new capabilities unsettling.

"A lot of good this sneaking around will do if we are just chasing ghosts!" said Ragnar. "I'm sure they are watching us go to all this trouble to be quiet and having a jolly laugh about it."

"Hey, have you noticed? We both seem to be merging with the darkness a little too well." Even though Ragnar was standing right next to him, Angus was unable to make out his silhouette.

"Of course I noticed!" Looking around for his now invisible partner, Ragnar could see the cavern darkness in flux as it morphed around their bodies.

"What in the world is going on with us?" asked Angus as they worked their way through the cavern complex. Slipping around a large limestone column they could see a brighter glow not far to their left.

"Over there!" Hurrying toward the light, Angus gave up being stealthy. Ragnar was hot on his heels.

"Look at the size of those stones!" exclaimed Ragnar, elated to see the energy crystals as both he and Angus hurried towards their glowing light.

"I win!" said Angus, reaching the glowing stones first. "Uhhhhhh…" The gnome's eyes opened wide as he felt a jolt of energy pulsing throughout his body. Putting out his hand when he reached his goal, he gripped the crystals protruding from the stalagmites on the cavern floor.

"Angus, look at them!"

"Oh no! They darkened as I touched them! How is that possible?"

"When we rejoin the crew we better not say anything with your elf friends around." The pulsing energy was so pleasurable that Ragnar could not resist touching the crystals himself.

"Do you think she might make an issue?" Basking in the glow of crystal energy, Angus closed his eyes and leaned against the rocks.

"Well, she is a Moonguard, sworn to protect the crystals that you and I just darkened," said Ragnar. "I wonder if she'll care… hmmmm… Of course she'll care, you fool! Should I draw you a picture? Do I have to remind you of the price you paid for not listening to me in the past?"

"Okay, brother. Okay! You're right!" laughed Angus. Nothing could spoil his good mood right now.

"But we will need to talk to Davissor about this in private later." Ever since the battle in the Dark Forest cave, something had felt different to Ragnar and he now realized that it wasn't just him.

* * *

"*Darkness!*" Waiting for all of the mercenaries to disappear into the upper chamber before he got to work covering their tracks, Killian cast a shroud over the mine carts that his heroes had left unattended. The goblins rushing through the caves to repel the intruders grew closer by the second, and he didn't want his heroes discovered just yet.

"*They are down this tunnel,*" said Sooga, using silent talk to communicate with Zik, whose ogres were closing in from the other side of the tunnel system. The goblin necromancer was controlling the zombies and ghosts charging along at full speed, along with sixty hunters.

"*We will crush them between the hammer and anvil!!*" cackled Zik, excited to have their quarry trapped between two strong forces. Everything was unfolding just as he had planned. Gurosh and his ogre warriors were hiding amongst the rocks and crevices and Zik cast a darkness spell to help shield them from view. By the time the intruders saw them waiting, they would be too deep into the trap to escape.

"Target the mage first!" Fingering his missing eye, Gurosh tried to make his new patch comfortable. Scowling at the shaman, he again swallowed the bitterness that Zik had been unable to save his vision.

With the mage dead victory will come easy, but the killing of a mage will be the hardest part. Agreeing with Gurosh's strategy for a change, Zik prepared to battle what he knew would be a tough opponent. Wondering if they had enough troops, he felt better reminding himself that the necromancers would command any of the goblin or ogre undead that rose as well.

"Where are they? Where are they?" Working himself into a rage, Gurosh wanted nothing more than for the action to begin.

"Be silent!" Just as impatient, Zik was listening for any sound that might indicate their enemy's arrival.

"With the goblins coming from behind, our ambush might be perfect," said Gurosh, disrespecting the shaman whenever possible. "There better be enough of them!"

"We have sixty goblins and twenty zombies coming to flank the rear, Gurosh!"

"The ambush is well planned then." Always looking to boost his status among the warriors under his command, Gurosh made sure they could hear him speaking.

"Of course the ambush is well planned, you fool," interrupted Zik. "I thought of it."

"The plan is as much mine as it is yours, Zik!"

"Quiet, Gurosh!! Be ready!" Hearing noises coming from down the tunnel, the shaman prepared to unleash hell.

* * *

"An el luminous!" Roaming ahead of the others as he illuminated his sword, Davissor sent blue-white light sparkling in all directions, the crystals in the cavern reflecting flashes of his sword's glow.

"This cavern extends in two directions, Llysander." Hoping her husband could provide some guidance, Kalahni didn't want to leave the search for Morrowyn in the hands of the mercenaries.

"Snow! Find Angus and Ragnar!" Giving her the freedom to run, Llysander was aware that the cat would know which way to go and she rushed off into the cave, happy to oblige her master.

"Easy Ahira..." Feeling a strong yearning come over him when he saw the crystals reflecting in the cavern, Garrett could tell by the way Ahira was acting that he was experiencing similar urges. Clamping his hand on the dwarf's shoulder, he tried to calm his friend.

"I'm going with the cat!" Ignoring Garrett's firm grip, Ahira spun free and charged after Snow.

Signaling his wife to look at the darkened crystals he had just passed, Llysander could tell from the tracks all around that Angus and Ragnar had been standing next to the crystals not long ago.

Acknowledging the direction of Llysander's hint, Kalahni's gut feeling was that their new companions might not mean them any harm, but it felt obvious that something was not right with this group. Putting her hand near the blackened crystals, she was careful not to touch them this time. Her energy began draining into them just by having her hands in the general proximity.

"Not so loud, Ahira!" Worrying that the reckless dwarf might bring unwanted trouble back with him, Davissor waved to make sure everyone was still following and hurried away after him.

"Hey! Are you guys all right?" Primed and ready for a fight, Ahira's adrenaline kept him from whispering.

"Quiet, brother!" Exasperated by the dwarf's noisy arrival, Angus shook his hand to slow Ahira down.

"What is it?" Crouching beside the gnome and following his pointing finger, Ahira looked down through an opening in the floor and below them he could make out two ogres talking.

"We have company," said Ragnar, whispering to Davissor as he joined the crew eavesdropping on the conversation below them. Concentrating on what the ogres were saying the team crowded around the crack in the floor.

* * *

"Where did they go?" said Gurosh, not happy seeing goblins pouring out of the tunnel with no intruders in front of them. Motioning for his edgy warriors to stand down, the last thing he wanted was for them to attack the approaching goblins.

"Did you see anyone?" Looking baffled as they approached the ogres, Halob and Sooga approached the group of ogres with similar dumbfoundedness. Not expecting this turn of events and just as perplexed, the ogre shaman shook his head.

"How could they have known we were here?!" Looking for someone to blame, Gurosh considered the shaman to be the most obvious culprit.

"Maybe they gated out?" said Halob, waiting for a sign from Sooga and not prepared for this situation. Glancing over his shoulder at Bogg, he wanted to be sure his champion was standing down. Like most pure warriors, it was difficult to control him when his emotions were running hot.

"Somehow they must have known we were here!" Pulling out his bone necklace to start an incantation, Zik thought Gurosh was the possible culprit.

"Why are we waiting here? Let's hunt for them!" said a voice from the back of the goblin mob.

"Silence!" growled Bogg, the muscular goblin in no mood for any impertinence. Standing next to Halob, he wanted to see for himself what the necromancers were doing.

"Moaann!" Shuffling towards Bogg as the champion watched the necromancer, the zombie's instinct was to protect his master.

"Control your zombies, Halob!" snarled Bogg, angry that the creature was hungry for his energy. Striking it hard with the pommel of his sword, the creature had approached within range and fell to its knees from the force of his blow.

"They found a way to the upper level!" said Zik, straightening up as he broke his trance.

✳ ✳ ✳

"Of course they were trying to ambush us!" said Ahira, watching the undead mill about through the crack in the tunnel floor. "Look at them! Those zombies are awful creatures!" Shuddering at the thought of their lifeless bodies, he saw one of them staring upwards as if it could sense that the team was there looking down.

"Shush now! Not too loud!" Watching the ogre shaman working his beads and trying to figure out where they had gone, Davissor knew the game was now afoot. Throwing up a misdirection spell, the mage cloaked the cavern around them in thick darkness.

"Lucky for us that we checked out that side passage," said Garrett, recognizing that they had just escaped entrapment between the two hostile groups below. Peering through the narrow crack, he was unable to get an accurate count of the enemy, but it looked like lots.

"Davissor, I'll be honest. I don't think it was luck." Speaking aloud the words that everyone else was thinking, Angus decided that now was the best time to explain what had been happening to them since the battle in the cave.

"Angus? Why do you say that?" Looking at his companions, Davissor could see that they were holding something back. "All right then, boys. It might be a good idea to let me know what all of you are being so quiet about, before the fight with the goblins and ogres begins. Assuming that you'd like to live today, that is."

"Something led us up here," blurted Ragnar. "There was a voice in all our heads advising us to stop and use that hidden passageway."

"This is an interesting development indeed. It appears we have an unseen ally. And it's pretty clear that you two have no idea what we are talking about." Davissor smiled at the puzzled expressions of Llysander and Kalahni.

"Bah! I say we drop the dynamite on them right now and get this party started!" interrupted Ahira, pulling the dynamite from his pack as he searched for something to ignite it.

"Easy tough guy!" cautioned Ragnar, putting his hand on Ahira's arm.

"Agreed Ragnar. Ahira, let's not give away our position just yet." Narrowing his eyes to communicate to the dwarf that settling down was not optional, Davissor and the team clustered back around the opening to try and get a better idea of their opponent's strategy. Although the ogres were speaking in the Shard common tongue, the mage had no problem translating as the minutes ticked by.

* * *

"The upper level only has two entrances!" said Sooga, repeating Zik's words.

"We can still corner them then!" Visualizing the attack as his adrenaline levels began spiking, Gurosh was more than ready to spill some blood. "Let us hurry to smash these intruders before they get away again!"

"Be careful! They are aware we are hunting them now!" Unable to pinpoint the adventurers' location but sensing they were nearby, Zik tried piercing the darkness with little success.

"I will take our troops back through the tunnels," said Halob, signaling Bogg to turn the hunters around and head back the way they came. "There is a side passage that leads to the upper level not far from here!"

"Let's get moving!" Bogg began pushing the hunters closest to him.

"We will cut them off in the main hallway!" said Gurosh, heading his warriors in the opposite direction towards the other passage leading to the upper level. "We will crush them between us! They will have nowhere to escape this time!"

Shouting as one, the ogres were itching for a fight.

"Remember they have a mage!" said Zik, shouting over the rattle of armor and weapons. "Fifty gold pieces to whoever brings me his head!"

* * *

"Well fellas, it sounds like we are still getting boxed in!" said Ahira. "I guess maybe that voice wasn't so helpful after all."

"Fifty gold pieces for my head? That doesn't seem like much of an incentive."

"It's enough for me, Davissor! I might turn you over myself!" laughed Ragnar.

"Maybe I should turn myself in! Although on second thought, I might need my head going forward."

"Ok, so do we gate out of here?" asked Angus, trying not to laugh. "We've already discovered that something is darkening the crystals. Is this enough for the elves? No point getting ourselves killed, is there?"

Squeezing Kalahni's shoulder to prevent an emotional outburst that might offend the mercenaries, Llysander tried warning them off with the look on his face. He figured that the mercenaries were just having a bit of fun with their newest companions, and while a Ranger understood the rough humor that often took place as tensions began rising before a battle, this was all new to his wife.

"No Angus, wait. I think we'd better be sure about these crystals first." Watching the storm of emotions rolling across Kalahni's face, Llysander indicated that the time for joking was over.

"So what shall we do about the goblins and ogres closing in then? I don't want to get my shirt dirty!" Snickering as he drew his crossbow, Ragnar displayed the obvious answer in his hands.

"We must fight, you fool!" shouted Ahira. "What's wrong with you?"

"Get the explosives ready, my friend," said Davissor, clapping Ahira on the shoulder. "Let's prepare them a proper Heroes of Karth welcome!"

"Where do we want to meet them in battle, Davissor?" Winking at Kalahni, Llysander caught her eye. Her eyes were bright and her bow was already in hand.

"Here is as good a place as any, my good Ranger!"

"Kalahni and Llysander, can we put one of your bows on each flank?" Checking over his sword, Garrett limbered up by swinging and jabbing it at the shadows on the wall.

"Of course, Garrett!" said Kalahni, understanding now that the jokes and ribbing were all just part of the acceptance process. "Thank you all for trusting us!"

"Good luck to you all!" Rumbling into the minds of the four heroes infected with his venom, Killian had been watching and listening to them prepare for the battle from deep in the darkness. Hurrying back to the shadow bridge, he hoped that none of the shades had noticed his absence.

"That blasted ghost just spoke to me again!" said Angus, searching all around.

"It wished us luck!" said Garrett as Ragnar and Ahira nodded their acknowledgment. "It must be on our side."

"Oh how I wish I was worthy of consideration for inclusion in the conversation with your grand spirit guardian!" Raising his eyebrows in mock annoyance, Davissor looked at Kalahni and Llysander to see if they knew about this mysterious voice. Both of them shrugged to let him know they did not hear anything either.

"Maybe the ghost doesn't like elves!" said Angus, mocking them.

"Perhaps you are right, Sir Gnome! Or perhaps my team are the crazy ones and only the elves exist in this reality!" This time both Kalahni and Llysander were in on the jokes and laughed like members of their adventuring party.

"We should get into position!" In spite of her initial reservations, Kalahni found herself warming up to these charming rogues. Always turning the conversation back to the serious task at hand was her nature, and she kept her focus on finding out more clues about what happened to Morrowyn. *This battle will bring me closer, my daughter. I know it!*

XV

DEFENSE OF STRATHMORE

"*The necromancers have too much power!*" Lifeless eyes burning in protest, King Ferrus's long taloned fingers gripped his sword as he tensed in preparation for this encounter.

"*How can one human necromancer escape your grasp?*" The dragon's shadowy form twisting as he clenched his jaws in anger, without a second thought he crushed the servant standing closest underfoot. News of the human necromancer's soul-saving act came as a shock to the dragon. Having conquered many worlds while bringing necromantic knowledge to those that allied with him, Karth was the first world that already had a sub-culture of necromancers in residence before he arrived. His efforts to persuade the human cult to join his side had ended in failure, but it would only be a matter of time before they were forced to join en masse. If they had now figured out a way of countering the Undead Curse by keeping souls from leaving the physical plane, he was not sure how controllable the zombies would be in his grander plan for conquest.

"*The necromancer managed to control many of my undead, turning them against me.*"

"*Useless mummy! How could you let this happen?*" Xeon wondered how many human necromancers existed. He needed more information before his plans derailed.

"*My undead army is far smaller and weaker now…*"

"*Do not cry to me, pathetic cur! Your weakness disgusts me! Are you sure she held the elf's soul? If you are wrong, your miserable life will be forfeit!*" Stretching his giant body upwards, Xeon snatched up the lifeless corpse of the servant lying under him, tearing it to pieces in frustration. Bloody chunks of flesh rained down on the stones separating him from his audience.

"I followed them from a distance and can confirm that the elf was still of her own mind and talking with the necromancer," interjected Killian.

"Gans! What is your pitiful excuse for not helping Ferrus?" roared Xeon, demanding a response even as he tore though Gans' mind. The dragon ripped deep into the shade's being, looking for answers as his victim's life approached its end.

"Killian commanded us to stay back with him!" Groaning in agony as the dragon exerted his overpowering strength, in desperation Gans tried deflecting the blame. Buckling under the overwhelming onslaught, he could only muster the barest of squeaks in protest.

"Master, the necromancer was stronger than we expected," explained Killian, not surprised by how the weakling Gans folded. *"If we attacked she could have used our shades against us. Only King Ferrus and his bodyguards were able to resist her..."* Twisting in agony as Xeon's anger focused on him now, he could feel Gans struggling to stay alive as the dragon now crushed and depleted them both. Keeping his composure under the pressure, Killian expected that Gans would not survive the dragon's terrorizing affront.

"You are all weak! She should never have escaped!"

Standing to the side King Ferrus was staying out of the way of the dragon's torturous castigation. Thunderstruck by the strength of Xeon's voice as it smashed against his mind like wild and endless surf, the mummy soon began feeling the dragon's acid tentacles eating their way past his defenses, pulling his life energy away as well.

"I did not want to risk losing anymore of my army!" Dropping his sword as he struggled to remain standing, King Ferrus soon gave in to Xeon's staggering brutalization of his spiritual energy.

"I brought your soul back from the dead and gave you that army, you pathetic maggot! I did that! How quickly you forget who is the master of your universe. I am your master, the one who owns your life and your death!" Regretting his alliance with this weakling mummy and questioning the worthiness of his shades, Xeon drained all of them of their life force as he writhed in fury. Gans and Killian hung on to their souls by the thinnest of threads while the mummy was on his knees screaming in agony.

"No more delays, shades! Take command of the undead and march against Strathmore. I want this necromancer dead! Mummy, you will stay behind and if you forget your place again I will terrorize what little is left of you before I banish you forever!"

Having felt Xeon's draining anger in the past, the shades were better equipped at handling the recovery. King Ferrus lay motionless on the ground, the flame in his eyes having dimmed to the slightest flicker.

"Gans, take the shades and gather all the undead at the crypt entrance," said Killian. *"I'll join you there in due course."*

"Yes master!" Now that the dragon had left him, Gans could sense Killian draining a trickle of his energy to speed his own recovery and putting some distance between himself and his general was a relief.

"Stay with me." Whispering to his two skeletal knight bodyguards whom he had moved out of sight of the dragon when all of the commotion started, King Ferrus did not want to disobey or argue with Xeon but he would not allow the removal of his two knights as part of this new arrangement. Struggling to his feet, the mummy had heard the dragon give command of his undead army to the shades. Disgusted by the prospect of slavery, for now the choice was no longer his to make.

"I will not fail you, Master," said Killian. *"I will destroy the town and raise the burial ground. I will return with a massive army of undead."*

"Above everything else Killian, I want that necromancer dead!"

"I hear and obey, Master." Turning away without another glance at the shattered mummy, the shade disappeared into the darkness, heading in the direction of the crypt entrance.

* * *

"This ointment should slow your decay, Lenowyn." Reaching over her, Tabatha rubbed some of the healing ointment over a spot on the elf's arm that showed obvious signs of decomposition. Before their eyes the flesh healed without leaving so much as a scar behind. "Now lie back and let me treat the rest of your wounds."

"Thank you Tabatha." Feeling awkward as the necromancer touched her, Lenowyn had no choice but to acquiesce. Allowing Tabatha to help her disrobe was embarrassing and the feeling of vulnerability was uncomfortable at first, but as soon as the ointment touched her skin she could feel the soothing medicine working its magic.

Working up from her feet, Tabatha motioned to lift her arms. As the necromancer was applying ointment down the side of her upper body, it occurred to Lenowyn that she had never considered just how stressful and tense her life had become.

"The elf healers should know all about these healing ointments," said Tabatha, remembering the harsh words spoken by Lenowyn when they left the crypt. "Why would they not want to help a fellow elf in need?"

"The moment they realize I am undead, the priestesses will cast their magic and explode my body, banishing my soul forever!" After leaving Tabatha outside the crypt, Lenowyn watched the decay start within minutes. It didn't take her long to accept that returning home right now was not an option. Images of the high priestess banishing the undead father and daughter, body parts and blood splattering everywhere, flooded her mind and illustrated the obvious truth.

"I think those elf priestesses need to lighten up!" said Tabatha, exasperated by how cold the elves could be. "Close your eyes. Your face needs help next!" Remembering how pretty Lenowyn was the first time she saw her, she smiled as the ointment restored her facial features.

"As I watched my skin rot I knew I had no choice. Did you mean it when you said you thought the other necromancers might try and heal me?" Thoughts of living like this forever brought her to tears and Lenowyn worried that all the necromancers together might not be able to help her.

Pausing the ointment application, Tabatha stared into Lenowyn's eyes. It would take more time for her to build complete trust in the elf but the necromancer suspected that she was safe with this hold over her physical body. "How about this. If you help defend the town and my cemetery, I'll take you to Barsoom and see if the rest of the necromancers can help you."

"That sounds like a fair deal," said Lenowyn, relieved to hear that there might be a way out of her predicament. In addition to repairing her skin, Tabatha's ointment was having a positive effect on her attitude as well, and she felt elated.

"Have a look and tell me what you think!" Applying the finishing touches to her face, Tabatha found it amazing how fast the healing ointment worked.

"Are you sure I should look?" Reaching for the mirror, Lenowyn felt a lump in the pit of her stomach. Before arriving in Strathmore she had caught a glimpse of her appearance reflected in a window. It had been difficult to control her emotions and look away.

"Oops! I missed your hands. Look at your face first and then I'll take care of them as well."

"Thank you Tabatha." Examining her face from side to side in the mirror, Lenowyn wouldn't touch it with her rotting fingers. Even knowing that the rot wouldn't rub off, she didn't want to take the chance of damaging her face again. Always very proud of her appearance, the mere thought of her face rotting off had given her fits.

"You look as good as new!" said Tabatha, satisfied with her handiwork. Gazing at Lenowyn as the elf looked at herself in the mirror, she blushed when Lenowyn caught her staring at her naked body. Embarrassed by her indiscretion, Tabatha changed the subject.

"I heard a voice in my head when we left the crypt."

"Oh? What did it say?" asked Lenowyn, putting the mirror down.

"It said my discovery might be the answer to the Undead Curse. I wasn't sure at the time what to make of it. I just wanted to escape from that crypt before the undead came pouring out after us."

"What discovery?"

"I think he was referring to you!" Grabbing Lenowyn's hands to rub ointment on them, Tabatha's enthusiasm was contagious.

"Of course! I should have realized that the Undead Curse turned me into this... thing. I should have become a zombie!"

"But I saved you in time. Don't forget about that!"

"You brought me back from death. I will never forget that. But I am still undead." Deciding that she was not ready to leave this world just yet, Lenowyn turned philosophical. *I wonder if most people welcome leaving this world. I wonder what happens next?*

"Your priestesses were quick to blame the necromancers for the curse, yet we might be the only ones that can save the world. You have to admit, the irony is delicious."

"I was wrong to generalize, Tabatha. You are not evil and I have always known that in my heart. I'm sorry for saying so."

"Apology accepted. You were a little messed up. You're not the first to misunderstand us, and I'm sure you won't be the last."

"Where did you get these?" asked Lenowyn, changing the subject. The necromancer carried two silver daggers with gem-studded handles sheathed in fine leather scabbards attached to her belt. The assassin couldn't help but admire their craftsmanship, lifting one from its scabbard for a closer look.

"They were my father's." Watching the elf hold and test the blade as she massaged more ointment onto her legs, Tabatha could tell that she was very proficient with weapons. "They are special blades designed for use against the undead."

"I sure could have used one of these when we were in the crypt! You are lucky to have them."

"There are many more undead coming, Lenowyn. You should take one of them. Perhaps you'll think of me when the battle is over."

"Thanks Tabatha. I will put it to good use, and I will think of you."

Putting the ointment and utensils away, Tabatha heard the undead under her control animate, raising their weapons. Running to the window, she gasped. "They are here! Hurry Lenowyn! They have arrived quicker than I had expected. Get dressed and meet me outside." With a quick motion to her undead, she grabbed her equipment, slipping out the door with the zombies right behind her.

"To arms! To arms!" Lenowyn heard the guardsmen mustering outside and it spurred her to move quicker. *At least they are not being sneaky about it. These undead are walking right up to the front gate!*

* * *

"There are hundreds of them!" Standing on top of the barricades, the sheriff's blood ran cold at the sight of the undead horde marching toward him. His men had created a wall out of anything they could carry. Their plan was to funnel the undead into one smaller defensive line. The strategy seemed more plausible when there were not hundreds of undead charging towards them.

"Stay together! Kill them one at a time!" Shouting encouragement to each other, the defenders took stock of their situation. Outnumbered at least five to one, those odds did not take into account the Undead Curse adding to the undead numbers as the defenders died.

"Where is Tabatha? We need her now!" Mayor Downey knew their only chance stood with bringing the necromancer's power to bear. The intensity of the zombies' moaning increased as they approached the graveyard.

"*Tear down the barricades!*" Gans had no intention of falling into the crude funnel, knowing that their biggest advantage lay in attacking from more than one flank. Sending the zombies to break through the barricades, he advanced the skeletons into the funnel, followed by the rest of the shades.

"*Leave the necromancer for me!*" Searching the assembled townspeople, Killian was unable to recognize her in the crowd but sensed that she was among the main group making a stand.

"Kreeeeel!" Screeching at the defenders, the skeletons vocalized their thirst for souls to feed on. Advancing through the funnel as one great wave, they hit the line of human guards hard and tore into their ranks.

"*Devour them all!*" Accompanying the shades compelling the skeletons forward but stepping back from the brink of joining in, Killian let the others rush past him as he melted into the shadows. With the first rush pushing hard at the guards, the undead began their murderous spree. Observing Gans hammering against the barricades, he watched the zombies working hard at smashing through the wooden constructs that blocked their path.

"Hold the line, boys! We can do this!" Swinging his sword in a wide arc, Ted struck one of the skeletons in the neck, sending its head bouncing across the ground in front of him. The faces of his men were exhibiting pure unadulterated terror, as most of them had never seen an animated skeleton before. The awful screeching of these creatures was enough to turn the toughest of his men into a mewling babe. The sheriff watched as, one by one, his men began falling to the fury of the undead onslaught. It would not be long before they were rising up against him as zombies.

"They are not easy to kill!" shouted the mayor as he severed a skeleton's hand with a quick chop. The creature did not slow down.

"*Kill the humans!*" screeched a shade at the fresh zombies that had risen from the dead guardsmen moments earlier.

"Mrroannn!" The zombie guards turned against the human guards that only minutes ago had been fighting beside them as comrades. The sheriff's men were losing their morale at a rapid pace.

"Protect the humans!" Stepping out from behind the line of guards to command the undead around her, the necromancer's will was stronger than the shades. In no time she had gained control of the nearby zombies and skeletons. Seeing her charge into battle with her own swarm of undead bolstered the guardsmen, giving them hope that maybe they had a chance.

"*The necromancer is here!*" Killian heard the cry from one of the shades on the front line.

"They are going to break through our barricades soon!" shouted the mayor, warning anyone who could hear him. Rushing towards the wooden walls, he and his men worked to prevent the undead from crashing through.

"Tab! Help them at the front!" shouted Lenowyn, looking at the sheer number of skeletons and gauging the area of greatest weakness. Charging into the midst of the horde, she dispatched a zombie with two strikes of her katana. Feeling more like her old self, it appeared as though the ointment had healed more than just her outward appearance.

"*Kill the other undead and protect the humans!*" hissed Killian, taking control of many of the zombies milling about, turning them against Gans and the zombies he was controlling. Now that the other shades were otherwise occupied he decided it was time to take care of his ambitious second in command.

"*Killian! What are you doing?*" Defending against the attacking zombies, Gans managed to kill the first small group that fell upon him, but a second and third wave followed right behind them and Gans began weakening.

"*You never should have challenged me! It is time for your reckoning!*" Tearing into Gans's mind, Killian began siphoning his second-in-command's life force. Weakened by the onslaught of undead, the shade had little resistance to offer against his master.

"*Master! Nooooo!*" Twisting out a final shrill cry before his energy faded to black, Gans' fading screech confirmed that his soul was forever lost.

"*The elf has an undead weapon!*" Screeching in pain as a dagger sliced into its side, the shade closest to Gans avoided the main thrust of the assault. Stepping back to evade the elf charging right at it, it was unable to react in time to the death knell of its comrade.

"*Maintain your positions. I am coming.*" Keeping the shades distracted from his murderous actions, Killian approached the main group of undead attacking the humans and took control.

Even with the help from the necromancer, the guardsmen were losing this battle. Outnumbered by the skeletons, their defeat was assured. Backed into an ever-shrinking space, the undead bones tore into them with unbridled fury.

"Whatever you're doing is not working!" shouted Ted, coming within earshot of Tabatha. "You need to control more of them or the town will be overrun!"

"I am trying, Ted! There are too many shades!"

"Hold the line, boys! Tabatha is trying to get us out of this!" Rallying the troops, Ted could see his guardsmen swinging with weary arms. It was becoming more obvious that this battle would all be over soon.

Hearing shouts of surprise, Ted looked over his shoulder as a shockwave rippled down the defensive line. The largest shade, accompanying a large number of undead, was now joining the battle. Ted had to blink several times to make sure he wasn't hallucinating, as this group of undead appeared to be slaughtering their fellow zombies and ignoring the human defenders. "Tabatha! You've done it!"

"One less shade to bother us!" shouted Tabatha in triumph as she sliced a shade to pieces with her dagger. "What have I done now, Ted?" Spinning around to see what the sheriff was shouting about, her blood ran cold when she saw the largest shade advancing with its personal mass of undead. Fresh anger infused her soul as she viewed this rude invasion of her personal space. This graveyard was her home, it was all she had left and she was not letting it fall to the undead. Locking eyes with the advancing shade, Tabatha readied herself to die protecting her family home.

"*Do not fear me, necromancer!*" Hailing her from across the battleground, Killian admired her strength. "*I will not let the undead win the day.*"

"*You're the one from the crypt! Why would you help us?*"

"*You hold the secret to the Undead Curse.*"

"*What are you talking about?*" Watching the shade order the skeletons around him to attack the undead and help the humans, another shade came within her range. Lashing out with her dagger, she sliced deep into its back. It staggered away as its life force poured out the gaping wound. Looking for her next target, she saw Ted appearing unsure of what was going on. "Ted! The large shade is with us! Rally your men, this battle is ours!"

"The large shade and his undead are on our side!" Causing his remaining troops to erupt in a loud cheer, the sheriff shook his head in disbelief. The shade's undead had joined the guardsmen and together they began routing the opposition. It was confusing, as one zombie or skeleton looked much like all the others, but the guardsmen were letting the undead lead the charge.

"*Shade! Why are you helping us?*"

"*I cannot stay and explain. There are other heroes that will help destroy my master.*" Watching with bitter satisfaction as the elf assassin killed the last of the shades, Killian prepared to deliver the message of failure to Xeon once again.

"*Who is your master?*"

"*Xeon has chosen this world as his next conquest. He is using the Undead Curse to help raise his armies and plans to drain this world of all its life force.*"

"*Why won't you stay with us and fight?*" The possibility of Xeon's involvement continued fuelling debate among the necromancers, and now Tabatha had confirmation.

"*My master does not know I am helping you. I cannot stay here. I must return to endure his wrath when I tell him that the battle was lost and his army of undead destroyed.*"

"*We thank you for your help today, shade.*"

"*Remember, there will be other heroes that will help you win this fight!*" said the shade, disappearing into the surrounding darkness.

✳ ✳ ✳

"Shade, no! What are you doing? My army is damned!" Speaking out loud even though he and his skeletal knights were alone, King Ferrus could do nothing but stand by and watch as Killian took control of the zombies, commanding them to attack the other undead. "This shall be your undoing, shade. Xeon will make you pay for this outrageous act with your worthless life!"

Sensing his anger, the skeletal knights raised their weapons and began edging towards the fight.

"*Stay here and guard me!*" barked Ferrus. The king remembered Killian's strength from their last encounter and dared not join the battle for Strathmore. It would all end soon regardless of his presence. Using the medallion once held by an ogre and given to him by Xeon, he was now able to initiate communication with the powerful undead shadow dragon.

"*Why do you disturb me? Where are you?*" roared Xeon, already furious that none of his shades were answering him. "*SPEAK!*"

"*Master, please. I had a suspicion that your orders would not be followed, and came to monitor the shades in the battle for the human town.*" Expecting that the dragon might kill him for not following the explicit command to remain close, the mummy couldn't resist this opportunity to raise his own station. After he explained what he had seen, the dragon would need him more than ever.

"*Disobedient CUR!! You shall pay for this transgression with your life!*" Screaming into Ferrus' head, the dragon was beyond tired of his antics.

"*Killian betrayed us and turned the undead against each other,*" squeaked Ferrus as Xeon's mind began crushing him. "*The shades are dead. Our army of undead has been destroyed while the necromancer yet lives.*"

"*What are you saying? The leader of my armies has betrayed me! How is this possible?*" Forgetting about the mummy, Xeon dropped all communication as he wrapped his mind around this new dilemma.

"*Are you there, Master?*" asked Ferrus, not sure he wanted to hear the answer.

"*Yes I'm here!*" Beating on his mind like a hammer on an anvil, the booming voice tore into the mummy, knocking him to the ground.

"*We need to regroup and prepare for all out war against the humans! It appears that I will have a use for you after all.*"

"*But I have no army.*" Pleased by how he had influenced the situation in his favor, the mummy's lust for power was endless. Ferrus sensed that today he had gained the leverage over Killian he had sought for so long. "*What is it you would have me do now master?*"

"*Come to Harrow Gate. Your crypt is now lost. By the time you arrive, I will have a new plan.*"

"*And what of Killian?*" The crypt was his base and he was even more upset at the realization that he would lose it as well because of the shade's actions today. The mummy wanted revenge as soon as possible.

"*I will take care of him myself. Make sure you do not let on that you saw him today. Travel to Harrow Gate at once!*"

"*Yes master.*" Hearing that Xeon would deal with Killian was what the mummy needed to hear.

"*When Killian arrives I will have everyone retreat to Harrow Gate. Killian will suffer for this treachery. I will not tolerate this!*"

"*I hear and obey.*" Surprised by the dragon's words, Ferrus felt substantial relief knowing that he did not have to deal with Killian.

"*When you arrive I will have a new army for you to command! Now go!*"

Left alone with his thoughts, King Ferrus stood pondering the day's events. Watching the humans racing about the battlefield as they mopped up the remaining undead, the mummy shook his head at how unpredictable the winds of fortune could be.

XVI

MIXING POTIONS

"A good morning it is," said Jujube to no one in particular, yawning as he stretched the stiffness out of his body. Staring out the gates and enjoying the early morning solitude, the shaman's apprentice had to admit that in spite of the obvious difficulties, he had been in better spirits ever since Morrowyn arrived. Straightening his short brown robe, he reached up to pull the hood over his head. The mountain air was below the point where water became ice and a few specks of snow chased each other to the ground outside. The random motion of the flakes was mesmerizing, and he stood at the portcullis longer than normal. Looking out past the overhang of the cavern entrance, he could see the mountain slopes wearing thick blankets of white.

"A good morning it is," he repeated. Basking in the cold mountain silence, Jujube used to feel depressed by the monotony of his life passing him by. However, he did not feel alone anymore and for the first time in a long while, he wasn't looking out at the mountains wishing to be somewhere else. Pausing for a moment, he thought about the day's tasks.

"Mor-o-win needs breakfast!"

"Fssstz!" The spiritual energy-draining staff stuck in his belt made a buzzing crackle. Pretending that it was agreeing with his new enthusiasm for life, Jujube caressed the magic stick like it was his pet.

"Come, you. We must get started on the chores." Turning from the heavy iron bars, he knew better than to wait for any response from the staff. "Let's get food from the pantry."

Plodding towards the kitchen, feet slapping against the cold stone beneath him, he had just started whistling his favorite tune when rustling outside the portcullis made his ears perk up.

"Goblin! Where is the girl?" A rough voice barking behind him snapped Jujube out of his daydreams and made him jump. Whirling around it shocked him to see an ogre warrior open the portcullis, marching inside the cave as if it were his own.

"How dare you come into the master's lair demanding answers!" Trying not to sound unsure as his heart raced, in an instant Jujube became paranoid and protective. *Why does he want to know about Mor-o-win? Has the master figured out the truth about her magic?*

"The Chieftain sent me to check on the girl. Is she still with fever?"

"Yes… Of course she is still sick! You cannot disturb her now! What is this about?"

"The Chieftain has decided that he wants her as his slave! Where is the key?" Seeing the shocked look on the goblin's face, the ogre snarled and sneered as he began rifling through the piles of bric a brac on the shaman's shelves, knocking piles of items on the floor.

"Wait! Zik! The shaman does not approve of this! He does not approve!" Disbelief and fear flooded over Jujube's soul at the thought of the girl falling into the chieftain's hands. *I have worked so hard at this! I risked my life!*

"Zik is not here and has no choice!" Anger boiling over at the challenge from this puny goblin apprentice, the warrior snapped his hand backwards, striking Jujube hard in his nose and mouth. The blow sent him tumbling under the kitchen table.

"Wh-Why??" Putting his hand to his mouth and feeling the wetness of blood from his split and swelling lip reminded the goblin to stay out of range.

"Your Chieftain has commanded it! Who are you to question him? Get me the key and open the cell now! If I find the key first, I will eat you before I take the girl!"

"Yes, yes, of course, master." Having been around ogres for a long time, Jujube knew better than to push back too hard. Ogres never seemed to make idle threats when it came to eating prisoners. Stubborn though, he tried one more time. "Do not waste your time with a sick prisoner, master. I will bring her as soon as she can travel!"

"Fine, goblin! But I warn you, it better be soon. When the fever breaks bring her to me! Don't make me come back here." Glaring at Jujube to make sure that he got his point across, the warrior turned and left, not caring to hear another word.

"We still have some time!" Whispering to the staff as he watched the ogre stomp away, the goblin knew that he would be back in a day or two at best and would not take no for an answer. Pondering how he could help the girl this time, something in his heart told him that in the hands of the chieftain, her remaining days in this life would be short. The flipside was that if he tried stopping the ogre from taking the girl he would also end up on a dinner plate. Returning to his room to sort through this turn of events, Jujube was so jarred and distracted that he forgot all about making breakfast and draining Mixer of his magic energy.

*   *   *

"Which potion are you making now, Mixer?" Trying to be quiet but unable to hold her tongue any longer, Morrowyn found his secretive nature annoying. Whenever she tried seeing what he was doing he would gather his ingredients closer and slam his big recipe book closed.

"I can't tell you, Morrowyn. It's a surprise. I just know you will love it." Mixer didn't know or care why Jujube was late arriving to drain him of his magic energy. All he knew was that he had been waiting a long time for a chance just like this one. Looking at the shackles around his leg, he tugged at them and smiled. He could not remember the last time he felt so much power emanating from inside. Perhaps now he could change his situation. With his full powers he was able to concoct more powerful potions, and Mixer knew just which ones would free him from this predicament, allowing him to exact his revenge. The situation with Jujube and the magic staff was going to change soon.

"Thank you Mixer! I just love surprises!" Tying her hair back to keep it from getting into all of the ingredients and bottles littering the table, the enchantment potion still affected her, making her feel just as comfortable in his cell as she did in her own.

"Don't worry, little one. I will show you how to make this special concoction later." Concentrating on the recipe's very specific procedure, Mixer mumbled whatever came to his mind.

"Well I'm almost done my potion!" chirped Morrowyn, thrilled to be completing her first healing draught. It had taken some convincing, but Mixer had agreed to show her the basics of potion-making despite his grumpiness. Sitting by his side and ignoring his obvious irritation, she worked hard at mastering the fundamentals he had taught her earlier. Mixing the ingredients for the very simple healing draught mixtures that he made for the ogres, she was finding the making of potions another of her natural talents.

This is easier than spellcraft. I wonder if he would let me help him with his duties. Having spent time with her father watching him prepare healing draughts, Morrowyn noticed that Mixer's method was very similar. With the recipe book propped open, the only difficult part for her was adding magic to the ingredients. She had heard that all elves have a certain amount of natural magical energy, and those that practiced would increase the level of magic that they could tap from their body auras. The more experienced a person was, the more energy emanated from their auras. She was not finding much to work with but at least her natural elven attributes provided enough for simple spells and creating minor draughts.

"Anam fo hc'nip a!" Adding more herbs to the mixing bowl, the primitive rhythm that orcs used for their magic words made her laugh every time she said them. They followed a simple magic enchantment and pronounced everything they chanted backwards in the common Shard tongue. It was like a secret code.

Seeing the girl smile out of the corner of his eye made Mixer frown. If she didn't add the proper amount of magic in relation to the measure of elements, it would be a total waste of his valuable ingredients. Hating that she found potion making so easy, the orc remembered it taking him years and many beatings from his master to learn the skills. All elves had these natural abilities and he hated all of them for it. The only thing keeping him from showing his murderous contempt for the girl was that he expected her to show him some elf magic once it was his turn. Maybe then he might discover and learn something a little more powerful.

"Hta ed fo hc'nip a!!" intoned Mixer, working at a furious pace on his latest concoction. Expecting Jujube's appearance at any moment, he worked his magic with single-minded purpose, not caring to pay much attention to the girl. *This will take care of my shackles!* Testing a drop of the potion on a spoon, he watched the metal bubble and melt.

∗　∗　∗

"What is Jujube going to do?" asked Wiz as he and the goblin reset the items on the shaman's bookshelf. The wizard found it unsettling to see Jujube so preoccupied and it was making him nervous. If the ogres could just show up one day and take the elf girl away as a slave for the chieftain, there was no guarantee that he wouldn't be next.

"I don't know!" shouted Jujube, raising his voice without thinking. The wizard's constant chatter was not helping him organize his thoughts. *She's just another elf prisoner. She doesn't matter.* The more he thought about his encounter with the warrior that morning, the worse his stomach felt and he was having a hard time concentrating on the chores right in front of him. The girl was as good as gone now that the chieftain wanted her, and the contradiction was that he didn't even know why he cared.

"Jujube will fix it!" Providing reassurance for at least the twentieth time, Wiz had confidence that the goblin would come up with a way to help the girl with whom he seemed so concerned. Thinking he was being helpful, every time he asked what Jujube was going to do, the goblin seemed more upset.

How can I protect her? Imploring his brain for a solution as he dusted off the spell books, Jujube had become preoccupied with putting the books back in order when all of a sudden it happened.

"I know! I know! I know!" he exclaimed, flipping through the pages of a big red book he had just pulled down.

"Know what? Know what? Know what?" Following behind the goblin and rearranging the books in their proper order, Wiz clapped his hands with excitement even though he didn't have a clue what they were talking about.

"I have a plan, Wiz!" Studying the human, Jujube wondered if the wizard could help him. Flipping through the pages of the spell book until he reached the page with his master's gate spell, he recalled watching the shaman cast it hundreds of times over the years and was pretty sure he remembered how it worked.

"Whoop! Whoop! Jujube has a plan!!" shouted Wiz, dancing around the room. "Jujube has a plan!! I knew he'd find a plan!! He's not as crazy as I am!!"

"Wiz! You must be quiet! I need your help with a spell! Can I trust you?"

"Fzzzt!" The staff crackled as Jujube twirled it around, reminding the wizard to settle down. It would play a big part in the coming days.

"Wiz helps! Wiz helps!" Hearing the staff and not wanting to feel the agony of its tickling, the wizard took a deep breath and huddled with Jujube. His eyes grew wide when he heard what the goblin needed him to do.

Explaining his plan out loud, Jujube became more convinced that there was no other option. Working together in the shaman's chamber, he and the wizard started learning how to cast the gate spell. If he could learn it before the ogres came for Morrowyn and before the shaman returned, there was a chance they could all gate away to safety.

As the goblin started practicing the ritualistic enchantments that were necessary for the gate to activate, the only part of the spell he did not understand was how to target a location. The shaman had adjusted the incantation so that gates would appear in predetermined locations, but the problem for Jujube was that he had never traveled anywhere with the shaman so he did not know where the gate would materialize. If he gated them into the middle of a crowd of ogres, they would all be on the menu that night.

It had been many years since he had thought like this and the plan was both scary and thrilling. Second thoughts began creeping into his frenzied mind and all of a sudden the whole thing seemed ludicrous. However, Wiz thought it was possible and Jujube wanted to help Morrowyn. Taking a deep breath, he took the next halting steps down the path towards freedom.

* * *

Morrowyn had been practicing for hours and succeeded in making three healing draughts. Pushing away from the table and stretching her neck and back, she was ready for a break. Smiling at Mixer, he motioned that she was not done, but she ignored his hints and made no move to continue.

"What time is it?" Wanting to go back to her cell where she knew there was some food squirreled away, Morrowyn felt tired, hungry and was becoming cranky.

"It's almost lunch and still no Jujube!" Ecstatic with the opportunity to create his potions unmolested, Mixer was curious as to why the goblin was ignoring them. *I wonder if he's dead!*

"Mixer, I'm hungry. Can I go back to my cell now?" Getting right to the point instead of trying to be polite, hours of hard work and constant pushing by the orc were weakening the effects of the charm. Morrowyn felt more like her old self.

"Yes, yes. Of course you are right. I almost forgot. It is time for elf magic now!" Finishing his last potion, Mixer felt confident that it would help him succeed with his plan. Shaking his head, he marveled at the opaque green liquid. The half-orc placed the potion in his shirt pocket and grabbed a smaller vial from the table.

"What do you mean?" She saw him take the small vial and pour some of its liquid onto his shackles. The metal began smoking and bubbling as soon as the potion touched it.

"Well Morrowyn, I am coming with you!" he announced, watching the acid work as expected on his shackles. "Now it's your turn to show me magic!" For what seemed like an eternity, the shackles around his legs had trapped him. Crackling as they smoked and smouldered, a slight tap against the table was all it took to break the clasps that had defined him as a prisoner for all these years. It was a momentous occasion and the orc knew just how he wanted to celebrate.

"But I'm tired and hungry, Mixer. I think I'd just like to have a snack and a nap." Seeing the evil look on his face, she realized the danger of saying no to him as the rest of the charm spell wore off. *I have a really bad feeling about him now. What have I gotten myself into?*

"Mixer has food for us to share!" Revealing his own stash of goodies, he grabbed the moldy meat he had stashed for just such an occasion. The potion-maker almost laughed out loud at the disgusted look on her face when she saw it hanging from his sweaty unwashed hands. Anxious to learn some elf magic, he pushed her out the door towards her cell. "We can eat in your cell while you show me your magic."

* * *

"Again! Again!!" Yelling encouragement as he jumped up and down, Wiz was helping all he could. It was precious little, but it was better than nothing.

"Par ipsu ori noom," chanted Jujube, waving his hands in an effort to cast the Moongate. For the seventh time there were sputtering sounds and a small puff of smoke but nothing else happened. Frustration cramped across his face every time he tried the spell.

"Heehee!" Laughing each time the spell ended with the sputtering noise and smoke, Wiz swirled around in the smoky clouds of burnt sulphur filling the room.

"Wiz! It's not funny!" growled Jujube, irritated that the wizard wasn't grasping the gravity of their situation. "This must work or we won't be able to help Mor-o-win."

"Jujube will fix it!"

"What am I doing wrong?" At first his plan seemed to have some merit, but as more time passed, he began appreciating the futility of this exercise.

"Again Jujube, again!!"

"What's the point, Wiz!?" Throwing up his arms in exasperation, the smoke was making him choke and he waved his arms in a futile attempt to clear some air.

"Again Jujube, again!!" Taking the goblin by the arm, Wiz stopped him from adlibbing and motioned for him to try it at normal speed with normal movements.

"Par ipsu ori noom," chanted Jujube, still not sure what the wizard was trying to make him do. This time there was a slight humming noise, then the familiar sputter and smoke. For a moment he was ready to lift his arms in celebration, but the realization of another failure made him slump down until he replayed it in his head.

"Again Jujube, again!!" Jumping up and down, pleased with the slight change in the result, the wizard could sense his improvement.

"Did you see it, Wiz!?" Feeling the wizard's approval and watching him become thrilled with the progress, Jujube joined him jumping up and down, but stopped when he realized how much time they were wasting.

"Jujube will fix it!" Growing bolder Wiz imitated the goblin, spitting back his words while grinning from ear to ear. "This must work or we won't be able to help Mor-o-win!!"

"Again, again!!" said Jujube, joining in on the imitation game. Taking a deep breath before casting the spell, the goblin wondered if he would ever get this right.

Walking down the stone passageway towards her cell with Mixer in tow, it felt just as she imagined the escort to the ogre's dinner table might feel. Dreading where this was going, she hoped that Jujube would intervene before it came time for her supposed elf magic demonstration. As the stress of her situation began overtaking her, she couldn't stop the tears.

"What! Why are you crying!!?" Sensing her uneasiness, he saw that the effects of his charm spell were almost finished.

"I am just so tired, Mixer. Must we do this right now?"

"You just need some food little girl." Pushing his greasy meat pieces in her direction, he motioned for her to eat all she wanted.

"I already have some food." Declining his offer, she grabbed the bread morsels stashed under her pillow.

"There you go! Now we can begin." Trying to sound sweet but failing, the half-orc's raspy voice growled out his growing irritation. "You just needed some food before we got started. Now let's go."

"Yes, yes, I guess I feel better already." Sitting on her bed looking up at him standing between her and the door, it was a cold realization that there was no way out of this.

"What spell will you show me first?"

"Well, maybe first you should learn the fire spell." She had been the most successful with this one, so decided to start with it and hope for the best.

"The fire spell!" shouted Mixer, excited by the sound of learning an elven fire spell, and wondering if maybe he could use it to roast the shaman. Maybe he could even replace him as master of this lair.

"To cast it you must first know the magic words." Enunciating each word for effect and feeling encouraged by Mixer's reaction, Morrowyn delayed as long as she could.

"Show me!! Show me!"

Chanting while working through the motions that Jujube had shown her and ending with the snapping together of the flint rocks that she now held in her hands, Morrowyn's face froze in horror when nothing happened. The silence in her cell was deafening. Looking up at Mixer, she could tell that he wasn't in the mood to be patient.

"Erif!" she tried again, and for a second time the spell failed to light on her fingertip. It had worked the one time in Mixer's cell, but she had no idea why it was failing her now.

"Erif!" barked Mixer, snatching the flint stones from her hands. Copying the motions with ease, he ended with a flame lit on the tip of his finger. Shoving the flame in her face to let her know how easy this spell was, he growled his dissatisfaction. This was not what he had in mind.

"Oh! I have a light spell!" offered Morrowyn, hoping that might appease him.

"This... is not... a fire spell!" The orange flame flickering from Mixer's fingertip revealed his angry countenance. His anger doubled and his patience melted away when he stopped concentrating on his finger and the flame burnt him before extinguishing "Now! Show me real elf magic!!"

"Wolf th'gil!" chanted Morrowyn, relieved to remember the words. The incantation was still emitting faint light from her bedpost and as she uttered the words it grew in intensity. Thrilled when she saw it working on the first try, the look on Mixer's face revealed his profound unhappiness.

Slapping the bedside table as he growled deep from within his throat, Mixer did not like where this was going. This girl was playing games and thought he was a fool.

Trapped in her cell, Morrowyn knew she was in danger. Looking over his shoulder and expecting Jujube's appearance, she wished now that she had listened to his advice about the potion-maker.

"Mixer please, first you must practice dimming and brightening the light spell on my bedpost." Chanting the words she made the light brighten, illuminating the angry expression on his face. With the charm spell now broken, the real Mixer was shining through and the elf was scared of what she saw.

"Ssenkrad!" barked Mixer, waving his hand to dim the light. Suspecting that the elf girl was backtracking on their deal, he was waiting no more. Not needing much encouragement to remember why he hated elves, he started envisioning how this girl was going to pay.

"Wolf th'gil!" chanted Morrowyn, brightening the light on her bedpost again. Mixer's expression made her wish she had left the cell dark.

"Elf girl! Last chance! Show me real elf magic! Show it to me now!" Expecting magic that would help him defeat Jujube and the shaman, her continued lying and mockery had pushed Mixer past the limits of his patience. Clenching his fists and panting, he began waving them in her face.

"That is all I know!!" she confessed between sobs. Horrified by his reaction, she saw his eyes change and knew without a doubt what was about to happen. Cornered in her cell, Morrowyn froze in fear as Mixer grabbed her arms and began shaking her.

"You don't know elf magic! You are just a rotten lying elf!!" Spittle flew from his mouth as he lost control of his temper.

"Please stop! Mixer you are hurting me!"

"You made me waste my charm potion!"

"NO! Mixer!!"

"You will pay for this!" Shaking her as hard as he could, her head snapped back and forth as the half-orc saw red.

"Jujube! Help me!"

"Quiet!" he screamed. "I always hated rotten elves!" Shifting his hands upwards from her shoulders, the orc's fingers wrapped around Morrowyn's throat and he began crushing her windpipe.

THE CREATURE
UNDER THE LAKE

"May I come close to smell you?" Thrilled by the presence of a new visitor after many years trapped and alone, Xamiss's curiosity was insatiable. "I only request that you keep your eyes closed."

"I suppose it would be fine." Shuddering from the damp chill in the cavern, Llythwain was drying off but in the cave's high humidity it was taking a long time. Closing his eyes and standing still, he heard the creature shuffle closer, and smiled as its warm breath took the chill away.

"I must say Llythwain, you look very young for an elf of your experience. In fact, you do not act like any other elf I have ever known."

"Well, I am different… I like spending time in my dream world." Hesitating to explain further, he wasn't sure if Xamiss was making fun of him. The creature's careful scrutiny was making him a little uncomfortable, and it was hard for him to stand still for this long. "My mother and father try and help me behave more like the other elves. They say it will help me fit in with the rest of them. They also say the way I think is a gift because my memory allows me to see things in my head with great clarity."

"There should be no doubt you are a gifted child!" Marveling at the boy's innocence, Xamiss recognized his advanced sense of empathy and curiosity. *This one has a great future ahead of him.*

"You can open your eyes again. Thank you for indulging me." Retreating back to his cloud of darkness, the creature resumed his questioning and probing. "So tell me, Llythwain. You have not revisited your time with Killian?"

"I have tried and except for scattered moments from the last week, I do not remember much of him or anything else from when the ogres took me."

"Young elf, I can help you remember."

"I'm... I am not sure..." Shivering in the cool cave air and caught off guard by Xamiss's offer, he wondered if he was shaking from the cold or the fear of so much unpleasantness. He wanted to know more about Killian, but maybe the ogres and goblins were better left forgotten.

"Do not let your fears control who you really are, Llythwain. Let me help you."

"But the nightmares..." Blocking out this part of his life seemed to help him be more like everyone else. He wanted to know more about his past, but because those memories scared him he felt vulnerable and would fidget when he thought about them. It had made fitting in with his peers a difficult process.

"Relax your thoughts, Llythwain. Use my magic to rest and dive deep into your past. I will join you in your nightmares, watching over you to keep you safe."

"I suppose it will be okay if you are with me, Xamiss." Feeling the pressure of the creature's encouraging words, Llythwain felt an obligation to try. He wasn't sure if facing his nightmares head on was the smartest approach, but resisting the creature's magic was impossible and as waves of warmth crept up his legs, he fell into a deep dreamy sleep feeling safe in the knowledge that at least he would not be alone.

* * *

"Gaffer? Hey Gaffer! Over here!" shouted Jaeyn. Waving when he saw the old man canoeing towards him, he was happy to see him back. "Don't worry Ran, we will find him." Consoling the dejected boy sitting in the back of the canoe, Jaeyn grabbed his shoulder and comforted him.

"What is all the commotion?" asked Gaffer, coming up alongside them and examining the elf. Based on the description from his captive, the doppelganger knew this must be the Ranger Scout that was in charge of watching over the children. Staring at Ran from the canoe, it wished it could have killed both boys instead of just the elf.

"One of the children fell overboard while fishing, Gaffer. We are heading out to search for him."

"Do you think he drowned?"

"He is a pretty good swimmer, but he's been out there for awhile now." Resting his hand on Ran's shoulder when he saw the boy's worried expression, Jaeyn gave him a reassuring smile. "We expect he managed to swim to safety."

"I'll help you with the search!" said Gaffer, turning his canoe around to head back out on the lake. "Where was he when he fell in?"

"We were over near the island," said Ran, pointing at the doppelganger's hideout. Paddling towards the island, as they got closer they saw no signs of life on its shore.

"LLYTHWAIN!! LLYTHWAIN!!" Hoping that he would just pop out of the rocks and wave at them, Jaeyn and Ran continued shouting his name.

"Maybe he's exploring the island," said Ran, trying to be helpful. "You know how he sometimes goes off into his own little world." No one noticed the old man's irritated reaction at the suggestion.

"Well young man, if he made it to the island he would be answering Jaeyn's call, wouldn't he?" Thinking fast, the creature didn't want them to investigate and find its lair. The impulsiveness of its action to go after the boys had interrupted its careful planning and the old man's remains were lying in plain sight. Shifting in its seat as it looked out at the island, the doppelganger saw that its plan was not turning out as envisioned.

"Well, maybe he is unconscious or injured!" Clinging to the faint hope that his friend might be there in need of their help and refusing to accept that he might have drowned, Ran ignored the old man and appealed to Jaeyn's sympathy. "We were right near here when he fell in."

"I don't see any sign of him floating, Gaffer." Looking across the surface of the water, Jaeyn searched for any kind of unusual debris. "I think Ran is right. At the very least we should search the island in case he came ashore disoriented. He could be anywhere."

"Can you swim, Jaeyn?" Unhappy with where this investigation was going, all of a sudden the creature had an idea.

"Of course I can Gaffer!"

"Swim around and check for the boy on the bottom. While you look out here, I'll paddle over and check the island. I'm too old to be bobbing around in the waves like a lost seabird."

"Good thinking, my friend!"

"Hey Llythwain! Are you there?" shouted Gaffer, paddling away from the searchers towards the island.

"I want you to promise me you'll stay in the canoe, Ran." Knowing he was looking for any way to help, Jaeyn didn't want to have to pull two boys from the lake in one day. "If I find him I'll need you here to help pull him into the canoe!" Taking off his shirt, as he prepared to dive into the water, he shouted at the old man. "Good luck Gaffer, and thanks for the help! I hope you are the one who finds him!"

"Llythwain!" shouted Gaffer, waving at the Ranger and paddling harder towards the island. The creature couldn't help admiring its cleverness as it rowed away.

*   *   *

"Xamiss! Where are you?" Recognizing where his mind was taking him, this time Llythwain felt much calmer in his dream than he had experienced before. With the help of the creature's magic his subconscious had relaxed, and he could see his surroundings with much greater clarity.

"I am here, young elf. Do not worry." Remaining silent, the creature let Llythwain control his mind with little outside influence.

"Where are you taking me?" Wrapped in the shade's essence, their journey this time was much longer, and as he rocked back and forth he found himself dozing on and off. The black void through which they were traveling appeared cold and empty whenever he snuck a glimpse.

"We have arrived." Stepping down from his spectral flight, spending the majority of the journey in silence had permitted Killian time to think and better understand his newfound self-awareness and free will. As the shadow-plane faded from his sight, the shade stood on the peak of a mountain overlooking a wasteland that stretched far off beyond the horizon.

Llythwain got to his feet, hearing the dry ground crunch with every step. Noticing the purple sky surrounding a small red sun, he recognized at once that this was not his world. Jagged orange mountains grew out of deep brown crushed sandstone, the barren landscape showing no obvious signs of life. Torn dead trees standing as the silent guardians of this uninhabited place brought a profound sadness to his heart.

"Where are we, master?" Speaking out loud as he stared at some bones scattered on the ground near the ruins of what appeared to be a house, signs that any form of life once lived here surprised him. His mind wrestled with the realization that his world was not the only one in existence. Discerning the outline of a gravel road winding its way down into a small valley below, he could make out orderly rows of broken dead trees littering the lower hills.

"Over here!" Bending to slide some rubble aside, Killian revealed a blacksmith's hammer. Picking it up, he grasped the handle as he stared at the destruction around them.

"This was once my home."

"Your home?!" Staring at Killian before looking back at the lifeless ruin of a world surrounding them, Llythwain couldn't hide his astonishment. "What happened here?"

"This place was once full of life, young elf. The dragon changed everything." Images of success and happiness were flashing behind Killian's eyes and a distant voice told him that the ruined structure they stood in front of had been large. Awareness of its method of destruction was eluding him.

"Is your family... gone?" Unsure of how to proceed with this conversation now Llythwain felt an instant kinship with the shade. Both of them stripped from their families, his empathy was bubbling over.

"Long gone, Llythwain. I believe I had a son, a daughter, and a wife. I do not remember the circumstances of their deaths."

"Why are we here, master?"

"I do not know for certain." Examining the scattered bones, Killian wondered if they belonged to members of his family. "This place was conquered a long time ago. I needed to see it again because you remind me of what I once had."

"Well, it is still a beautiful place." Marveling at Killian's world, Llythwain could picture the magnificence of this land. He imagined how the house would have looked and what the people living there would have done before it was all destroyed.

"My master commands me to take a servant," stated Killian, struggling with the overwhelming compulsion to follow Xeon's commands. Turning others into shades had never been a struggle before, yet now he hesitated and was not sure if he could go through with it. Taking two stiff steps closer, he towered over the boy.

"Killian, no! You do not have to listen to him!" Fear creeping up his legs, Llythwain stood rooted in place.

"I am sorry Llythwain." Grabbing the elf's arm, he prepared to strike.

"I don't want to be a shade! I don't want to be a shade!"

"Silence!" Rising over the elf, he became enraged by the boy's insolence. The Master had a firm grip on Killian's mind now, and was demanding he have a new servant. The independent thoughts filling the shade's mind mere seconds earlier had leaked away. Reverting back into his role as the Master's slave with ease, without warning he thrust downwards and struck a sharp blow to the child's arm.

"No! Killian don't!" Struggling to break free, Llythwain felt his entire body go numb as the shade's talon scratched his arm. A strange light-headedness washing over him, the boy went limp in Killian's grasp.

"I cannot do it!" roared Killian, stopping as the venom began seeping into Llythwain's bloodstream. Resisting Xeon's pull had taken all his strength, but in the end he may have been too late. The elf lay prone and unmoving, and as Killian looked into his eyes it was obvious that a small amount of venom had invaded his blood.

"Uhhhh… Killian no! What is happening to me? Am I a shade now?"

"I am sorry, Llythwain. I could not stop myself in time and a drop of my venom entered your blood." Wanting to show this strange boy who reminded him of his own son some comfort and affection, Killian could not remember how. "Because so little venom was administered, you appear to be fine so far. The typical transformation is quite quick, so while you may not become a full shade, in time you may gain some aspects of one."

"What do you mean, master? Will I live or die?" Curious about what would happen, the feeling in his fingers and toes was returning.

"When a shade injects venom it is always in a very large quantity. The venom takes over your mind and body in the blink of an eye. I took control of my will in the moments before that happened and very little of my poison passed into your blood. You still have your own mind. You have survived so far."

"I can feel it in me though. It feels warm. Will it kill me?"

"I don't believe so Llythwain, but to be honest, I don't know. It appears so far that by injecting only a drop or two of venom you are retaining your independence and your life."

"I don't want to be a shade!" As his emotions boiled over, without meaning to or knowing why, he willed the shadows near him to congregate. The abrupt expenditure of energy used up everything he had left and slumping to the ground, Llythwain sobbed dry tears.

"Easy boy." Gathering the elf up, Killian wrapped him in black essence and willed the shadows to take them back onto the cold road above. *"It is time I took you home."*

"Home?" Passing in and out of consciousness, weak from the changes still occurring in his body, the power of that word nevertheless brought a light to his eyes.

"*Bringing you here was wrong,*" said Killian, feeling strange emotions brimming at the surface of his otherwise stoic exterior.

"*What will you tell Xeon about me?*"

"*I will tell him you did not survive the venom,*" said Killian, re-evaluating the sight of Llythwain controlling the shadows for that brief moment. "*I am done being the dragon's puppet.*"

"*I knew you could resist!*"

"*Yes, you were right young elf.*" Stopping the dragon from repeating on Karth what had happened on his own world had become paramount to Killian. He promised himself that from this point onwards, he would avenge his family at all costs. Administering only a light kiss of venom would allow him to create demi-shades that could still generate independent thoughts while gaining the powers of a shade. The potential impacts were enormous.

"*Killian? Am I really going home?*"

"*Yes Llythwain. I am taking you home now.*"

"*I am going home,*" whispered Llythwain, tears welling in his eyes. Long ago he had accepted that life with his family was over. He had built walls protecting his mind from the abuses of the ogres and goblins. Knocking those walls down was not taking long at all.

"*You will survive, Llythwain.*" Killian began formulating a plan to change things forever but needed his new friend to stay silent. Willing him to sleep on the long journey back to Karth, he inserted instructions deep in the elf's subconscious. "*You will remember nothing.*"

"*I will remember nothi...*" Falling into a deep sleep as they traveled through the void, Llythwain's body jerked and twitched in response to the venom and adjusted to its new existence.

"*Goodbye my son,*" said Killian, letting Llythwain down with care now that they were near his home on Karth. Hearing the sound of someone approaching, the shade wasted no time disappearing into the shadows, not giving the elf another glance.

"*Interesting!*" Satisfied with what he had seen in Llythwain's dreams, Xamiss released the sleep spell's hold. Pondering the depth of the boy's past, he waited for the elf to recover and wake.

✳ ✳ ✳

"Hey Jaeyn, where did Gaffer go?" asked Delorion. Seeing his Ranger Scout staring out across the rolling swells of the lake deep in thought, the captain wanted to see if he could offer any emotional assistance.

"He went up to the main cabin, Delorion." Focusing on the island, Jaeyn's inner voice kept nagging at him. *Why did Gaffer leave the camp without a word and without any of his things?*

"What is bothering you? Is it anything besides Llythwain? We must accept that the boy drowned. You did everything you could, Jaeyn."

"Not quite everything!" Stepping back into his canoe, Jaeyn's face reflected his determination. "I must take one more look."

"It will get dark soon. Do not stay out too long, or we will have to send out a search party after you as well."

"Don't worry," he said, a grim smile playing across his lips. "I won't be long."

Stroking with power rowing towards the island, Jaeyn peered across the surface of the lake in case Llythwain was somehow still afloat amongst the swells. Guiding the little canoe close to the island shore he identified a safe spot to land, being careful not to slam into the rocks jutting from the water. There was no sign of Llythwain hanging exhausted between the slippery boulders. Arriving where the rock face leveled off, a small beach allowed him to carry his canoe up and out of the water.

"You seemed a little too distracted for my liking, Gaffer." Speaking out loud now that he was alone, the memory of the old man's odd grin as he paddled away on the search earlier kept flashing in Jaeyn's mind. "Let's see why you seemed so fixated on this island."

The island was tiny as far as islands are concerned, but there was a large stand of trees wrapping around a sheer cliff that dropped away to deep water. Beaching the canoe, Jaeyn found it strange to see fish bones littering the sand. Further investigation uncovered a rock that had marks consistent with use as a tool. Something was on the island and had perched on the large boulder facing the camp.

"Someone has spent time here. Were they living here or spying on us?" Drawing his dagger, the Ranger crept towards the trees filling the cracks between the tumbled boulders leading down to the water. With all senses on high alert, his training took over and he examined every blade of grass for evidence of habitation. It was clear from the way the grass was bent that the path down from the cliff edge had been used often. Moving inland through the trees, he stumbled upon a small cave opening located between boulders facing away from their camp.

"Hello?" Standing back with his dagger ready, Jaeyn waited in silence for several minutes for any reaction to the sound of his voice. Hearing nothing out of the ordinary, he stepped closer to the entrance and saw more fish bones scattered about. The odor emanating from deep in the cave was nauseating. Covering his nose with one hand, Jaeyn stepped inside the gloom and let his eyes adjust.

"Mrmmm!" As soon as Gaffer realized that the person entering the cave was not the creature returning, the old man began making as much noise as he could muster. Stiff from having his mouth gagged and arms tied for so long, he was fragile from the lack of food and water. Seeing the elf walk into the cave, Gaffer thought he was hallucinating again.

"Gaffer! What is going on here?" The sight of the old man, naked and bound with his head covered in dried blood and deep bruising on his throat, shocked Jaeyn into action. The scout hurried over to untie his bonds, helping him to be more comfortable. *Why would anyone beat this harmless old guy and leave him for dead? And who is that Gaffer back at the camp?*

✻ ✻ ✻

"Xamiss! I can remember everything now!" Piecing together the last bits of the mystery removed a weight from Llythwain's mind that he had been carrying for years. "You were right, there was nothing to be afraid of at all!"

"Your story is rich and interesting, Llythwain. I would never have guessed that such a young elf could have experienced so much."

"I hope you mean that in a good way!" Sharing all the intimate details of his life with a stranger that he had never even seen was embarrassing, and Llythwain felt a little sheepish. "I'm not sure what to make of it all just yet."

"It looks like Killian ended up being your friend," said Xamiss, wondering if the shade venom had any long-term effects. "Most times powerful friends are a good thing. How long has it been since this happened to you?"

"It has been almost two years." Stretching his legs and arms before standing, he was still groggy from the forced sleep and could hear his stomach growling. 'How long was I asleep?"

"Not long, perhaps a few hours at most. I must admit, time has little meaning to me down here. Are you worried about getting back to your friends?"

"Well, I'm sure Ran will be worrying about me." Looking around the cavern, Llythwain saw the crack where he had arrived and began preparing to leave. He hoped the creature was agreeable.

"You're right of course, you better get going." Losing his company so soon was not what Xamiss had in mind, but he understood that not letting Llythwain go made him a prisoner. "I enjoyed your short visit. You have given me a lot to think about."

"I enjoyed this too, Xamiss. I mean that. As you said, making powerful friends is a good thing and I am glad to call you my friend."

"Will you come see me again some day, young elf?"

"I promise I will come back again," said Llythwain, empathizing with the loneliness of the creature beneath the lake. "Are you sure I cannot tell anyone?"

"Remember your promise. It is very important to me."

"No worries, Xamiss, I was just checking. I won't tell a soul. Goodbye my friend! I'll miss you!"

"Thank you, Llythwain. Safe travels my friend." Surprising him, he felt a pang of emotion tug at his heart as the elf disappeared. It would take some time to settle his mind down from the excitement of the past day's events, and Xamiss was already anticipating the opportunity to speak with him again.

XVIII

THE AMBUSH

"There are several goblins at the entrance and four hunters hidden above on the hilltop!" Swooping in close to the waiting Rangers, Maedyn transformed back into an elf as his feet hit the ground. Pointing at their hiding spots, the druid stopped to catch his breath.

"Archers above!" shouted Llaen, his Rangers bursting from the trees. Arrows raining down on them, the goblin archers protecting the entrance from above were dead before they realized what was happening.

"Let's not waste time," said Llaen, signaling his Ranger Scouts to move forward into the mine. Flanked by archers, the Rangers felt confident approaching the entrance and let their eyes adjust to the darkness once inside.

"I'll be right there! Don't wait up!" Recovering from his hurried flight, the sudden decision to move had taken Maedyn by surprise. He had been counting on a few minutes to recover.

I knew I shouldn't have eaten just before I got here. Puffing as he tried catching the Rangers, a strong stitch in his side was preventing him from moving too fast. Up ahead he could see the scouts joining the ranks of the rushing Rangers just as they filled the entrance.

"To my side!" shouted Llaen, the Rangers next to him closing ranks as they charged into the disorganized goblins left to block the oncoming attack. Holding his blade overhead, the captain tore into the first line of defense with the power of adrenalin pumping through his veins.

"Look out! Behind you! It's an attack!!!" Shouting a warning, Madi saw the rush of elves charging towards them. Like a true rogue, while yelling for his companions to form a line of resistance he slipped away from the fight. The young thief knew that this battle would not end well for them as most of the goblins had followed orders to join the hunt for the intruders deep inside the mines. Their flimsy defense would not hold against an organized troop of elves. Swords drawn against the wave of invaders, his companions pushed forward regardless of the fact that they were facing superior numbers.

Sneaking from shadow to shadow as he moved away from the battle, Madi threw himself prone on the ground when he heard a loud crackle. A shimmering blue portal appeared in front of him, the Moongate preventing him from disappearing deeper into the mines where he planned on hiding. Peeking up with one eye, Madi saw what he believed were two Spirit Walkers in hooded dark gray and purple robes step out of the portal and stand almost on top of him.

"It has started!" Oramix could hear the sounds of metal clashing not far from where he and Zira stood. "Those we seek are down this tunnel. Follow me!" Looking down he saw a goblin lying on the ground staring back at him. Seeing no threat, the Spirit Walker ignored him and walked away.

Madi had already constructed a story to explain to the Spirit Walkers why he was so far away from the battle when they turned away from him, dashing down the same side passageway that he was just about to run down himself. The rogue had never seen a Spirit Walker before but he had heard stories of them and their missions from the Gods. *At least I know now not to go down that passage.* Shrugging his shoulders, he searched for an alternate route.

"The Curse!" screamed an elf, yelling out a warning as the fallen goblins began rising again as undead zombies.

This battle is already lost! That didn't take long! Upset that his companions were not putting up enough of a fight to give him sufficient time to escape, Madi slipped back into the shadows and skirted the bloodshed at the entrance. The thief never looked back as the sounds of fighting and dying grew distant behind him.

* * *

"It's too quiet," whispered Llysander, watching Kalahni's back from the rear of the group. Davissor had adjusted the arrangement of the mercenaries so that she was in the center. The Moonguard had healing abilities and the mage wanted her protected so that she could heal them on the fly. Affecting the undead was also a key part of their defensive planning and Kalahni had that ability as well. Ahira and Garrett would be their front line with Angus and Ragnar taking the wings.

"Let's stay quiet. We do not want our adversary knowing that we are here." Expecting that his words would have little effect, the mage had known his companions long enough to understand that his crew could not stop talking.

"How will staying quiet help when they already know where we are?" barked Ahira.

"The dwarf has a point, and I'm not talking about the one hidden under his helmet!" laughed Angus, poking Davissor in the ribs. "Let's talk it up and have some fun. We can show these goblins how we laugh at their supposed strength and numbers."

"We are doomed!" said Kalahni, rolling her eyes. Glancing back at Angus, she wished he could be serious for once and just listen to Davissor without always offering an alternate opinion. Gripping her bow, nerves were getting the better of her.

"We have our rear protected by your husband," whispered Davissor, reassuring her. "With your healing and my spells I am confident we will come out of this with nothing less than success."

"Using the power of the crystal in my sword, I have placed a protection aura around us as an added safeguard," said Garrett, winking at her. Wanting to demonstrate his prowess in combat to the newcomers, Garrett was still annoyed that he had been rendered helpless during their last meeting with the goblins at the cave.

"Listen fellas, there are hundreds of them and only eight of us, including the cat!" Flexing his arms while gripping his double bladed battle-axe, Ahira thought this was the best time to be honest. "I know it's strange to hear this coming from me, but this time I have a bad feeling."

"You are right, Ahira. It is an unfair fight. They should get more troops to even this out!" Trying to help Kalahni relax, Ragnar frowned at Ahira, indicating for him to dial back the negativity.

"How are you doing, my warrior wife?" whispered Llysander, reaching up to put his hand on her shoulder. Feeling her relax under his touch, Llysander smiled and squeezed a little tighter.

"I'm okay." Lowering her bow, she took her husband's hand for a moment and let his strength buoy her.

"Okay elves, enough of that lovey-dovey stuff," teased Garrett, hearing the noise of the enemy coming from the tunnel ahead. The mercenaries were confident in their skills and abilities but the moments before an upcoming battle were always the most tense and difficult part of the job.

"Listen, Ahira and I have figured out how we will keep track of our kills. Whoever lands the crushing blow gets credit for the kill even if another helps with the death blow!" Refusing to keep quiet as the noise around them grew, Garrett enjoyed the confidence boost that boasting brought.

"You don't stand a chance against me, knight!" said Ahira, getting pumped up now. Voices and the sounds of marching echoed from the walls all around them.

"I have been waiting for this day, my brother," replied Garrett, drawing his greatsword and gripping the hilt. "I think you might be underestimating my strength." Swinging and slashing his blade in front of him, he looked back at Kalahni and winked.

"Bah! My axe can kill five at a time!" snarled Angus, twirling his weapon overhead and refusing to listen to anyone trying to outshine him when it came time for talking about battle prowess.

"Come on, brother! You can't think you'll beat me with that woodchopper, do you? I'd let you count my kills but I'm afraid you will run out of fingers and toes!" Banging his sword hard against his chest, Garrett was about to expand on the reasons for his guaranteed contest victory today when the expression on Kalahni's face stopped him short.

"RRRAAAAAA!" Roaring ogres interrupted the heroes' chatter as a hail of spears rained down on them. Entering the cavern ahead of the goblins, the ogres looked fierce as they rushed forward and stopped every ten strides to toss another volley.

Raising their arms overhead out of instinct, the deflection aura that Garrett had cast over them shielded everyone from the projectiles and they watched the spears bouncing off in all directions.

"Ready with the dynamite?" Nodding at the mage, Ragnar and Angus ran off towards their positions.

"For the Heroes of Karth!" shouted Ahira, not waiting for anyone to join him before taking the battle to his enemies. Slowing their approach at the sight of the dwarf charging at them alone, the ogres looked dumbfounded. Adding to the bold counter-attack, Garrett ran after the berserker with his sword raised and ready to strike. As soon as Snow saw the two mercenaries running into battle, she sprinted on their heels, protecting their flanks from behind.

"Davissor now!" shouted Llysander, judging that their opponents had gotten close enough. The Ranger's tactical training told him that they didn't want to lose any momentum. The mercenaries' plan was to concentrate all their initial attacks on one side so that they would not have to worry about two strong flanks once the melee began.

"Gnin th' gil!" Releasing a blast of lightning from his fingertips, the crackling bolt tore through the ranks of the ogres rushing forward, lighting up the entire left flank of their attack. Electricity ricocheted from one ogre to the next, shocking and scorching over half their flank before the knight and dwarf had even arrived. The lightning bolt was random and the ogres that survived the first blast screeched in surprise. Before they could react further, the mage let loose a second blast, paralyzing more of them.

"Zik! Where is Zik?" roared Gurosh, shocked at the ease with which the mage was dropping his warriors. The shaman's toolkit would be necessary if they were to have any chance against him.

"I am here, Gurosh!" Pushing his way towards the front of the ogre line, Zik hit the ground as a blast of lightning shot past him. A volley of arrows from the elves ripped into the ogres just in front of where the shaman stood moments ago.

"Attack! Go now!!" roared Gurosh, knowing that a concentrated attack from his remaining warriors could still deliver a heavy blow.

As the ogres leapt to close on the intruders, Ahira was the first to meet the onslaught, his axe slicing across two ample bellies with one wide arching swipe. Unfazed by his attack, the ogres countered with two hard blows against the dwarf's armor.

"That's one for me!" Skewering an ogre warrior without breaking stride, the knight buried his sword to the hilt in the creature's body, the force of his thrust pushing its corpse into the path of another. As the stumbling ogre tried to regain his footing,

Snow's powerful jaws closed around his neck. The cat felt the spurting of hot blood as she tore out his throat and let him drop to the ground.

Hearing arrows whistling around him, Gurosh winced at the memory of the elf arrow burying itself in his eye not long ago. Instead of rushing into combat, he searched for the source of the lightning bolts. Locating the mage would be critical for their success, although he could see that victory was already beginning to slip from their grasp.

"We have the upper hand!" shouted Llysander, surprised at how well things were going.

"Now you've done it, elf!" Laughing at Llysander's verbal indiscretion, Angus shouted over the din. "Something will go wrong and it will all be your fault! I thought you were a seasoned warrior!"

Targeting his bow on the middle of the ogre ranks, the smile dropped from Lysander's face as a chill ran through his body. *That shaman... I recognize him! He is one of those that we seek!*

"Llysander! What is it?!" Seeing the expression of fury roll across her husband's face and following his icy stare, Kalahni knew in her heart that this shaman was one of the ogres that had kidnapped their daughter. Dropping a charging warrior with two well-placed arrows, she gave notice to Angus and Ragnar that the goblins were approaching from behind them now. Leaving her position and letting the gnome and dwarf fight on their own, she slipped through the confusion to Llysander, standing motionless and glaring at the shaman.

Using two large boulders as cover, Davissor continued letting loose his lightning strikes. Seeing Kalahni make a sudden move across the line to join her husband, he wondered what was so important resulting in her abandoning their initial strategy. Turning away from the ogres he adjusted his attack to focus on the fast approaching goblins.

Furious at how easy it was for this small group of mercenaries to beat the ogres down, Zik searched for the source of the lightning attacks. These assaults were far beyond anything he could defend against and the shaman was insane with jealousy knowing that a far more powerful mage was making him look weak. Gurosh began yelling, pointing at something in the boulders. Following Gurosh's arm, Zik saw the elf mage turn away from the ogres to address the goblins rushing from behind. Smirking at his good luck, the shaman had one spell that he hoped would take out this powerful mage from behind, once and for all.

"That's four for me now!" shouted Ahira, attacking with abandon. "I'm two ahead!" Striding close to two ogres, his blade severed a leg just above the knee. As the ogre toppled Snow pounced with a roar, overcoming his resistance with ease.

Watching his comrade die a gruesome death, the other warrior didn't recover fast enough and took a hard slash across the midsection. As he stood in shock watching his viscera tumble onto the ground, the blade of the dwarf's axe cracked through the center of his skull, dropping him on top of the mound of gore.

"We're tied!" Keeping track of his own kills while watching the dwarf to make sure he wasn't cheating, when Garrett saw Snow tear that warrior apart he knew right away that Ahira would count that one as a kill. Parrying an attack from his next target, out of the corner of his eye he spotted the two ogres he had just slain rising again, this time as undead zombies.

"Learn to count, you fool!" roared Ahira, shaking his head.

"None of those count as kills! We are both at zero! They have risen again as undead so you must kill them again to make it count!"

"Blasted human! You're making up the rules as you go along!" Flabbergasted at the nerve of the knight, the dwarf glared at Kalahni using her Moonlight power to send beams of white light tearing into the undead ogres, burning their flesh away before he could strike at them. "Hey that's not fair! This elf stole my next kills!"

"You should have stayed home with your children, evil elf!" Charging the elf woman, his face distorted in hate, with an overhand sweep of his blade a goblin warrior knocked her square in the chest before she could react. Admiring his handiwork, the goblin realized that her armor was well crafted and the hit had deflected without penetrating. Charging at the elf again, the angry warrior intended on finishing what he had started.

Spinning from right to left, Kalahni used the goblin's own motion to bring him crashing to the ground. The goblin's sword nicked her arm on the way down but she never felt it. Loosing two arrows at point blank range, he was dead before she regained her feet.

"Kalahni!" Unable to leave his position, Llysander's arrows kept the other goblins from joining the attack on her. Watching his wife fight on her own he wished that she had stayed home with Llythwain, but found himself smiling at the ease by which Kalahni took down her opponent.

From the rear, the bulk of the goblin troops were almost on top of the mercenaries but Davissor slowed their advance with several well-placed lightning bolts.

"Fellas!! The dynamite!" shouted Davissor, getting Ragnar's attention at the exact moment that the ogre shaman let out a shrill screech. The mage had no chance to react as the fire spell exploded right between the two boulders where he stood, engulfing him in flames.

"Davissor! No!!" Catching a glimpse of the mage-filled conflagration dropping to the ground, Llysander's heart sank as he turned back to the battle at hand. *This shaman must die! For Davissor! For Morrowyn!*

"The explosives are charged and ready!" shouted Ragnar, as he and Angus scurried behind cover and leaned on the plungers.

The fury of the blast took both sides of the conflict by surprise, the combatants falling to the ground as the concussion ripped across the cave. Those facing the tower of orange flames and smoke saw a storm of goblins, both parts and whole bodies, spinning through the air with great velocity, bouncing and splattering against the cavern walls. A massive cloud of dust and debris filled the confined space, large and small rocks raining down and causing grievous damage to anyone without protection.

"Oh no! I think Llysander cursed us!" said Angus recovering from the ringing in his ears. Sticking his head out from behind the rocks protecting him from the blast, he witnessed a large mob of dust-covered goblins rising from the ground as undead zombies. "Fellas! I think our fun might be over!"

"Come with me, this battle is over!" Approaching Pooga to stop the shaman from advancing with the rest of the goblins, Oramix looked over the goblin shaman's shoulder and caught a glimpse of Zira making her way towards the ogre shaman.

"What are you saying? Where are you taking me?" said Pooga, outraged by the interruption. Eyes widening when he recognized a Spirit Walker the shaman relented, following him away from the battle and down a small side passage.

"Brother, we're in trouble now!" As the undead began lurching towards them, moaning as they thirsted for their energy, Ragnar spun and looked at Angus. As the rogues' eyes met they knew that two of them battling this many zombies were not going to be successful.

"That's three more for me!" shouted Ahira, still playing the game with Garrett even though he knew that without the mage their group had become overmatched.

The onslaught of zombie ogres was pressing in on him from two directions and his fight had become defensive. Spinning and slashing, it was all he could do to stay alive.

"Come with me, this battle is over!" Stepping in front of the ogre shaman, Zira looked back and saw Oramix leading Pooga away from the battle.

"Who are you? We are winning now! Step aside puny goblin!" Scowling at this stranger standing in front of him and blocking his path Zik rushed forward, slapping her with the back of his hand and sending her tumbling into Gurosh. Returning his attention to the battle, he saw two elves glaring at him with familiarity. His face cracking into an evil smile, he recognized that these elves must be the parents of his captive. Ignoring the goblin's warning he strode towards them, intent on inflicting pain.

"What do you mean the battle is over?" said Gurosh, hesitating as the Spirit Walker regained her feet. Not knowing who she was, the brashness of her approach had made the warrior stop and think.

Straightening herself, Zira accepted that the ogre shaman's fate was now sealed, but looking into this warrior's eyes she knew that the gods would approve of her saving him instead. It was clear that great things were still possible for this one. She would be able to find success in this assignment yet.

"Control your zombies! Attack the elves!" Commanding the closest necromancer to move forward and finish off the elf archers, Zik failed to notice Zira stealing away with Gurosh in tow.

"I killed your girl! I killed her!" Making sure the elves heard the words in the common Allegiance tongue echoing across the cave, Zik guessed that the woman must be the girl's mother. Feeling an impact in his shoulder, he glanced down and saw the feathers of one of her arrows protruding from the joint. Infuriated by her puny attack, the shaman decided to crush her spirit before he ended her life.

Reaching into his pouch, Zik pulled out the prayer beads he had taken from the girl's bag. Making sure the elves could see them hanging from his hand overhead, he licked his lips and with an obscene grin stared right at them.

"I ate your little girl!! She screamed for you as I chewed off her arms and legs!!"

Frustrated by the sheer numbers attacking them, Llysander and Kalahni had switched to swords for the close quarter fighting, but as soon as the shaman began boasting about killing Morrowyn, neither parent could hold back their anger. Their concentration and focus were on reaching the shaman, but from both flanks their enemies smashed into them, beginning to overwhelm their defenses.

"Brothers! We appear to be in trouble!" Shouting in desperation over the noise of the goblin zombie surge, Angus knew that this time help would not be coming to save them.

"I am over here, little brother!" shouted Garrett, his sword swinging in wide arcs as he cut down zombie after zombie. The waves of undead seemed endless, and it was becoming obvious that the light on the candle of their lives was growing dim.

Forgetting all about counting corpses now, Ahira just finished one opponent when four more came rushing at him. As the dwarf tired, the effectiveness of his blows began dropping, and it was taking more hits to kill his foes. Seeing Llysander and Kalahni overwhelmed, he was working on getting into a position to help them, but like the others he was beginning to recognize that this battle was almost lost.

"Let them see my face before you slay them!" screamed Zik, instructing the necromancer without thinking. Charging towards the elves, he wanted to stare them down one more time before they tasted death. He would drink their blood tonight.

"Kill the necromancer and shaman first!" Pointing right at them from the cave entrance, Llaen recognized that in order to kill the snake, they must first sever the head. The Rangers were eager to comply, nocking their arrows and letting them fly.

Zik's grinning face changed from glee to horror when a Ranger arrow pierced the necromancer's skull standing beside him, killing the goblin before his body hit the ground. Without the necromancer's control the zombies ran amuck, attacking anything with life force, including goblins and ogres. Watching the mayhem spreading around him, the shaman now understood the goblin's warning. Wheeling around as he forgot about torturing the elves, the shaman looked for a way out of the death chamber.

"Brothers! We might yet survive this! Look!" Desperation giving way to elation, Angus could see the Rangers cutting a swath through the milling zombies.

The sound of elven forces joining the battle had captured the remaining goblins' attention. As they turned away to protect themselves from the zombies and Rangers, Llysander was able to protect Kalahni, giving her time to switch back to her bow. Training it on the ogre shaman, she grit her teeth in a rage fueled by hatred that she had never known before today.

"Morrowyn!" Pulling her bowstring with the strength of profound grief, Kalahni let her arrow find its target. In spite of the tears blurring her vision, the arrow was dead on its mark, the ogre dropping to the ground mid-stride. Zombies fell on him from all directions, trying to catch his energy before it disappeared into the air. The shaman's fall triggered the release of an emotional torrent for Kalahni, being the final act in the search for her daughter. As tears poured down her face, she continued destroying her enemies with clockwork precision.

Heading for the nearest pathway out, Zik never saw the arrow carrying word of his death. Flying with extraordinary velocity, the projectile pierced his neck at the base of the skull and smashed through his vertebra, the shards of bone tearing out his throat as they exploded outward. Tumbling to the ground as his head snapped forward and his legs buckled, the shaman clenched his teeth with the expectation of how he was about to die. Before gurgling his last breaths, the ogre experienced a brief moment of euphoria as he squeezed the elf girl's prayer beads and replayed the elf woman's look of loss over in his mind. It was his final joy as the weight of the zombies tearing at him took the remainder of his life force.

"Is that all they've got?" exclaimed Ragnar, relaxing enough for jokes now that the Rangers were taking some of the pressure. He had forgotten all about Davissor but seeing Angus run to the blackened boulders marking the mage's last known location was a stark reminder of how close they had come to losing this battle. Looking back at Llysander and Kalahni, he considered that not everyone would have an appreciation for humor right now.

Stepping between the two boulders, Angus could make out a form still smouldering from the ogre's fire blast lying in the crater left by the explosion. Seeing no movement and with his heart heavy, Angus rolled the limp mage onto his back.

"Is that you Angus? It's about time you checked on me." His eyes fluttering open through the soot covering his face, Davissor groaned with every movement.

"Davissor?! You're alive! But how? I saw the blast that hit you, brother. I expected the worst!"

"I thought the zombies would find me as I lay here. I guess the soot masked me just enough." Coughing and wheezing as he recovered his strength, Davissor struggled to sit up.

"Remember this?" Holding up his hand, covered in soot was the Ring of Dahar obtained on one of their previous adventures. "It turns out this ring has fire resistance properties. Without it I would have burned to a crisp!"

"Morrowyn is dead!" cried Kalahni, hacking a goblin into pieces even though it was long dead. Looking up she saw her husband approaching, and dropped her weapon with a clatter. "We failed her, Llysander. We failed, the ogres ate her and we will never see our daughter again!"

"The battle is over, Kalahni!" Trying his best to console her, Llysander was overcome with his own storm of emotions. He had never let the possibility of Morrowyn's death creep into his mind and had no idea of the correct response to this situation, now that it stood staring him in the face. Letting his anger boil over, Llysander lifted the prayer beads to the sky as he blamed the goddesses for their incompetence and cruelty. Dropping the beads as Kalahni rushed into his arms, they squeezed each other until they could no longer take a breath, collapsing to the ground in a sobbing heap together. In this cave full of the stench of the dead and the panting of the living they felt alone, struggling with the pain of eternal loss.

$$* \quad * \quad *$$

Leaning against the rock, Davissor knew now that their quest had come to an end. Happy to be alive, he joined the others giving Kalahni and Llysander some time and space to grieve.

Using mining carts to haul the bodies of their enemies outside of the cave, the Rangers created a huge pyre and burned them. Smoke billowed and rose several hundred feet into the night sky, alerting all other goblins within range that this battle with the elves could be counted as a loss.

Watching Llysander consoling Kalahni brought more than a few tears to Llaen's battle-hardened eyes as he shared the pain of his friends. There is an expectation that warriors will lose their lives in battle and soldiers enter into that brotherhood knowing what to expect, but losing a child in such a horrific way was unbearable. *The goblins and ogres will pay a terrible cost at the hands of the elves down the road.*

"They ate our daughter. They ate our daughter." Her voice trembling, rocking back and forth in her husband's arms, Kalahni blamed herself. For hours they sat embracing, coming to terms with the pain and anguish that would live with them for the rest of their lives. "If I had prayed more, Morrowyn would have lived!"

"Kalahni! Please be reasonable. This is not your fault," cried Llysander, shocked by her raw emotional state. "Listen, we must leave soon. I will check with Llaen to learn the best way for us to get home. The goblins will soon regroup and attempt to expel us from their lands." *We may have exacted some justice today, but I vow to return and hunt down every Shard creature in these mountains.*

"I am not going home with you, Llysander! I cannot... My life as I have known it is over. I will return... to my mother!" Her words stabbing deep into his heart, Kalahni rose and left Llysander surrounded by the Rangers and the dead.

*   *   *

Hurrying down the passageway with Pooga and the two Spirit Walkers, Gurosh was happy letting the goblin lead. There had been no need to remain any longer once he realized that there was no chance of victory. Entering the passageway, he looked back just in time to see Zik fall and die. No longer would he have to worry about him meddling and competing for the chieftain's favor. Gurosh knew that Bigglum would not welcome the news of their defeat but at least he would gain a solid footing as second in command. As they sped along the dark corridor, Gurosh kept wondering what had gone wrong with their plan. He had many questions, but his suspicious mind was sensing treachery. With the defeat still bitter in his mouth, he swore to himself that there would be a reckoning one day soon.

"Shhhhhh! They are hunting us!" whispered Oramix, raising a hand to quiet the group.

"We must move faster!' The stress of being a fugitive was fraying Pooga's nerves. Hearing footsteps behind them, the shaman's eyes widened with fear.

"Wait for us!" shouted Sooga, panting as he and Bogg caught up with the group. "We have been running as fast as we could but I think some elves are chasing us!"

"Wait! I saw you die! And what of this one?" Examining Bogg, Gurosh could see the goblin dripping blood and dust and having difficulty standing. Suspicions running high, the ogre was not taking any chances with undead.

"That was Halob!" Furious that they had somehow managed to lose the battle, Sooga was happy seeing others in front of him but tired of running and ready to give up.

"We cannot stay here," interrupted Zira, seeing at least ten Rangers closing in on them. "The elves are almost upon us!!"

"Gate us away! Hurry!" shouted Gurosh, not wanting to face any Rangers in this enclosed space.

"Par ipsu ori noom." There was a hum and flash, and the shimmering blue portal appeared in front of them. Gurosh could already feel the arrows piercing his back. Pushing past the rest of the group, he dove through the portal before anyone else had a chance to react.

"Escape while we still can!" Ushering everyone into the Moongate, she could see the elves taking aim from afar.

XIX

BARSOOM

"We finally made it," whispered Tabatha, grabbing Lenowyn's arm in excitement. "I can't believe you've never been here before! Barsoom is the largest city in the world!" Seeing glimpses of ocean shoreline breaking through the forest after three long days on horseback was elating. Following the road out of the woodlands, the caravan made its way through fields of grains and legumes, the port city of Barsoom stretching out alongside the ocean in the near distance. One of the greatest wonders of the world of Karth, many finely crafted buildings of varied architectures stood within its miles of high stone walls. As they drew near the towering front gates, Tabatha found the thought of all the adventures taking place on the streets inside overwhelming.

"It looks amazing!" Having heard that Barsoom was a melting pot of many different cultures, the contrasting building styles in various districts highlighted the mix of races and philosophies living together within its walls. Thinking back to her education, Lenowyn could still hear the priestesses describing this place as sacrilegious because of the mosaic of different cultures and religions. The elven district was easy to spot from afar, displaying a large church towering high above most of the other buildings, the holy symbol shining on the top. Recognizing the buildings of her people brought a pang of sadness, knowing she could not risk visiting that part of the city. Her current undead state would be detected with ease by the priestesses and they would waste no time destroying her.

"The elf buildings are quite beautiful," said Tabatha, noticing the direction of Lenowyn's gaze. "Don't worry, Lenowyn. You'll find that in Barsoom there are many beautiful and interesting things to see."

"I'm sure there are. The elf market is something I would have loved wandering through though." Baring her arm to show Tabatha that the gray wrinkled skin was forming again, Lenowyn made her point clear. "I can never risk going there looking like this. My people would kill me."

"Barsoom! Halt and dismount to enter!" Silencing Tabatha and Lenowyn as the procession pulled to a stop, a guardsman stood blocking their progress. They were all on horseback except for the mayor who had a team of six horses pulling his enclosed wagon. The carriage was bright red and festooned with wooden carvings from the driver's box to the rear boot. The driver rode on top accompanied by the sheriff who had already hopped down to assist the Mayor.

"We have arrived, Mayor!" said Ted, knocking on the wagon's door.

"Did you say we are there, Sheriff?" Opening the small sliding window to squint out at everyone, Mayor Downey remembered instructing the guards to stop before reaching the gate entrance so he could freshen himself up from the long journey. The mayor tried to not let this oversight irritate him as he swung the wagon door open, wanting to appear dignified while his stiff body betrayed the journey's fatigue. Facing the ocean and breathing the salty air, he attempted to brush away the crumbs and creases of the last three days.

"We made it in good time, sir."

"It will be good to stay at the palace again. Please fetch my hat, Ted." Sending the sheriff away while he stretched his arms and legs to work out the kinks, Mayor Downey was straightening his stringy white hair when he noticed Tabatha staring at him, and he motioned her over.

"Sorry, Mayor. I didn't mean to stare." Thinking about recent events as she watched him, Tabatha decided that she still did not trust his motives even though she seemed to be enjoying much more respect from all the townspeople including the Mayor since saving Strathmore.

"The King has learned of your abilities and the fact that you saved our town. Life is about to change for you, my dear," said the mayor, buttoning his shirt while he spoke. "I already sent a message and the King's Council replied, informing me that there will be a Necromancer Proclamation!"

"What does that mean?" asked Tabatha, not sure if she should just pack her horse and leave right now. As long as she had been alive her profession was always shunned. Necromancers like her had created and maintained a secret society where they could practise their skills without fear or judgement. *Did I just fall into a trap? He will probably have me arrested at the palace.*

"It means that every town will now have a necromancer representative appointed, Tabatha. Henceforth, necromancers will help guard against the curse and will no longer need to hide their profession. The King is holding a ceremony in honor of our saving the town."

"That... is wonderful news..." *There must be a catch. This mayor doesn't do anything for nothing.*

"I want you to be Strathmore's representative! You will continue to manage your cemetery and help control the undead for us and in return you will even receive a salary."

"That is very nice of you... I think..."

"Your hat, Sir!" Forcing a smile towards Tabatha, Ted interrupted the conversation then walked away.

"Listen, there will be a special ceremony at the palace and I am requesting you be there, Tabatha!" Knowing she was awkward and introverted, the mayor used his most stern voice to help her understand that this was not negotiable. "I will need you on your best behaviour. Do you understand me?"

"Yes Sir!" Staring at the ground and dreading the attention, Tabatha was happy hearing she would be the representative in Strathmore and that the cemetery was still hers to control. She had worried that the mayor might still try exhuming and burning all of the corpses interred there.

* * *

"I'll give you four silver for this dress," said Lenowyn, looking disinterested. Tabatha had convinced her to explore the open bazaars to find something more suitable for the coming ceremony at the King's court. Her current wardrobe of battle-worn armor and ripped cloth was ill-suited to this civilized environment.

"Six silver coins," said the shopkeeper, refusing to lower her prices any further.

"We'll take it!" Pushing forward to hand over the coins, Tabatha shot Lenowyn an appreciative grin. "This is my treat!"

"Don't take her money! I can pay my own way!" protested Lenowyn, offering her own coins. Dismissed by the merchant, she gave up on paying for it. More exploring of the bazaar had yielded some interesting jewelry and after looking one more time at her new dress, she knew that it would complete her look.

"You will look great!" said Tabatha, admiring the way the dress brought out a softer and more alluring side to the elf.

"Thanks for being so kind, Tabatha." Lenowyn felt more awkward than ever. She could only remember demonstrating selfishness and dislike towards Tabatha, yet she always received kindness in return.

"It might not be the elf market, but admit it! You had fun today!" Ignoring the strained silence between them as they walked the streets, Tabatha felt good to be back in the familiar surroundings of Barsoom.

"Alright, I'll admit it. Your bazaar is very interesting." Shaking her head as they kept walking, Lenowyn thought about the speed with which life could change direction. Not that long ago her mission was to assassinate all necromancers, and now she found herself tied to one who had saved her life. *If the priestesses could only see me now, walking in this huge city, enjoying the company of a human necromancer.*

"Hey! Come on!" Leaving the bazaar and turning west, Tabatha took them in the direction of the docks. The smell of the salt breeze got stronger with every step.

"Where are we going now?" asked Lenowyn, her head on a swivel as she tried remembering landmarks to orient herself within the flow of life.

"When I was younger my father sent me here to study. I lived in this part of Barsoom for a few years and know this area like the back of my hand! I want to show you a few of my favorite places while we're here."

Strolling along the cobblestone streets by the harbor, they could see a vast array of different sized ships loading and unloading cargo. As much as Tabatha was happy to be back, she realized that it was much better having a friend to keep her company. Turning the corner away from the shipyard, the streets became narrower, the tall yellow buildings with orange tiled roofs making the change in districts quite obvious.

"I went to school here!" Stopping to examine the yard of a large four-story building nestled amongst the huge trees lining the street, memories flooded Tabatha's mind.

"It looks like a great place to learn!" said Lenowyn, impressed with the simplicity of the surroundings. Several ornate plants and trees and a small garden on either side of the main walkway lead students to the double-door entrance. Lenowyn could almost picture a much younger Tabatha running up to the door and disappearing inside.

"Not far from here is one of my favorite places," said Tabatha, hesitating before elaborating further. "We can get some food and relax. It's been a busy day so far," she finished, hoping no further explanation was necessary. Having brought it up before thinking things through, she decided to continue with her idea and hope that she did not regret introducing Lenowyn to this part of her life.

"Food sounds good to me, Tabatha. What is this place called?" Having noticed the hesitation in the girl's voice, her training as an assassin kicked in and she stared into the necromancer's eyes trying to discern what she was thinking. Lenowyn made a mental note of her current surroundings, trusting that she was not in any danger but intending to investigate Tabatha's turf in greater detail when she got the chance.

"It's called the Black Tomato." Turning before there were any more questions, she headed off down the street to show her new friend her old haunt.

$$* \quad * \quad *$$

A pastiche of smells and sounds assailed them as they entered the Black Tomato, their eyes taking a few seconds to adjust from the bright sunlight outside. Lenowyn started looking around for a table but froze when she saw a redheaded woman jumping to her feet.

"Tabatha? I can't believe it!"

"Who is that?" whispered Lenowyn, her eyes narrowing as she prepared for trouble. The woman was human, close to Tabatha's age and dressed in a similar style of clothing. The assassin noted that the other females sitting with her appeared uncomfortable, their body language indicating that they and the necromancer all knew each other, but this group of women was less than thrilled to see either of them standing there. *I wonder why they would have a problem with me.*

"That. Is Linda." Taking a deep breath, she closed her eyes in preparation.

"Linda is my ex-partner."

"Tabatha! How are you?!!" Rushing over to give her a big hug, Linda straightened her hair and stepped back to look Lenowyn up and down.

"Interesting, honey. It's pretty clear to me that this elf is one of us."

"Excuse me. This elf's name is Lenowyn," replied Tabatha, pushing her glasses up on her nose while taking a step closer to protect her new friend. "She's undecided right now." Linda was invading her personal space and she felt conflicted. There was no denying that she still had feelings for her ex and missed her touch, yet something was different. Watching the other girls glaring at her was a stark reminder of why they broke up in the first place. Pulling away from Linda's body, Tabatha moved close enough to Lenowyn that their arms and hands were bumping together.

"I'm Linda!" she said, flashing a seductive smile at Lenowyn. "I'm Tabatha's partner."

"You were my partner, you mean, until you decided you wanted more variety!" Seeing the way Linda was looking at Lenowyn reminded Tabatha of the day they had met in The Black Tomato years ago. That familiar seductive smile was bewitching and she found her reaction to it surprising. *Why am I feeling jealous? Who am I jealous of? Linda or Lenowyn?*

"Oh Tabatha! One mistake and you toss me away like a broken arrow. Lenowyn dear, do you mind if I steal your Tabatha away for a few minutes? We need to clear this up!"

Lenowyn stared back at the two humans, unfazed and emotionless. She had no words.

"Sorry Lenowyn." A tight smile breaking across her face, Tabatha squeezed the elf's hand. "Grab us a table, I promise I won't be too long."

∗ ∗ ∗

"Grab us a table, I promise I won't be too long!" Shaking her head, Lenowyn's mind was spinning. First she had to process the realization that Tabatha was a necromancer. Even knowing that killing her meant that they both would become undead, it had been difficult for the assassin to put aside her mission. Hearing that the girl was also attracted to the same gender was a lot to absorb. She had heard about this form of attraction but had always imagined it was nothing less than depraved. Conservative elf religious culture taught that same gender attraction was wrong and Lenowyn had never had any reason to doubt it. Yet here she was on the verge of being undead, wearing human clothing, and having lunch with a necromancer who admitted an attraction to the same gender. *If the priestesses could only see me now!*

"Lenowyn? I can't believe it! I thought you were unsuccessful at your escape!"

Shocking her out of her deep thoughts, the male voice sounded familiar. Snapping her head up, Lenowyn recognized the elf staring back at her in disbelief.

"Kethus?" Wrapped in a red silk robe, the mage was drinking wine and smoking a long wooden pipe. Enjoying a meal in close company with a human male, he looked casual and relaxed, explaining why Lenowyn hadn't recognized him sitting there. Her heart jumped when she realized he was a possible link back to the priestesses. If he reported to them that he had seen her here, she would be in grave danger indeed.

Enjoying an intimate dinner with his partner, Kethus had been in the middle of telling him the story of the assassin and the exploding zombies. Looking up to take a draw on his pipe the mage came close to choking when he saw Lenowyn sit down at the table next to him. On the verge of panic, upon closer inspection he realized she had been with the woman standing with the necromancer moments earlier. Trying to relax, when he replayed his memories from the time he saw her walk in until the time she sat down, all of a sudden he began smiling. The mage could tell right away that Lenowyn had feelings for the necromancer. She hadn't noticed him yet, but he still worried that she might discover his preference and report it back to the priestesses. Instead of worrying about his possible discovery in Barsoom, he decided to just be straight with her.

"Lenowyn!" he shouted, jumping up from his chair to give her a hug. Looking back at his partner, Kethus winked to let him know everything was all right. Inviting himself to sit at her table, he grabbed her hand and hoped she wouldn't try to run away.

"I am so happy to see you here, Lenowyn! We should talk about everything you are seeing and feeling though. It's not healthy to keep your feelings bottled up inside, no matter what the priestesses might say."

"Kethus, I am so confused!"

"I have no doubt that you are feeling confusion, Lenowyn. I can see that you like her! We elves have a lot to learn about the ways of the world."

"What?! Tabatha is just a friend! I don't appreciate your insinuations and I do not approve of your behavior either." Glancing over his shoulder she caught a glimpse of Linda reaching over and brushing Tabatha's hair back from her face. It bothered her, but she forced her focus back to the mage.

"You will lose her if you wait too long," cautioned Kethus. "Listen to me, I know what kind of internal conflicts you are feeling. They will weigh you down and block you from taking action. Please don't make the same mistakes that I made."

"Did they send you to find me, Kethus?" Ignoring his words and being as blunt as possible, with a little time to think things through she decided to overcome one worry at a time.

"Lenowyn, believe me when I tell you that I am not here to find you. Although I am curious to know why you are here and how you survived the crypt?"

"I would rather not say." Sneaking another glimpse at Tabatha, she looked back and made sure she had the gray dead skin on her arms covered. "It's… complicated."

"It seems to me that life becomes more complicated when you only look to yourself for solutions. You can confide in me," said Kethus, knowing that the only way he would find out if she would be reporting him to the priestesses was convincing her to trust him. "We share more mysteries than you might think. Look at where you found me and whose company I am enjoying. We both know the elves would cast me out if they discovered my secret."

"Kethus, I worry…" Looking again at Tabatha and Linda, the high priestess's direct order to kill all of the human necromancers flashed through her mind.

"Lenowyn, if your concern involves telling me Tabatha is a necromancer, I already know. In fact, many others in this place are also necromancers, including the red-haired Linda that your friend is sharing a drink with right now."

"How do you know so much, Kethus?" When they traveled together she found the mage annoying and sneaky, but it appeared as though her initial impression of him was inaccurate. Speaking with him one on one was eye opening.

"Come on, Lenowyn! I am a mage," he laughed. "And I have been coming here for years. I know many of the patrons, some of them quite well indeed." It was so obvious to him that she was not the same individual as the one he had traveled with, but rather than prying, he wanted her to come forward with the information he was seeking. He stopped talking and gave her the time and space to think.

"I died that day in the crypt." Breaking the silence with unintended drama, Lenowyn's eyes bored into those of the mage, waiting for his reaction. "Before the end, Tabatha found a way of keeping my soul bound to my body. But with the Curse, I rose as undead and I am bound to her for protection." Even though she felt comfortable with him, old habits died hard. Gripping the hilt of her katana in case he didn't like what she was saying, it was an unconscious and unwelcome reaction. The assassin returned both hands to the tabletop.

"I am seeing the truth hidden in the rumors." Taking a sip of wine, the mage considered her words. "The necromancers were already told of a zombie elf that had been able to keep its mind and soul intact. I should have guessed it was you they were talking about."

"Tabatha can provide more explanation as to how the process works. But I am a... zombie... and my body would be rotting away if it were not for her healing salves."

"This is an amazing discovery, Lenowyn. You have become an important part of the research towards ridding ourselves of this curse. If not for your pallid eyes there would be no telling that you carried the affliction!"

"Tabatha promised to approach the other necromancers to see if they could cure me."

"Ha ha! The ironies in life!" chuckled Kethus, shaking his head. "Did you know that as the elves are proclaiming necromancers as the cause of the curse, the humans are about to decree them as heroes?"

"I didn't know about the human decree until I arrived here, but it makes perfect sense to me now! I can't believe how much respect I have lost for the priestesses and elf religion in general."

"They sent me here as their ambassador, Lenowyn. They want to try and influence the humans to attack the crypt and wipe out necromancy forever."

"Wait until they hear that the humans are hailing the necromancers as heroes," laughed Lenowyn, certain that Tabatha would also see the humor in this dichotomy.

"Relations between elves and humans will be at an all time low, but since the elves depend on Barsoom as their major trade route there is little that they can do about it."

"Kethus, I can't believe I am sitting here with you enjoying myself!"

"I feel the same way," said the mage, echoing her chuckle. Finishing his wine, he prepared to get back to his dinner.

"Kethus?" said Tabatha from over his shoulder. She had noticed Lenowyn with the elf mage and rushed to her friend's defense. She wasn't sure if the assassin was in trouble but she could not hide the concerned look on her face.

"It's okay, we were enjoying ourselves." Happy that Linda was not with her, Lenowyn grabbed Tabatha's arm and pulled her into a seat. "He is not who I thought he was and we have had an enlightening conversation."

"Ladies I am sorry but my friend and I have to get going! Perhaps you both should join us for breakfast tomorrow! We could meet at the Morning Owl?"

✳ ✳ ✳

I knew it. Wrapped in her black hooded cloak, the assassin had watched the palace gates for hours from her rooftop vantage point. Her patience had paid off.

"Show yourself!! What is your name??" It was after midnight and the guard was not expecting anyone to be leaving the palace at this late hour.

"I am Tabatha Shadowsong," the person responded. "I am restless tonight and am going for a long walk."

"The city is a different place at this time of night. You are safer staying within the palace walls."

"I have lived in Barsoom for many years, guardsman. I appreciate your concern."

"As you wish, Tabatha Shadowsong. Be safe." Looking up at the tower, the guardsman signaled his comrades to open the gates.

Where are you off to, my little Tabby? Sneaking off to see your old friend, perhaps? Slipping off the roof, down the fire escape and onto the street in mere seconds, the assassin crept from shadow to shadow, blending in with the darkness as if she had been born a part of it. Lenowyn had mapped out all the possible routes away from the palace, so she knew at once which way Tabatha was heading.

That guard was right. I need to be careful without Lenowyn with me. His warning was not just empty words and Tabatha knew that the streets of the city at night were a rough place for anyone alone. Nevertheless, when she received notice of the secret society's emergency meeting she could not refuse to attend. The complication was that on this journey she could have no special friend accompany and protect her. Only necromancers had permission to attend so bringing Lenowyn was not an option.

Watching Tabatha head towards the docks, Lenowyn saw her take the same route the two of them had used earlier in the day. The assassin hurried through the cobblestone streets, passing her quarry while staying deep in the shadows. Having a good memory of what was ahead, she wanted to get in front of her and cross the bridge unseen.

"I thing am I a little drunk." Struggling to keep up with his friends as they crossed the bridge, the dishevelled man could hear them laughing and assumed it was at him. The alcohol added fuel to the fire of his temper as he staggered along behind them.

"Blast!" Observing this crew from the shadows of the empty guardhouse at the end of the walkway, Lenowyn saw that these were five large men, all drunk and not an intelligent looking one in the bunch. She needed to get across before Tabatha arrived to discover her follower, but she also did not want her friend to risk facing this crew alone. The necromancer lacked fundamental fighting skills and it was quite probable that she would lose out in a struggle with any one of these brutes. With mere minutes before Tabatha reached the walkway, the assassin would need to work fast.

"You have no tolerance for strong drink, John! Perhaps we should put a dress on you!" Watching their friend holding onto the rails of the walkway, the group laughed harder.

"Hey! You guys should leave here now or this will not end in your favor!" shouted Lenowyn, her katana drawn in one hand and the jewelled magic dagger Tabatha had loaned her in the other. To any sober person she looked threatening enough, but to men filled with liquid courage she was nothing but enticing.

"Oh ho! It is our lucky night, boys! Come to Papa little one!" said the largest of the drunkards, opening his arms wide. The rest of the group thought this was hilarious.

Guessing by their reaction to her that respect for women was not their hallmark, Lenowyn decided that reasoning with them was not going to work. Before the large man could say another word she attacked, knocking him unconscious with the hilt of her sword. Whirling to face the rest, she hoped that her quick attack would convince them to move along.

"Take your friend and leave! Now!"

"Okay now you asked for it!" Another of the men shouted as two more rushed at her, arms outstretched and trying to grapple.

"Wash out you idiots! She hash her shords drawn!" said John, trying his best to sober up.

The men proved no match for the elf and as they came within range, the tip of her blade tickled their ample bellies. If she had wanted them dead it would have all been over by now, but fear was her goal. She just wanted them to get the point and leave. Spinning around she saw another man rushing at her holding a dagger. Like a striking snake her blade shot out, nicking off the tip of one of his fingers and causing him to drop his weapon with a clatter. Sweeping his feet out from under him as he stood staring in disbelief at his wounded hand, the man's face smashed hard into the cobblestones.

"I'm dying!" he cried, putting a bloody hand up to his bloody face.

"Leave now or I will turn that statement into a prophecy!" Positioning herself so that there was an obvious way for the drunkards to escape, Lenowyn became as threatening as possible. *Please leave. I don't have much time left.*

"Let's get out of here!" shouted John, and within moments the men had disappeared, leaving the street empty again.

Just in time. A last scan of the street showed no danger, and slipping over the side of the walkway, she melted into the shadows once again as Tabatha walked by.

* * *

Looking back to make sure she wasn't followed, Tabatha slowed down to peer into the shadows. Instead of entering The Bald Eagle Tavern from the front, she cut through a small alley to a side door. Looking around once again, she then knocked three times.

"It's dark outside," growled a man's voice, answering the knock as a tiny shaft of light shot out into the night.

"I don't mind the dark," replied Tabatha, stepping close enough that her whisper would project through the crack in the door. "With the moon so bright, I can find my way easily enough."

The shaft of light extinguished and after a moment of silence, the door creaked open. Slipping inside, she disappeared as the door clicked shut.

About to take a closer look, Lenowyn heard the click of approaching footsteps. Melting back into the shadows, she held her breath as an older man in a fancy suit and cape walked within a few feet of her hiding spot. Studying him as he turned down the side alley, she noted that he had a feather perched on his hat and was carrying a wooden cane topped with a large skull and tipped at the bottom with silver. Stopping in front of the side door, he also knocked three times.

"It's dark outside," the man's voice growled down the shaft of light.

"I don't mind the dark," Feathered Hat replied with an even tone. "With the moon so bright, I can find my way easily enough."

Once again the light disappeared and there was silence before the door opened and the man slipped inside.

Gaining access seems easy enough, even for an undead elf! The moon is dark tonight. Luck is with me so far.

Pulling her hood low, she took a deep breath and approached the door, knocking three times.

"It's dark outside," growled a man's voice, the dusty sliver of light shooting out from a small panel in the center of the door.

"I don't mind the dark," replied Lenowyn, looking at the stars twinkling in the dark sky. "With the moon so bright, I can find my way easily enough."

The panel snapped shut and there was a moment of silence before the door creaked open, giving Lenowyn a view of a short hallway ending in stairs that appeared to go below ground. Stepping over the threshold she passed the growling man sitting on a chair behind the door. Nodding his welcome, he motioned her towards the stairs.

Arriving at the lower level she could see a gathering of at least twenty people taking part in the ale and food. Tabatha was across the room and seemed to know most of the people assembled here. *What is going on here?* Looking for a decent place to observe the proceedings, Lenowyn stuck to the wall as she scoped out her surroundings.

Blending into the back of the room, she found a small storage alcove and was able to slip inside unnoticed, hiding behind some boxes where she could still see most of the attendees. Making herself as comfortable as possible, she began the process of making mental notes.

∗ ∗ ∗

"Ok everyone! I think we're all here!" A handsome man attired in a black pinstriped suit and scarf walked about the room greeting everyone. "Please take your seats so that we may get started."

"Tabatha! Over here!" shouted Linda, sitting next to Feathered Hat. She had kept a seat open next to her, and she beamed when Tabatha walked over.

"Tabatha! How nice to see you!" said Feathered Hat, standing to offer her a warm handshake.

"Wilfred!" said Tabatha, taking his hand and hugging him in greeting. "It is delightful to see you again! Are you still teaching at the school?"

"Silence everyone, please!" Raising his hands to quiet the room, Pinstriped Suit motioned to his left with a deep bow before returning to his seat. A hush came over the assembled group.

"Greetings everyone!" A heavyset man walked to the front of the room wearing an elegant black suit and white shirt. Hanging on his chest was a silver necklace centered by a skull dagger pendant.

"For any of you who do not know me, I am Professor Wulfgar Valentini, and I am your host this evening."

"We all know who you are Professor!" screeched a heavyset woman holding a tankard of ale. "You taught every one of us at the academy!" Wrapped in a tight purple dress, several buttons may have become unfastened this evening, accentuating her features. Taking another swig of her beer, she smiled at everyone while wiping foam from around her mouth.

"Thank you Sally. It is nice to see you again as well. Friends, I called this meeting because as some of you may have heard, tomorrow the king plans to unveil his Necromancer Proclamation!" Waiting until the chatter had died down, it was apparent to Wulfgar that many were just hearing about this now.

"This will mark the first time that necromancers will be allowed to practise their profession out in the open without fear of judgement or persecution."

"What happened that the king is deciding to do this now?" said Wilfred, speaking for many in the room.

"Can we trust his word?" said Sally, belching after draining her tankard. "Maybe it's a trick!"

"Or maybe someone amongst us saved Strathmore by using necromancy, convincing those in power that there was value in our art!" bragged Linda. She had been gossiping about Tabatha ever since her friend had returned to Barsoom.

"Tabatha! Is this true?" asked one of the women who had been sitting with Linda at the Black Tomato. "Linda told us that's what happened but we assumed it may have been a little bit of an exaggeration."

"Hi Allison. Well, I guess it is true." Flustered and embarrassed by the sudden spotlight, Tabatha realized that the whole room was staring at her. Fidgeting with her glasses, she cleared her throat and smiled.

"Friends, not only did Tabatha save Strathmore, but she also discovered a weakness in the Curse!" Coming to her assistance, Wulfgar jumped back into the conversation.

"Well, Tabatha? What do you have to say about that?" A man wearing bifocals, a white long coat with a brown shirt and an orange bow tie spoke up now. "Please tell us about the weakness!"

"Hello Sigmund. Well, I discovered if you cast a raise dead spell…" Starting to explain the process, Tabatha looked at Wulfgar to make sure she had his blessing to continue. He nodded for her to continue." If you cast it just as someone is dying while in the vicinity of the curse, the body becomes undead but the soul remains attached!"

"Astonishing!" Shaking his head, Sigmund clicked his tongue in thought. A renowned scholar of necromancy, he had many more questions but remained quiet so that others might speak.

"That's impossible!" interjected Sally, others nodding in agreement. "What proof do you have of this weakness? You don't look experienced enough to save a town!"

"Sally, I've heard enough of your lip tonight! Tabatha saved an elf assassin just as she was dying!" Glaring at the doubters in the room, Linda dared them to press her further.

"You did what?" Frowning at Tabatha, Wilfred wagged his finger. "That was poor judgement, my dear. I have heard rumors of an assassin sent by the elves to hunt down and kill all necromancers!"

"Everyone knows the elf priestesses cultivate a deep fear and hatred of our kind!" Agreeing with Wilfred, Sigmund shook his head.

"Everyone, wait! Lenowyn has become my friend! I came here hoping someone could help cure her of the Undead Curse!" Hearing a few snickers from the crowd, Tabatha felt her heart sink.

"It does not matter who she saved!" shouted Linda, standing beside her friend in support. "When did we become so judgemental? The point here is I have seen this zombie elf for myself. I could feel her undead form and even control her. I spoke with her and can verify that Tabatha's claims are the truth!"

"I might be able to help your friend," said Sigmund, his brain whirling with ideas.

"But what does all this mean?" asked Allison, looking to Wulfgar for answers.

"It means that because of Tabatha we can now rise up and be proud of what we are!" said Wulfgar. "The times are changing and I feel that the rise of the necromancers is imminent. No longer will we need to hide and be afraid of discovery!"

"We will even receive compensation for our services now, from what I have heard," added Wilfred. "The king will ask that each town and district employ at least two of us to help protect against both the curse and the undead!"

"In fact, we already have an assignment list written up for when the time comes," said Wulfgar. "I don't want to leave anything to chance. Don't be fooled, my friends. This transition in philosophy will be difficult for many to accept. Please do not let your guard down for an instant!"

"I am joining you in Strathmore!" whispered Linda. "Won't that be fun?"

Peering out from behind her wall of boxes, Lenowyn was struggling with the idea of necromancers being an accepted part of society, but she would be willing to accept their help to become normal again. *This ought to be interesting. The priestesses will never accept it. I shall have to keep an eye on Linda. There is something about her that I don't trust.*

XX

ESCAPE

"Wicked rotten elf! You have no powers! No powers at all! You cheated Mixer!" Pushing Morrowyn backwards and grabbing her by the throat, the potion-maker's mouth screeched mere inches from her face. "No more crying! Mixer hates your stupid crying!"

"No! Mixer! Stop it! Stop!" Kicking and fighting the attack but unable to get away from the strength of his grasp, Morrowyn flailed her arms, battering her assailant with all her strength. Her defense had little effect and she felt the orc's fingers tightening.

"Help! Joojooooo...!" Screaming with her remaining breath, the high-pitched squeak echoed down the cellblock. As Morrowyn's strength waned and her vision began to fade, she had a vision of her mother waving from the back door of their home. She wanted nothing more than to wake up in her mother's arms, feeling the comfort of her strength and protection.

"Silence! I have had enough! I... will... kill... you... today!" Gritting his teeth and growling, shaking her back and forth with all his might as his fingernails sunk into her throat, the red wave of rage blinded Mixer from noticing a jumble of movement behind the cell door.

* * *

"Again! Again!" shouted Wiz, yelling encouragement as he jumped up and down. The goblin was making progress. His latest attempt to conjure a Moongate had made one flicker for several seconds.

"Par ipsu ori noom!" Sweaty brow wrinkling with concentration, once again Jujube heard the sputtering sound and saw a small puff of smoke. *The portal is right there! What am I missing?* Taking another deep breath and glancing around the shaman's chambers, Jujube knew that if the ogre returned right now and saw what they were attempting he and the wizard would have no chance to explain the mess and smoke. There was no going back to the life he had known for so long.

"Hee hee! Again! Again!" Laughing as he danced in circles, Wiz appeared to be having the time of his life.

"Wiz stop! It's not funny! We have to get Mor-o-win away from here before the ogre comes back for her!" Wishing there was some other way the wizard could help him, Jujube felt his confidence slipping away.

"What's that you say? Morrowyn?" Cocking his head as a cry for help from down below tickled his ears, Wiz almost fell as he stopped. "Did Jujube hear something too?"

"Oh no! What is Mixer doing?" The thought making his blood run cold, Jujube dropped the spellbook and ran as fast as his legs could carry him down to the cellblock with Wiz following close behind.

"Morrowyn is in trouble! Morrowyn is in trouble!" Keeping his distance in case he needed to make a hasty escape, Wiz had been around too long to rush into any situation.

"Mor-o-win! Where are you? Mixer! I forgot to check on them! Wiz, if there is a problem I am going to kill Mixer!"

* * *

With savage glee Mixer watched the elf girl turning blue, but as she gasped her last breaths, the pile of bones behind the door began stirring. Animating in a matter of seconds, the skeleton's burning eyes focused on the creature attacking the one whose protection was its responsibility. With two strides it was on top of the half-orc, beating him with boney fists hardened by magic.

"Ow! What? Get off! Aah! Stop! Stop!" Forced into releasing the elf to defend against the ferocious assault, with his mind still clouded by rage the potion-maker was unable to switch gears. The skeleton took the upper hand with mindless ease.

Sprinting into the cellblock, Jujube and Wiz went straight to Mixer's room. The door hung open, the cell was empty. The sounds of struggling were coming from down the corridor in Morrowyn's room. *Why isn't Mixer locked in his cell? What is going on down here?*

"Mor-o-win!" shouted Jujube, running to her cell and kicking the door wide open. With widening eyes as his brain processed the scene, the goblin tried to make sense of the violence transpiring in front of him. Morrowyn lay lifeless on her bed, purpling bruises on her throat. The skeleton was beating Mixer senseless. It was a spectacle out of Jujube's worst nightmares.

"You did this! YOU!" Noticing Jujube standing in the doorway, Mixer's bloody mouth hung open in shock. "I WILL KILL YOU, GOBLIN!"

"Mixer!? No! What have you done?!" Moving the magic bones into Morrowyn's cell one night when everyone was asleep, Jujube was unsure why but it had felt like the right thing to do. Imbuing them with the magical instructions to guard her, he didn't ever expect it would be necessary. Seeing her lying motionless on the bed, he hoped the skeleton had not been too late.

Gathering his remaining strength, Mixer flung himself away from the skeleton and rushed at Jujube. Swinging in all directions he managed to land a few hard blows on the goblin before the skeleton caught him again and continued its relentless beating.

"You better not have killed her!" yelled Jujube, falling back into Wiz as the potion-maker's barrage caught him off-guard. Pushing the half-orc away as the skeleton caught him again, Jujube let his servant complete its assigned task.

"I… HATE …!" Spitting a final torrent of venom before his strength gave out, the half-orc's arms dropped as his eyes began glazing over. No longer encountering any resistance, the skeleton wrapped its arms around Mixer's furry head and with a single violent twist, snapped his neck with a loud crack. The potion-maker slumped to the floor, bleeding from dozens of wounds.

"Cease!" said Jujube, commanding the skeleton to stand down from its duties. Seeing how easy it had been for the skeleton to kill Mixer, he had a momentary panic attack wondering if he still had control of it.

Sensing no further threat to the creature under its protection, the skeleton stood still, waiting for his next command word.

"Mor-o-win!" Rushing to the girl's side, Jujube and Wiz gave her a cursory examination. The terrible bruises on her throat were growing but she appeared to still be breathing. It was a relief, but she needed help surviving this day. Commanding the skeleton to carry her and follow, they hurried back to the shaman's chambers.

Laying the girl on the bed, Jujube ran to the cupboard and pulled out one of the healing draughts lined up on the top shelf. Knowing that it was one of Mixer's concoctions, he delighted in the irony. Kneeling beside her, he began dribbling the elixir into her mouth. Whispering a quiet prayer as he poured it, his eyes lit up when she coughed, gasping for breath. The potion's magic deepened as she awoke, the bruises on her neck fading as Jujube and Wiz watched in relief.

"Jujube?" Coughing as her eyes fluttered open, Morrowyn's last memory was the sound of Mixer's rage and the stink of his breath in her face. She could still feel his weight pinning her against the bed.

"Drink Mor-o-win. You will live," whispered Jujube, his affection obvious.

Elated that the potion was working, in the back of his mind the goblin was aware that they had to get moving before the ogres returned. Leaving the girl to sleep off her ordeal and let the healing potion take full effect, he and Wiz returned to conjuring the Moongate. For hours they worked, trying different combinations of ingredients, different intonation and volumes of incantation, but the fizzling puff of smoke was always the end result. It was almost morning when exhaustion caught them, the wizard asleep on the floor and Jujube's head planted on the shaman's table.

* * *

Jujube wondered how Mixer could still be alive. The potion-maker was yelling at him from inside his cell, banging a tray against the bars. The banging was deafening and Jujube could not make out what he was saying. Concentrating as hard as he could, the goblin turned his head from side to side to see if maybe one of his ears wasn't working. Back and forth, back and forth, faster and faster, until without warning the cellblock dissolved into a cloud of haze.

"Goblin! Open the gate!" roared an ogre's voice, banging on the heavy portcullis with his club, furious with the delay. Turning to his two companions, the warrior motioned for them to step up and help. "The Chieftain demands the girl today!"

"Wha?" Rubbing his eyes and wiping the drool from his face, Jujube looked around and realized it was late morning. A chill ran down his spine when he understood what was happening.

"Open the gate, goblin! I've come for the girl!"

Wiz and Morrowyn had startled awake, terrified by the racket. Watching Jujube rushing about the room, grabbing assorted supplies and stuffing them into pouches, Morrowyn had no idea what was going on but the look on his face was one of pure unadulterated fear.

"No, no, no, no!" Panicking before running down the hallway towards his room, Wiz was too tired for thinking and needed some time to gather his thoughts.

"The ogre is coming for you, Mor-o-win!" His heart racing as he tried to figure out a plan, for once Jujube was thankful he had locked the portcullis but under the pressure of the brute strength of the ogres, it would not protect them for long.

"Grab supplies and get ready to leave! This spell will work or we will all die!" Shouting as he rushed around the room grabbing anything he thought might be useful and shoving it into his sacks, Jujube left the rest for the girl and began working on the gate spell. The continued pounding of the ogres was making it difficult to concentrate.

"Jujube, what happened to Mixer?" Trying to make sense of what was happening, the goblin's panic energized her and as she hopped out of bed, Morrowyn tried to organize what he had already packed.

"Par ipsu ori noom," chanted Jujube, the desperation in his voice obvious as he notched another failed attempt. "Mixer is dead! Just hurry!"

"Goblin! Open the gate now!" Roaring as their rage mounted, the ogres had been joined by several more who had brought a huge trunk to use as a battering ram.

"Jujube, I don't want to die," cried Morrowyn, hearing the iron bars groaning as the ogres began smashing them with the heavy ram.

"Find Wiz!" Giving the skeleton an order, Jujube frowned when he saw the elf girl frozen with fear.

"No time! No time to be afraid! We need supplies! Blankets! Hurry!"

"Yes! Yes! Sorry!" Jujube's tone and volume did its job, breaking fear's hold on her mind. Grabbing a sack from the corner of the room Morrowyn filled it with blankets and other items she thought might be important.

"Par ipsu ori noom!"

"Mixer's recipe book! We need that!" Rushing off towards the potion-maker's cell, pleased that she could be useful, Morrowyn forgot that the path to the cellblock would take her right past the portcullis now teeming with ogres.

"Mor-o-win! Come back!" Putting down the spell book, Jujube rushed out of the chamber after her.

"Wiz in trouble! Help! Jujube!" Pushing back against the Mixer zombie outside Morrowyn's cell, Wiz used his staff to block the undead creature from getting close, but was running out of strength.

Morrowyn was so focused on acquiring the recipe book that she had blocked out all other distractions. A loud crash startled her out of her hunt as she darted past the cave entrance and looking up, for a second she locked eyes with an ogre larger than the rest. Standing in front of the gate, he was shaking it loose with all his might. Her eyes widening, she picked up her pace and ran towards the cellblock.

"The elf girl is free!" roared Bigglum, furious with their inability to break through the gate. Smashing at it with renewed rage, his eyes blazed imagining what he would do to everyone inside the cave when he got past the iron bars.

"Hold on Wiz! Jujube is coming!" Rushing past the wizard into Mixer's cell, Morrowyn saw the skeleton arrive to help the wizard and she could hear Jujube's flapping feet from down the hall. Ignoring the chaos outside the door, she focused on finding the recipe book buried in the mess of ingredients and containers.

＊　＊　＊

"Par ipsu ori noom!" Waving his hands in panicked agitation, the fear on the goblin's face was becoming more obvious every time he tried the spell and failed.

"Jujube, please! You must do it slower!" Even having no real practical experience with magic, Morrowyn knew right away the spell would not work for anyone with these quick movements.

A thunderous crash of iron and rocks echoed into the chamber from down the hall followed by a momentary silence. The sound of heavy footsteps approaching the shaman's room caused the hair on Jujube's neck to stand straight up.

"Kill them all!" roared a deep voice a second later.

"Par ipsu ori noom," chanted Jujube, taking a deep breath and moving his hands at the pace he remembered from many years ago. This would be his last chance before death, and he stared at Morrowyn to keep his focus. Images of times spent with her flashed across his memory, a warm feeling welling up from the pit of his stomach, all the fear and frustration transforming into a vibration that rang in his ears. The heavy stomping getting closer pushed his panic to near overwhelming proportions but with herculean willpower the goblin blocked it out. The crackling of the Moongate was his reward. The gate shimmered like a blue gem just above the floor.

"Hurry Mor-o-win! Jump into the gate!"

The Moongate had formed in front of her, reflecting in her eyes, now wide with amazement. Ordering the skeleton to protect and follow them, Jujube pushed the other two into the portal first. Taking a final nostalgic look around the room he had cleaned for so long, the goblin gasped when he saw the energy draining staff lying on the floor near the doorway. Rushing to grab it, Jujube looked up just as an ogre barged into the room.

Seeing the blue portal as he rounded the corner, Bigglum's eyes fell on the goblin near his feet holding a bag full of the shaman's spell books in one hand and the magic staff in the other.

"Nasty goblin thief!" Smashing his club against the floor in rage, Bigglum swung his club and connected with the apprentice's shoulder before he could make another move, knocking him across the room towards the portal.

"Uhhh!" Holding onto the staff and the bag of goodies as he went tumbling across the floor, the blow knocked the wind out of him. Dazed and disoriented, Jujube raised his head just in time to see Bigglum rushing toward him, club raised to crush him where he lay. The rest of the warriors were pouring into the chamber behind their chieftain, looking for the prisoners.

With no time to catch his breath, Jujube stumbled backwards away from the chieftain and avoided the club whistling over his head. Falling through the portal just as it began closing, the roaring voices of the ogres quieted as he landed in the snow.

✳ ✳ ✳

"Jujube made it work!" shouted Wiz, hugging Morrowyn as the goblin dropped to the ground in front of them.

"You did it, Jujube! You did it!" said Morrowyn in disbelief, helping him to his feet.

"Look out!" Crashing backwards into the wizard, Jujube knocked them all out of the way. As he looked back at the closing portal he saw an ogre hurl his club, the heavy wooden weapon shooting over their heads. Rolling over to make sure everyone was still in one piece, he could not believe what had just happened. *I cast a Moongate spell! I did it! We just escaped the ogres!*

Surveying their surroundings, Jujube could see that they were higher up in the mountains than the ogre village. The wind was brisk and cold, snow capping the peaks as far as the eye could see.

"Where are we?" Searching the skyline with the hopes of finding some landmarks that would tell her they were in elf territory, Morrowyn saw nothing familiar. Taking a deep breath of the crisp air she examined the skeleton standing next to her holding onto two large sacks.

"Ha ha hoo hoo!!!" Rolling in the snow not far from the others, Wiz clapped his hands, grinning from ear to ear. The wizard had long since given up any hope of seeing the outside world again.

"I think we are high up in the Snowy Owl Mountains! Let's get some blankets and get covered up. It's cold!" Grabbing one of the large sacks from the skeleton, Jujube pilfered through it and handed each of them a thick piece of cloth.

"Why did you bring us here?" asked Morrowyn, not worrying about the cold just yet.

"The ogres will look for us. We should not celebrate too much until we are far away. This was the safest place I could remember. Even the shaman would not think to search for us here."

"I can't believe this! Thank you for saving us Jujube! Which way do we go now?"

"We have to go that way!" Pointing even higher, the mountainside was not steep and Jujube hoped that they could all manage the trek. "There is no going back, so we must go forward!"

"Jujube, I would like to go home," said Morrowyn, wrapping the blanket around her when she saw the steam rising from her mouth.

"Home now is with my goblin tribe!" announced Jujube, shocked by his own words. "They should not be too far from here." For so many years he had stared out the portcullis bars each morning, imagining what he would do if he returned to his people. The reality of returning both excited and scared him. *Will they even remember who I am?*

"Will they hurt us?" Relieved to be away from the ogres, Morrowyn was still trapped. "I've heard that goblins and elves don't like each other in the real world."

"We will protect you, Mor-o-win!" promised Jujube, pointing at Wiz and the skeleton. "Together, we will have lots to offer the chieftain and they will welcome us into the tribe!" Wrapping a black blanket around his shoulders and over his head, he had no idea if they were going to get a friendly welcome or not, but knew they would freeze to death if they didn't get moving. There was no other option for them, so with the energy staff in one hand Jujube jumped up on a boulder facing his little band of fugitives.

"Follow me to a new beginning!" he proclaimed, waving the staff and eager to begin this part of their adventure. Jumping down he started off with Wiz marching close behind him.

"Are you coming or not?" Shouting at Morrowyn over his shoulder, the wizard worried about the ogres and did not want to lose any time in case they came looking for them.

"I'm coming! Wait up!" Watching Jujube lead with the wizard and skeleton in tow, she was left with no choice but to follow and hope for the best.

* * *

"I am so tired!" said Morrowyn, catching up when they stopped to take a break from picking their way down the scree-covered side of the mountain. Dragging her feet the last few hours, she had been busy as she followed Jujube down the mountainside.

"How much farther?" Looking back in the direction they had come from, it was impressive to see how far they had worked their way down through the narrow crevasses, but she had lost track of the number of days they had been hiking and all she wished for now was to be somewhere warm.

"Soon! Soon!" Giggling as he imitated the goblin's words, this game was amusing Wiz without end as they hiked through the mountain passes.

"I don't even have to speak anymore!" laughed Jujube, tired of trying to convince him to stop the imitation game. Doling out a handful of berries to each of them, he hoped the mouthful of food would provide enough energy to keep going for a few more hours. Not wanting to admit anything to his traveling companions, Jujube no longer knew for sure if they were even on the right mountain.

Shoveling the berries into her mouth, she took a swig from one of the healing potions to chase the dried fruit down. The liquid left her feeling invigorated. As she hiked, Morrowyn kept her eyes open for the special plants that she had read about in the recipe book, and by mixing those she found with some of the ingredients taken from Mixer's cell, she had been able to make each of them a healing potion.

"Good girl!" said Jujube, seeing her eyes light up after drinking the elixir. They had precious little food with them and game at this elevation was scarce. Without Morrowyn's potions they would already have died, the liquid's magical energies keeping their energy and spirits high. Taking a swig, he had already quaffed half of his share and it was worrying him.

"One more step and my arrows will pin you and your friends to the trees!" announced a figure speaking the Shard tongue, interrupting their repast. Stepping out in front of them, bow drawn and pointing at Morrowyn's heart, the figure oozed strength and confidence. Growling at the intruders, a white giant cougar walked out from behind the boulders to stand at her side.

"Snow?" gasped Morrowyn, regretting her voice as soon as it left her mouth. This cat was not Snow and these were not her friends. Her heart sank a little, even if she was a little relieved that someone had found them.

"Dark One! Forgive me!" said the goblin huntress, bowing her head while being careful not to look into his eyes. It struck her as odd to see a Dark One out here in the woods, but she was not about to question a necromancer. Seeing this dark-robed goblin commanding a skeleton and waving a magical staff, it was natural for her to assume he was powerful. "Master, my name is Kitt. I am yours to command!"

Taking the time to collect his thoughts before he spoke, Jujube could see that this huntress was not from his tribe. With little food and nowhere to go, he had no other choice. It seemed that risking their lives was becoming a habit. "Take me to your chieftain! The Dark One commands it." *What is a Dark One? Why is she calling me that? It must be this blanket!*

"What is happening?" Relieved when the goblin lowered her bow, Morrowyn was studying her in great detail. They were about the same age and physical size, but this girl appeared to be exploring the mountainside alone without any worry. Big cat aside, confronting a group of strangers outnumbering her four to one was a huge risk.

"Silence! No talking!" hissed Jujube, turning his head to wink at Morrowyn. Pointing the energy staff, he zapped her to show the huntress that he was in charge of his prisoners.

"Hee hee!" giggled Wiz, seeing a new game to play. When Jujube pointed the staff at him and shook his head, the wizard stifled any further laughing.

*   *   *

"The prophecy! Brothers, the prophecy is coming true!" Watching from the shadows as the huntress led the strange group into the village, Tana made the decision to act. The Guild Master had received secret instructions from Kar not long ago. The God of Thieves had foreseen this moment. "We must protect the Dark One. There can be no mistakes!"

Escorting the Dark One with two prisoners and a skeleton into their camp, Kitt was aware that everyone had stopped to watch her take them to the chieftain's massive hut. Proud of being the one to find them, she puffed out her chest, ignoring the staring eyes of the crowd.

"I will kill the shaman. You must remove all of his apprentices!" Handing each of the assassins a dart tipped with poison, Falani gave them his final instructions. "One shot, one death. The gods demand it." Signaling the assassins to fan out among the assembled crowd, the Guild Leader pointed them towards the large central hut surrounded by totems.

"Hurry!" hissed Tana. "The high shaman is with the chieftain. He will not accept the Dark One and the shaman and his apprentices will rally behind him to provide their support."

"No worries, brother. The Dark One will not lose. The high shaman will face him alone!" Watching the drama playing out in front of the chieftain's hut, Falani's eyes followed the assassins positioning themselves to engage the unsuspecting shaman apprentices.

"A Dark One! A Dark One is here!" Shouts of amazement rose from the crowd as all eyes focused on the newcomers.

"Jujube! What is happening?" Staring in amazement at the goblins surrounding them and following the gaze of the crowd, Morrowyn focused on the guards at the front of the main hut. Pulling back the tent flaps, they revealed a large warrior accompanying an older goblin dressed in patched leather and adorned with many bone necklaces. The older goblin wore a strange looking skullcap covering half his head.

"That is the chieftain and the high shaman!" Remembering most of the protocol but unsure how to handle it, he signaled her to be quiet. "I must challenge the high shaman so we can remain with this tribe!" Ordering the skeleton to step forward, he gripped his energy draining staff with whitening knuckles and readied himself for combat.

"Jujube, I thought these were your people!" When they saw her talking and moving around, two of the guards made threatening gestures. Morrowyn retreated to her spot and waited.

"Who are you? Why are you here?" Unimpressed by the short goblin with a human and elf girl as prisoners, the chieftain eyed the skeleton but was unable to gauge its strength.

"I have journeyed many miles. I have traveled over mountains and crossed many rivers. I have come to this village to challenge for a place in this tribe!" Stepping forward with the skeleton at his side, Jujube waited for the high shaman's inevitable hostile response.

"You do not look like a Dark One to me!" Grabbing his staff and stepping forward, the shaman hissed like a stepped on snake. Searching the crowd, he wondered why none of his apprentices were rushing to join him.

"Mighty Chieftain!" shouted a tall warrior, breathless from pushing through the crowd. Infuriated by the warrior's interruption, the high shaman nevertheless allowed it, wanting to give his followers time to arrive.

"Speak warrior!" granted the chieftain.

"The shaman and apprentices are all dead! They have been poisoned!"

"You did this!" Pointing a crooked finger at Jujube, the high shaman's eyes were wild with rage.

Before he had the chance to attack, Jujube pointed the magic draining staff and started the process of collecting the high shaman's magical energy. Just like he did with Mixer what seemed like such a long time ago, he made sure that the process was slow and painful. Catching him off guard and with no backup, a surprise attack was their only hope. It might be called cheating by some observers but for some reason none of the shamans remained alive to challenge him. He had no idea what had happened to them, but he felt substantial relief knowing that there would only be one adversary to battle today.

"I demand a place in the tribe as the chieftain's new high shaman!" shouted Jujube, staring the chieftain in the eye as the magic staff crackled with energy.

"Aaaargh!" Writhing in agony from the full drain of the staff tearing at his every nerve, the high shaman paid a high price for underestimating Jujube's cunning. Not expecting this powerful an attack from a dishevelled goblin wrapped in a blanket, he had no opportunity to respond. As his energy drained away and he slumped to the ground, the skeleton began its relentless pounding and clawing.

"Dark One!" shouted the chieftain, stepping forward to stand beside the high shaman, crushed to his knees by Jujube's attack. "We shall respect your power. All will welcome you into our tribe!" The chieftain's heavy double-sided axe provided an abrupt end to the challenge, the former high shaman's head bouncing on the ground with a hollow thud.

There had been rumors amongst the tribes of the Dark Ones' viciousness. Today this tribe had all bore witness that the rumors were true.

"Now we are home!" Relaxing on a pile of furs, reflecting on what he had just accomplished, Jujube marveled at the day's successes. Defeating the high shaman meant that he took possession of his former adversary's hut and belongings, and once the rest of the tribe had left them alone he was able to stop all pretence and be himself again.

The hut's front area was for guests to sit in a circle and discuss important issues with the high shaman. Many furs covered the floor and leaning against the walls were carvings of various gods. Beautiful works by skilled craftsmen hung at random intervals and in between, the decorated canvas walls showed scenes of goblins living in harmony with nature.

"It is beautiful in here!" said Morrowyn, astonished to see so much artwork. Growing up in the world of elves, she would never have guessed that goblins were so talented. Remembering the lessons telling her that they were savage creatures with no religion or culture and marveling at the detail in these paintings, Jujube's statement did not register in her consciousness.

"They are preparing a feast for us!" said Jujube, peering through a crack in the wall. Sitting back on the furs, he shook his head in awe at how the gods seemed to be favoring them. He had been hopeful to find his old tribe and maybe convince that high shaman to let him return as an apprentice. It was going to take some time to gain a full understanding of what had just transpired. *Someone was helping us and killed the shaman and the apprentices, but I don't know anyone here. I don't know anyone anywhere!*

"High shaman!" said Wiz, bowing down and interrupting Jujube's quiet brooding. "I think the feast is for you, not us. I hope you will remember us tonight!"

"This is home?" As his words sunk in, Morrowyn wasn't sure how to react. Jujube had helped her escape and she was grateful for his friendship. As they had traveled across the mountains she recognized her true friends and saw how Mixer's influence had come close to poisoning her relationship with them. It was almost a fatal lesson. Sitting across from him now, Morrowyn had to accept that she had no way of leaving goblin territory without them catching and killing her. Pinestone and her parents were in fact no closer than before, but at least there were no shackles on her leg and no immediate threat of death looming over her shoulder.

"Yes, my young shaman apprentice! This will now be our home!" Grinning as he placed one of the high shaman's many headdresses on his head, Jujube then took a necklace made of many bones and draped it around her neck. "I am going to need your help, Mor-o-win. A High Shaman has a lot of responsibility within the community."

As Jujube kissed her forehead to welcome her as his apprentice, the warmth Morrowyn experienced made her feel safe amongst friends. *Perhaps this won't be so bad after all.*

XXI

THE ROAD TO SHADOW

"Gaffer, what happened to you? Jaeyn said you left camp with no explanation?" Standing alone with the human on the shore, Delorion had only met him once before and thought he was harmless. The search for Llythwain had been called off for the night and the crowd had returned to their respective cabins to rest. However, the old man was acting strange and seemed pre-occupied.

"I needed some time to cool off. Jaeyn upset me." Staring off into the darkness and mist, his gaze remained focused in the direction of the island. Needing to come up with an answer right away, the doppelganger was caught off guard. Targeting the Ranger became the easy excuse.

"Please Gaffer, tell me what happened." As the Ranger in charge of the camp, Delorion felt the conduct of every Ranger under his command was serious business. Jaeyn was the youngest scout and this would not be the first time his mouth was discovered working faster than his brain.

"He insulted me, telling me I did a poor job of fixing the dock! I don't think he likes humans."

"Now, now Gaffer. Perhaps you shouldn't take him so literally, although I do wish he would take more of my advice. Even tonight, he was adamant that he had to check the island for Llythwain even though I advised him to wait until morning."

"What? Why would he do that?" Thinking that the search was over, the creature was stunned. Having Jaeyn snooping around on the island was not expected. *Why can't these elves just leave it alone? The child drowned, his story is over. Focus on the rest of your children!* Trying to pierce the lake's misty cover, the creature began formulating a plan.

"He left to check out the island a while ago. Who knows, we may be searching for him in the morning as well."

Organizing its thoughts, the doppelganger saw motion in the fog. *Here he comes. It's time to leave.* Taking a few small steps away from Delorion, it prepared to make a move.

"Jaeyn! Over here! Did you find him? Look Gaffer, it appears like there are two people with him!"

"I will run to tell the others!" shouted Gaffer, rushing away from the dock toward the cabins. Looking back to get a glimpse of who was in the canoe, the doppelganger already knew it needed to get away as fast as possible. *I won't make this mistake again! Next time no one lives!*

"Jaeyn? What is going on? Gaffer is that you...? But? Gaffer was just here talking with me!" Helping Llythwain out of the canoe, he was glad the boy was okay but he couldn't stop staring at the Gaffer slumped in the front of the canoe. Half-naked and gaunt, the old man was covered in scratches and bruises. Looking up the hill towards the camps, Delorian saw the other Gaffer running into the trees.

"Delorion! That is not Gaffer!" Jumping out of the canoe, Jaeyn grabbed his leader by the shoulder. "Sound the alarm! The old man that was with you is some kind of shape shifting lizard creature! We must capture it!"

Word of Llythwain's recovery spread through the camp like wildfire. Cabin doors flung open as everyone ran to see what was going on, making it difficult for the Rangers to get organized. Jaeyn's voice was drowned out beneath the waves of commotion surrounding Llythwain's safe return.

"Everyone! Please get back inside your cabins!" Knowing that there was a murderous lizard creature on the loose, panic ensued and the Rangers had their hands full managing the crowd.

"Sound the alarm! Everyone is to stay locked in their cabins until further notice!" Taking control when he saw the frustration on Jaeyn's face, Delorion's voice carried more weight. The camp was buzzing and while most followed the instructions to get back to their bunks, several of the older children continued hanging around to see if they could help. The Rangers following the creature's path stooped to inspect its tracks and Delorian joined them. "Rangers, to me! Get the children back to their cabins!"

* * *

"Llythwain! What happened to you? What are the Rangers panicking about?" As soon as the elf closed the door to the cabin behind him, Ran began grilling him. "Why do we have to lock our cabins and stay inside? What happened to Gaffer?" Having spent the last twelve hours mourning the loss of his friend, throwing his arm over his shoulder and welcoming him back seemed to help his brain accept that his friend was alright.

"That creature tried to kill me, Ran!" Pausing to think through what he could say in light of his promise to Xamiss, Llythwain had every intention of staying true to his word. "It took Gaffer prisoner and stole his identity!"

"Gaffer?! Wait! What?" gasped Ran, his mouth hanging open in disbelief. "I was talking to him not that long ago! So the half-naked man that was in the canoe with you is the real one? And the one I was talking to was a creature who had copied him?"

"Yup! Jaeyn found him tied up on the island!" Flapping his hands as he basked in the attention, the excitement of the night was still pumping through Llythwain's veins and he could feel his heart thumping. "And the creature is still loose!"

"Look there's Jaeyn!" Peering from the window to see if he could figure out what was going on, Ran could not believe what was happening. "He is with the other scouts and they are pointing into the forest! They are going to chase that thing and try and catch it!"

"I saw the fake Gaffer run off," said Llythwain, joining Ran at the window. "They must have found its trail."

"So what happened when you fell in the water?" Watching the Rangers disappear into the forest following the creature's tracks, Ran was unhappy with their forced captivity. He took solace in the fact that at least he was able to learn more details about what had happened to his friend.

"I didn't fall in! The creature pulled me in."

"What does it look like?" Realizing all of a sudden that he could have been the one that the creature pulled under, Ran thought about how long he could hold his breath. *I wonder if I could have survived.*

"It was hard to see in the water. It looked kind of like a half human and half lizard with no tail and bulging eyes."

"Was it trying to keep you under the water? Was it much stronger than you?"

"Yes it was holding my leg and I was struggling to get away, so I kicked it. It let go but chased me deeper."

"No way! You were lucky to get away!"

"It grabbed me again and started pulling me back up. I swam as hard as I could, dragging it down with me. When I was too deep for it, it let go of me. Then I pretended I drowned. When I stopped swimming it left me alone. I got back up to the surface and didn't see the canoe so I swam to the island and was so tired that

I passed out right on the shore." Unwilling to tell the truth, Llythwain hoped his story sounded real. *I must keep my promise to Xamiss.*

"Jaeyn found me after he found Gaffer and brought me back to camp." Thinking back to what happened with Xamiss and what he had learned about his relationship with Killian, Llythwain's mind was racing. Turning away from Ran to peer out the window, his thoughts strayed to the squirrel in the forest the day the ogres took Morrowyn. *Things are starting to make sense now.*

"That is amazing, Llythwain! You sure fooled that thing! Way to go!"

That's why the squirrel died! I drained its life! Distracted by his inner dialog, he was no longer acknowledging Ran's presence and just stared out the window. Noticing his arm where Killian had struck him, the skin looked gray and wrinkled. It was horrifying, but fascinating in equal measure. *Xamiss was right. I am becoming a shade and will need spiritual energy, just like the other undead! I am becoming an undead shade!*

"Blasted elves!" growled the doppelganger in Gaffer's voice, watching the Rangers examine its tracks and knowing they would soon be hot on its heels. "This old man's skin will not work for me anymore." Weighed down by its disguise, it was having trouble running fast and with the chase started, a change in strategy was necessary if it was going to avoid capture.

"Say goodbye Gaffer!" it hissed, tearing away the human-looking skin, first on its hands and arms and then with its talons free, tearing apart its face. Green ooze ran in globs, puddling on the ground while the creature ripped off the rest of the meat, revealing the shiny green scales underneath. Dropping the stinking mass of flesh to the ground, it stepped away and shook itself, enjoying the feel of the night breeze against its real skin.

"What a waste!" Upset at having spent so much time morphing into the human only to peel it away in a matter of hours, keeping the human disguise was not an option. In its natural form the scales would reflect the foliage, camouflaging it with ease. "Let's see if you can find me now!"

Sniffing the air, it realized that its pursuers were closer than anticipated. Inching under the thick brush, it blended into the foliage at once. Circling towards the water and covering its tracks, the creature grabbed a low hanging branch, hoisting itself into the canopy where it could observe the Ranger team chasing it through the forest.

Motioning to the other scouts to wait, Jaeyn stopped when he found the remains of the creature's human form. Wisps of steam rose from the pile of meat, indicating that the creature could not be far away.

"Disgusting! The smell is incredible!" gasped Delorion, staring at the gore. "I think I might have stepped in some of it too." Drops of green blood had splashed across the ground amongst the fallen leaves and lifting his boot to inspect it, he began wiping the heel in some tall grass.

"It looks like that thing crossed the river!" Following the trail to just below where the doppelganger had hoisted itself up into the trees, one of the scouts shouted his report up the bank to his leader.

"Jaeyn, take the Rangers and check the other side of the river!" Still wiping his shoes clean of the creature's body fluid, Delorion decided to wait for them there.

Surprised to see the Rangers falling for its simple ruse, the creature took the opportunity to move closer to Delorion. *The hunted becomes the hunter in the blink of an eye.* Flexing its talons, it prepared to strike.

"Keep searching for the trail while I circle back to get a canoe!"

"As you wish, Delorion. Let's go, Rangers! Move!" Wading into the water first, Jaeyn didn't want to waste any time. Still angry about how the creature had tricked him, he was impatient to find it and was sure it hadn't gotten too far away yet.

Positioning itself as close as possible to the Ranger, the creature tensed as it prepared to attack. The elf was still distracted by the mess on his boot. *I never would have thought that the old man still had a purpose.* Waiting until the other Rangers had crossed the river, the doppelganger moved without a sound, dropping on top of the elf before he had a chance to defend himself. In a matter of moments the creature had torn out his throat and the Ranger lay choking and dying on the ground.

Dragging the limp body into the water, being careful not to alert the other elves, the creature knew its time as this latest particular elf would be short-lived. It had decided on bigger aspirations in life than being a humble Ranger.

Showing only the barest sliver of a moon, the dark night sky allowed Llythwain to see the stars hanging cold and silent above Mystic Lake. It had been a week since the incident with the creature and the camp was still in an uproar. The Rangers had lost its track across the river and now Delorion was missing. That situation was terrible, but what was more upsetting to Llythwain was the news that his sister had been killed by the ogres. His father had arrived earlier that day, taking him out on the lake for several hours to talk about what had happened after he and his mother had left Pinestone that day. Instead of coming to the camp, for some reason his mother had returned to Thantos and sent his father to break the news to him alone. *Morrowyn is gone forever. The elves are at war with the goblins. My mother is living with grandmother and refuses to return to Pinestone. Our family will never be the same again.*

Llythwain had no more tears left to cry. Staring out across the lake, he searched for solace in the vast emptiness above his head. Having informed him that afternoon that they were leaving for Thantos the next day, his father told him that he would be returning back to the camp soon. The war with the goblins might last a long time and for now, no one was safe in any of the towns. Ran had promised to keep his bunk safe while he was away and that made Llythwain feel a little better, but he needed to talk with someone else to calm his agitated mind.

"Killian, are you out there?" Remembering everything that had happened now, he had so many questions for the shade. The darkening patch of skin on his arm was now almost all the way around. The metamorphosis into a shade was happening, and he wondered if Killian knew this would happen.

Trying to meditate while sitting on his bunk earlier that evening, Llythwain had decided that the lake shore might be a better place to try his luck at contacting Killian. Slipping outside the cabin without making a sound, he knew that Ran would have a million questions and if the elves found out that he was becoming undead, there was no chance of any of them helping him with anything. Elven hatred for the undead was cultural and ingrained from birth.

"Killian, are you out there?"

"Llythwain? Are you all right? Can I help you?" Happy to have sensed Llythwain's presence, the creature under the lake could hear the boy's thoughts and felt the disappointment of his call to Killian disappearing into the sky's blackness.

"Xamiss! I have had better days, my friend. But tomorrow I am leaving for a while." Failing to reach out to Killian was frustrating, but getting a response from the creature was a welcome surprise.

"What happened, Llythwain?"

"My sister is dead. The ogres killed her, Xamiss! My mother no longer wants to come home. My father is here now and is taking me to Thantos to visit her."

"*I am sorry to hear about your sister, young elf. It will be good for you to see your mother again. Perhaps when she sees you, it will help her to heal.*"

"*I hope so, Xamiss. I miss her a lot. I should be back in about a month. My father has to rejoin the Rangers in the war with the goblins and right now it's not safe for anyone to go home. He promised to visit me as often as he could and teach me how to be a Ranger. And my cat Snow will be staying with me at camp when I get back.*" So much was changing so fast it made his head spin, but talking to Xamiss always made him feel a little better. Learning the ways of the Rangers was something he was always told would wait until he was older, but Llythwain felt he was ready and was pleased that his father had changed his mind.

"*Has Killian ever answered your call?*"

"*No, I've reached out to him several times but I never hear anything back.*"

"*Have you tried controlling the darkness again?*" Persuading Llythwain to focus on his powers instead of his conversion to undead was an important diversion. The opinion Xamiss kept to himself was that even if the boy existed as a demi-shade for years, the venom would take over at some point in the future. The positive was that Killian had somehow managed to overcome the poison's influence even after being completely consumed by it, so there was still a faint hope of survival, but Llythwain needed maturing before he could understand.

"*The darkness! Of course! What if I used it to communicate?*"

"*Try thinking about the shadow bridge and traveling on its dark roadway, Llythwain. Perhaps it knows where Killian is at any given moment.*"

"*Killian, can you hear me?*" Discovering the connection with the dark had opened his mind and gave Llythwain the ability to see through and control the darkness as if it was a looking glass. The process enthralled him and he played with the darkness every chance he got. Noticing his shadow standing on the shore beside him, he willed it to move away, wrapping it together with the other dark patches.

"Focus on the roadway, Llythwain."

"Killian, can you hear me?" Motivated to concentrate harder, the black fog thinned and Llythwain was certain he could view patches of the onyx road shimmering before him. *"I can see the road, Xamiss! He is still not answering me. Killian! Killian!"*

"Stay focused!"

"Come to the Gates of Palos!" The voice was faint, the words fading in and out from what sounded like a great distance, then nothing but silence.

"Killian? Is that you?"

Feeling weak from the effort, Llythwain sat on a boulder as the concentrated darkness dissipated and the roadway disappeared from his mind.

"I lost him Xamiss."

"You did well, young elf! You had better stop for now. The paths of communication exist only for those who can see the signs. You are close, but need practice. Promise me you will wait until I am with you before trying again."

"All right. I promise." Dragging his body back to the cabin to get some sleep before their early departure, Llythwain took his time so that no one would notice his midnight adventure.

"There may be dangers in the darkness that we do not know about! I suggest leaving the darkness alone for now. We can practice more once you come back to the camp."

"Sure thing, Xamiss." Manipulating the darkness had drained his energy and the toxins in his blood were screaming for replenishment. He would have to be careful as the venom's effects progressed.

"Goodbye Llythwain! Safe journeys!"

"Goodbye my friend! I will think of you often!"

The splash of the first bells chiming reminded everyone that the Gathering would start in one hour. Watching elves bustling about preparing for the event, Llysander and Llythwain could see the crowds dressed in their finest clothes and accessories. Examining Llythwain and himself, both attired in worn and well-traveled Ranger clothing, Llysander smiled knowing how Kalahni's mother would react when she saw them. Norin never approved of anything he did. Strolling along Thantos' inner palisade in no particular hurry, they had arrived at the capital city earlier in the day and worked their way to the inner gates of the castle, stopping to speak with many Rangers along the way offering their condolences on Morrowyn's death.

Cordoned behind the protected walls of the inner palisade and separated from the common area beyond the outer palisade, the priestesses' dwellings were separate from the general public. Controlled by armed Moonguards, unauthorized entry into the religious district was not permitted. Arriving at the front gate, Llysander and Llythwain waited for one of Norin's servants to escort them to her home.

"Where is mother?" blurted Llythwain, walking ahead of his father, excited to see her again. Following the servant towards a section of larger dwellings, he rounded a corner and saw his grandmother's home standing before him. It was the largest mansion in the compound and was an architectural marvel. His mind filled with memories as he marveled at the decorations and holy statues perching on the window ledges.

In the doorway stood his grandmother, wrapped in the formal white silken robes of the high priestess only worn at important events like the Gathering. The silk making up the outer layer of her robe was woven so fine as to be transparent, encircled by floral designs that appeared as though they were floating. Not even Llysander could deny the garment's beauty.

"High Priestess Tulaanos!" said Llysander, greeting her with a deep bow that hid his grin. Noticing her disapproving expression and the obvious dislike for him displayed by her body language as he approached, he stifled the urge to laugh in her face.

"Nima!" yelled Llythwain, excited to see his grandmother. It had been many days since he had spent any time with her, and so much had changed.

"Llythwain!" Giving them each an awkward hug, the priestess made sure her robes were not creased. "You do not need to be so formal with me, Llysander. You know you can call me Norin."

"Nima, where is my mother?"

"She is getting herself ready for the Gathering, little squirrel. Just as you both should be doing. I will have my servant bring you some wash towels. And clean clothes."

"When can I see her?" Following his grandmother up the marble stairwell to Kalahni's floor, Llythwain peered down every hallway hoping he would see his mother waiting for him.

"Your mother has taken a vow of silence. She is busy in prayer right now, and only once the Gathering is over will you be allowed to visit with her. Llythwain, the vow of silence is a sacred pact between your mother and the Gods. You must promise me that you will respect it!" More concerned with her son-in-law's reaction, Norin stared at Llysander as she spoke to her grandson.

"Of course, Nima!"

"I left you something in your room, little squirrel!" said Norin, stepping aside to let him run past.

"Thank you!" Thundering up the rest of the stairs, his mother had an entire floor devoted to her and her family and everything looked just like it was the last time Llythwain visited. Running down the hall he disappeared into his room.

Clapping her hands, Norin summoned two servants to the top of the staircase. The high priestess could hear the second bell ringing and was anxious to leave for the church.

"Bring some towels and fill the wash basins for my guests!"

"Yes high priestess!"

Leading Llysander up the rest of the stairs, Norin took him into her daughter's bedroom. She had noticed his face redden with anger when he found out about Kalahni's vow of silence and knew he wanted to react, but so far he had remained silent.

"You can stay here with Kalahni if you like," said Norin, smirking at Llysander as they stopped in front of a large chest sitting open next to the bed with Kalahni's Moonguard garments folded on top. "But with her vow, I guarantee you she will not speak a word to either of you."

"Thank you for your hospitality, High Priestess Tulaanos. I'm sure that the vow of silence will make her an excellent listener, unlike her mother!" Lifting Kalahni's bow to inspect it, he waited for the priestess to leave him alone with his thoughts.

"She will not need those things anymore, Ranger!" snapped Norin, not getting the reaction she wanted and pushing his emotions harder. "Kalahni is leaving the

Moonguard and accepting the priestesshood!" Standing back, she let her words sink into Llysander's consciousness. Wanting nothing more than to laugh at his failure as a husband, she was wise enough to know when to pull back.

"What have you done?!" shouted Llysander, infuriated with the old priestess and unable to control himself any longer. "She would never forsake her family and go back to being a priestess on her own!" Squeezing the short bow with whitening knuckles, he imagined how satisfying it would be to sink an arrow between the old woman's eyes.

"If she had stayed a priestess in the first place, Ranger… Morrowyn would still be alive!"

"You call yourself a high priestess and yet you behave like a goblin! If she had stayed a priestess, Morrowyn would never have been born!"

"I'm off to church now!" said Norin, ignoring his last words and turning her back to leave. "I reserved a spot for the both of you in the very back row. Make sure you wash yourselves well. Your strong smell will offend everyone around you."

∗　∗　∗

With the sound of the final bells signaling that the Gathering was starting, the tardy faithful rushed into churches around the city. Those that lived behind the castle walls attended the main cathedral towering above most of the other buildings. Its slender tower, topped by a shining holy symbol, was studded with the four life crystals surrounded by massive silver bells. The white prism crystal represents all colors and depicts the balance between good and evil; the green crystal represents nature and all living things; the purple crystal represents the stars and heavens that contain everything within it; and the yellow-gold crystal depicts the richness in life that allows everything else to co-exist and flourish.

The Gathering is the most important and sacred act of worship in elf life. Going to the Gathering is the only way an elf can fulfill the Commandment to keep holy the seventh day and it was the only opportunity to receive the Holy Spiritual Energies from the four life crystals.

"Over here!" said Llysander, his hands still shaking with rage, his spirit broken by Norin's cruel treatment. Leading Llythwain to the back pew, he stopped to dip his fingers in the holy water, tapping its waters against himself and his son while making the sign of the four life crystals. *This is a habit I need to break. There is nothing sacred about this place or its leaders.*

"Let us hear the word of the Goddess Shifra!" shouted high priestess Brotah, starting the sermon on time.

"I do not see mother!" whispered Llythwain, his voice carrying to all those around him as he strained his neck to see over their heads. The terse frowning from the worshippers caused him to sink back into his seat in embarrassed silence. Seeing that his father wasn't concerned by his talking he ignored the looks of those around him and lost himself in his dream world, not caring about the sermon, but his ears perked up when his grandmother's voice addressed the crowd to join her in the Rite of Penance. This was the moment when everyone was to think about his or her sins and wash them away. Llythwain could not help wondering how they would react if they knew he drained that poor squirrel of its life energies.

"I see your mother!" Poking his son to pull him from his daydreams, Llysander waved at Kalahni in hopes of drawing her attention to the back row. He was quite sure that Norin would forget to mention their presence to her.

"She smiled at me!" whispered Llythwain, staring at his mother on stage in her priestess gown.

"Everyone must join us for the prayer and hymn of the adoration of the Goddess Silverymoon!" Signaling for the congregation to kneel and pray, Inunis stood with her hands raised to the sky.

Over time the voices of the priestesses blended together as Llysander fixated on Kalahni throughout most of the remaining proceedings. Hoping to make eye contact with her, he grew sleepy as the homily droned on. Expecting to see Llythwain asleep, the boy was very focused on the sermon now that they had started with the Creed, addressing the current concerns about the war with the goblins and the Undead Curse.

"The goblins," shouted Norin, her voice reaching every ear in attendance. "The goblins are evil incarnate and they do not care that nature is withering away around us! Let us support the lords who will wipe out the goblins who threaten our very way of life!"

"Hear us, Goddess Silverymoon," the crowd chanted back to the high priestess.

"The human lands have rotted away and now our lands are threatened as well! Some of our forests are starting to show signs of decay. We must wipe out necromancy from all walks of life so that our lands can thrive once again!"

"Hear us, Goddess Silverymoon," the crowd chanted as one.

"The undead are rising up and they are killing us in our own towns. The humans have allowed their farms to disintegrate, their livestock threatening them as undead creatures," screeched the high priestess, her voice at a fever pitch. "May we strike down all undead creatures and banish them below where they will scream for eternity!"

"Hear us, Goddess Silverymoon," agreed the crowd.

Grimacing at those last words from his grandmother, Llythwain stared at her with a horrified look on his face. *I am becoming an undead shade. I don't want to scream for eternity!* Pulling on his sleeve to make sure it covered the gray skin of his arm, Llythwain hoped that no one had noticed it sticking out while he sat there.

Watching his son out of the corner of his eye, Llysander saw him shrink in fear at his grandmother's words. *What is Llythwain hiding? There is something going on with him. This bears further discussion soon, I think.*

XXII

A New Adventure

"*Come to the Gates of Palos!*" Echoing in Garrett's mind, the persistent whisper woke him from his deep sleep again. This was the third time he had heard the raspy voice since returning to Whistlewood Manor in Chatham to recuperate from their adventure in the mines. Cutting through the curtain between sleep and wakefulness and just before his eyes opened, he could see a dark onyx roadway stretching off into the distance while feeling the now familiar pull on his mind. Resisting the urge to follow, Garrett rubbed at the throbbing in his neck as he roused his lethargic legs to move. The pain of the wound was gone, but the scar was turning gray and gave him a strange sensation whenever he drew a deep breath.

Stretching as he stood, the knight reached for his linen undershirt and pants hanging next to the plate mail on the wooden armor rack. Throwing the dusty tunic over his head provoked a sneeze, a wet roar echoing down the hallways of the manor.

"Listen fellas! Garrett is awake now too!" Laughing at the racket from upstairs, Angus had been the first to awaken from their common nightmare this morning.

"Hey Garrett! Did you hear that blasted voice again too?" Watching the knight hang onto the banister and nod as he made his way down into the great hall, Ragnar shook his bearded head. "When I get to those damn gates, someone will be wishing they never met me!"

Curving upwards around the massive central fireplace, the staircase disappeared into the ornate lamps hanging from the high ceilings of the great hall. The second floor of the manor was set aside for each of the adventurers' chambers, with Davissor occupying the largest apartment. His anteroom extended around the tower hugging a cliff that overlooked the Great Sea.

Accommodating a hundred guests with ease, the great hall at Whistlewood Manor had seating for all on benches lining the dark oaken tables. The room had witnessed many important guests over the years, but this morning there were only the usual suspects.

Chuckling at the sight of his friends sitting at the largest of the oak tables with their ale tankards overflowing, Garrett always admired the ability of dwarves and gnomes to drink alcohol. The key to the human's success with the tankard was knowing his limits and letting others do more of the heavy lifting. The sun had only just cracked the horizon today and the tired mercenaries were already half-drunk. The lack of sleep added an edge to their usual jovial attitudes.

"What are you staring at, longhair?" Belching as loud as he could while stretching his arms wide, Ahira raised his mug to take another mouthful before slumping back over the table.

"It's the third time I've been woken up by that nasty voice!" said Garrett, slapping the bleary-eyed, stuporous dwarf on the back and laughing at his terseness, relieved to discover that he was not the only one having the nightmare. "You guys saved some of that ale for me right?" *This is not going to end well for any of us. There is no way we can ignore this for much longer.*

"Come to the Gates of Palos! Woooooo woo woo!" said Ragnar, imitating the raspy voice while raising his hands in the air and pretending to be a ghost. "What kind of voice is that and where in hell's dry dead forest is Palos?"

"I'll tell you who it is. It's that blasted creature in the caves that did this to us!" shouted Ahira, straightening himself with a righteous indignance born of little sleep and lots of ale. "We should have finished him when we had the chance!"

"What the hell is happening to us?" said Angus, the concerns of the others weighing down his usual ebullient personality. "Come on, let's get it all out on the table."

"The scar where I was bit is turning gray and dead!" Pulling his tunic down so the others could see his neck, Garrett leaned in so they could all get a good look.

"The scars on my arms are looking just as bad!" said Angus, surprised by the state of Garrett's neck.

"And how is it I can control the darkness, boys?" Concentrating on the shadows near the ceiling, Ragnar willed them to draw closer. "Now you see me and now you don't!" In seconds a cloud of dark fog covered him. Practising this manipulation of darkness ever since they returned from the battle at the mines, he was starting to get pretty good at it.

"Demonic!" gasped Ahira, taking another large swig.

"Amazing!" exclaimed Garrett, impressed with the swirling shadows.

"I think we were cursed by that creature!" said Angus, willing the darkness around Ragnar to dissipate so he could see his face. "Maybe we should have already told Davissor."

"We needed to wait until we were away from the elves!" Sliding his hand out of the swirling shadows to rest on Angus' shoulder, Ragnar squeezed to emphasize his point. "You saw how crazy they get with necromancy and the undead."

"And don't you just love the elves' Necromancer Proclamation!" laughed Ahira, shaking his head in disbelief. "These elves have become full of mistrust and hate. It's outrageous!"

"Preaching to wipe out all the undead is one thing I don't have a problem with," said Garrett. "But to also target human necromancers is going too far. Do they want a war with everyone?"

"Ok, but let's focus on what is important for us! We need a healer, fellas!! The elves can fight whomever they want for all I care, as long as we get fixed. It's either that or amputation." Poking at the darkening skin, Angus wondered what it would be like to be a thief with no arms.

"Listen brothers, the dwarven healers can help us!" Wiping foam from his mouth, Ahira got up to pour himself another drink. "Their rune magic has special healing powers that are in tune with both the living and the dead. Wait a minute. Did I just suggest going to the dwarves for assistance? Somebody help me, I must be drunk…"

"Are you kidding me, Ahira? I'm surprised you would even suggest that! I thought you were long done with our brethren." Ragnar was aware that the Rune Masters were quite proficient with healing magic, but would never have been the one to make that suggestion knowing Ahira's past issues.

"Yeah, I guess I was done with them! But now that we all need help, I suppose I am willing to let bygones be bygones! Besides, we just need their help. It's not like I will be buying property in Rochdale. We get in and we get out!"

"Ok, but how will we convince Davissor to let us venture to the Iron Spike?" said Ragnar. "The dwarves are at war with the orcs as we speak. The route to Rochdale will take us right past Orc Helm!"

"I think we should just tell him what is happening to us!" said Garrett, looking at the others for consensus. "There is a good chance he will have some ideas to help and to be honest, I'd be surprised if he doesn't already suspect something."

"Listen longhair, we don't even know when he's going to be back!" said Ahira. "And why do we care what he thinks anyways? We are the ones with this blasted pox!"

"Wait a minute! He is our brother and our leader!" said Angus, standing on his chair. "We can't just exclude him from our plans!"

"He is also part elf, Angus!" said Ahira, reminding them of the obvious. "Should we take the chance that when he finds out we may be turning into undead, he decides that turning us over to those priestesses is the best thing to do?"

Pondering that question and how to get the mage to agree with their plan to visit the dwarves as they sipped their ale, the Heroes agreed to hold off telling Davissor about their predicament for a little while longer. It was a risk but wouldn't hurt anything in the short term and perhaps they could get this decay-thing corrected without telling him at all.

∗　∗　∗

Exiting the elven council chambers, Davissor crossed the courtyard with their final payment tucked away in his black coat. There had been no arguing that the Rangers had needed to rescue the Heroes of Karth from the mine, and because of that the lords were adamant that a change in the terms of the original agreement was appropriate. Davissor had made his points clear but the elves were having none of it, so agreeing to a twenty five per cent reduction in their fee kept everyone on good terms. It was still a good rate of return and there would be more work in the future.

As he walked through the rows of merchants on his way out of town, a stout looking dwarf with bright orange hair and full beard walking in the opposite direction caught his attention. Kitted up in a stylish white shirt, hand-stitched green and white patterned kilt and accompanied by an entourage of bodyguards wearing chainmail and plate shoulder pads, it was an unusual sight in the Thantos market. Davissor stopped for a closer look.

"Dantor!?" *What is the ambassador from the Iron Spike doing here today? I hope he has forgotten about that incident with Ahira!*

"Huh?! Davissor!" Recognizing the mage at once, the top hat and black overcoat unmistakable, the ambassador stopped in his tracks. "Are you coming from the council meeting?" Dantor's spies had reported that the mage and his band of heroes were on a mission for the elven lords and had returned a short time ago.

"Why, yes I am old friend!" Raising an eyebrow at the dwarf, Davissor marveled at the efficiency of the dwarven spy network. "How have you been? How are things in your corner of the world?"

"I'm doing just fine, good sir. But I can say with great confidence that the Iron Spike has seen better days!"

"What is going on, Dantor?" Glancing over at the bodyguards, Davissor examined all the people within earshot. "Perhaps we should discuss this over a drink? I could use a little something to calm my nerves after that council meeting."

"You know me too well, Davissor!" Strolling away from the merchant area, Dantor and the mage settled on a small tavern away from the crowds. Having traveled to Thantos for the purpose of finding Davissor, this chance meeting couldn't have worked out any better. Besides, he was never one to pass on a drink. Interacting with the Heroes of Karth meant interacting with Ahira, but he was willing to swallow his pride for the good of the clan. "Guards, please give us some space.

Leave me to talk business with Davissor. Feel free to enjoy yourselves. We are among friends in Thantos!"

"You heard him, boys!" The guard captain motioned for the rest of them to relax and join him for some ale. They took a table not far from Dantor and Davissor, keeping their eyes on the crowd.

"Davissor, is it true that you discovered crystals being darkened in the Mines of Taas?"

"Unfortunately Dantor, I can confirm that rumor. With my own eyes I observed a goblin necromancer blackening a group of crystals, soaking up their life energy while his undead gobbled up any stray morsels that escaped him. I believe this to be the cause of the Curse of the Undead. In fact, I am certain of it. The elves now believe they have discovered a way to stop the curse from spreading further."

"Blasted goblins!" said Dantor, slapping his hand on the table. "Do they not care that this curse rots away all our lands?"

"We defeated them at the mines, but it was a hollow victory. There is a high likelihood that many goblin tribes will now rise up together because of that defeat. The elves are facing a full-scale war. It wasn't what they were looking for and they gave me a light roasting in the Council Chambers today."

"Two large tankards!!" shouted Dantor, catching the bartender's attention.

"Our Rune Masters want to meet with the elves. They believe the curse's effects can be reversed and not just stopped."

"I hope they're right!" said Davissor, knowing that the dwarven healers had the best chance of succeeding. Renowned for their skills at metallurgy and geology, next to the Moonguards the Rune Masters knew the most about the four life crystals.

"Why wouldn't they be right?" Snarling at Davissor's doubt, Dantor took a mental step back to calm his pride. *I wonder if hiring this group again is the right choice.* Taking a big mouthful of ale, he ignored the mage's quizzical stare.

"All right Dantor, tell me the real purpose of your visit. Are you in need of our services again?" The mage had been in this business for many years and knew his clients well. There could only be one reason why the dwarf was here and so willing to have a drink. This was a calculated risk, but Davissor could read the dwarf's body language and thought he already knew the answer to his question.

"There you go!" Slapping his now empty tankard down on the table, Dantor signaled to the bartender for a refill. "You know me too well, Davissor!"

"Listen my friend, I also know you don't like asking for help, so your troubles must be reaching extreme levels," said Davissor, lowering his voice to keep their conversation civil. Several of the tavern's other patrons had glanced over at the noise of the dwarf's mug hitting the table.

"You don't know the half of it, Davissor. The very world has shifted underneath our feet!"

"Is it the orcs?"

"Those blasted orcs! All the outer clans have either fled to Rochdale or suffered capture by the orcs and made into slaves! The damn orcs breed like ants so that even when we think we have crushed them, it seems like there are more than before."

So the rumors are true. Now that the elves face all out war with the goblins they will not be able to offer much aid to the dwarves. That is why Dantor is looking for us.

"Orcs are the most vile and wicked of the Shard races, enslaving any that get in their path. We would all like to see them eradicated, Dantor. How are you progressing on your tunnels to the human lands?"

"We are more than halfway there!"

"Excellent! So it is moving faster than planned."

"Not quite. We were progressing well until this latest setback. Now we find ourselves faced with swarms of kobold miners digging and searching for our tunnels."

"Kobolds!" said Davissor, remembering his dealings with the ancient humanoid dragon creatures. "So they have allied themselves with The Shard! It seems the balance of power has shifted in your region! You can't hold off the orcs on the surface and the kobolds from below at the same time!"

"Now you know why I am here. We need help with both the tunnels and the orcs. We need the tunnel to Barsoom completed within four years."

"Oh ho! So you need our services again. I knew this day would come. I just had to be patient!"

"Wipe that damn grin off your face, mage! This is hard enough as it is."

"Tell me you request the pleasure of the services of the Heroes of Karth, or else we may not be able to help you!" said Davissor, providing the dwarf with a gentle mocking. "I would like to hear you say the words. And be sure to say please!" *Ahira will be so excited to hear this!*

"Baah! You stinkin' elf!" Looking up at him in hopes of seeing a sign that this wasn't necessary, Dantor saw nothing on the mage's face indicating this was a joke. "Yes we need your damn services! Please Davissor! Don't make me grovel!"

"That's the spirit!" laughed the mage, breaking the tension and drawing a hearty laugh from the dwarf.

"The usual price?" Expecting a hike in the fee, Dantor was ready to pay whatever was necessary.

"The usual amount will be fine, my friend. I understand that you are in a, shall we say, delicate predicament and are desperate to repair our relationship." Hoping that Dantor appreciated the empathy in his voice, Davissor let him off easy. "Half now and half upon conclusion of our business?"

"Deal!" proclaimed Dantor, offering his hand.

"The Heroes of Karth are now at your service!" said Davissor, shaking the offered hand with gusto.

Pulling out a sack full of gold and gems, Dantor slid it across the table to the mage, who wasted no time squirreling it away inside his coat.

"I knew you wouldn't pass up this adventure!" Relaxing in his chair, Dantor allowed himself a satisfied smile.

"We will meet you in Rochdale. Safe travels!" Shaking Dantor's hand again, he left the tavern in a hurry in case anyone unsavory saw him pocketing the sack of gold and gems. Slipping through the crowds in the merchant area, he made his way back to the quiet spot in the courtyard. Without an audience, he cast his Moongate and disappeared.

* * *

"Hey, hey boys! He is finally back!" shouted Angus, spotting the Moongate shimmering in the corner. As Davissor was stepping through into Whistlewood's great hall, Angus ran to get him a tankard of ale.

"Good day Mr. Fergusson. Nice of you to join us!" Standing to stretch his legs, Ragnar was glad to see the mage appear. The mercenaries had all placed bets on what amount the elves would agree to as their final payment. Being an eternal pessimist, Ragnar had wagered it would be the lowest amount.

Returning with the full tankard, Angus moved his red coat off the chair next to him and invited the mage to sit.

"Brothers!" shouted Davissor, striding up to the table and slapping Ahira on the back.

"You finally made it!" said Ahira, Davissor's exuberant greeting causing him to slop some of his drink on the table. "What kept you this time?"

"Did you get our payment?" Anxious to see the bag of loot and find out which of them had won the wager, Angus was all eyes as Davissor pulled out the chair and leaned on the table.

"In fact, I did get our payment. And it seems that I have good news and bad news from Thantos." Davissor's eyes sparkled as he built the requisite amount of anticipation for the announcement. "It's up to you. Which do you want to hear first?" Knowing Ragnar and Ahira would ignore that question, he was tingling with anticipation at the thought of revealing this new adventure to his surly dwarven colleagues.

"The bad news!" Seeing the mage's mischievous smile, Garrett recognized right away that he was playing with them. The only way to get to the endgame was to hear the bad news first.

"Bah! Who cares?" grumbled Ahira. "Why don't you just hurry up and tell us without playing games?"

"Behold the bad news!" Tossing a pouch of gold and gems on the table, Davissor waited for the inevitable reaction. "The elves withheld twenty-five per cent because we needed rescuing."

"They call that a rescue?" said Garrett, throwing his hands in the air. "What is wrong with them?"

"Those filthy elves!" fumed Ahira. "We risked our damn lives in there!"

"I win! I win! Boys, you can pay me now or pay me later. Just don't forget to pay me!" Laughing as he jumped to his feet, Ragnar was quick to rub in his victory. "Okay Davissor, we played your damn game. Now tell us the good news."

"The good news is that I ran into an old friend of ours." Winking at Garrett and Angus who were both grinning and enjoying the fun, the mage went silent and waited for someone to respond with the obvious.

"While I think we all agree that might be interesting, it hardly qualifies as good news. Does this old friend have a name or do we have to guess that as well?" said Angus, setting Davissor up to unleash his big surprise. It was obvious that the mage was having a hard time containing his excitement.

"His name, my impatient friends, is… Dantor!"

"DANTOR!!" Jumping to his feet, Ahira picked up his chair and threw it across the room. "That is the last name I ever want to hear and you know that!"

"Just because you two had issues doesn't mean we can't take his money," said the grinning mage, stepping out of the way of the bouncing furniture.

"Davissor, I thought you said this was good news!!" Ragnar was not half as bothered by the thought of Dantor as Ahira but the direction of this conversation irritated him all the same.

"Easy boys! That is not the good news to which I was referring!" Pulling out the second bag of gems and gold coins, the mage flung it on the table. "This is the good news!!"

"Money, money, money!" Watching all the gems and gold coins spread out onto their large oak table, Angus's eyes grew wide. "Brothers, I love my job!"

"That bag of loot has a funny smell! Where did you get it from?" Grabbing his ale tankard, Ahira drained it dry. He shook his head as memories of past dealings with Dantor flooded his mind.

"You already know who gave it to me, Ahira."

"I can't believe that you accepted a job with Dantor again," said Ragnar. "Is it the blasted orcs?"

"Not just the orcs. Kobolds are invading their tunnels. They can't fight them all off at the same time. He seems very desperate."

"Of course he is!!" Furious now that he understood what was going on, Ahira stood clenching and unclenching his fists. "I refuse to help him. You can't pay me enough this time."

"Davissor, is this adventure in Rochdale?" Elbowing Ahira, Garrett looked around and raised his eyebrows at the rest of the group.

"Of course it is in Rochdale, Garrett. Where else would it be?"

"Rochdale is where we will find the Rune Masters!" Laughing out loud, Angus could no longer contain himself. They had just spent the morning discussing ways of convincing Davissor to let them travel to Rochdale.

"What are the odds?" Chuckling under his breath, Garrett couldn't believe their luck.

"It must be fate!" Staring at Ahira, Ragnar winked at his angry fellow dwarf. "I wonder what our old friend Dantor has been up to all this time? It should be fun catching up!"

"Right, right, of course. I haven't been to Rochdale for a long time." Choking down his reluctance, Ahira was painted into a corner. "I guess visiting the Rune Masters might be a good idea while we are there. You know, just to say hello!"

"All right then, boys. I'm not sure what is going on here but I'm glad to see you've all come to the same conclusion." Looking at each of his heroes, searching for a clue to their thoughts, Davissor decided that he would just go along with the game for now. *These guys have something planned and don't want to tell me. I'm sure I will find out soon enough though.*

"It's nothing, Davissor. I was just having a moment," said Ahira.

"Yes, me too. A moment!" Raising his tankard to toast their new adventure, Ragnar stifled a snicker. "To having moments!"

"Excellent then! I'll admit I was a little worried when I first came back, but I'm glad you boys are able to see the logic in working with Dantor again. The dwarves are desperate and have money. We want money and are looking for adventure. Everybody wins!"

"To the Heroes of Karth! And to having moments!" Knocking his mug against Ragnar's, Angus was glad to be heading north to try and find out more answers about what had happened in the cave. Making a wagonload of money while doing it was better than he ever imagined!

* * *

"Come to the Gates of Palos!"

Hounding him from his deepest sleep, the voice was relentless. It demanded his immediate attention. Hung-over and in a weakened mental state, Angus had no choice but to obey.

"Yes master." Willing the darkness to wrap itself around him, in moments a radiant black road became visible. As he stepped with caution onto the dark ribbon stretching into the darkness, the voice urged him onwards.

"Come to the Gates of Palos!"

Taking several reluctant steps, he looked back and watched the darkness close around his bedroom until he was alone and immersed in this strange new place. The safety of his room and everything he knew was gone. Surrounded by suffocating blackness, the ribbon emitted a faint glow but even after his eyes adjusted he struggled with the closeness of this unfamiliar environment.

"Come to the Gates of Palos!"

Appearing to have a life of its own, the road contorted like a living being, twisting and turning, compelling him to take a few more awkward steps. Before long he was almost running.

"Come to the Gates of Palos!"

"*I am walking as fast as I can, Master!*" Following the glow as the ribbon danced him through the void, Angus moved closer to what appeared was its edge. Unable to decipher if he was looking up or down, all he could see was more darkness beyond his position. Stumbling closer, a strange panic overcame him and he was somehow certain that by stepping off the roadway he would drift away and be forever lost.

"*Come to the Gates of Palos!*"

"*I hear and obey!*" His subconscious burning through its stores of energy, he became less and less capable of resisting the strange voice's siren call. A sudden change in his environment cut through the fog of fatigue and sent warning bells ringing in his ears. Slowing the frenetic pace of his passage, he willed the darkness surrounding him to thin and began hearing unfamiliar voices all around.

"Open the gates, ogre!" Deafened by the rattling chains and bumping bodies, Angus dared not move. That was Shard tongue! It sounded big enough to be an ogre or an orc. *What have I gotten myself into here?*

"Hurry! Let them pass!" Garbled voices were shouting but Angus was frozen inside the blanket of darkness. Wanting nothing more than a mug of ale and a return to his bed, discovery was imminent. *What am I supposed to do now? Where are my brothers when I need them!*

"*Come to the Gates of Palos!*"

"*I must obey!*" Answering the voice's call, he stepped out of his dark cocoon into nothing less than a pure nightmare.

"I have traveled a long way to Harrow Gate! King Ferrus demands an audience with Xeon, the master of us all! I will not be refused access!" Swinging his fists, a giant mummy stood with his back to Angus, ranting at the ogres in front of the gate.

"Take the mummy to the master!"

"*Come to the Gates of Palos!*"

"*I am coming, master!*" Stepping out from behind King Ferrus, the gnome was walking into what appeared to be a world of giants. The two skeletal knights accompanying the mummy were his equals in size, and the ogres they addressed were not much smaller. No one noticed the tiny being standing in their midst.

Striding past the ogres and up a steep incline, King Ferrus and his entourage made their way past the gates to a tower on top of the mountain. With his shorter legs pumping, Angus struggled to keep up.

Studying the expanse of mountaintops stretching into the horizon, a cold sweat formed on his back. The tips of the mountains resembled the bumps on a dragon's back. There was no mistaking where he was standing. *The Dragon Spine Mountains! What is happening to me?*

"*Come to the Gates of Palos!*"

"*I am coming master!*" The compulsion to move towards the voice was overwhelming. "*I hear and obey master!*"

"Open the portal to the shadow world!" roared King Ferrus. Standing on top of the citadel and whipped by the cold mountain winds, a circular stone portal stretching at least sixty feet in diameter rested on the platform at the top of a stone staircase. Waiting at the foot of the stairs for his audience with the dragon, King Ferrus was waving his arms in anticipation. "Dragon! Where is the army you promised me?"

That portal is large enough to fit an army through! And something is moving in it! Gasping in disbelief as the center of the blue stone portal began shimmering,

Angus was unable to comprehend the scope of the drama unfolding in front of his eyes.

"Xeon is coming!" "Xeon is coming!" Shouting out warnings as it became clear what was happening, the ogres cowered in fear. Even King Ferrus dropped to his knees as the shadow dragon manifested and thundered through the portal.

"Bow before your master!" commanded Xeon, his claws leaving deep grooves across the stone platform. Flanked by three undead skeletal dragons, the four massive creatures crowded the wide platform as they screeched and roared at the assembled masses below.

"Bow before your master!"

"*I hear and obey!*" Cowering in the crowd, Angus had nowhere to hide. *Don't look at it! Don't look at it! Oh please, don't see me here!*

"King Ferrus! Approach me now!"

"Yes Master!" Rising from the ground, the mummy climbed the stairs to meet the dragon. It was the moment of truth. If Xeon was going to kill him, this would be the time and place. As he reached the platform, Ferrus stopped and stared in disbelief. Behind the skeletal dragons, an endless army of undead were massing on the other side of the portal.

"King Ferrus! Take command of my army of undead and help me destroy this pitiful world!"

"No!" Hearing those words Angus screamed in terror. Raising his head, eyes wild with fear, he found himself staring into the baleful yellow eye of the dragon. Terrified to his core, he pulled the darkness tight around, desperate to disappear anywhere before the dragon caught and destroyed him.

"Angus! Wake up, man!" Woken by the bloodcurdling screams coming from the gnome's room, Ragnar ran across the hall and kicked open the bedroom door to find him tied up in knots in the blankets of his bed. Tearing the fabric back to reveal his face, Ragnar began slapping him out of whatever nightmare was consuming his mind.

"Hey! Who's hitting me now? Stop that! Stop it!" Surrounded by the familiar feeling and smell of his bed, Angus stopped struggling and poked his head out of the blankets. Seeing Ragnar standing beside his bed, it took him a minute to reorient himself.

"Are you alright, brother? What were you seeing that made you scream like that?"

"I know where the Gates of Palos are!" shouted Angus, jumping up from bed.

EPILOGUE

"Can someone please come and check on me?" Feeling agitated and flushed, Cassandra called out for the midwife. Based on everything she had been told about giving birth, her experience so far had been irregular. In truth it was not just her pregnancy that felt strange. Ever since she and Braigon had married, their relationship had seemed different. Becoming emotional as she remembered the joy she had felt when they first met, Cassandra's contractions were getting more painful but she knew the real reason for her tears was not from giving birth.

"It hasn't been an hour yet. The midwife will come when it's time," said the birth companion standing next to her.

It has actually been more than an hour, but who's counting? Lying in her bed, surrounded by healing salves, birthing equipment, and other paraphernalia and following the loud rhythmic beat of a small candle which sat on top of her belly, Cassandra watched the magical flame bouncing to match the beat of the fetal heart of her child.

Slumped in an uncomfortable chair next to her bed where he had spent the night watching the candle flicker, Braigon was slipping in and out of sleep.

"Listen to me! I think the baby is coming!" Feeling the contractions coming closer together, the baby's heartbeat was growing stronger and Cassandra sensed she was becoming feverish.

"She'll check on you soon," said her birth companion, looking in the other room for any sign from the midwife. Submersing a small towel into cold water, she rung out the excess and placed it on Cassandra's head to cool her temperature.

"I really think I need to be checked now!"

Following an irritated sigh from the other side of the curtain separating her birthing room from where the midwife was staying, Cassandra heard the sound of agitated footsteps. Making a quick examination without so much as acknowledging her existence, the midwife turned to Braigon. "I need to fetch the healer. Whatever you do, do not tell her to push."

Was she kidding? Who did this woman think she was talking to? Cassandra felt vindicated regarding her need to be checked, but the midwife might as well have asked her not to breathe as not to push!

In a flash, a flurry of activity transformed the room. The birthing companion lifted Cassandra's legs into stirrups while Braigon rushed to her side and gave her a hand to squeeze from the pain of the contractions. The pain continued to grow and before long she was screaming in agony.

"Try not to push!" The birthing companion was becoming concerned by Cassandra's heavy bleeding. The intense and irregular contractions were difficult for the new mother to handle. "We need to move her to the birth pool!" she announced. Waving at Braigon to help, the two of them managed to lift her to the pool of warm water that had been prepared earlier.

Her husband massaged her head while the water's heat helped to relax Cassandra's tense muscles. The calmness and peace she felt was short-lived though, as the pain soon returned with a fury.

"Braigon! Help me!" Writhing in agony, Cassandra could see the water turning dark with her blood.

"Find that midwife now!" Yelling at the birth companion, Braigon chased her from the room in a panic. Locking the door, he turned to his wife once they were alone, taking her hand in his and squeezing it hard.

"What is happening to me, Braigon? Is our baby alright?"

"The baby is fine!" hissed Braigon, his voice becoming raspy and foreign. Grinning with evil satisfaction, the lord was amused by her obvious confusion and decided to reveal his secret. "The mother of a doppelganger child always goes through birth like this."

"What? Who are you?" Looking into Braigon's eyes, Cassandra knew now what had been troubling her all these months. Even though the physical features were her husband's, this creature was not him. "No! What have you done with my husband?"

"Oh he is long dead, my love. And I'm sure he would be happy to know that I have taken such good care of his wife for all these months!"

"What? Braigon! Oh no! No!" Mourning the loss of her husband, at the same time Cassandra felt somewhat relieved to learn that this creature was not him. As he had changed over the last year she had started to hate him, but in truth it was this creature she hated. *My sweet Braigon! You are still my true love.*

"I'm afraid so, my dear. And if that was not enough excitement, I have one more surprise for you today." Putting his lips right next to her ear, he watched as her eyes began closing for the final time. "When a doppelganger child is born," he hissed. "It first kills then eats its mother."

About the Author

Born in Rouyn-Noranda, Quebec in 1968, Grant Hamilton went to a small high school with less than a dozen people in his graduating class. The small class environment provided some distinct advantages, with his teachers being able to devote more time and attention to individual students. Grant's teachers encouraged his storytelling ambition and subsequently one of his poetry works was published. This small success was the catalyst for Grant's writing passion, fueling the energy to finish high school with a major in enriched English classes at Brookfield High. After obtaining a B.A. at Carleton University with studies in Film and English literature, Grant's fertile mind continued to flex as he wrote short stories and poetry to be included in future anthologies.

During this time, fantasy books and board games were becoming very popular and were a heavy influence on Grant. Warhammer, Dungeons and Dragons, Lord of the Rings, The Hobbit, Forgotten Realms: The Crystal Shard, and Dragonlance: Dragons of Autumn Twilight are some of his favorite books and games.

Grant was married in 1999 and as a civilian Project Manager with National Defence and the Canadian Armed Forces, has continued to develop his writing and communications skills. His second youngest son Gregory Hamilton was diagnosed with autism, resulting in his family re-inventing themselves by down-sizing their home and income, his wife leaving her job to home-school their son with special needs. Raising someone with high functioning autism opened Grant's eyes to a part of the world about which he knew very little. He has reinvented himself as a champion of autism and as part of that challenge, Grant made the decision to raise autism awareness by writing a series of fantasy novels that includes an autistic hero modeled after his son.

The Heroes of Karth series is the result of his experience and passion coming together like a perfect storm, creating a world for readers of all ages to enjoy and expand upon for many years to come.

DOPPELGANGER!

Sign up for our newsletter and name the doppelganger for a chance to win a **HEROES OF KARTH** : Deathmatch Trial Pack.

DETAILS AT WWW.HEROESOFKARTH.COM